NICHOLAS: THE LORDS OF SATYR

APHRODISIA BOOKS are published by

Kensington Publishing Corp.
850 Third Avenue
New York, NY 10022

All Kensington Titles, Imprints, and Distributed Lines are available at special quantity discounts for bulk purchases for sales promotions, premiums, fund-raising, and educational or institutional use.

Special book excerpts or customized printings can also be created to fit specific needs. For details, write or phone the office of the Kensington special sales manager: Kensington Publishing Corp., 850 Third Avenue, New York, NY 10022, attn: Special Sales Department, Phone: 1-800-221-2647.

Aphrodisia and the A logo Reg. U.S. Pat & TM Off.

ISBN-13: 978-0-7582-2039-4
ISBN-10: 0-7582-2039-1

First Trade Paperback Printing: August 2007

10 9 8 7 6 5 4 3 2 1

Printed in the United States of America

NICHOLAS: THE LORDS OF SATYR

ELIZABETH AMBER

APHRODISIA

KENSINGTON PUBLISHING CORP.
http://www.kensingtonbooks.com

PROLOGUE

Satyr Estate, Tuscany, Italy
1823

It was Moonful and a Calling night.

The Lords of Satyr met silently in the sacred gathering place at the heart of the family's ancient vineyard. Instinct had driven them here. Need fueled them.

They paused beneath a large statue—the most imposing of those that ringed the isolated glen. Above them on a pedestal, Bacchus stood frozen in stone. Grapevines wreathed his hair, and a wine goblet was extended in one hand as though he were offering a toast in celebration of what they were about to do.

The first shaft of moonlight dispelled the murk, drenching the lords in its silver, revealing their nakedness. Almost in unison, they were seized by cramps that rippled cruelly over their taut bellies. They bent low, their features contorting into grimaces. Raw groans that were a blend of pain and pleasure erupted from their throats as the last physical change of the Calling night occurred.

Nicholas, the eldest, recovered first.

His eyes made a quick survey of the glen. It was protected, he knew. Strangers never came here. When Humans wandered too close, they were repelled by a force they didn't understand.

He willed himself to uncoil and stand, relieved that the turmoil had passed. He hated the feeling of helplessness that always accompanied the Change. He couldn't afford to be vulnerable, even for so short a time. There was too much at stake.

It would be dangerous for anyone to see him or his brothers like this. He was a freakish creature now, fit only for a harem or brothel that catered to those with a taste for the bizarre. Just the sort of place he might frequent, were he in a particular sort of mood.

He touched himself, slid a thumb and two fingers along newly awakened flesh from root to crown. His thumb found the drop of moisture in the crease at his tip and idly smeared it.

The last Change of Moonful had gifted him with this new shaft of bone and sinew—this second cock ripped from his own flesh. It extended high and hard from his pelvis, and twitched with hunger. Only slightly smaller than the enormous cock already rooted just below in his thatch, it craved relief as much as its twin. He soothed it, stroking. Mimicking the welcome it would soon find between female thighs, as he waited for his brothers to undergo a similar change.

At his command, ribbons of swirling mist spun in the glen and then stilled, shape-shifting. Iridescent forms rose from the vapor and solidified into Shimmerskins—insentient females who had serviced the Satyr since ancient times. Their soft hands caressed his newly furred haunches, offering comfort.

Moments later, the three lords moved apart to pursue their individual pleasures. Their instincts were more animal than man now, their minds riveted on one goal.

The Shimmerskins moved before them like lush automatons, each dutifully preparing to fulfill the role for which she'd been designed. Eagerly, they padded to the small tablelike altars dotting the glen. Their smiles were vacant, their movements gliding.

Breasts and abdomens met cold granite as they bent forward over the stone slabs, with their legs widespread and their bare feet planted in the moss. Orifices automatically moistened and readied as they prostrated themselves, awaiting the pleasure of the lords, just as countless legions of their kind had offered themselves here over the centuries.

Each brother chose a Shimmerskin and nestled close behind her.

Moonlight caught the cobalt glitter of his eyes as Nicholas stood over a golden Shimmerskin. With his thumbs, he pressed the ruddy, straining tips of his cocks to the anal and vaginal openings on display. Like his brothers, he needed two female openings at once for his first mating of this night. His second cock required only a single ejaculation and would afterward retreat inside him until next month's Moonful.

His palms flattened upon the stone on either side of her hips. He didn't prepare her as he would a Human woman. Shimmerskins didn't feel pain. Or pleasure, though they faked it well.

A low rumble welled in his chest as he stared down at her smooth, glimmering back. With a harsh growl, he plunged deep.

She moaned as her kind always did when he breached one. Nearby, her sisters echoed the lonely feminine sound. It meant nothing, he knew. Everything they did was programmed to incite male passion. He had but to imagine an action and she would perform it, no matter how obscene or debauched.

He drew back and plunged again, and again. Dual stabs sacrificed her to his rhythmic grind. Her tissues worshiped his cocks like wet fists, tugging him toward release with methodical precision.

Distantly, he felt his brothers' exultation in their rut, and it fueled his own. Satyr blood linked them, causing them to share emotions at times of heightened stress.

For long moments, the stark slap of heated flesh was loud in the hush of the glen. Nick bucked with mindless, merciless strength, scarcely registering the attentions of the other Shimmerskins whose hands entwined and caressed him, as they awaited a turn.

Fauns, nymphs, faeries, and maenads sculpted from rock and forever locked in carnal embraces gazed down on the scene with lusty approval. Bacchus smiled indulgently, pleased.

Rapture spiraled, each brother's passion building on that which another experienced. For a time, Nick lost himself to the animalistic mating.

Eventually, his sacs drew up, tightening. Raw need twisted in his gut.

Three triumphant shouts of release sounded almost at once. Hot, wet seed blasted forth. The Shimmerskins' inner passages convulsed in acceptance.

Nick's breath sawed in his lungs in the aftermath of the anguished, empty gratification.

He gritted his teeth against new pain as his second cock, now satiated, receded from the Shimmerskin's anus and back into his pelvis. The razor's edge of need hadn't dulled. But he would require only one female opening now.

The golden Shimmerskin faded into the nothingness from which she'd come. Nick took a fresh victim under him.

Masculine commands and grunts mingled and floated on trails of mist. All were captured by a gentle breeze as the three Lords of Satyr slaked their lust until dawn.

1

Lord Nicholas Satyr lifted the dagger from the desk before him, anxious to have the task ahead complete. The blade flashed, reflecting the intensity of his strange pale gaze, before twisting to slice through the tasseled cord encircling the roll of parchment.

The missive's arrival that morning had been both unexpected and unwelcome. Dispatches from ElseWorld were infrequent and usually portended mischief of some kind. Trouble was already threatening the vineyards, which lay at the heart of Satyr lands. He could spare little time for any nonsense.

As the cord fell away, the coiled document unrolled with a will of its own, releasing a faint hint of magic into the room. Nick spared a quick glance for his younger brothers, Raine and Lyon, whom he'd summoned an hour ago from their adjacent estates within the Satyr compound. They would have sensed it, too.

Raine stood at the window, hands clasped at his back as he surveyed Nick's manicured gardens. Whirls of fog obscured the tangled forest and grapevine-covered hillsides beyond. He was, as usual, meticulously outfitted in gray, his cropped hair and garb as restrained as the early spring morning he observed.

Restless energy crackled from Lyon as he prowled Nick's salon, wending his brawny frame among elegant furnishings and curious artifacts. Occasionally he paused to examine one of his brother's newer acquisitions in his pawlike grasp, but he didn't linger. He was impatient to learn the document's contents and return to the business of overseeing his property.

Nick's fingertips tingled from the hum of ElseWorld magic caught in the parchment, but nothing in his face revealed his thoughts as he read. Over the course of three decades, he'd learned to disguise his emotions. They'd all found it necessary to hide their true natures, having grown up half Human, half Satyr in an EarthWorld intolerant of their kind.

Turning from the window, Raine glanced toward the parchment. "Is it from an Elder?"

Nick nodded, a curt inclination of his dark head. "King Feydon himself."

Lyon halted midstride and whipped around. "What the devil does *he* want?"

The leather of Nick's chair creaked subtly as he shifted all six and a half feet of his well-muscled form. "It seems he has managed to sire three Earth daughters."

Raine digested this news in silence, a slight stiffening of his shoulders the only indication that he'd heard.

Lyon snorted in amusement. "That randy old goat of a Faerie Elder sent us a birth announcement? From his deathbed, no less."

Not fully grasping the import of the news, he blithely twirled a globe of EarthWorld upon the tip of one finger. Jeweled continents, sapphire oceans, and an emerald dragon or two sparkled in the candlelight.

"His announcement is somewhat belated," Nick clarified.

"The birthings occurred some twenty years ago. Apparently he's had an attack of conscience at this late date. And it's his dying wish that we remedy the situation he leaves behind."

Raine folded his arms, suspicion coloring his eyes a stormy gray. "And how precisely are we to do that?"

"According to his instructions, we are to locate his progeny and marry them," said Nick.

A bark of astonished laughter escaped Lyon. "What?!"

Nick tossed the parchment on the desk. "Read it yourselves if you doubt me. And have a care with my orb, Lyon."

Lyon looked down at his broad hands and saw they were very nearly crushing one of Nick's precious objects. His strength belonged to the outdoors and served him well in the Satyr vineyards. However, it didn't suit Nick's fashionable rooms, and he constantly had to be on guard lest he fatally upset something.

Grimacing, he set the globe back to rest in its cradle and headed for the letter on Nick's desk. He snatched it up and read aloud.

> *Lords of Satyr, Sons of Bacchus,*
> *Be it known that I lie dying and naught may be done. As my time draws near, the weight of past indiscretions haunts me. I must tell of them.*
> *Nineteen summers ago, I fathered daughters upon three highborn Human females of EarthWorld. I sowed my childseed whilst these females slumbered, leaving each unaware of my nocturnal visit.*
> *My three grown daughters are now vulnerable and must be shielded from Forces that would harm them. 'Tis my dying wish you will find it your duty to husband them and bring them under your protection. You may search them out among the society of Rome, Venice, and Paris.*
> *Thus is my Will.*

"This is absurd," Lyon muttered in disgust. He slapped the letter to Nick's desk, causing the crystal bottles in the inkstand to rattle. The small act of violence did little to mollify him, and he turned to prowl the room again as though he were a caged animal seeking escape.

Raine took up the parchment and silently scanned its contents, assessing each phrase, searching for nuances of meaning. When he finally set it aside, his expression was grim.

He'd been wed before, three years earlier, but the marriage had ended in disaster within months. He had no plans to marry again. But he didn't speak of that now.

"Interesting that Feydon chose to produce three *female* offspring, and in locations so obligingly convenient to us," he remarked.

Nick slanted him a considering glance. "Almost as though he intended his daughters for us from the beginning."

Lyon swung around. "Seven hells! Do you suppose he spawned them on purpose in some misguided attempt to saddle us with wives?"

"Now that he has slipped into the shadows between life and death, we can only guess at his motives," said Raine.

Nick leaned back, causing his chair to protest once more. Candlelight flickered, glancing blue highlights off the jet black of his hair.

"It would be like him, however. We're the only of our kind left in EarthWorld, and he has long made clear he felt it our duty to procreate so Satyr lands won't fall into Human hands. Our properties need heirs, yet we have shown ourselves reluctant to sire them. He may have felt such an action justified."

"'Forces that would harm them,'" Lyon quoted from the parchment. "Do you think he means forces from his World or ours?"

"Or could it simply be a ruse to ensure our involvement?" asked Raine.

"If so, it's an effective tactic," said Nick. "Feydon knows our protective instincts would cause us to act if his children are in danger."

"It's an unfair obligation to thrust upon us," said Raine.

"Damn right, O Master of Understatement," said Lyon. "It's blatant manipulation."

"Manipulation or not, it makes our decision regarding a course of action or inaction a rather pressing matter," said Raine.

"Surely we must take some action," Lyon said, voicing reluctant concern. "These FaerieBlend females can't be left to fend for themselves. Can they?"

He and Raine looked to Nick.

"If we're to believe Feydon's missive, the females he mated were unaware he bedded them," said Nick. "That being the case, both mothers and daughters are innocent of any deceit directed our way."

"It's likely the daughters don't realize they're of Else-World," said Raine.

"Though they must be feeling the quickening pulse of Faerie blood," said Lyon.

"And misunderstanding its meaning if there's no one to guide them," said Nick. "'Tis a troubling notion."

"But not at all tempting," Raine stated baldly. "I've no interest in marrying again."

Nick and Lyon exchanged glances.

"Marriage to a half-Faerie creature could succeed where one to a Human failed," said Nick.

Raine shrugged. "Nevertheless, I'm unwilling to experiment."

Lyon ran blunt fingertips through the tangle of his thick tawny hair. "I find myself in agreement with Raine. I've no interest in tying myself to a woman not of my choosing, be she Faerie or Human. Isn't there some way to protect Feydon's daughters short of marriage?"

"How? Shall we hound their footsteps over the years to

come in order to guard them against trouble?" asked Nick. "They will have us arrested."

"I still say marriage can be avoided. Why not simply bring them to Satyr land and let them roam about as they please?" suggested Lyon.

Nick laughed, and Raine shot him a pitying glance.

Lyon looked affronted. "What? They will be safe here under our protection."

"Like your other pets?" asked Raine, referring to Lyon's menagerie of exotic animals that ranged freely on Satyr lands.

"They're females, not livestock," said Nick. "They will never agree to so ridiculous an arrangement. We must husband them and bring them under our protection. I see no other way."

Raine eyed his older brother. "You seem strangely committed to the idea of marriage after so little consideration."

Nick flexed his wide shoulders, straining the seams of his waistcoat and causing the subtle design in the dark teal brocade to shimmer. It was an unusual coat selected from among the treasures of his ancestors. Something about it pleased him. But then, he relished the unusual.

"Granted, the notion of marriage was unlooked for," he said. "But as I reflect on Feydon's edict I realize it provides a certain . . . opportunity."

Lyon gave him a look of false commiseration. "Poor Nick. Have you lacked for the attentions of a sufficient bounty of females all these years? You should have spoken sooner. Raine and I would be glad to share with you some of the legions angling for our portion of the Satyr coffers."

Raine smiled, a fleeting lift of one corner of his mouth. "He makes a point, big brother. We've all had more than a few opportunities to shackle ourselves over the years."

"We need heirs," said Nick.

Raine and Lyon stared at him in surprise.

"My thirtieth year approaches. You trail me by only two

years, Raine. And you by merely four, Lyon. Who else are we to sire sons and daughters on if not these FaerieBlends?" Nick demanded, gesturing toward the parchment. "They are by nature half breeds, a blend of EarthWorld and ElseWorld, like us."

"But unlike us, Feydon's daughters have Faerie blood in their veins," Raine reminded him.

"And the Faerie are volatile," added Lyon. "Who knows what diverse bag of tricks they may possess?" He shuddered.

"My material point is that while Human women might find certain of our ways strange or distasteful, a Fey wife would be less apt to present any objection to the manner in which we might presume to quest for heirs," said Nick.

"But what sort of heirs will they provide?" Raine asked, shaking his head. "A half-Satyr husband mating a half-Faerie wife? What kind of children can come of it?"

"If we don't intervene, it's probable the FaerieBlends will marry and mate with Humans. What offspring do you imagine might come of that?" Nick asked pointedly.

Lyon rammed his hands into the pockets of his sturdy trousers and sighed. He dressed the part of a vintner, wearing rumpled trousers, a nubby cotton tunic, and greatboots. "You're right. Neither they nor their children will know what to make of their abilities. That could prove disastrous."

A brittle tension settled over the room.

"The Satyr have always looked after the Faerie," Nick said decisively.

Lyon sighed. "It appears settled we must marry them. Bacchus, what if mine is stupid? Or offensive? How will I stand to bed her?"

"As I understand it, marriage and protection are our only obligations," said Raine. "Feydon's missive stated no requirement to mate or sire offspring."

Nick's eyes sharpened on him. "True."

"You would bind your wife to a childless marriage?" asked Lyon. "Bind yourself to one?"

"The choice will be hers, the facts put to her before we marry," said Raine. "I want no Blended children who will suffer the alienation of finding one foot in EarthWorld and one in ElseWorld while not properly fitting in either."

"What of the wine?" asked Lyon. "Our heirs must carry on our work in the vineyards when we're gone."

The vine-covered hills at the center of the Satyr compound produced grapes, which were made into wine each season. Labeled *Lords of Satyr*, it was hotly sought by the wealthy and titled throughout Europe and beyond. Some whispered that Satyr wine possessed magical properties, which it in fact did.

The brothers' trio of estates was strategically placed at triangulated points along the borders of an ancient forest, like guard towers at three corners of a fortress. At the center of each estate stood an ancient castle with extensive gardens and grounds that met and eventually mingled with the trees of the magnificent old-growth forest. The forest in turn ringed the base of the sloping hills of the vineyards, which formed the central core of their lands.

Theirs was ancient ground chosen by their ancestors for a special purpose—to serve as a sacred joining place for Else-World and EarthWorld. In centuries past, many Satyr had secretly dwelled here, protecting the portal that led between worlds. Now there were but three.

Raine flicked a speck of dust from his immaculate jacket, the expression in his gray eyes opaque. "Your offspring are welcome to my share. Let that settle the matter."

"For now," Nick relented.

Raine shrugged.

"Then it's only left to determine which daughter we select," said Lyon.

"Rome is most convenient for me," said Nick. "Any objections?"

"None. I'll take Paris," said Raine. "Damn, I abhor traveling."

"Traveling? To Paris? I'll remind you I'm left with Venice," said Lyon. "The journey there will be excruciating after the rains."

Raine quirked an eyebrow. "It should be no hardship since you travel there to meet buyers with regularity."

"Still, it's a bad time to be away. Many of my animals are in foal," said Lyon. "And the vineyards need watching."

"We can exert enough of our combined Will to bolster the forcewall around Satyr lands for weeks," said Raine.

"Why take unnecessary risk? It's my opinion some of us should stay," said Lyon.

"Agreed," said Nick. "I will go first. Once I secure my bride, your searches can follow."

Raine and Lyon assented, and soon thereafter, all three turned to the door.

Once outside, Nick breathed deeply. "The vines begin to awaken. I will make haste."

Eyes of sapphire blue, ashen gray, and tawny gold locked for a potent moment and then slid apart as the three Lords of Satyr were dispatched into the late morning mist.

2

Tivoli, east of Rome
Two weeks later

*S*he was here.

Excitement thrummed in Nicholas Satyr's blood as he caught the tantalizing hint of Faerie magic riding on the air.

He surveyed the swarm of humanity at the afternoon festivities now underway in the Renaissance gardens of the Villa d'Este. The wildly integrated assemblage of jugglers, musicians, and costumed artisans mingled with Rome's social elite. Most had ventured the twenty miles for a day in the country, as he had.

But they had come for different purposes.

Neither the fountains nor the other entertainments on offer held his interest at the moment. He had other business here. The business of finding a specific prey—one who was destined to become his wife.

For the past week, Nick had attended every such social gathering of any consequence in the offing in Rome. It now appeared

Feydon had miscalculated. The first of the Faerie brides wasn't to be found in Rome after all. Today he'd taken a chance he might locate her here, in nearby Tivoli instead. His hunch appeared to have borne fruit.

Still, he'd wasted precious time tracking her in Rome. Thus occupied, he hadn't buried himself in feminine flesh for days, a considerable dearth for one of Satyr lineage. He would find remedy in the arms of his meretrice—or mistress, as the English more politely called their bought whores—later that evening.

Nick strode into the crowd, his concentration focused on his task. His keen olfactory senses sorted through perfumes and natural Human odors, searching, testing, rejecting.

There was no question King Feydon's daughter lurked somewhere in this throng of Italian and English society.

But where?

Amid the greenery, enormous hats with dancing plumes vied for attention with swagged, embellished skirts. Since Napoleon's fall, fashions had turned away from high-waisted, slim-fitting gowns in favor of a more romantic look. Waists were now well cinched, and skirts belled across the landscape like oversize parasols.

His height allowed him to gaze easily across the sea of faces, passing over the male ones and pausing on those of the females. It was unlikely he would know her by sight. She would be hiding any outward manifestations that might betray her parentage, as he did. No, he would have to rely on scent alone.

Pausing at the base of the steep steps leading to the gigantic Water Organ fountain, he looked toward the statue of Bacchus, seeking inspiration. Instinct had him turning to stroll the Avenue of One Hundred Fountains. Here mythological creatures and gargoyles lined the path, spouting and sputtering with cascading waterworks.

He stilled, his interest sharpening. *There it was again.* A faint but unmistakable Faerie fragrance. He started in its direction, only to be brought up short when a fleshy hand gloved in canary yellow tapped his shoulder.

"I say! That you, Satyr?"

Nick turned to find two couples with whom he had a marginal acquaintance. The persona of respectable aristocrat slipped over him like a carefully constructed cloak. He gave them a polite nod. "Lord and Lady Hillbrook. Signore Rossini, Signora Rossini."

Today's event had been organized at Lord Hillbrook's instigation. Wealthy Englishmen such as he commonly wintered in Italy, often sojourning well into spring to escape England's chill. But the first hint of Italy's infamous summer heat always saw them scurrying homeward.

"Unusual to see you at one of our little occasions," Lord Hillbrook enthused. He stroked his profuse side-whiskers, which pointed in a dozen directions as though uncertain of the direction his conversation might go. "Honored to have you."

"I don't visit Tivoli as often as I might like. But as I happened to be here, I wouldn't miss one of your functions," Nick commented affably. "'Tis a credit to its hostess."

Lady Hillbrook preened under his praise. "You Italians are so temperate in your weather. In England it would be difficult to hold an open-air event this time of year, fearing rain."

"Ah, but there can be such a thing as too much sunshine. Our vines welcome the occasional spring shower," said Nick. "Too little rain makes for puny grapes."

"Speaking of which, you haven't forgotten we're in for fifty cases at the auction this autumn," Signora Rossini reminded him. Though it was warm, she wore a tight-laced crimson gown that was making a heroic effort to cinch her ungainly proportions into some semblance of an hourglass shape. Perspiration dotted her upper lip and brow, and she occasionally mopped it with a monogrammed handkerchief.

Lady Hillbrook discreetly nudged her husband with a satin-covered elbow.

"One hundred cases here," Lord Hillbrook was prompted to add.

"Sending for it on the sly as usual?" Signore Rossini asked.

Hillbrook nodded, rocking on his heels. "English laws are quite set against sales of the bottled stuff, you know. The practice of selling it by the measure continues, so we're forced to purchase on the sly or become bottlers if we're to drink."

He moved his walking stick toward Nick's calf as though to nudge him conspiratorially. He wisely thought better of it and merely asked, "I suppose you'll be asking an obscene amount for your vintage this year, eh? Yours seem to be the only vines spared from the current blight."

Nick tensed. "We've been fortunate in that we've seen no signs of it so far."

"'Tis said every field in Europe has been affected by the pox. Some devastated," said Signore Rossini. "And no cure in sight. I understand no one is even certain of its cause."

"The matter of the blight has naturally been of great concern to my family. As I said, we count ourselves fortunate that so far our fields remain unaffected," Nick replied coolly.

"Odd, that," mused Lord Hillbrook.

"Scusi?" Nick turned his full attention on the gentleman, who promptly withered under his piercing stare.

Satyr lands were protected by the ElseWorldly powers he and his brother interlaced around them. Therefore, their vines hadn't been afflicted thus far with the dark spots that had begun to appear on the vines of nearly every other vineyard in Europe. He'd known it was only a matter of time before Humans began to speculate on the reason his fields had been spared.

"I say, meant nothing by it," said Hillbrook, flushing to match Signora Rossini's gown. "Everyone knows the Satyr label is impeccable. Nothing odd at all, really. No doubt it's simple dumb luck, er—"

His wife frowned and shook her head, causing his words to dwindle away.

"I assure you dumb luck isn't what protects us," said Nick. "While the blight persists, every precaution has been undertaken to protect our grapes from its ravages. It's difficult to know how to limit exposure, since its cause remains unclear. However, we limit access to our vineyard and take care that contaminants are kept out."

Signora Rossini leapt into the awkward silence that fell. "Really, such talk is too serious for so lovely a day. Now, Lord Satyr, you must tell us. Have you visited the botanical exhibits yet?"

Enthusiasm sparkled in Lady Hillbrook's eyes, and she leaned toward her companion. "The study of flora is all the rage in England. I myself have indulged and have acquired many interesting specimens."

Nick smiled with easy charm. "Indeed? I regret I haven't yet had an opportunity to explore the exhibits. You will excuse me? I find I'm most anxious to investigate." With a cursory bow, he left them.

Setting the matter of the pox aside for the present, he once again threaded through the crowd, stealthily sorting, considering, and discarding. As he passed the Fountain of the Dragon at the center of the gardens, the young ladies daintily plied their wiles, vying to turn the head of one of the obscenely wealthy Satyr lords. If he could but find such tenaciousness in field workers, he would engage them in employment at his vineyards in an instant.

Their eyes said they wanted him—or at least his riches. But they knew nothing of his true nature. For if any of them had an inkling of the strength and depth of his dark physical passions, he was certain that even his vast fortune wouldn't cause them to view him as a candidate for marriage.

As afternoon purpled into evening, the delicate scent of Faerie wafted on the cooling air, teasing and then withdrawing. He circulated, playing a children's game of getting hot, then cold, then hot again as he patiently tracked it.

Eventually, as he neared the fish pools, the thread of magic grew steadier, telling him she was close. His hunting instincts sharpened.

He circled a veiled tent set amid others between two labyrinth herb gardens. An assortment of young English and Italian ladies and their beaux mingled there, chattering.

When his approach was noted, feminine heads lifted, as though scenting prey. Several ladies promptly forgot the gentlemen to whom they'd been speaking. Lacy fans fluttered faster.

She was here, somewhere among them.

"Have you come for a reading, Satyr?" chirped one of the young Italian bucks. "Don't believe in the stuff myself, but it's a bit of fun, I suppose."

One of the ladies knocked the young man's arm teasingly with a haphazard bouquet she'd obviously picked from the herb garden. "It's not *reading*, Signore. It's fortune-telling the mystic offers."

"That's what I meant," he replied, rubbing his arm in mock pain. "Palm reading, isn't it?"

Nick surveyed the tent. It was white, with great swoops of tulle flowing at its corners and a flag decorating its pinnacle.

Anticipation gripped him. She was inside. He was certain of it.

"So, there's a true mystic in residence?" he inquired, fishing.

"Si. As we speak, my sister's within, having her fortune told," said the young man, whom Nick now recognized as the son of Signore Rossini.

Was it to be his sister? If so, he sincerely hoped she bore no resemblance to her mother. Lyon's fears on the matter of his intended's attractions resounded in his head. Suddenly, he wasn't quite so anxious to peek inside the tent.

Her appearance didn't matter, he reminded himself. As her husband, he would mate her only as often as duty required. In turn, she would produce his children and not object when his cock sought true satisfaction away from her bed.

Still, when the gauzy veils of the tent parted to expel Signore Rossini's sister, Nick nearly sighed in relief. She was an Italian beauty. Her gown was a stay maker's delight, its shot silk waist nipping in to reveal curves far shapelier than those of her mother. Dainty ribbons tied under her chin held a straw bonnet so profusely decorated with bluebirds that it appeared surprised to find itself sitting on her raven curls rather than in an aviary.

As she slid forth from the enclosure, another young customer slipped past her and into the tent. Nick caught a glimpse of the bowed figure in gypsy garb seated within.

"What did the mystic say?" one of the other ladies asked Rossini's sister.

"Yes, Bianca, do tell us," added an English girl. "We're giddy to know."

Signorina Rossini parted her lips and then faltered when she noted Nick's interest.

Once introductions were dispensed with, he stepped closer to her than propriety allowed in order to kiss her gloved hand. An invisible aura of Faerie magic enveloped him at her nearness.

So it *was* to be the Rossini girl then. That his search was over so abruptly caused him a moment of disorientation, as though he'd run to the brink of a cliff and now found himself teetering on its edge.

Satyr weren't especially talented at probing the minds of

others, but he plied what skills he possessed, hoping to learn what he could of her.

Her thoughts told him she found him attractive, but her expression had already informed him of that. He felt frustration when he couldn't read further evidence from her that she was Faerie, until he realized her own lack of awareness of her heritage would naturally render her thoughts blank of it.

She seemed a sweet, biddable girl, and she was undeniably beautiful. If his instincts were right, this one would prove a good choice.

That it was her mother King Feydon had cuckolded surprised him. A discerning libertine, Feydon typically chose only the most beguiling of mates. But perhaps Signora Rossini had been more pleasing to the eye in her youth.

Bianca shifted uncomfortably, and he realized his silent study had grown too intense. He bowed. "It is indeed a pleasure, Signorina Rossini."

"Signore," she said, curtseying. Her voice was an awed whisper, brimming with wonder and a trace of fear that he had deigned to mark her with his attention.

"May I inquire what sort of fortune you were given that brought such a charming blush to your cheek?" he asked, hoping to set her at ease.

"I'm to meet a handsome dark-haired gentleman," she blurted.

Her bevy of friends darted glances at him, giggling.

Bianca blanched when she realized what she'd revealed and to whom.

"And when you meet this gentleman, do you plan to share a dance with him?" Nick inquired with unusual care. She was one of those sweet-tempered creatures who inspired gentleness in those around her.

"Oh," she said, her brow knitting. "All of my dances are spoken for."

"Couldn't you spare just one for Lord Satyr?" her brother

encouraged, obviously beginning to realize what his sudden interest in his sister might mean to the family's fortunes.

Nick was certain the Rossini clan would easily accept him, as would their daughter. She had no doubt been trained well in her duty and would grace his home and bed and give him no trouble. Their marriage would cause scarcely a ripple in the comfortable pattern of his life.

Only the formalities were left to undertake. He would speak to his attorney in Rome tomorrow and claim her as his as soon as a wedding could be arranged.

"But that wouldn't be proper," she said.

Nick was taken aback for a moment until he determined she was referring to the question of allowing him a dance. "You're right, of course. How unfortunate for your dark, handsome gentleman and all others who have missed their chance for a turn on the lawn with you tonight."

"Um, yes," she said. She blinked, appearing mesmerized by his smile.

Really, this was too easy, he thought. While pleased at her lack of artifice, he couldn't help but wonder if the lure of her simplicity might dull in time. It didn't matter. Husbands of his rank spent little time in their wives' company.

And every Faerie had hidden depths. He wondered what magic her demure manner concealed.

The drape parted as the tent emptied its latest client.

"Going to try it?" asked one of the youths as the mystic's most recent customer was expelled. He sounded hopeful, no doubt assuming the ladies wouldn't divert their attention from Nick until he left them.

Nick offered an arm to Bianca. "Since I'm to be denied a dance, will you accompany me inside to have my fortune told?"

Bianca's startled eyes darted to her brother.

"With your brother's permission," Nick added.

"Go ahead, Bianca," said her brother. "The mystic is chaperone enough, and I'll be right outside."

"But I've already had my fortune told," she reminded them.

"I haven't, however," said Nick. "And I admit I'm daunted by the notion of approaching a true mystic. You have obviously navigated these waters and survived. I beseech you to come along with me that you might shore up my quaking will."

Bianca still hesitated. *Probably wondering if Mama would approve,* he thought.

He employed his considerable powers of persuasion. "Your eyes tell me you possess a generous spirit. Surely you can find it in the kindness of your heart to make a decision in my favor."

"Why, all right. Of course I'll accompany you," she agreed. Then she leaned closer to offer, "But the mystic isn't terribly frightening, really."

With a nod to her brother, Nick held the drape aside and bade Signorina Rossini enter before him.

3

Within the tent, Jane Cova listened and rolled her eyes at the gentleman's blandishments. Was his lady really wooed by such practiced flattery? She'd seemed to hang on his every word.

For a very different reason, Jane had done so as well. One could learn a great deal about a potential client by eavesdropping on what they said prior to entering the tent. With enough information, an entire fortune could be fabricated for someone, as she had cause to know. Not that her talent was all subterfuge.

The cobweb drape at the tent's entrance fluttered. She prepared herself to greet the new arrivals, adjusting her head covering to partially conceal her youthful features. A few strands of her moon-colored hair escaped the wrap, but she didn't bother to tuck them away. They would be mistaken for gray in dim light.

The betraying softness of her hands was carefully hidden with black lace gloves that left only her fingers bare. She rounded her shoulders to foster the perception she was wizened beyond her years. The crude corncob pipe she slid between her lips was unlit. It, too, was designed to age her and disguise her voice. It was effective, but holding the stem for any length of time was painful. Her lips were already bruised.

A male hand parted the drape, allowing some of the gloom inside the tent to escape. At the sight of those strong fingers, an odd awareness prickled over her. Uncertainty quickened her pulse. Inexplicably, her every intuition and instinct urged her to flee.

She flattened her palms on the table and half stood and then hesitated. Rarely did she gainsay such feelings. Still, she hadn't yet earned the coin she'd hoped for today. She'd arrived late to the event and found the tents occupied with other vendors. Only when the prior inhabitant of this tent had recently vacated had she entered and begun to ply her trade.

The assemblage was wealthy and the evening young. What to do?

Before she could decide, her new customers came inside. Jane recognized the pretty signorina as an earlier visitor. Her color had heightened under her suitor's attentions. But she was harmless enough.

However, the gentleman who shadowed her was a different matter.

His gaze when it met hers was a jolt to the senses. How unusual to encounter an Italian with eyes the color of blue mirrors. Heavily fringed with dark lashes, they reflected what he observed, giving away nothing.

Skin of golden olive marked him as a man of Italian blood. His strong brow, sculpted chin, and jutting blade of a nose marked him as obstinent.

Taken altogether, his features combined into a striking, if haughty, aristocratic face that sat atop a muscular frame. His height was commanding and surely reached to six and a half feet. Blessed with such a surfeit of good looks, he appeared a god among mortals.

"Leaving?" he inquired, noting her uncertain pose.

Jane faltered and then simply stared into those strange eyes. She stood frozen in indecision, knowing she looked the idiot. But she couldn't seem to help it.

At her continued silence, the man's brow rose in question. He'd politely seated his lady, fetched an additional chair for himself from somewhere outside the tent, and now stood patiently waiting for her to be seated. Perhaps he was accustomed to striking women dumb at first sight.

"I hope my gold will prevail upon you to tarry?" he asked gently.

The pipe slid from Jane's slack jaw. She barely caught it before it bounced on the table. The mishap had the effect of pulling her eyes from his, thus breaking the spell. Her legs wobbled, forcing her to sit.

Embarrassed, she gathered her wits and straightened to find him seated, studying her.

Hoping to divert his attention, she began to caress the crystal ball before her. Though she didn't really employ it in her trade, it helped foster the illusion in people's minds that she was a gypsy fortuneteller.

"What are you called, mystic?" Nick asked. His Italian was shaded with a slight accent, she'd noted. But the language sounded comfortable on his tongue and was most likely his native one. His English was fluent but less certain. She guessed he'd been schooled in England or by an English tutor, at any rate. The commanding timbre of his voice indicated he was a man accustomed to having his demands met, which implied he was wealthy.

"Jane," she replied.

He settled back in his seat with a smugly amused expression. "Jane the mystic?"

Signorina Rossini looked puzzled. "I thought your name was Madame Fibbioni."

"Jane be me given name," Jane lied, lapsing into the fractured cockney-Italian blend she'd developed for such occasions.

"Well, Madame Jane Fibbioni," said Nick, "what is your usual fee for reading palms?"

The signorina answered for her.

"I tell me fortunes singly," Jane announced, belatedly remembering to disguise her voice as a throaty cackle.

"Oh!" said Signorina Rossini. "In that case, I should withdraw."

Jane drew in a breath of alarm. She couldn't take him alone! The idea was horrifying.

A masculine hand over the signorina's stopped her from rising. "Hold a moment. Would triple your fee convince you to make an exception?" he inquired of Jane. He lay the money on the table atop the beaded scarf she'd draped over it.

Jane stared at his coin in indecision.

"Is business so robust you can turn down such an offering?" he cajoled.

No, it wasn't. With a sweep of her hand, she raked the money into the coin purse in her lap.

"Yer takin' a chance lettin' yer lady hear yer future," she warned. "But if it's yer wish, then oiyl see if the spirits be willin'."

"Grazie. We shall await our fortunes at the spirits' leisure, dear mystic," he said.

"I make no claim to the title of mystic," she told him with a shake of her head. "I be a simple teller of fortunes."

"Do let her tell yours first," encouraged Signorina Rossini. "It's very exciting."

Nick smiled down at her.

The pretty signorina hardly struck Jane as the type who would appeal to an earthy male such as this. However, he appeared to be truly under the spell of her attractions. His look when set upon her was hungry enough to make her own skin tingle under its indirect impact. No wonder the signorina had fallen for his honeyed words.

From the distance came the eerie sound of water being pressured through the pipes of the grand Water Organ in the garden for the guests' amusement. Jane fiddled with the strings of the coin purse in her lap, loathe to begin what must be begun.

"Begin by placing your hand in hers," the signorina prompted to Nick.

"As you command."

His hand settled onto the scarf within Jane's vision, palm upward. Something about the shape of those long, blunt fingers both repelled and compelled her. The blue pulse at the inside of his wrist throbbed warm and strong, his life force vibrant.

Beneath the table, she tugged the lacy gloves low. Nothing but her fingers must be bared on him.

Then she sat forward, touching. The tips of his fingers curled in response, brushing sparks over the tender underside of her wrist through the lace.

Desperately she traced the terrain of his palm, willing the images to come. His fate line ran unbroken through the valley of his palm—a man of exceptional self-control. His heart line showed him to be shrewd. The padded Venus mount at the base of his thumb was plump. A man of vitality, health, and stamina.

Her abilities as a fortune-teller weren't a total ruse. She could learn something of a person through touch. At least, enough to satisfy the average customer.

But the remarkable abilities that had come to her with the onset of puberty had recently begun shifting. They were slowly draining away in some areas while increasing in others. Her ability to read Humans became less reliable with each passing of the moon. She prayed it wouldn't fail her now.

A sigh of relief left her lips when the mind mist enveloped her, calming her with its familiarity. Her eyes drifted shut, and she drew her fingers over him, occasionally following a crease or dusting over a mount. Just the barest, minute mixing of skin oils was all it took for a simple telling of fortunes. It was important to avoid melding. If she bonded further, parting sometimes caused her pain.

"I see a forest," she began. "An ancient forest. It surrounds a flourishing garden covering many hillsides. I see three brothers, three splendid homes."

She opened her eyes and pondered him curiously. Only Nick noticed how refined her accent had become.

"Lord Satyr owns a large estate in Tuscany, along with his two younger brothers," supplied Signorina Rossini. Her voice trembled with excitement that Jane had guessed correctly.

Jane smiled at her. Now she had his name and residence. People were so free with information. Really, it made her efforts quite simple at times.

Nick eyed her sardonically. "My estates and family ties are no secret. You will have to do better to earn your coin."

If she'd been wise, she would have fabricated a silly fortune and released his hand as soon as possible. It was no doubt what he expected. But she was overcome with an irrational desire to prove herself.

She ducked her head and continued.

"I see material wealth. Power. Passion." She slanted him a glance through her lashes. "Concealment."

A subtle tension invaded his skin.

Signorina Rossini giggled. "Passion! Goodness! And what could you be concealing, Lord Satyr?"

His hand shifted so his thumb interlaced Jane's two smallest fingers, stroking the tender skin between them. Deliberately?

She was amusing, he thought. Her fingers were soft, her skin unlined and youthful beneath her ragged crone disguise. His curiosity was aroused. He shifted on his seat. *He* was aroused.

Annoyed that she had caused his need to flare when it couldn't be quenched, he smiled, flirting. Just to rattle her.

As Jane stared at the full curve of his mouth, sudden shocking visions dashed at her like storm-tossed waves. She saw him in another time and place. He was standing. The muscles of his naked chest flexed and rippled in soft candlelight. Or was it moonlight? His features were raw and savage, and eyes glittered as he stared intently at—something. A woman. She was before him, bent over some sort of table. W—what was he doing to her?

She gasped, realizing they must be copulating. Blushing, she snatched her hand away. The vision snapped off as though a door had slammed shut.

Flames of interest lit his eyes.

Surreptitiously, she wiped her fingers on her skirt. This was insane. What was she doing melding so closely? What if he were to rip off her disguise and report her doings to her aunt and father?

In a panic, she began to pack her belongings. His gold be damned.

"You've only told me a mix of obscure speculation and what I already know to be certain. What of my fortune?" Nick demanded.

It was impossible to look at him now. What if he read the truth of what she'd seen? Of him doing *that*. It was wrong that she'd observed him in such a private moment. Evil that she had the despicable ability.

"'Tis a pleasure to report all yer prospects be excellent! I see only good fortune in yer future," she predicted hastily. "And there'll be a bride for ye soon! One with pretty blue eyes."

There—that should please his companion.

Smiling, she turned to Signorina Rossini and pretended to realize her identity just then. "As for yer young lady—I've previously given her a fortune, tellin' her she would meet someone dark and handsome."

Here she turned back to Nick. Not daring to meet his gaze,

she stared at his chin. Already a blue-black cast shadowed his jawline, though it was only early evening. For some reason, this small confirmation of his virility alarmed her all out of proportion to its import.

"Yer appears to fill the bill, good sir. I'll leave you to it then."

She gathered the trappings of her fortune-telling trade in the table scarf, loosely tying its fringed ends. Holding the makeshift bundle to her chest, she rose to leave.

But the muscular god stood as well. Was he being polite, or did he intend to block her exit? By now, she'd dodged a sufficient number of men along Tivoli's streets that she'd become wary of their bold hands.

Determinedly, she moved forward, shying an arm's length from the formidable wall of his chest. Lord, he was tall. A vision of him naked and straining flashed in her mind, and she nearly moaned in despair.

"I mustn't tarry. The, uh, spirits call me away," she informed the toes of his boots. They were midnight blue, nearly black. And there was a pattern etched on them of writhing vines that entwined some sort of mythological creatures. How odd.

She felt him smile at the top of her head. He sought to toy with her, did he?

Though the eyes she lifted to him shot green sparks, her voice was mild. "Please stand aside, signore."

"Lord Satyr?" his companion asked uncertainly.

At her voice, he seemed to come back to himself. He shifted, parting the drapery at the tent's opening.

Something nagged at Nick as the gypsy's bent figure scurried beneath his arm and outside, but he couldn't determine the source of it.

He stared after her, loathe to let go of an unsolved puzzle. "Strange one, that."

"Well, she is a fortune-teller, after all," Signorina Rossini reminded him.

She was right, of course. He shook off the feeling that something wasn't quite as it should be and turned back to his companion. He had more important matters to attend to.

He pondered whether to tarry alone with her in the tent's confines. Her brother would report the indiscretion to her parents, which would likely facilitate their consent to a quick wedding.

Instead, he watched his hand part the drape, and he escorted her outside. Uncertain as to why he had done so when lingering within would have been to his advantage, he attempted to engage her in conversation apart from her acquaintants.

Putting a question to her regarding an upcoming ball was enough to incite her interest. As she was one of those young ladies who required little attention in order to prattle on about inconsequential matters, it took only a small portion of his mind to keep up his side of the social discourse from there. Another part of his brain returned to puzzle on the episode that had passed inside the tent.

A moment later, he realized he'd missed much of what Signorina Rossini had said. He stared down at her and recognized his uppermost emotion for what it was. Boredom.

Worse still, the Faerie scent that had once cloaked her had dramatically faded. In fact, it had all but disappeared.

He stepped back from her. *Seven hells!* It wasn't she after all!

If he stayed by her side any longer, society would have him engaged to her no matter what his preference. His mind racing, he drew her into the flock of her friends, who quickly included her in their midst.

The gypsy fortune-teller. It had to be.

But King Feydon had claimed he'd bedded a highborn woman, not a gypsy. Had the girl fallen on hard times?

His chin lifted, and he searched the wind. There it was. The very faintest hint—the merest thread of Faerie spice.

Eyes narrowed, he scanned the grounds, questing, and found the formal entrance at the north end of the gardens. There. The arch of glass over the walkway. The very portal through which the fortune-teller had recently fled. With her departure, the scent of Faerie had fled as well.

Abruptly he excused himself from Signorina Rossini and the cluster of guests. He ignored the almost unanimous start of surprise at his curt withdrawal. Features honed with determination, he began his hunt anew.

Outside the garden gate, he trod the expanses of lawn, passing the occasional fountain or pond. Beyond, when the greenery turned to the paving stones of a thoroughfare, he instinctively headed toward the Aniene River.

He caught sight of the fortune-teller again some distance ahead, scampering over the wide uneven bricks underfoot. She traveled alone, foolish girl. It was a fashionable area, but she could easily find herself in trouble in the nooks and crannies of these twisting streets.

Now and then she became lost from his sight, for she had nearly a fifty-yard lead on him. But his gait was longer than hers, and he easily gained ground.

Occasionally she glanced back as though sensing his pursuit. He kept to the shadows, hidden.

After some blocks, he saw her enter an ironwork gate leading to a private town house. From an alley across the lane, he assessed the dwelling and found it well kept and luxurious, though unostentatious. Was it that of her family, or was she a guest in another's household? Or a servant? Was she already wed? Would her relatives prove difficult?

So many questions, and no answers to be had this night.

In ElseWorld, Satyrs sought their mates in a more forthright manner than was the custom of Human society. Unfortunately that meant he couldn't follow her inside and take her with him tonight.

Fortunately he could display infinite patience when it was required. Tomorrow he would visit his attorney and determine the nature of her family. Their financial circumstances and social standing would inform him regarding how best to proceed.

Briefly he wondered at the danger to her person about which King Feydon had hinted. The house she'd entered appeared innocuous, like dozens of others along the street. However, he had more than a passing acquaintance with the secrets that ordinary stone walls could conceal.

The clatter of carriage wheels drew his attention. A portly man sat in the passing open-air coach, his eyes closed and an expression of agonized delight on his face.

When his conveyance hit a pothole, a flustered feminine head popped up from between his sausage thighs. Her hair was mussed and her lips moist. For a moment, her glance tangled with Nick's. She boldly eyed the swell of his crotch and winked.

A prostitute. A very comely one. He smiled his admiration, and she smiled back. Then, with resignation, her head ducked over the signore's lap once again, and the carriage rattled out of sight.

With no more reason to linger, Nick slipped back to the garden and hailed his private coach. His physical needs could be denied no longer.

Overhead, clouds had gathered and thickened, obscuring starlight. But the heavy tautness in his loins told him the moon was waxing. It was a dangerous time for one such as he to be without a woman for so long.

The Calling would occur three days hence, at Moonful, as it did with monthly regularity. When the night sky's orb hung swollen and round, his passion would unleash. It was essential he curtail his business here in Tivoli and return to Satyr land before the Calling overtook him.

Hours later, he entered the sumptuous abode of Mona, one of his favorite meretrici in Rome. She greeted him effusively, and he found himself engulfed in her bosom and smothered by the falseness of her perfume. For the first time he felt vaguely repulsed by its brazenness, so unlike the delicate fragrance he'd tracked earlier that evening.

He pulled away and saw she had readied herself for him. She was dressed as he liked, in a manner which proclaimed she'd once been part of accepted society. No bawdy-house woman here, but rather a figure that might have graced the finest ballroom if she hadn't fallen into financial difficulty and chosen this profession as a way out.

Her mild plumpness and elegance pleased him. His taste in women varied, but on the whole he preferred them cultured and genteel—at least on the outside.

A movement in the salon doorway attracted his notice, and he turned to observe another of her kind waiting in the dimness beyond. He'd sent word ahead that he would be calling. Mona had obviously prepared some sort of entertainment for him.

The other woman wore a scarlet bombazine gown that appeared determined to bind its wearer as tightly as his trousers restrained his burgeoning cock. Though the gown's design bordered on prim, its waist was sharply curtailed and its bodice forced her ample bosom high.

Marking his interest, Mona waved a manicured hand toward her companion, inviting her closer for his inspection.

"I hope you don't mind," she teased throatily, linking her arm with his and the other woman's to draw their threesome more intimately together. "My sister will be joining us."

Giggling, the younger version of his meretrice jiggled coyly, purposely attracting his gaze to the undulating globes that swelled precariously above the neckline of her gown.

"Angela!" Mona scolded. "Lord Satyr comes to us seeking

refinement, not the behavior one might expect from a whore of the back alleys."

The younger woman straightened, chastised.

Nick smiled at her, flashing even white teeth. Her expression melted as she quickly fell under his thrall.

Both women had lush figures but were different of feature. He doubted they were related. Still he gave Mona high marks for the creativity she displayed. The fantasy of having sisters attend him was always quite diverting.

Nick shook off the notion that such pleasures, though as necessary to him as breathing, had come to seem empty in recent months. The addition of a wife and children to his household would prove a welcome distraction from a growing awareness that there was a void in his life.

"Vino, signore?" asked Mona, pressing her bosom into his arm. Candlelight flickered on the bottle she lifted from the liquor cart. It bore the Satyr Vineyard emblem, an embossed SV.

He nodded.

A soft hand grazed the fabric over his crotch, as though by accident. Her supposed sister. He ignored the overture for the moment and lifted the glass that was poured for him, anticipating the first swallow.

The intimate touch at his trousers grew bolder as the shimmering liquid spilled over his tongue. The tart sweetness tightened his taste buds even as the skilled fingers released his engorged prick to the caress of a feminine mouth.

Ah! There was nothing like the taste of Satyr . . . wine.

4

Wine! It disgusted her!

Jane kicked the empty bottle she'd tripped over just inside her aunt's gate.

Normally she wasn't so clumsy. But after leaving Villa d'Este, she'd been rattled by the bizarre notion that she was being pursued. A few more steps and she'd be on the stairs leading inside Aunt Izabel's town house.

She picked up the wine bottle for closer examination and rubbed her thumb over the raised insignia molded into its side—"SV."

When she'd lived in London, she'd discovered many such bottles in various hiding places. This one was her father's, no doubt, as all the others had been. So much for her aunt's prophesy that the move from London to Tivoli would cure his intemperance.

She wrinkled her nose at the vinegary smell of the bottle's dregs.

What did he find so necessary in this fermented brew that

he'd thrown his life away on it after their mother had died? And how ironic, when the contents of bottles such as this one had been the very cause of her death! For the coachman who'd driven her the night her carriage had overturned had been intoxicated.

The clouds overhead parted, and the bottle caught the moonlight, momentarily shooting amber starbursts. Anger bubbled up. Under her fingers, the glass heated and rattled. Cracks formed over its surface as though it were arid soil too long denied rain.

She tossed it away. Arcing in midair, the bottle shattered in a soft explosion, sprinkling the path with golden jewels.

Gratified, she stepped over the shards and scurried up the stairs. Her bundle was a comfortable weight against her thigh, heavy with coins and the trappings of her secret occupation.

The coin purse hidden in her armoire grew fatter by the week. One day soon, she would take her sister and leave this place. The money would buy them food and lodging somewhere in the countryside. It would buy anonymity. Security.

Upon reaching the town-house door without discovery or mishap, she breathed a sigh of relief. Her step light, she lifted the latch and let herself in.

From the window above, Jane's aunt Izabel took careful note of her homecoming.

"Jane has returned from her nocturnal wanderings," Izabel observed. "In an effort to escape the tightening nuptial noose, she goes on her jaunts more frequently."

"She'd best keep herself chaste for Signore Nesta," muttered the figure that shadowed her. "Think you she visits another man?"

Izabel's laughter trilled. "Jane? Hardly."

A stealthy masculine hand slid over her shoulder and dusted her collarbone. Hesitantly, as though unsure of its welcome, it delved under the neckline of her nightgown to capture a breast.

Izabel registered the intrusion with a distant corner of her mind and decided to allow it.

At her lack of resistance, the palming of her flesh grew bolder. Familiar fingers found and twisted the small silver ring that pierced her nipple, drawing a sigh from her.

"Come to bed, my love," the man coaxed.

Izabel let the window curtain swish back into place. Her eyelids drooped, and she leaned against the warmth behind her.

Turning her, he lifted her breasts from their lacy confinement and latched onto the nipple nearest his mouth. The slurp and pull of his lusty nursing caused a pleasant tugging sensation in her womb.

The folds of her gown brushed the backs of her legs, gathering in his fists. Cool air touched her naked bottom as his hands gained the access they sought. Gripping her twin swells, he kneaded.

Fondly, Izabel gazed at the head rooting at her nipple. She stroked his wavy dark hair, so like her own.

He was useful, this stepbrother of hers.

And he was always so agreeably impatient to have her. Outside her bedchamber, rules of propriety had to be observed. There, he could treat her only in a fraternal manner. And on many nights, she deemed it wise to refuse him the use of her body even in private chambers. Denial only served to whet his appetite.

Should she let him have her tonight? It wasn't wise to make him too certain he could take such liberties at will.

However, she had reason to be grateful to him. Six months ago, he'd brought his daughters to live in her home. The value of her younger niece remained uncertain. At the moment, it was Jane who was of primary interest.

Soon her eldest niece would be made to wed. Signore Nesta had already proven his ability to sire sons. He would no doubt whelp more on Jane with satisfactory haste. And through Jane's children, dreams long in the making would be realized.

"Let me fuck you, Izzy. Please," her companion begged.

A sense of feminine supremacy sent a charge of lust sizzling through Izabel's veins. She delighted in his pent-up frustration.

Tugging his hair, she pressed his lips to rub across hers. The taste of the wine she'd provided was tart and cool on his tongue. Pulling away, she whispered to him in the darkness.

"You may fuck me in good time. But for now, allow me to—" She let the words hang in the air between them. He caught her meaning, and his eyes lit with anticipation.

Her smooth lady's hands slid down his body, shaping his ribs and then his thighs until she knelt in a pool of silk and lace before him. His shaft twitched and pulsed, tenting his robe just below its sash. A small circle of pre-cum dampened the satin.

Her lips twisted. While a woman's desire was easily concealed, a man's was always so pathetically obvious. The power in this act was hers. His desire for her allowed her to control him.

Gently she parted the fabric.

His ruddy crown bobbed forward, its slitted eye leering at her. His shaft wasn't especially large, though it had felt so the first time it had come inside her. She'd been so young then, her body untried.

Since that day, she'd delighted in trying many things with him. And with others. It was her nature to revel in pleasures of the flesh. Unlike his former milquetoast English wife.

The odor of male musk strengthened as she widened the opening at the front of his robe. Leaning forward, she ran plump, dry lips along his length. Burying her nose in the thicket of hair at his root, she inhaled the slight sourness, a comfortable and familiar smell peculiar to him. She pulled back to swirl her tongue around the under ridge of his crown and then flicked his seeping slit, enjoying his groan, enjoying the salty taste of cum and unwashed flesh.

He rested fingertips on her shoulders and braced his legs. As though from a distance, she watched her hands weigh and fondle his testicles and then grasp his length and guide it forward. Her salivary glands squirted, preparing the cavern of her mouth for the task ahead.

At the first wet stroke, the muscles of his thighs tensed and jerked. The firm O of her lips undulated his crest and then slid to his root. He moaned as her fists, mouth, and tongue worked in unison, coaxing him in the strong, milking way he liked best.

Though her mind roamed elsewhere as she drove him toward his release, she was truly eager to please him. In the end, it was she who'd benefit from his desire.

For this act upon his flesh, he would do anything she asked of him.

For this and other private pleasures she bestowed, he would betray his own children, turn a blind eye to her plans for them.

For this, he had allowed her to kill his wife.

She had never understood why he'd married that dry English vacca in the first place. The marriage had caused him to abandon her—his dearest stepsister—in Tivoli so he could share a home with his erstwhile wife in London.

When he'd no longer been readily available to fuck her, Izabel had been furious. She had married herself to an elder in her church, who'd been so agreeable as to keel over and leave her a wealthy widow within the year. Nevertheless, for all the nights she'd been forced to spend beneath the old rutting buzzard, she blamed her stepbrother and his marriage. Even now, his betrayal stung.

A firm squeeze to his testicles caused him to buck, stuffing his cock deep. A pinch to the tender skin of his inner thigh reminded him the pace was hers to set. He yelped at the light punishment and clenched his buttocks, trying to remain compliant.

His letters to her during his marriage had often complained of his wife's deficiencies in the bedchamber, of his disappointment that his efforts with her had sired only two children, and both of them girls. Izabel had read the details of their coital incompatibilities with relish and invigorated hope. She had carefully plotted her rival's downfall.

When he and his family had occasionally visited, she had made sure the former Lady Cova noticed the unusual closeness she and her stepbrother shared. On that last fateful visit he and his wife had made to Italy, she had flaunted the incestuous relationship until Lady Cova had been goaded into openly acknowledging her awareness of it. And her disgust for it. So naive.

In so doing, Lady Cova had shown herself to be a threat. Their enemy. If she were to expose their secret to the world, few would understand. By then, her stepbrother had grown tired of his wife's cold English bed. He had quickly seen the wisdom of dissolving the marriage in the only way open to them.

His wife's death.

Arranging it had proven surprisingly simple. Just three bottles of rotgut wine for the coachman and a shallow cut to a carriage axle that ensured it would break along its trip. The rest of her plan had been equally easy.

Following Lady Cova's demise, the bereft family had come to Italy, and Izabel had opened her home to them. It pleased her to know society at large thought well of her willingness to care for her nieces and to see to a betrothal for Jane. Appearances were so important.

Amusing how things had worked out in the end. Her stepbrother's marriage to his English milksop, which had once so pained her, now worked to her advantage. The match had produced Jane.

Jane, of unearthly parentage, who was of a good age for marriage.

At last.

Her stepbrother's length swelled and grew more determined within her mouth as she competently sucked him off. Only when his cream finally spurted and dribbled down her throat did she rise and lead him to her bed.

5

Jane knelt on the brick path that wound through her aunt's garden and jabbed her small spade into the soil, loosening and turning. She discovered a sickly patch of variegated applemint and lifted it.

"Poor dear. Not to worry. I'll fix you right up. I wonder, which of the mulches would you prefer?"

"Do they ever talk back?" a girlish voice teased from behind her.

Jane gave a start and glanced over her shoulder to find her younger sister, Emma, grinning at her.

She smiled and shrugged, casually moving so her body shielded the bed where she'd been working. "If they could, I imagine they'd be denouncing our aunt's previous gardener. He neglected them shamefully."

"But they're improving under your care," said Emma, craning to see Jane's handiwork.

Jane was unsurprised to notice that Emma held a book in her skirts. She motioned toward it, hoping to divert her sister's attention. "What do you have there?"

Emma held up the leather-bound tome and opened it to a particular passage she'd marked with a strip of velvet.

"It's Carl Linnaeus' *Philosophia Botanica.* I have decided to attempt to plant a floral clock such as he describes. Just imagine being able to tell the time simply from the blooming and fading cycle of a blossom."

Jane's brows rose. "The horologium florae? Many of the plants he suggests for the clock are wildflowers, are they not? Will you be able to locate them all here in Tivoli?"

Emma shook her head. "'Tis unlikely. But I've begun a survey to determine the opening and closing hours of native Italian plants. In place of any plants I cannot collect to match the twelve Linnaeus describes, I shall find substitutes that reflect the same timing!"

"Brilliant!" Jane enthused. Both sisters were intensely fond of botany. While Jane's interest lent itself to actual tactile work among plants, Emma's tended toward a more scholarly endeavor.

"Read to me while I finish up here," Jane invited. "I've forgotten precisely which plants the clock calls for."

Emma situated herself on an ironwork bench and began reading aloud.

Jane positioned herself so her interaction with the plants couldn't easily be observed. There were some secrets she must keep safe, even from Emma.

Under her care, loam enriched. Tendrils sprouted and curled lovingly around her fingers. Weeds shrank away. Foxglove and orange blossoms sprang to life. Wilting snapdragons perked and brightened, their color intensifying as if by magic.

If only she could work such magic for her sister.

For she was deeply worried about Emma. Of what she might become—a creature like herself, possessed of an unnatural strangeness that must be hidden.

In mere months, Emma would reach her thirteenth year. For

Jane, the change from girl to woman at thirteen had naturally meant moving from padded stays into the restriction of corsets. But at the same time that society had dictated her body be forced to morph into an hourglass shape, another equally unstoppable metamorphosis had begun within her.

Though Emma knew nothing of Jane's bizarre abilities, their mother had. And that knowledge had caused everything to change between them. Her mother had stopped loving her, stopped touching her, and had watched her with new wariness. Jane had soon learned to conceal much of what she was.

Concealment. The word put her in mind of the lord with the pale blue eyes who had visited her tent at Villa d'Este.

She arched her back, stretching.

"Jane!"

At their aunt Izabel's summons, the sisters exchanged hunted looks.

Emma jumped up and pulled at Jane's arm. "Let's hide."

Jane forced a teasing grin to her lips. "Save yourself. Go finish your reading elsewhere. It's me she wants."

"Jane!" the shrill voice called again, nearer this time.

Emma mimed a face of comical terror and then grabbed her book and scampered away.

Jane understood her sister's feelings completely. With reluctance she stood and removed her apron.

Her aunt tsked in annoyance when she saw her.

"Your fascination with this grubby garden is beyond my understanding. Just look at you. Filthy!"

Izabel smoothed Jane's hair into place, and Jane let her. She tried to pretend such brusque assistance was offered with familial kindness.

"Disgraceful color. But there's naught to be done about it, I suppose," said Izabel.

Jane ignored the insult. Her pale blond hair, pointed chin, and fair English skin were very like her mother's. While Emma had inherited their father's ash-brown hair and eyes, Jane mirrored nothing of him.

Izabel dipped her handkerchief into the small garden fountain. When she returned, it was to scrub dirt from Jane's cheek with dimpled, beringed hands.

Jane had avoided the touch of others for years, out of necessity. She only permitted it when it was unavoidable or to earn necessary coin in her fortune-telling.

"What does my appearance matter?" she asked, ducking away. "I have no plans to venture out."

Slapping the soiled cloth onto the stone rim of the fountain, Izabel frowned, etching lines around her lips. "We have a guest. Or, rather, *you* have a guest."

"Who?" Jane asked warily.

"You shall see. It will come as a welcome surprise, I'm sure."

With trepidation, Jane followed her aunt into the salotto. There she found her father waiting, along with a signore who was becoming all too familiar to her.

Both men stood when the ladies passed through the tall white and gold doors.

"Buon giorno, Signorina Cova," the visitor told her in greeting. Though his mouth smiled under his dark mustache, his small eyes did not. His checked waistcoat was well fitted and tasteful, his trousers creased. His dark hair was slicked and styled. He was as fastidious and presentable as he was repulsive.

"Buon giorno, Signore Nesta," Jane replied.

Her hand was briefly enfolded in his cold, dry one. He wanted something from her. She felt it. But what? His touch had been too brief for her to meld yet too long for her to bear.

Her aunt sat a distance away, leaving her the chair closest to their visitor. Jane remained outwardly placid as he examined her in an appraising way, with his head slightly cocked as though attempting to determine her value.

She twitched her skirt in annoyance.

He said something in Italian to her aunt and father, and the three of them laughed. Her grasp of Italian was good, but he'd spoken colloquially and too quickly for her to catch his meaning.

"You're well since we last met?" he inquired in heavily accented English.

"Yes. And you?" she replied.

"Molto bene, grazie."

An awkward moment passed.

Her aunt sought to fill it. "The gardens are so colorful this time of year, aren't they, signore? Jane has such a way with the plants. She's making our gardens the liveliest in the neighborhood."

Jane's eyes widened. Suddenly her gardening skills were of value?

Signore Nesta nodded at Jane. "You would have suggestions to offer for the gardens at my villa, perchance? You must visit."

Jane opened her mouth to decline, but her aunt stepped on her words.

"Oh, yes, we shall endeavor to visit quite soon." She frowned at Jane. "Niece, Signore Nesta's cup needs filling."

Jane picked up the teapot and perfunctorily filled his cup.

When she leaned forward to hand it to him, Signore Nesta's eyes dropped from her face to her form. She fought the impulse to cover herself. The lecher!

He smirked. "Salud!" he said, offering a mocking toast as he took the cup.

Though the conversation continued to flow around her, Jane didn't participate further unless a direct question was put to her.

It occurred to her that Signore Nesta's attention and avid glances meant one thing. That he wanted to wed her, in order that he might touch her with carnal familiarity.

Though she was uninformed regarding the specifics of what happened between married couples in private, she knew husbands expected to put their hands and lips on their wives. To somehow join their bodies together, producing children.

She didn't want the signore's hands or lips on her. In fact, now that she'd ascertained the nature of his interest, she felt physically under threat in his presence. He put her in mind of a particular kind of cuspidate, an ivy that pleased the eye but given enough time overpowered and suffocated every living thing around it.

Signore Nesta certainly knew more of the marriage bed than she. His wife had died bearing a third son to him in less than three years. He was still a young man, and she was very much concerned she was slated to become his next brood mare.

If she must marry someday, she'd prefer a husband who paid her scant attention, or maybe one with impaired sight. Signore Nesta's gimlet eyes watched her every twitch. For that reason alone, he wouldn't do.

The very last thing she needed was an observant, interfering husband. Such a man would quickly discern that all wasn't right with her. He would realize she could do . . . feel . . . know . . . things that others couldn't. Such a man would denounce her when he learned her secrets and discovered what she'd become.

Because whatever she was—she could no longer believe herself to be truly Human.

6

Late the next morning, Izabel dabbed her prim lips with a crisp napkin and then broke the silence pervading the dining room. "'Tis an incredible stroke of luck."

Dressed in elegant peach satin, she sat to Jane's left at one end of the oblong, damask-draped dining table. Jane's father, who more than filled the delicate chair at the opposite end, looked up at her words.

"We must accept with haste lest the offer be withdrawn," Izabel went on.

"Umm-hmm," Jane murmured. Her attention was on the book lying open in her lap, half hidden below the lip of the table.

It was Homer's *Odyssey*, which she'd enjoyed many times before. But today she studied one particular passage with new interest.

Homer mentioned a curative called allium moly. Hermes had given it to Odysseus as a protection against the magick of Circe the sorceress. Dare she hope it might prove to be the cure for her strangeness?

The idea had come to her yesterday when Emma had read to her from Linnaeus. Both he and the botanist Dioscorides had also spoken of the moly's curative properties.

They'd described it as the moly she knew, which bore a simple yellow flower. Some termed it lily leek, while to others it was known as sorcerer's garlic.

She longed to discuss the matter with her sister, though without revealing the reasons for her interest. However, the chair opposite her was empty, since Emma was at lessons with her Italian tutor upstairs.

"Well? Do you not agree?" Izabel's tone had grown strident.

Jane tore her attention from the book. Alarmed, she realized both her aunt and father were staring at her expectantly. What had she missed?

"Um, I'm not sure. . . ." she ventured. She reached for a croissant, filling her mouth to avoid finishing.

"Suffice it to say we find him satisfactory," Jane's aunt informed her. "You must accept him as your husband."

Homer hit the floor with a muted *thunk*.

"What the devil?" Her father ducked his head under the crisp tablecloth to see what had caused the noise, leaving Jane to stare at her aunt.

"My w—what?" Jane asked faintly.

"Your husband, girl! What do you think I have been going on about for the past ten minutes?" Izabel picked up a serving spoon, surreptitiously admiring her reflection in its polished silver before she dipped it into the soup.

"Signore Nesta has offered?" Jane squeaked, fighting panic.

"No, not Nesta!" scolded Izabel. The ladle clinked to the table, as though adding an exclamation point to her annoyance.

"Someone else wishes to be my husband?"

"Not just someone," her aunt continued. Her eyes sparkled as she leaned forward to divulge her precious nugget of information. "'Tis Lord Nicholas Satyr!"

Jane's head jerked back. The man from the tent? He wanted to marry her? Her mind sought to bend itself around the news and couldn't.

"Impossible."

Izabel's lips thinned. "A gentleman of wealth and standing has requested your hand in marriage and you say 'impossible'?"

Bewildered, Jane shook her head. "It must be some sort of jest. He doesn't even know me."

"He claims a prior acquaintance," said her aunt.

Jane was shocked into silence by this information. Had he seen through her disguise at Villa d'Este last week? Still, why now did he press his suit after twenty minutes of conversation with her at a fair?

"He came here?" she asked.

"And visited your father this very morning."

Her head swiveled to her father.

"He's titled, at least," he mumbled into his plate.

"Yes, the name of Satyr had long been inscribed in the Libro d'Oro della Nobiltà Italiana," added Izabel. "You will do no better for a husband."

That the man's family was listed in the registers of Italian nobility maintained at the offices of the Consulta Araldica made his offer for her even more absurd.

Jane ladled soup from the tureen into her bowl and strove for a rational tone. "But I'm not ready to marry quite yet."

"You wish to be a burden upon our household until your dotage?" asked her aunt.

No, Jane wanted to scream. What she wanted was to be accepted by her family for who she was—what she was. To be loved. But she no longer hoped for such things. Experience had taught her not to expect them. Even her own dear mother had found her too abnormal to love. Her father had ignored her because she wasn't a son. Now she sought only freedom for herself and Emma.

"I sensed no attraction between us," Jane murmured almost to herself.

Her aunt's brows slammed together. "I thought you didn't know him."

A vision of the man from the tent—naked, engaging in carnal activity with an unknown woman—crept into her mind and was instantly banished.

"Only the barest facts. He's a libertine, isn't he?" Jane hazarded.

Izabel shrugged. "Should he prove so, as his wife you will be perfectly situated to influence him into curbing his ways."

"He doesn't strike me as a man easily influenced."

"Again, you show the lie in your claim to be unacquainted with him," said her aunt.

Her father frowned, appearing to suddenly awaken from a trance. "Is there some reason Satyr presses for this marriage?"

"Presses?" Jane echoed.

"He asks for a wedding within days," her aunt informed her.

"Have you been meeting him on the sly?" her father barked. His eyes fell to Jane's slim waist, and his hand fisted around his table knife upon which was speared a piece of venison.

Jane leaped to her feet and threw her napkin to the table. "No! I simply cannot accept him, and certainly not so soon."

Her aunt rose more slowly. "You most certainly shall accept him, or it will go ill for you."

"Now, Izzy," her father chimed in, belatedly attempting to calm the waters. He flapped his hands, birdlike, in an up-and-down motion indicating they should be seated. Izabel sank to her chair, and Jane followed suit.

"What's your objection to Satyr?" he asked Jane.

"I know nothing about him!" she very nearly shouted. "What are his habits, his conversation, his reason for wanting to wed me? Too many things to enumerate."

Her aunt's palm slammed the table, making the silver rattle.

"Goose. What does it matter? As his wife, you will join one of the wealthiest families in Italy." Her tone altered. "But I won't force you. If you prefer to take Signore Nesta to husband, then so be it."

"N—Nesta?" Instantly Jane saw new merit in Lord Satyr's proposal.

"Are you a magpie? You must know he wants you," said her aunt. "Don't you desire a home of your own? A family of your own?"

Jane recalled that Lord Satyr had brothers who lived in proximity to him. Did they have families? Would the extended Satyr clan provide Emma and her with the welcome and acceptance their current situation lacked? He was wealthy, her aunt had said. Emma would have fine clothes, schooling. Safety.

Her heart clenched. She would do anything to keep her sister from harm. Anything. Even this.

"All right," Jane said quietly. "If I must marry, I'll have Lord Satyr. If he is serious. But—"

"There's nothing more to discuss on the matter," said Izabel.

Jane rushed on. "But I will only agree to wed him if you and father will allow Emma to come and live with me in his home."

Without consulting Jane's father, Izabel gave a curt nod. It was painfully obvious who now made the decisions concerning the girls' futures. "We will inform Lord Satyr of your consent."

7

A few days later, Jane sat hunched over her aunt's delicate French writing desk, attempting to read the document before her. Strong emotions blasted in her direction from every side.

From the upholstered sofa came Izabel's determined anxiety and her father's belligerent suspicion. From the chaise opposite the desk, the attorney's speculation. And from the man sitting with his back to the window, a hum of something indefinable.

Jane glanced toward the mauve shadows of her aunt's study where her would-be husband lounged, observing them all with those shocking blue eyes.

Why didn't he speak?

"Maybe he has mistaken you for someone else," Emma had suggested when Jane had told her the news of his offer. "Imagine his embarrassment if he comes calling and discovers his fiancée isn't the correct one!"

But Lord Satyr had made no such demur upon seeing her when he'd arrived that morning.

Her eyes dropped to the sheaf of papers that had earlier been thrust under her nose by his attorney. It was impossible to comprehend the words on them while everyone in the room scrutinized her with such rapt attention.

The attorney inched the papers closer to her hand in an unsubtle attempt to coax her into signing.

"Will you explain this to me?" she asked him, tapping a particular codicil with her pen nib. Her voice sounded unnaturally loud in the quiet room.

"It's your marriage contract. You are to sign here," he replied, indicating a blank area on the final page.

Did he think her witless?

"May I take a private moment to study it?" she asked.

Her aunt tittered nervously. "Don't be absurd, Jane. That could take all morning. And Lord Satyr might mistake it to mean you distrust him. Sign your name and be done with it."

Jane sensed a restive movement in the shadows. A man rose from the chair. The man from the tent. The one who wished to marry her. Lord Nicholas Satyr.

"Don't concern yourself, my lord, she will sign," Izabel cooed prettily. But when she turned to her niece, her eyes were frosted slits. "Won't you, Jane?"

"I would speak to Signorina Cova in private," said Lord Satyr. The low rumble of his velvet voice caressed Jane's nerve endings, causing the pen in her hand to tremble.

"Certainly, signore," said Izabel, leaping to her feet. She tugged Jane's father toward the door.

The attorney tossed her an encouraging wink as he ushered himself out, hard on their heels, folding the double doors shut behind them.

Jane stared after the trio, appalled. Her aunt knew the impropriety of leaving an unmarried female in the sole company of a gentleman. What was she thinking?

She turned to find Lord Satyr inspecting her.

"No pipe?" he asked, his lips curving slightly.

It took her a second to comprehend his meaning. The corncob pipe from her gypsy fortune-teller costume, he meant. So he *had* seen through her disguise.

She shrugged. "The occasion didn't seem to call for it."

His smile broadened.

He was extremely handsome, even more so than she remembered, if that were possible. Emma would think him a knight in, well, a dark waistcoat. Now that she studied the coat at close range, Jane saw that it bore a black-on-black design depicting bizarre beasts with tails and wings intertwined with vines and flourishes. On another man it might have looked outlandish, but somehow the peculiar coat served only to accentuate his masculinity.

Nick noted and accepted her interest in his form as useful. Some thought him vain, he knew. But one couldn't live to nearly thirty years of age and not be aware of the effect one's looks had on the feminine sex. He knew his features were arranged in an appealing way and used the knowledge to his advantage in social and business dealings. Beyond that, his own attractions were of little interest to him.

Her scent had teased at him since she'd entered the room. It was of spring and new sky and of crushed blossoms and cool, shaded earth.

He shifted closer, wanting more.

Satisfaction zinged through his blood at her nearness, stiffening his cock. There was no doubt this time. Everything about her proclaimed her to be of ElseWorld heritage. In the way of the Faerie, her face and form were delicate and ethereal, her manner and movements graceful.

Stilling, he allowed himself to savor her, to bask in the joy of discovering the woman he would take to wife. The urge to claim her—to mate her here and now—swelled in him, taking him off guard. The need shouldn't be so strong.

Several days earlier he'd traveled home, returning to Tivoli only yesterday. The sole purpose of his trip had been to take part in the Calling along with his brothers. It was possible to perform the ritual away from his estate, but when his mind and body were given over to the Change, he was vulnerable and preferred not to be among strangers.

When he spoke, Nick gave no clue as to what he'd been thinking. "You're reluctant to sign. Why?"

Jane's gaze darted to the door and then back to him. "You must know your offer comes as a surprise."

"A happy one?" he inquired.

"In my aunt's view, at least," she replied with a tight smile.

"And in yours?" he asked.

"In my view," Jane confided, "you are too fickle. At Villa d'Este, you were quite fixed on another young lady, as I recall."

"Ah!" Something shifted in his eyes momentarily, making her wary. "I can't explain my behavior the other day beyond saying that once you left the gardens, I realized a definite attraction in your direction existed. I apologize for the necessity of making formal arrangements for our marriage through your guardians. It's done this way here in Italy."

"It's arranged in much the same way in England, as you must know. But even there, men and women learn something of one another before they marry." She spread her hands in a gesture of confusion. "How can you want to wed someone you don't know?"

"From what I have observed at your English balls, there is little interaction before an engagement. Women dress like flowers to attract men to their honey. A few dances, a very few words, and men soon find themselves husbands."

"I wasn't dressed to attract when we met."

"How lucky for me then that I saw through your disguise."

He was too glib. Annoyed, she tried to read his thoughts.

Nick felt her press at the gates of his mind. Her touch was purposeful but weaker than his will and easily blocked. No doubt this was not her strongest talent. Briefly he wondered what that would prove to be.

Concealment. It rolled from him in waves. Jane's gaze shifted away. He wasn't the only one concealing something.

"I sense some underlying reason for your suit of which you aren't apprising me. Otherwise, why the rush?" she went on.

"It's difficult for me to be away from my land for great stretches. I recently decided it was time to marry. Now, I'd like to get on with it," he said.

"And any woman would adequately suit the position? Even one who tells fortunes in disguise for coin?"

"I have numerous requirements in a wife."

"I'm interested to know what they are," she snapped. "I bring you no title, no wealth, no land. I'm unremarkable."

She had no idea how wrong she was. "I have sufficient titles, wealth, and land that I needn't go seeking them in a wife. I only require an intelligent, well-bred lady of marriageable age who will bear my children."

"Under your requirements, you would find hundreds of suitable ladies."

He spread his hands, feigning regret. "Alas, the laws of Italy decree I cannot marry hundreds. I've chosen you."

"But for all you know, I could be unchaste." She leaned forward meaningfully. "Or a candidate for bedlam."

"Are you?" he inquired.

She drew back. "I'd hardly reveal it if I were."

He smiled, enjoying her. "It's of no moment. Our contract allows me to annul our marriage on several counts, including those you mentioned. Come, unlike your aunt, I would not have you ignorant." He drew her to sit at the desk. Leaning over her, he began to outline the meaning of each paragraph of the agreement in turn.

"Here I require you to accept the surname of Satyr rather

than keeping that of your father, as would be customary in Italian marriages."

His desire to stamp his name on his wife didn't surprise her. But it was the least of her concerns.

"And here it says the marriage may be annulled for a number of reasons."

"Voided, you mean?" she interrupted. "As though it had never existed?"

He nodded, and she marveled at his conceit in suggesting such an idea.

"As you see here," he went on, enumerating the clauses, "I may petition for annulment in the event you prove not to be virginal."

She blushed furiously at this, glad her bent head hid her reddened cheeks.

"Likewise," he continued matter-of-factly, "I may do so if you deny me husbandly rights, prove unfaithful, or if you don't produce an heir within a reasonable amount of time."

"The latter is hardly fair," she pointed out.

"But necessary. And, in the event of an annulment, I will of course provide a comfortable allowance for you."

Hope rose within her. With such a settlement, she and Emma could be free. Able to live as independent women.

"Am I too plainspoken?"

"On the contrary," she told him. "Your lack of subterfuge inspires trust."

"Sufficient trust that you will agree to my proposal?" he murmured above her.

Jane stared at the words dancing across the page, her mind examining the choices open to her.

If they married, she would have access to his lands. On that ancient ground, plants such as moly might exist that could help her—help her sister—before it was too late. Definitely an argument in favor of wedding him.

But he would touch her. Could she keep herself from melding? He didn't strike her as a man who would miss much of what she was. An argument against.

Still, he no doubt had business interests that would often take him from home. Perhaps he would spend so little time in her company he'd never notice his wife was an unnatural freak. A plus.

And he wasn't Signore Nesta. A definite plus.

"Do you enjoy children?" Nick prompted, breaking into her thoughts. "More specifically, are you prepared to bear mine?"

She stood and slid from the desk and him. If she could be certain they wouldn't share her taint, she would gladly bear his children. She would shower them with all the affection her family had denied her.

A few feet away, she turned, clasping her elbows with her hands.

"One cannot predict the likelihood or timing of heirs with any great certainty."

Secrets flashed in his eyes. "Thus my inclusion of the clause. Make no mistake—the production of heirs is of paramount importance in my association with you. Should you prove unable or unwilling to provide them, I must have the freedom to form an alliance with another."

Approaching her, he tilted her chin up and waited until her eyes met his.

Surprisingly, no visions came to her at his touch.

"Do you understand what that entails?" he asked.

She glanced at him sharply. Did he refer to childbirth or to . . . ?

"Do you understand what will happen in our marriage bed?" he clarified.

She wriggled, and he allowed her to shrug free. "Your questions are premature. Before we reach an agreement, I have requirements of my own."

He folded his arms, half sitting against the desk. "Go on."

"My sister, Emma. You know of her?"

He nodded.

"Since our mother's death, I have provided for Emma's care. If I were to wed, I'd wish to have her with me, to raise her as my own daughter. And I'd want to keep a promise that was made to her that she might attend the school of her choosing. She's quite intelligent."

"Of course," he agreed easily.

"It may prove costly," she cautioned.

He lifted his fingers in a careless gesture that was innately Italian. "Its cost is of no consequence."

Jane released a breath she hadn't known she'd been holding. How easily that had gone. Perhaps managing him would not prove difficult after all.

"Was that your only condition?"

"I have one other," she said. "I've been used to certain freedoms in my choice of hobbies. I'd like to continue with them, unhampered."

"Fortune-telling?"

"No," she said, refusing to blush. "That was strictly for coin."

He tilted his head, considering her. "Then may I inquire as to the general nature of this other hobby?"

She realized she was twisting her hands and forced them to stillness, folding one atop the other at her waist. "'Studies' is more accurate. Botanical studies." She stifled the impulse to prostrate herself with further explanations and pleas.

He examined her a moment more and then replied easily and without reservation. "As long as they don't endanger or shame you or my family in any way, you may keep your hobbies."

She sighed. "That's what I find so difficult about this marriage business. Why is a husband entitled to give a wife permission or withdraw it simply because he's male? In truth, I would prefer to abide in a single state."

"'Tis a husband's obligation to protect his wife and family. And consider that if you never marry, Signore Cova will continue to control your future."

He was right, she knew. Until she amassed enough wealth of her own, she would never be free of male domination.

A feeling of entrapment squeezed her chest. Why was she continuing this farce? She should tell him no and be done with it. Bearing his children was simply too great a risk. And if he but knew the depth of her strangeness, he certainly would not want children of her.

Instantly, an idea born of desperation came to her. There was a way, it whispered. There were herbs said to prevent impregnation. Such herbs would let her marry him and lie with him yet ensure she would not conceive.

It was deceitful. And he would eventually annul the marriage when no heir was produced. Until then, she and Emma would have a home. Afterward, they would have the allowance he promised.

From beneath her lashes, she studied him. Did she dare trick him in such a way?

Taking her survey of his person as an invitation, Nick moved closer. Grasping her upper arms, he drew her against him.

She allowed the embrace and even mustered the courage to rest her palms on his chest. Taut muscle and bone underlay his waistcoat, and below that a steady heartbeat.

Without warning, the coat under her fingers faded into translucence to reveal sculpted planes of male flesh that bunched and flexed as he moved in undisguised passion. She fisted her hands and forced the vision away.

Her gaze roved higher.

Dark spiky lashes framed the remarkable blue eyes that studied her in turn. A flush of good health angled along his cheekbones. The haughty line of his aristocratic nose and straight brow proclaimed his good breeding. He exuded confidence from his very pores.

His will seemed to reach out to her, tickling her mind, pushing her into acceptance of him.

Again she wondered why so beautiful and wealthy a man was so determined to have her.

He moved his hands along her upper arms to cup her shoulders, idly brushing thumbs over the hollow above her collarbones. Fingers slipped around to cradle her skull and tease tendrils of her hair along the shallow groove at the back of her neck.

She shivered. But it wasn't due to the same fear Signore Nesta had engendered. This man's touch was unsettling but not at all distasteful.

For so many years she'd avoided human touch and had become unused to it. Even holding hands with Emma was something in which she rarely indulged. The risk of melding was too great. Yet she wasn't melding with him now. Was the ability dissipating, or was she developing sufficient skill to rein it in when she chose?

His head ducked close, and his voice rumbled at her ear. "Come, what's your answer, Jane?"

Her mind raced. If she worked at it and held her emotions distant, perhaps she *could* stop herself from melding with him by choice.

"I'm not at all certain this course you have set is wise. But if you're determined upon it, then, yes," she heard herself say. "I say yes."

Before she could reconsider, he took her arm and led her back to the desk. When he pushed the stack of papers aside to display the last one, she briskly signed her name to the contract.

Blue mirrors smiled into pools of limpid green. "You do me an honor, signorina."

8

Izabel lost no time in informing her dearest friends of her niece's lofty engagement. Fortuitously, the monthly meeting of their society had been scheduled for the following afternoon.

As always, the five women gathered at the Cova family home, where Izabel and her stepbrother had grown up. Unoccupied and without servants in attendance, the house and gardens had assumed a neglected air but not yet fallen into true disrepair.

After their parents died, she'd kept the abandoned lodgings especially for the purpose of hosting her friends at these events. It was a far cry from the perfection of Rome's seven hills where their ancestral predecessors had once gathered. Centuries ago, those hills had rung with the frenzied cries of the original maenads, the Sisters of Bacchant. They and their followers had enjoyed the freedom to worship the god of the grape and to practice their rites uninhibited by lawmakers of the day.

How things had changed! It was now prudent that they— the last remaining descendants of the Sisters of Bacchant—perform their rituals in secret. This secluded garden and grotto provided adequate shelter and privacy from the life teeming outside the gates. One must make do.

The other four members of her society stared in surprise after Izabel imparted the news of Jane's impending nuptials.

"But what of my son?" demanded Signora Nesta, a frown creasing her forehead. "You know I wanted your Jane for him."

Signora Bich patted the other woman's hand consolingly. "She's right, Izabel. You had struck a bargain."

Izabel sipped her wine, a luxury she openly permitted herself to enjoy to excess only in this setting, among these particular friends.

"Satyr won't keep my niece forever," she explained. "If all goes according to plan, your son will have her in good time. Though by then, she will be slightly used."

Signora Natoli chortled at this, and all eyes fell to the quiver of her massive bosom. Encased in satin, the orbs were hidden from view for the moment. But that situation was certain to change within the hour. Izabel ran her tongue along her lower lip, catching a droplet of tangy wine.

"What can you be planning, Izzy? Do tell us," Signora Ricco encouraged.

"Through Jane's marriage, I intend that we will gain access to the inner recesses of the Satyr compound," Izabel informed them.

A stunned silence prevailed for a moment.

"For the purposes of our Society?" ventured Signora Natoli. "In order that we might meet there?"

"Naturally," said Izabel.

"Even wed to your niece, Lord Satyr is unlikely to be influenced into allowing us access to his estate," scoffed Signora Nesta. "He won't turn his back on centuries of exclusionary practices."

"She's right, Izzy. It's common knowledge that only vineyard workers, servants, and those with specific business are allowed on Satyr land," said Signora Bich.

"If influence fails, there are other means," Izabel pointed out.

Signora Natoli giggled. She was as usual the most quickly affected by the wine and was well on her way to giddiness. "Oh, dear. I fear Jane's husband may meet with an unfortunate end."

"Risky," said Signora Nesta, her gaze speculative.

"However, it can be done," said Izabel. "And once he's disposed of, control of his estate will fall to Jane."

"What of his two brothers?" asked Signora Bich.

Izabel waved her glass in a careless gesture. "If they interfere, they can be dispatched."

"And if your niece manages to bear her husband's offspring before he's done away with?" Signora Bich persisted. "Judging by the look of him and tales that circulate, Satyr is quite capable of mounting her with regularity."

"Why, that is part and parcel of my very plan," said Izabel. "Only imagine the sons they might produce if the strangeness in Jane's blood is mixed with that which we suspect the Satyr possess. With him gone, we'll school her offspring to our viewpoint. And in time, when her sons are of an age to produce life-giving seed, we will mate them with my younger niece."

"And with ourselves, I'll warrant!" added Signora Natoli. Her cheeks and the upper swells of her breasts were beginning to flush with the wine.

"Salud!" toasted Signora Ricco. "Maenad blood mixed with that of the Satyr. We'll sire a dynasty!"

"But why don't we simply undertake to mate with the three lords immediately ourselves?" asked Signora Bich. She stirred a finger in her wine and then licked it. "I for one wouldn't mind bearing a Satyr offspring, if I can first enjoy the begetting."

"The Satyr are too careful," said Signora Nesta. "Though it's said they sow their seed far and wide, no children have come of it. Men built such as those surely cannot be sterile."

The others nodded.

"But if there is a child, will your niece give it over into our care?" asked Signora Bich.

Izabel glared at her. Signora Bich could be such a stickler for annoying details that were quite easily dealt with. "When the time is right, we shall initiate her into our society with a set of the ancient rings. They'll lead her into seeing our way of thinking on the matter. If Nesta still wants her after her she is ringed, he may have her."

"But if she's truly inhuman, the rings' powers may not affect her," argued Signora Bich.

Izabel rolled her eyes in exasperation. "In that event, we'll arrange to have her judged an unfit parent based on her various abnormalities. But these are trifling matters, and we have much time ahead to consider them. On to the next order of business."

Signora Natoli clasped her hands in delight. "Ah, yes! Our good works."

Five heads turned toward the nearby grotto.

Through the dappled shadows, a pair of dark eyes met theirs, the terror in them heightening.

Izabel stood and moved closer to admire their captive. The others trailed in her wake. "I see we have procured the necessary ornament for our festivities."

The young man lay at a slight incline, securely lashed to a stone slab. Other than the handkerchief stuffed in his mouth, he was naked.

Signora Bich nodded. "We rescued him from a difficult life on the waterfront."

"He ate hungrily," added Signora Nesta.

Izabel's eyes narrowed on the fellow's shrunken shaft. It was slack with fear but had definite potential. "A fine rescue."

The other ladies marked the direction of her gaze and tittered.

Izabel stroked the captive's stubbly jaw, her expression kind. His eyes bulged, and a shudder rippled over him.

"Will you take wine?" she asked. It was a rhetorical question. The gag always made them thirst.

His head bobbed. Behind her, the splash of liquid reached her ears. The ceremonial goblet was handed to her.

"I'll remove the cloth from your mouth so you may drink," she told him. "But you must promise to keep silent."

Again, he nodded. She removed the gag slowly, making sure he was as good as his word.

When she handed the cup to him, he drank thirstily. They watched to ensure he swallowed a sufficient quantity.

"Enough," said Izabel, pulling the cup away before he'd finished. The aphrodisiac properties of the drugged wine affected people differently. If he were too impaired, his performance would disappoint them.

She brushed the hair from his eyes. They were a lovely brown, the color of a hazelnut.

"What's your name, signore?" she inquired.

His lower lip trembled.

"Come now, don't be frightened," she coaxed.

"Carlo," he croaked.

"So strong." She smoothed the backs of her fingers along his ribs and lower over his belly. His muscles jerked in repudiation. "And so beautiful."

"Please, signora, release me. Please." His voice rose in distress.

"Soon."

He twisted to escape the gag, but the ladies held him. When it was replaced, they left him again.

Gold chalices inscribed with ancient symbols were brought

out and filled with aged wine poured from a decorative urn. Together, the Sisters swayed in the soft sunlight, chanting their ancient runes.

Ties and hooks opened under the caress of feminine fingers. Silk and linen clung and rasped and then slid away. Sighs of relief sounded as flesh, creased and marked from binding corsets, found freedom. With the easing of physical restraints came the further easing of moral ones.

Izabel searched out Signora Natoli and watched as another peeled the fabric from her friend's monumental breasts. Signora Natoli's eyes found hers and then darted away. She was always so charmingly bashful when first revealed.

Soon all five women stood naked in the deepening afternoon shadows, save for similar jewelry worn in a place so peculiar that it would have shocked society to know of it. Identical rings of silver lanced their nipples, ten loops winking in the waning light and firmly set into the tenderest of olive skin.

When each daughter had come of age, their own mothers had initiated them. Decades earlier in a solemn ceremony, the silver had been driven into their flesh, forever marking each as maenad. The exquisite pain of the piercing was still fresh in Izabel's memory. It was said to rival that of childbirth.

A hand grazed Izabel's breast. Fingers came between her legs from behind and squirmed their way inside her cunt. A thumb poked for the opening between her bottom cheeks, stuffing itself deep. She arched at the intrusions, knowing she mustn't cry out and risk being overheard by passersby beyond the garden.

Signora Natoli's breasts bobbed within easy reach of her lips. Izabel stifled the urge to moan by plugging her mouth with a brown nipple. She sucked in cold silver and supple flesh. Signora Natoli's head fell back, and she sighed.

Another of her companions, she cared not which, nudged Izabel's legs apart. A tongue teased between her thighs, lapping at her clit. She welcomed the touch of a woman's mouth there, so discernibly different from that of a man.

Feminine voices murmured comforting sounds as they attended to her. Lips and fingers worshiped her for long minutes, and her lust spiraled.

When sudden, sharp need twisted, she pulled away from her caretakers before it could overwhelm her. Turning, she stumbled toward the grotto.

She found him in the shadows, bound and gagged as they'd left him. His eyes had begun to glaze with the effects of the tainted wine. Good.

Behind her, the others' attentions moved on to Signora Nesta. Her turn with him would come next.

Izabel straddled him where he lay on the slab. With fingers made clumsy from wine, she spread her frilled labia over his cock. He was thick now, hard from seeing their nakedness. She smiled into his eyes, riding him, slowly slicking him with her ooze.

Under her, he bucked awkwardly.

She cupped his cheeks, kissed him.

"Have you ever fornicated?" she whispered.

He nodded, flushing.

"Naturally. But there is no doubt much that remains to be learned. My friends and I have schooled many in the ways of pleasing a lady in coitus. There are few more valuable skills for a man to have."

Lifting his head, she directed his eyes to their undulating genitals. When she had his attention, she stopped moving her hips and raised herself slightly. With two fingers, she parted her pubic hair and showed him her moist, gaping gash.

"Would you like to come into me here?" she queried softly.

His head bowed in quick assent, his eyes shining with drugged lust.

"Very well, then. I will begin your education. But first you must promise to remain an obedient, quiet student. Can you do that?"

She looked into his eyes, glimpsed the wanting, and pulled the gag from his mouth.

"Si. Grazie," he said. His voice was calm now and wine-slurred.

Quickly she released the bindings on his torso and legs, leaving his wrists and ankles loosely hobbled.

She led him a few feet away by means of a lead string. Her pussy was swollen now and aching for him.

Tugging, she pulled him to the lush grass. "Come," she told him. "Lie with me."

He lay on his back, and she linked the lead string between his wrists to a stake that held them raised over his head. They would slacken his bonds later and toy with him in other ways.

Weapons were at the ready if he attempted to flee. But the aphrodisiac usually sent any thoughts of escape from a captive's mind.

His staff bobbed high and vulnerable against his furred belly. She grasped it in her fist, running her thumb over the moisture at his cock slit. He didn't resist. He needed her now, needed the relief she could provide.

"If only women were blessed with such fine organs, men wouldn't be necessary at all," she heard Signora Nesta murmur. The others laughed quietly, a distance away.

Izabel enjoyed the way he whimpered as she slid the ring over the tip of his cock and downward. It lodged in place at his root, ensuring he would remain engorged throughout the night.

Eager now, she squatted over him, her knees sinking into dewy earth on either side of his hips. His penis twitched in her grasp as she led it to an angle that suited her.

"Please." His was a desperate whisper.

"I know," she crooned.

The puffy slit between her thighs stretched as she sank over him. Her sisters had prepared her well, and he came into her easily. How nicely he filled her! She wiggled her hips, forcing him as deep as possible, letting him take her weight.

Her eyes fell closed in rapture at the sacred moment of the first taking. Delicious.

Already, she teetered on the edge of orgasm. She humped him hard a dozen times or more, coming quickly.

After she'd fucked him, she lingered, watching Signora Nesta spread her dimpled haunches over him. Izabel's fingers found the slickness within herself and drew it over her clit. It pulsed with remembered pleasure.

Turning away, she found the wine. Nearby, two mouths suckled the teets of a woman, who lay sighing in ecstasy upon the grass. Signora Natoli's bosom was always much in demand.

Izabel sipped, observing, and then went to kneel between Signora Natoli's legs. Tipping her glass, she dribbled its sparkling chill over her friend's thatch, causing her to gasp in surprise.

Signora Natoli's dark eyes were on her now, and Izabel tossed her goblet aside. With her thumbs, she widened the woman's cinnamon slit and then pressed her mouth to it, sucking at her sweet wine.

Izabel's pale ass rose high in the air, begging. Even now, one of the others left Signora Natoli's bosom. Hands caressed her bottom, and thumbs spread her cheeks. Finger fuck or tongue? Which would it be? She groaned into Signora Natoli's cunt, anticipating.

As dawn came, Izabel let herself into her city town house by a side door, taking care not to disturb anyone. She took the steps and then moved stealthily down the hall, passing her bedchamber door.

She intentionally didn't wash before joining her stepbrother in his bed.

He rolled on top of her when she woke him and kissed her. His greeting was sleep-slurred, his first caresses lethargic.

Suddenly his head jerked back. His eyes widened, alert as he searched her face. "You come to me from another's bed?!" he accused.

She smiled, taunting, and felt his shaft harden in reluctant response.

"You dare come to me drunk with some other man's wine and smelling of his cock?" he demanded. His face was thunderous.

Izabel reached low between their bodies to find and stroke him. "Don't scowl and bluster with pretended outrage when this says otherwise." Her firm squeeze on his cock made him wince. "Yes, I have been well fucked by another this night, and you're aroused by the smell of him on my skin. Don't bother to deny it."

"Damn you."

She widened her legs under him and flung her arms to the sides in open invitation. "Come inside me, brother," she crooned, "and feel the welcome of another man's cream."

With a harsh grunt, he rammed his cock into her gaping slit, reddened and abused from recent screwings. She folded her arms and legs over him like a beetle capturing prey.

The bed quaked and jolted under his angry pumping as he punished them both for the truth of her words.

The body of a young man was fished from the Aniene River long after the Sisters of Bacchant had forgotten him and moved on to other victims. His wrists and ankles were chafed, officials noted. And a dainty handkerchief of fine lawn was stuffed in his mouth, holding his ruddy lips wide in a silent scream.

9

Just shy of two weeks later, Jane found herself ensconced with her sister in a lacquered carriage emblazoned with the Satyr crest. They were outside the chapel, waiting for her husband of less than an hour to join them before traveling the short distance to the celebratory luncheon her aunt had organized.

Nick had returned to his home in Tuscany immediately after their engagement, so she hadn't set eyes on him again until that very morning when he'd arrived on horseback flanked by his brothers. In the chapel, the three Satyr lords had towered over the congregation of her aunt's friends, looking invincible. Though many had whispered and stared in awe, all three men had appeared oblivious of the mass scrutiny directed their way.

On their part, Raine and Lyon had covertly studied her with equal measures of suspicion and curiosity. If they were searching for flaws, they would find them. Perhaps not on the surface, but probe a little deeper and they were there.

However, once outside after the wedding, the brothers were all politeness as they offered felicitations. The manner of their congratulations had told her a wealth about them as individuals.

Raine had placed a restrained kiss upon her bare wrist and bid her a solemn, "Welcome to the family."

Whereupon Lyon had sighed, nudging him aside. "Don't let my brother overwhelm you with his enthusiasm," he'd told her teasingly. "We have long been without the grace of a female upon our lands. You are indeed welcome to the family."

His golden cat eyes had sparkled as he planted a brotherly kiss upon her lips. As opposed to Raine, he'd appeared reluctant to release her, and she'd worried a melding might occur. When Nick cleared his throat, Lyon remembered himself, tossing her a mischievous smile before moving away.

It had been Lyon who'd charmed Emma on immediate acquaintance, and Jane had seen her sister's disappointment when she realized Nick was to be Jane's husband rather than his youngest brother.

But with his benevolence in allowing Emma to ride to the feast in the carriage, Nick now found himself on the receiving end of her sister's adoration as well. Upset at the impending loss of her older sister, Emma had become a sponge desperate to soak up any kindness.

The two sisters had settled themselves in the carriage facing away from the driver, leaving Nick the better seat. Emma's nose was already buried in a book, something she was rarely without.

Jane twisted the Satyr family's sapphire-and-emerald-encrusted wedding ring on her finger and then smoothed her gown. Nick's money had paid for it, an ivory damask with several flounces along the bottom edge, a design of seed pearls over the bodice, and gigot sleeves. She wore orange blossoms in her hair, a symbol of chastity and fertility.

Twitching the window curtain, Jane watched her new husband make his farewells to his brothers outside. It was a busy

time on their estates, he'd told her. So his brothers would return home immediately, and Nick would follow on horseback
after the wedding feast. That would leave her to travel in his
wake by carriage.

She caught the fleeting look that passed between the threesome and turned her ear to the window to catch her husband's
lowered voice.

"I have her," she thought he said. Odd phrasing. He spoke
as though she was some sort of prize he'd obtained through
specific effort.

"I'll begin my search," Raine replied.

Search for what? Jane wondered.

His brothers departed, and Nick made for the carriage. She
dropped the curtain before he could catch her spying.

The large table in the sala da pranzo of her aunt's home
glinted with silver candlesticks, cutlery, and platters laden with
food enough for three dozen wedding guests. All had been
beautifully prepared and purchased with Satyr funds.

Jane glanced longingly toward the staircase as they passed it,
wanting nothing more than to go upstairs, sink into her bed,
and hide. But of course this wasn't to be. The last of her belongings were being packed into traveling trunks even now.

She felt eyes on her and turned to meet the intent gaze of
Signore Nesta. He'd been at the wedding, so it followed that he
would be here. After all, his mother was one of Izabel's inner
circle.

Unconsciously she scooted closer to Nick.

"A particular friend of yours?" he inquired, noting Nesta's
approach.

She shook her head.

"May I kiss the bride?" Nesta inquired of Nick when he
reached them. Sensing the other man's covetous nature, Nick
placed a hand at her waist, staking claim.

"You must ask her for such a favor," he said.

Jane glanced at him in surprise, wishing with all her heart he'd refused. The one time a husband's domination would have served her, and he'd bungled it. Now she had little choice.

"Of course," she agreed woodenly.

Nesta wet his lips and then moved to grasp her.

"No hands," Nick ordered coolly.

"W—what?" asked Signore Nesta, his voice affronted.

"I said no hands," said Nick. "But now that I consider the matter further, I've decided no kiss either. You will excuse us?" He steered Jane toward the table.

A muted giggle escaped her at Nesta's shocked expression.

"You're amused?" Nick asked. From his tone it was obvious he wasn't.

"Grateful," she answered. "I didn't want his kiss."

"Then you should have said so." Nick's clasp relaxed, and she suddenly wondered if he'd been jealous of her, his newest possession. His expression gave nothing away as he saw her to her seat and took his place beside her.

During the meal Nesta stared at her from time to time, but he'd ceased to concern her, now that Nick had dealt with him.

She in turn stared surreptitiously at her new husband. At his hands stroking his fluted glass, wielding his knife, lifting a napkin to his lips. His fingers moved with sensuous grace and patience. She shivered with an indefinable emotion at the thought of them moving over her.

"Here, Jane. Have some wine. It will calm you," said a friend of her aunt's seated next to her.

Jane searched her mind for the woman's name and managed to find it. Signora Bich. She didn't mention her mother's death or the role spirits had played in it but simply told her, "Thank you, but I don't take spirits."

Signora Bich's laughter trilled, drawing attention. "You have wed a winemaker, yet you refuse to drink wine? But, how amusing."

"Winemaker?" Jane echoed. "You're mistaken."

"I assure you I'm not. Lord Satyr and his brothers are the most famous winemakers in all of Italy," said Signora Bich.

Jane swiveled her eyes to Nick and froze at the confirmation she read in his face.

"Demon bastards!" A loud male voice echoed through the dining room, ripping through her thoughts and severing all conversation. The clinking of china and crystal faded into silence.

"Fucking Satyr! Fucking my daughter!"

Across the white linen, Jane and Emma exchanged chagrined glances.

"Oh, no," mouthed Emma. "Father!"

"I'll see to him," murmured Jane.

She and Izabel leaped to their feet at the same time and dashed to the vestibule.

Signore Cova halted at the sight of the two women rushing toward him, but it was Jane his stare accused. His raised fist held her heavy coin purse, and he shook it in her face so its contents rattled.

"How come you by this, girl?"

Jane's fingers curled, wanting to grab. "It's mine."

"I know that, wicked child!" he raged. Spittle popped and sizzled on his lips like grease on a griddle. "It was found hidden among your belongings as they were packed. How did you come by such a sum? Have you been whoring? Been with Satyr? Is that why he wants you so badly?"

He towered over her, his expression menacing, his breath reeking of spirits.

"Silence, Cova," said Nick, coming to stand behind her.

Her father paled at whatever he read in Nick's eyes above her head. With a mighty thrust, he flung her coin purse across the room. When it hit the wall, it exploded, sending silver and gold flying. Coins pinged off the vases and thumped the drapes and then clattered to the floor. Finally the last one rolled to a stop, leaving only dull silence.

Cova weaved on his feet, viewing the destruction with satisfaction.

Jane stared at the money, tears filling her eyes. It had been her safety net. If things went badly in her marriage, it would have bought her and Emma an escape.

She made a convulsive move to reach down and scrabble after the coins, but Nick forestalled her. Placing a hand at her back, he guided her through the nearest door and onto the veranda.

It came as no surprise to Nick that Signore Cova was a drunkard. His attorney's investigation of Jane's household had been thorough.

But he'd been taken aback tonight by his wife's feelings on the matter of wine. Would they color her view of him? Of his family?

Jane pulled away from him and went to stare blindly at the the view beyond the railing. From the distance came the sounds of her father being forced from the room under the determined strength of several footmen and her aunt.

"You see what you have married into?" she murmured. "I did warn you to take more care in your choice."

"Every family has its quirks," said Nick, leaning idly against the doorjamb to study her. "Some make wine. Some imbibe too freely."

She shook her head, defeated. "I apologize for my father's behavior. It's inexcusable."

"Signore Cova chooses to be both intemperate and immoderate in his consumption. It's nothing to do with you. Or me."

She looked at him over her shoulder. "But you do make wine?"

He nodded.

"And probably drink it." Shaking her head at her silliness, she returned her gaze to the view. "Of course."

"Winemakers tend to appreciate libations slowly. Few are drunkards."

She whipped around wearing an agonized expression. But her voice was quiet when she spoke. "I don't drink spirits. I won't become like him."

Something twisted inside Nick. He couldn't bear that she suffered under the mistaken belief that the sot in the next room was her true father. If there were a Cova family predisposition to alcoholic excess, it wouldn't affect her. She had no Cova blood. But now wasn't the time to explain that.

"Is he often like this?" Nick asked, nodding toward the vestibule.

Jane shrugged, and Nick didn't press. He noted with approval her reluctance to share family secrets.

"You can honestly claim you never drink to excess?" she persisted.

"I'm no stranger to occasional overindulgence," he confessed. "However, I can assure you that you haven't consigned yourself to marriage with a swill pot."

He moved to take her satin-covered shoulders in his hands, and she lifted uncertain eyes to his.

"No thoughts of reneging, Jane. You've given your word in your aunt's church, and your signature on the wedding documents has satisfied the courts. I'll do my best to be a good husband."

She lifted a hand and rubbed her temple. It had been a long day terminating a tense week and a half since their betrothal.

"Come, you are tired," said Nick. "I'll summon the carriage. It's past time to depart."

"P—please, may I go with you?" a voice begged.

Jane looked beyond Nick to find her sister in the doorway. She went to her, wanting to link their hands but not daring. Instead she placed a palm on her arm, where fabric would separate their skin.

"Now, you mean?" asked Jane.

Emma's eyes darted to Nick and then away, unsure of him. She bobbed her head, looking pitiful.

A curious melting sensation assailed the region of Nick's heart when the two turned beseeching glances his way.

"I will speak to Signore Cova," he said.

"You will speak to me," said Izabel from the doorway. "Jane's father is indisposed."

"Very well. As you heard, my wife doesn't wish to be parted from her sister so soon. Jane travels alone with footmen while I ride ahead to attend to business. Emma would provide good company if she comes with her now."

Izabel shook her head. "It wouldn't be proper for newlyweds to take a child."

"Emma is welcome in my home," Nick persisted. "Jane and I will make time for ourselves."

"No. 'Tis my final word," said Izabel.

Tears of frustration filled Emma's eyes, and she dashed off toward her room without another word.

"I'll see to her," said Jane, anger tightening her voice.

Izabel accompanied her upstairs, as though concerned she might abscond with Emma via window. Thus the remaining time Jane spent with Emma was dear but besmirched with their aunt's presence and the knowledge that they would soon part. When Emma slid into a doze, they left her.

In the hall, Jane blurted the question uppermost on her mind. "Did you know he made wine?"

Her aunt merely smiled as they headed downstairs. "But of course. Everyone knows."

"Why didn't you say anything? You know my feelings on the matter!"

"Lower your voice, girl," said her aunt, motioning toward Nick where he waited below them. "As his wife, it'll be your duty to urge him toward restraint."

Jane looked at Nick, standing solid and strong just a dozen steps below them. If there was any restraining to be done, she imagined it would likely go in her direction rather than the reverse.

"Is your sister settled?" he asked when they reached him.

"For now, but she'll be distraught when she awakens," Jane told him. "I'd rather not leave her."

Nick frowned. "I must return to my estate. It's a critical time for the vines."

"I could join you later," she suggested.

Before he could answer, Izabel reminded her, "Your place is with your husband."

"Of course. But—"

"Jane, you will observe the traditions," said Izabel. "We will discuss Emma when you're receiving again."

This time Nick didn't dispute her aunt's decision.

With a heavy heart, Jane allowed herself to be ushered away.

10

As previously arranged, Nick rode ahead toward his estate in Tuscany on horseback. That left Jane to follow him for three bone-jarring days, alone in a luxurious private coach.

A trio of armed coachmen accompanied her, riding at the fore and aft of the carriage emblazoned with the Satyr family crest. They negotiated her meals and lodging along the journey and guarded the door of her assigned chamber each night as though defending England's crown jewels.

The roads between Tivoli and his home near Florence proved adequate. The mud from winter rains had largely dried, and the terrible dust of summer hadn't yet kicked up. However, by afternoon each day the shaking of the carriage caused her eyes to blur too much for reading, so she adjusted the blinds to watch the passing view.

As they traveled northward, the landscape gave way to a mixture of hills and plains dotted with squat, angular buildings of peach, bone, and ochre brick. Fleecy clouds hung in the cerulean sky above occasional farmyards, Romanesque churches, and cylindrical stone granaries.

On the last day of her trip, she suppered at an inn in Florence and then traveled on another hour. The sun had crimsoned low on the horizon by the time her husband's home came into view. She was shocked to see that it was a castle!

Perched on the side of a slope covered with fruit trees, it dominated the surrounding landscape, announcing its splendor to the entire countryside for a distance of many miles. An impenetrable stone wall that was likely a remnant of earlier fortifications stretched from either side of it, preventing entrance to the grounds beyond by any means save the front gates. The wall encircled a vast forest crowned with hillsides patchworked with ribbed rows of what she assumed to be grapevines.

Ahead, the castle loomed closer—majestic, impregnable, and out of scale with its surroundings. The broad sweep of grassland before it was parted like hair on a human head by a single curving road that took her conveyance ever higher.

Too soon, the carriage passed through the castle gates. Jitters bubbled inside her. She'd hoped for some time to become acquainted with her husband and his home upon her arrival. But as the carriage wheels clattered over the drawbridge, it was late. Time to retire.

In the courtyard, one of the footmen assisted her from the carriage, and she stood on the pavement a moment feeling at a loss. To her surprise there were no servants about. Nick opened the massive front doors himself and greeted her as the footmen saw to her trunks.

Her new husband was well turned out in his customary colors of black and white and appeared more relaxed and congenial here than he had in their previous meetings. She, on the other hand, was dusty, travel stained, and tense.

"Welcome to Castello di Blackstone," Nick told her in velvet tones, drawing her up the steps and into the foyer. "Have you dined?"

"Si." She'd had little dinner, but she knew she couldn't eat.

Inside the castle, she glanced around curiously and saw he possessed all the trappings of a wealthy gentleman. Above the grand entrance, the Satyr coat of arms bore a carved sash emblazoned with the words GUARDIANS OF THE GATE. Colorful tapestries depicting scenes of revelry and feasting draped the surrounding walls, which rose to a coffered oak ceiling with ornamental details highlighted in gold.

A wizened servant dressed in formal attire suddenly appeared, his steps echoing across the herringboned Italian marble floor.

"Have the footmen deliver her trunks upstairs," Nick instructed. "And the coachmen should see to the horses before retiring."

The servant nodded, never glancing at Jane, and then scurried outside with an idiosyncratic sort of prancing gait. A word to the footmen sent her trunks to a side entrance, and from there she presumed they would make their way to her new quarters.

"Where are all the other servants?" Jane asked when she and Nick stood alone.

"It's late," Nick told her. "All have gone, save for a single maid who awaits you in your chamber."

He had dismissed the servants? Why? What did he plan to do to her that he wanted no servants about?

"Come." He turned and led her toward the staircase. Together they scaled polished travertine steps, with columned balusters. Gilt-framed paintings lined the way, and from within them the hooded gazes of his ancestors weighed her.

At the head of the stairs, they moved down the long hallway, their footsteps silenced by the nap of a Persian carpet. She watched the floral pattern pass under her skirt, thinking that the next time she tread this expanse, she would no longer be a virgin. It was a peculiar concept.

Ninety-four, ninety-five . . . She counted ninety-six steps from the base of the stair until they arrived at her bedchamber door. Of course, his steps covered more ground. She would count them next time and take an average.

You're being ridiculous, she told herself.

"A bath awaits. I will come to you shortly," her new husband informed her. With an abbreviated bow, he left her standing outside what she assumed to be her bedchamber door.

Shortly? The word ricocheted in her brain, spurring her into a flurry of activity. She darted inside the room he'd indicated and closed the door behind her.

She hated it when people employed such imprecise terms, especially about important matters. Her mother's "shortly" had often meant an hour. But for all she knew, his could mean but a moment. He mustn't catch her unprepared.

Her room was beautiful, with a high vaulted ceiling colored pale olive. A wreath of roses was painted in the center, from which hung a fluted glass chandelier.

A maidservant came shyly forward and introduced herself in halting English as Martine. At the knock on the door, she went to open it, and Jane's trunks were trotted in.

Once the footmen had departed, the laborious process of removing her female garments commenced. First her dress and then her corset, until she at last stood clad only in her chemisette. The maid reached for it, but Jane drew back.

"I require privacy for bathing," she murmured.

The maid looked surprised but merely curtseyed in assent. She carried a bucket of steaming water from the fireplace and added it to water already in the tub to reheat it.

"I shall unpack your trunks?" she inquired.

"Si," Jane told her, forcing a smile.

Slipping behind the painted screen, she disrobed and bathed hastily, not wanting Nick to return before she finished.

She peeked around the screen and saw that Martine was sorting through her belongings, hanging clothing in the armoire and settling bottles and brushes on the dressing table. She seemed in an unusual hurry to complete her duties and be gone.

The maid's nervousness communicated itself to Jane, and her hands shook as she dried herself and took the nightgown Martine had tactfully draped over the screen. Only after the wisp of silk slid over her head to fall in folds at her bare feet did she emerge into the room.

While Martine was bent over the trunks, Jane presented her back to the mirror. Her quick inspection relieved her when she saw that the gown did in fact cover her shoulder blades. She'd specifically requested of her aunt's dressmaker that this be the case, but there hadn't been time to try it on to ascertain whether the drape was as ordered.

The maid came to stand behind her. "E bella," she enthused as she took down and brushed out Jane's hair.

"Grazie," said Jane. To her embarrassment, she couldn't control the tremor in her voice. The maid shot her a sympathetic smile. Jane looked away from the pity that shaded her eyes, and her gaze fell on her reflection in the mirror.

She sucked in a shocked breath. While she'd been concerned only with the proportions of the back of the gown, her aunt had engineered the rest of it into a design that seemed far too provocative.

Under other circumstances, she might have luxuriated in the slide of the cool, fine fabric across her skin. Enjoyed the faintly scratchy texture of the lace insets of the low, rounded bodice that barely concealed the tips of her breasts. She might have appreciated the design in its entirety, except for the fact that she knew a man—a veritable stranger—was going to view her in it.

When her maid determined she was sufficiently perfumed and primped for her husband's impending visit, she gave her an encouraging smile and departed.

Jane's reflection showed she was now properly prepared to become a wife, at least on the surface. On the inside, it was a different matter.

Again she checked her back in the mirror, shifting this way and that to determine what movement might reveal.

Satisfied that the gown covered her secrets well enough, she moved to the window and pulled the drape aside. She breathed deep of the calming, verdant odors of eucalyptus and pine cooling down after the warmth of the day. From somewhere in the distance came the notes of a wind pipe being played.

A row of cypresses speared skyward on the horizon, inked silhouettes against a blue-black sky. The moon was a thin sliver that shed little light on the grounds. Somewhere out there lay a shadowy forest filled with ancient plants.

Did it contain the curative she sought? She planned to find out. And soon.

Emma's future, and her own, depended upon it.

Nick entered her bedchamber moments later wearing a full-length brocade robe loosely belted at the waist. His gaze fell on the empty bed, and then he spied Jane at the window.

Her gown rustled as she turned, stirring his senses. He inhaled her essence, now familiar to him, and felt the rightness of her seep through his marrow.

An instinctive, wholly masculine desire to give her his child-seed came over him. But he resigned himself. No child would come until he took her in a Calling, weeks from now.

Fortunately he was a patient man.

The nightgown she wore sat uneasily on her, he saw. She probably believed it too revealing. His gaze narrowed on the rosy points that puckered the lace at her breasts. Her shadowy triangle was faintly visible through the folds of silk at the apex of her thighs.

She shifted, and an effervescent trail of rosewater and Faerie glamour teased at him.

Sudden heat surged to his groin. His arousal thickened and throbbed, readying.

The speculative way he was staring at her, as though she were a bone and he a hound, did nothing to set Jane at ease. She crossed her arms in an X, inadvertently plumping the swell of her bosom more enticingly above the low neckline.

For some reason, Nick winced and shifted his stance. "Is the chamber to your liking?" he inquired.

Her eyes surveyed the room. "It's beautiful. Larger than I expected, as is your home."

A strained moment passed between them.

"Perhaps you would find yourself more comfortable if you were to lie down," he suggested with soft amusement.

Of course! How thickheaded of her. He wanted to get on with the coupling, and that was best achieved lying down. Even she knew that much.

"All right," she acquiesced.

She moved to the bed and shifted the coverlet aside. Then she lay on her back, positioning her legs straight and her arms flat on either side of her. Her gaze sought the underside of the canopy's tented pinnacle, from which swags of buttery yellow swooped outward to four tall bedposts. The pulse of her heart thudded heavily in her ears.

Nick shrugged from his robe and draped it over the railing at the foot of her bed.

The impact of his casual nakedness was shocking. She stared. How could she not? He was extraordinary.

Unclothed, his broad shoulders appeared even more strongly molded. Dark hair lightly dusted his forearms and well-muscled legs and shadowed a powerfully built chest. The pelt tapered lower, spearing toward his groin. There, where the thicket grew dense, was that part of him that Izabel had explained would come into her when it was fully ready.

A nervous flutter tickled in her chest at the size of it. How much more ready would it become?

Unaware of her misgivings, he joined her on the bed, sitting close so his hip warmed her calf. He faced her in a relaxed fashion, with one leg crooked on the bed and the other braced on the floor. She tried not to look at that part of him that concerned her most, the rigidly engorged shaft that lounged on his thigh like an overfed snake.

His palm startled her, slipping under her hem to settle on the slender ankle closest to him.

"Did you choose your gown?" he asked. Her eyes flew to his and were captured by pale blue.

She shook her head no, the action mussing her golden hair on the pillow. "My aunt."

He nodded as though she'd confirmed what he'd been thinking. The gown's gossamer fabric followed the movement of his hand as it eased upward along her leg.

There was no shame in this. Allowing it was her payment to him. In return, he would welcome Emma and her into his home.

She concentrated on keeping herself from melding, praying his touch on her would not be prolonged.

The nightgown slid above her knee.

What if this joining somehow intensified her own strangeness? He would be here, a witness to it.

The silk slid higher still. Her breathing constricted.

He seemed suddenly to become aware she was trembling. His hand paused, resting heavily on the bunched silk he'd drawn to shape the bone of her hip. His brows furrowed as his gaze raked hers.

"You knew this would be part of it," he said evenly.

"Yes," she murmured.

"Is this virginal fears then?"

She nodded jerkily, embarrassed by his plain speaking. When he hesitated, she made an uncertain gesture. "Please, just . . ."

One side of his beautiful mouth slanted upward. "Get on with it?" He toyed with the soft fabric and then appeared to reach a decision. Flipping the hem high, he bared her naked to the waist.

She flinched when he grasped her knees and lifted them wide, exposing her most private flesh to his view.

A long moment passed as he surveyed her, his newly acquired property.

Carefully she kept her eyes averted, and it somehow helped distance her from what was happening. From thoughts of whatever was going to happen. She longed to close her legs. To cover her nudity and roll away from him. To go—where? She had no other home now.

She lay motionless, letting him look.

Her aunt had been her only source of information regarding what her husband would do tonight. "Don't fight him," she'd advised obliquely. "Lie calmly, and he will lead you in your duty. Whereupon, you must exhibit neither shameful lust nor repugnance."

When Jane had pleaded for more information, her aunt had reluctantly shed further light on the mechanics involved in marital duties. From this, Jane had discerned her husband was going to somehow place that jutting male part of himself inside her.

Something brushed her mound, disturbing the curls covering her privates and igniting curious sensations. Blunt fingers searched with businesslike intent, quickly finding the untried slit hidden within her crisp-soft down. Without warning, a fingertip pricked and then delved inside as though a thermometer intent on taking her temperature.

A startled sound escaped her, and her grip bunched the coverlet.

He didn't acknowledge her exclamation but merely continued to watch his hand work between her legs.

The vision that had come to her in the tent resurfaced. In mere seconds, it would be her beneath his sculpted, straining body. Copulating with him.

His finger probed deeper, chafing and stretching, feeling impossibly large. He drew it out and dipped in again, intruding farther each time. The invasive friction felt beyond uncomfortable, the intimacy of what he was doing virtually unbearable.

A sudden terrifying thought struck her. If a finger caused this much distress, what would happen when he performed the marital act? How would his huge other part—that thickened shaft—ever fit?

Her eyes darted to his lap, and she shuddered in dismay. Had it gotten bigger?

He exhaled on a note of frustration and drew his finger free of her. In one smooth motion, he left the bed.

Unease shot through her. Was he giving up? What if he decided to annul the marriage? If he sent her back to her aunt's, she might find herself enduring this sort of treatment in the bed of Signore Nesta. Or worse.

Quickly she levered herself up on one elbow. "I'm sorry. Please don't leave, signore. I won't inhibit you further."

He shot her an unreadable glance as he made his way to her dressing table. The clink of bottles and containers told her he'd begun to sort through the items her maid had placed there when she'd unpacked Jane's things earlier.

Candlelight danced like butterflies across the sleek, well-formed contours of his back and buttocks. With covert fascination, she studied the column of sinew and bone that now jutted at an upward angle from the dark thatch of his groin. Its girth had swollen as thick as her wrist! Blood-rich veins roped its length, painting its bulbous tip a dusky red. The idea that he possessed such a barbaric appendage and would want to join it with her was so extraordinary as to seem ridiculous.

Seconds later, he returned with a jar she recognized. Jane lay back against the coverlet, watching him.

Removing the lid, he tilted the pot so she could see its contents. "Cream," he informed her unnecessarily, "to ease my entry."

Her eyes widened, but she only nodded.

Two large fingers scooped inside the pot and came away with a sizable dollop of cream. Again, he sat alongside her.

"Open your legs."

Finding her knees clamped tightly together, she quickly complied with his instruction.

Long fingers massaged the cream through her intimate folds, occasionally dipping inside her with brusque, matter-of-fact movements. He seemed almost detached from what he was doing, as though he were a doctor and she a patient.

The slick movement of his hands felt soothing, oddly pleasant.

When his touch left her momentarily, it was to smear the remainder of the cream on his erection. Her eyes followed his stroking fingers, mesmerized. She blushed when she realized she was staring, and she looked away.

The mattress dipped, and his massive body levered over her, obliterating the light, like a dark cloud claiming her with shadow. His legs moved between hers, kneeing them wide to receive him.

A muscular forearm planted alongside her bore his weight as he reached low between their bodies with his other hand. Grasping his shaft, he stroked it along her creamy furrow until his blunt tip was seated at her opening.

He drew his arm back up alongside her.

Within the warm cavern of his chest, Jane held her breath,

every fiber of her being taut with the awareness that a man's thighs were entangled with hers. That his heart was pressed to her breast. That his male appendage was poised to imminently breach her most private feminine place.

How strange it all was!

Without warning, his hips flexed forward. Her slit parted valiantly at the initial incursion, struggling to envelop his crown. Jane silently cursed nature for designing men's bodies with so little consideration. Shouldn't the fullest girth of his male appendage arrive at the base of his shaft rather than the tip? Far more sensible to let the lesser circumference of the rod pave the way for the larger crown.

Head lowered and back arched, her husband watched their bodies couple.

She stared at the vein pulsing along the side of his neck, saw his jaw clench. What did he feel as he eased himself inside her by slow, deliberate degrees? His rigid features gave away nothing.

She squirmed beneath him, worrying at the increasing pressure and discomfort of penetration.

"Relax," he rasped. "I don't want to hurt you."

You already are *hurting!* she wanted to shout. She folded her lips inward and held them firmly between her teeth.

Left little choice, her nether lips eventually gulped and swallowed, granting his plum passage into the vaginal throat beyond. The feeling of fullness intensified as he prodded onward, pausing only when he met the barrier inside her. She sensed his glance brush her face, but she didn't meet it.

All her mental energy was focused on rejecting the body that was attempting to fully link with hers. On wishing him anywhere but in his current position.

God, it wasn't going to fit! He must be made too large or she too small. Couldn't he tell?

He battered against the pliable barrier with gentle force and then several more times with increasing urgency. Suddenly his buttocks tightened and his hips bucked forward. He took her by surprise, and she cried out as his thickness irrevocably punctured the fragile wall.

He tunneled deeper until the inky fur of his genitals mingled with the crisp curls of her own. Until bone met bone.

"Oh!" Her breath came and went in quick, silent puffs. She shrank into the mattress, trying to escape the stinging, burning, impossible pressure. The weight of his hips anchored her fast.

"Are you all right?" he asked gruffly.

Her fingers hurt. Why did her fingers hurt? She flexed them and felt warm flesh. Without conscious thought, she'd begun clutching his sides in a vain attempt to repel him. Yet she hadn't melded! Her palms fell to the bed beside her.

"Yes," she said, despising the quaver in her tone. "Is it nearly over?"

"Almost," he assured her, sounding strained. "Are you ready for me to continue?"

Lie calmly and he will lead you in your duty.

She took a deep breath. "I—yes, my lord. Signore."

At her words, his hips pulled back and then sawed forward. Again and again, he repeated the softly punishing rhythm. His man sacs thumped dully against her with each thrust.

Oh, God! In spite of the cream, the friction was intense. As the ceaseless stroking continued, she grew desperate. His solid length scraped every nerve ending she possessed. How long would she have to endure it? Her aunt hadn't said how long.

Hurry. Finish. *Finish!* she silently begged.

Gradually she sensed a change in him. His breathing grew harsh, and he began to plunge and retreat with a more fixed determination. His thrusts turned sharp and forceful, almost brutal.

She lay under him unresisting, doubting he was even aware

of her as a person as he worked himself in her with single-minded purpose. She was merely there to serve as a receptacle for his passionate emissions, as fertile soil in which his precious aristocratic seed might take root.

Hands gripped the cheeks of her bottom, lifting and grinding her hips to his. She gathered the impression he was hurtling toward some sort of conclusion.

At last, he groaned hoarsely, a harbinger of his finish. A strong burst of semen shot from him, singing her inner walls with its hot, fluid gush. More spurts followed, flooding her. He bucked again, one last time, as though intent on wringing the last of his seed into her.

For long seconds, his massive frame draped hers in the humid aftermath of his passion. An impulse to hold him to her, to comfort him and smooth the warm muscles of his back swept over her. She tucked her fingers tight to her sides.

When he recovered, he disengaged and eased off her to stand beside the bed. The fire in him was banked now, she saw, and his hooded gaze was unreadable.

His satiated shaft hung in smug relaxation from its moist springy nest at the juncture of his thighs. He stood without modesty, unconcerned that he was fully nude before her, a virtual stranger.

Cool air found the copious wetness between her thighs. She folded them together, finding her tired muscles slow to respond.

He'd worked so hard with her, and for nothing. She'd taken the preventive herbs daily for the past month. There would be no child born of tonight's joining.

Bending, he twitched her gown down her legs and resettled its hem at her ankles. She sensed his attention drift from her and on to other matters.

"Buona notte," he said softly. Throwing on his robe, he

moved across the room. He'd left it unbelted, and it momentarily billowed behind him like a cape. With a *snick*, the door adjoining his bedchamber swept shut. He was gone.

Limp, sore, and vaguely dissatisfied, Jane turned on her side and curled into a fetal position. She tried to ignore that unfamiliar slickness between her legs, and the inner ache that was a result of the way her body had just been used. The pot of cream mocked her from her nightstand, a reminder.

Ducking her head, she tried not to dwell on the most mysterious aspect of their encounter—that it had left her with the disturbing desire for something more.

11

The following day, Nick secreted himself in his office at the edge of the estate. Nothing that might betray his family's ties to ElseWorld existed here, where he conducted matters of commerce. The room was intentionally unremarkable, meant to proclaim Satyr wealth and status but not invite comment.

Due to his recent absences in Tivoli, he now found his calendar filled with a succession of appointments. Vendors arrived at his door in a steady stream. Coopers came offering freshly toasted oak barrels from France and Hungary. Cork sellers came from Portugal.

Messengers came bearing wedding gifts. News of his marriage had obviously circulated even beyond this world, for parchments of congratulation—some vaguely threatening—arrived from several of King Feydon's descendants. They bore news that the the king no longer lived. Nick swore aloud when he read that no heir had been named. There would be a fight for his throne.

Having married Jane, Nick was satisfied that he'd largely fulfilled King Feydon's request. Having mated her on Satyr land, he'd initiated the bespelling that would keep her from harm in all the years to come. With each successive coupling, ancient forces that protected his land and all who dwelled within would weave more securely around her.

Would it be sufficient against the threat to which King Fey had alluded? Time would tell.

For now, Jane was merely another piece of business he'd taken care of and would take care of again on succeeding nights as was his duty. Or so he told himself when thoughts of her crowded at him.

He could not allow her to cloud his mind. Especially not now that Raine had traveled to Paris on his bride quest. Nick felt the loss of him in the imperfect balance of the forcewall at the perimeter of their lands. He and Lyon must remain particularly vigilant during their sibling's absence.

In the late afternoon, bottles were delivered by H. Ricketts & Co. Glass Works of Bristol, England. These new machine-molded bottles had been patented only two years earlier. He'd purchased some last year and been pleased with them. They were more uniform in size and shape than those of blown glass they'd used previously.

He pulled out one of the bottles and brushed the pad of his thumb over the SV insignia. The stamp helped set their wine apart from the typically unlabelled bottles of competitors.

The demand for their wine would be stronger than ever this year, due to the pox's devastation in other vineyards. But he never took success for granted. His family's very survival hinged on it.

Healthy vines would ensure that the secret aperture between ElseWorld and EarthWorld that was hidden on Satyr land remained secure. Healthy vines would ensure his children's legacy. Healthy vines would allow him and his brothers to live on.

All three of them attended the vines throughout the year, involving themselves in overseeing the process of thinning, pruning, and the eventual autumn harvest. But there were hundreds of other duties involved in winemaking.

Nick's particular expertise was in considering all aspects of the business at once and making certain that everything occurred in a timely manner leading to a productive harvest and auction. As the eldest, he felt a tremendous responsibility toward the family business.

Raine kept the necessary ledgers. But his true fascination was in the chemistry of fermentation, the racking of the wine, and the blending sciences.

Lyon's passion lay with working the land itself and in supervising the workers. At the final auction, he charmed the guests, cajoling exorbitant prices for each bottle.

Like his brothers, Nick's physical rhythms moved in time to that of the vines. Spring was a time of euphoria when his body particularly reveled in earthly pleasures.

With a will of their own, his thoughts drifted to his new wife. Giving her his seed for the first time last night had been surprisingly satisfying. His father had told him that much greater fulfillment would come with the first imparting of childseed. He was eager to find this out for himself.

Patience.

Thus far, he was well satisfied with his new acquisition. Jane had proven herself a virgin and gave every impression she was cultured and chaste, traits he required in a wife. Qualities altogether lacking in the woman with whom he'd lost his own virginity and others he'd dallied with over the years since his first sexual encounter.

As a young man, he'd learned there were two distinctly different kinds of Human women in EarthWorld. Some were lusty and welcomed men between their legs. Others took no pleasure in sex.

His father had taken great pains to make him understand that wives were to be chosen from the latter pool. That conversation had ensued after he'd unexpectedly stumbled upon his father dallying with a kitchen maid in the cellar. He'd been a young lad then, but the memories were fresh. . . .

Fifteen-year-old Nick froze, unable to look away from the sight he'd come upon while taking a shortcut through the kitchen cellar. He'd been on his way to the caverns on Satyr land, where he planned to expand his collection of fossils. But all thoughts of his expedition left him at the sight of his father crowding a maid into the corner between two pie safes.

As his father's fingers had freed the maid's generous blue-veined breasts and begun kneading them, Nick's hands had flexed on his spade and bucket.

The maid lifted her skirts.

Nick's nostrils flared. His olfactory sense was already well developed, and the aroma of her cunt, mingled with cinnamon and hot apple from the cooling pies, teased at him.

His father worked the front of his trousers free and then insinuated himself between her thighs. At his first mighty shove, she gave a curt shriek. It was followed by feminine sounds of discomfort that quickly turned to groans of enjoyment as his father's hips established a steady rhythm.

Feminine giggles and encouragements joined with masculine grunts as his father heaved into her with growing force.

Nick knew he should go but found he couldn't look away. The earthiness of it fascinated him.

When they'd finished, the maid spotted him over his father's shoulder. She whispered something, causing the older man to whirl around in dismay, inadvertently displaying his cock.

Chagrined, he fastened his trousers and stuffed his tunic inside the waist, speaking ruefully to his son over his shoulder. "Caught us at it, eh, Nico?"

He swatted the maid's rump, and she took herself off, still buttoning her blouse and straightening her skirt. She tossed

Nick a saucy look he imagined meant she might enjoy having him between her legs one day. His cheeks burned even as his young loins involuntarily tautened.

As he set his clothing to rights, Nick's father noted his fascination with the maid. His appreciative gaze followed his son's to watch her shapely backside disappear down the hall.

"A lusty woman such as she welcomes a man between her legs," his father said. "Not all women do."

"How does one know for certain when a lady is that type?" Nick asked with increased interest.

His father sighed, placing a companionable arm across his shoulders. "I suppose it's time we had a discussion about such matters."

Nick found himself ushered upstairs to the study. There, amid the ledgers and books, his father proceeded to tell him about the two types of women to be found in EarthWorld.

"You're yet too young for such dalliances, but one day you will experience the overwhelming desire to dip your flesh into feminine honey. You'll find many obliging women such as yon kitchen maid with whom gentlemen such as ourselves may slake our lust. But her type are so separate a being from those ladies we must marry as to be another species."

Nick felt a surge of manly camaraderie at his father's willingness to discuss such adult, masculine subjects as lust and fornication with him. "In what ways are they different?" he asked.

"As a rule, wives welcome their husbands in the marital bed, only as it is their duty to procreate," his father explained. "A husband's taking of his wife should be a brief exercise, and she will take no pleasure in it. However, it is necessary to couple with one's wife at regular intervals in order to weave the protection of Satyr Will around her."

"And the other kind of women?" Nick prodded.

"Ah!" His father grinned. "Those are the ones with whom we may slake our baser, carnal urges."

"Servants?"

"Where they are willing," said his father with a shrug. "And without fear of contracting a pox or siring a bastard, thank Bacchus."

Nick looked confused.

His father leaned forward. "You will come to greatly appreciate the differences between us and Humans in this area. Unlike Humans, we aren't troubled by the various diseases communicated through fornication. And while the cocks of Human men issue seed that takes root as it wills, it's only possible for the Satyr to put a child in a female's belly during the Calling. Even then, we can decide whether or not our seed will be potent."

His father turned reflective for a moment, and Nick sensed he was thinking of his own wife, Nick's mother, who was long dead. She'd been Human, but a strain of Satyr blood had touched her family in the distant past, giving her the ability to bear the children of his father, a full-blood Satyr.

"But do take care not to become enamored of one woman to the exclusion of others," his father went on. "It's unsafe to reveal too much of what you are even to a wife."

Nick had often seen his father's wistful eyes follow his mother and had wondered why he kept himself from showing more affection toward her. Now he began to understand.

"Where are willing women other than servants to be found?" he asked, hoping to turn his father's attention to happier things.

His father eyed him. "There are establishments where carnal women can be had for coin. But it's too soon for such talk. When you're of an age, I'll show you such a place."

Eventually his father had made good on his promise. But not until after Nick had already seen to the losing of his virginity.

That event had occurred some years later with an especially bold upstairs maid. After Nick had achieved his full height, she'd begun to flirt openly with him, often finding occasion to brush her body against him in the hallways. She'd pretended such happy accidents were unintentional, but the coy looks she'd given him said otherwise.

One morning, she dared enter his bedchamber while he lay slumbering. She'd feigned chagrin and said she'd meant only to change the bed linens. But her eyes were keen as they lit on his penis, distended with its customary morning fullness. He'd seen the spark of lust in her eyes before she'd made her apologies and departed. Afterward he'd noticed several other maids eyeing him with increased interest.

When she chanced upon him one afternoon in the hall outside his bedchamber, she boldly took his fingers and lay them full upon her bosom. Covering his hand with hers, she stroked it over her bountiful flesh.

Leaning close, she whispered at his ear. "Would you care for a poke, young lord?"

She hadn't needed to make her offer twice.

Nick glanced around in search of a suitable dallying place. The linen closet? His bedchamber? Surely they couldn't couple in those locations. Anyone might chance upon them as he had his father that day in the cellar.

"Meet me in an hour near the knot garden wall," she'd told him. Then she'd withdrawn his hand from her bosom and given his cheek a playful tap. "Naughty boy."

Meet her he did, feeling nervous and excited and wondering how it would all begin. She'd been there, waiting for him as promised, and had shown him a nook in the garden where they could be hidden. She'd loosened her blouse's ties then, lowering the neckline so he had unfettered access.

Obliging her, he'd rubbed and fondled her breasts, marveling at their fullness and thrilling at his good fortune. She'd hastened matters herself, unfastening his trousers with her plump fingers and pulling forth his stiffened cock.

Her wide eyes and coarse compliments bespoke of amazement at his male endowments. Later, her lavish groans and lusty giggles had followed the reception of his shaft inside her.

He'd spent himself within her quickly and thrice more that afternoon. They met in secret by the garden wall almost daily thereafter over the next weeks. She was eager and appeared to require nothing of him other than their fleeting fornications amid the lemongrass and thyme.

Belatedly she'd often expressed concern he might have gotten her with child. His father had explained his first Calling would occur when he achieved another year of age. Until then he couldn't impart childseed. However, he offered her no reassurances. His half brother Raine had warned him that Humans were afraid of such abilities they didn't understand.

The maid's furtive, scheming glances had soon caused Nick to wonder if she secretly hoped to conceive his bastard so as to give her some sort of hold over him. When his father discovered the affair, he was relieved to put an end to it.

Afterward his father decided to introduce him to a similarly accommodating group of women more befitting his station in life. The promised trip to a brothel had occurred.

The bawdy establishment was awash with scantily clad women, but none so forward as the maid had been. Nick quickly discerned that sexual matters were conducted more subtly in such establishments. After a low-voiced negotiation with his father, an attractive lady had taken Nick's hand. She'd ushered him into a private chamber, sunk to her knees, and slid his trousers to the floor.

"You have a fine cock, Master Satyr," she'd complimented. Then she'd placed the aforementioned appendage between her rouged lips and proceeded to attend him in a way that was new.

He'd been ready for her again almost immediately. Before he put himself inside the passage between her legs, she'd inserted a sponge moistened with vinegar she'd explained would prevent conception.

A thin string attached to the sponge allowed her to easily remove it after they copulated. Before their second coupling, he did the honors with the sponge, curious to experience all aspects of this most pleasurable activity. There was no way to explain to a Human that there existed such an oddity as a man who could control his childseed. So he continued the deception he would carry on with all Human women he mated with thereafter.

Since that day, he'd never wanted for willing females to warm his cock. He had explored many avenues of gratification, some he was well aware his conservative peers in society would consider shocking or even aberrant. However, as long as a woman was of an age and willing, he placed no limits on what passed between them.

Over the years, it had been gratifying to discover how bold females could be, how amenable to suggestion. At least, a certain type of woman.

Such pleasant memories had his cock stiffening to the point of discomfort within his trousers. He glanced at his timepiece, willing the hours to pass so he could again approach his new wife's bed.

12

He'd shielded himself from her. It was Jane's first thought upon awakening the morning after her wedding night. Normally, at such close quarters she'd have been unable to stop herself from melding. Somehow he'd prevented it. Or was she simply gaining some control over the ability?

She removed her nightgown and examined the rusty streaks on the back of the skirt. Blood. Her inclination was to scrub the stain away. But her aunt had bade her save this evidence of her virginity as proof, should her husband require it. She wadded the garment and stuffed it into the far corner of a drawer.

A maid appeared to draw her bath. Jane instructed her that she would bathe in privacy and slipped behind the screen to do so.

She found herself moving somewhat gingerly. The worst soreness was naturally in the area where her husband had joined himself to her. But her body also ached in other unusual places due to the unaccustomed exercise.

Embarrassed to think the maid might notice, she dismissed her after dressing. Then she practiced walking before her mirror, making sure not to grimace or stride in an ungainly manner. It wouldn't do for her difficulties to be observed by anyone.

Jane half dreaded an encounter with her husband. How did one act with a stranger after having seen him naked? Even more to the point, after he'd seen her thus? Would the memory of what they had done together be in his eyes?

She measured out the herbs she must take each morning to prevent her husband's seed from taking root in her. Sprinkling them in a glass of water, she swallowed it, wincing at the bitter taste.

When hunger drove her to seek breakfast, she left her chamber and went downstairs. She peeked into several rooms along the hall, finding that many housed collections of various sorts.

In the sala grande, she found numerous displays of flasks, amphorae, and urns. These artifacts mingled with newer items of obvious expense. All were relics of her husband's winemaking trade.

Another room held alabaster carvings, shards of pottery and glass, exquisite shells and geodes. Yet another housed a full-sized stone sarcophagus carved with scenes of an afterlife imagined by ancient Etruscans. There were classic busts with pompous expressions, sections of frescoed fragments dating back centuries, and gold florins stamped with lilies.

It appeared her husband was a collector of treasures and curiosities. She could almost imagine herself in a museum!

Downstairs Jane found herself in a large circular-shaped salon della feste. A dozen evenly spaced windowed alcoves rose to a balcony and then beyond to meet in the center of the domed ceiling. Empty sideboards sat along one wall, and the dining table was bare. Judging by the sun, it was nearly noon. She rarely slept so late and had likely missed breakfast.

Still, she was unusually ravenous. Where was the staff?

She ventured in a northerly direction and opened a door to

what turned out to be the kitchen. Inside she found a number of servants bustling about. Every one of them paused in their work, silenced by her entrance.

"Buona mattina, signora."

Startled, she whirled to find a male servant standing in the doorway behind her. She recognized him as the one who had ordered her trunks upstairs last night.

"I'm Signore Faunus, the estate manager," he said, bowing and moving past her in that sprightly two-step way of his. "My duties include oversight of the other servants and personal attention to Lord Satyr. And of course to any members of his family residing here at Blackstone. If you require anything day or night, you are to please let me know."

Though he spoke formally and treated her with deference, the servant had an agelessness about him, and a hint of mischief twinkled deep in his eyes. The upper curves of his ears rose slightly to points, lending an elfin quality to his features.

"I see. Thank you, Signore Faunus. I wonder if you could tell me. Is—is his lordship still about?"

"The master is out and left instructions that dinner be delayed for his late return this evening."

"Grazie," she replied, reddening at the absurdity of a servant knowing more of a husband's schedule than his own wife.

It annoyed her that Nick had left neither word of his whereabouts nor any indication regarding what she should attempt to accomplish during his absence.

"May I get anything for you from the kitchen, signora?" Signore Faunus asked.

"Yes, some lunch," she decided suddenly. "I'm going for a walk."

He snapped his fingers at one of the maids, and she stepped forward. "I will leave you in good hands." He bowed again and took his leave.

"A picnic lunch?" the maid ventured, once he'd gone.

Jane nodded. "Nothing elaborate. Cheese, bread, and fruit?"

"Si, si, I will see to it," the maid said, rushing to gather the makings.

While she waited, Jane studied the kitchen. Running a household wasn't her forte; however, she supposed she would get used to it once she dove in. But she would spend today acclimating to her new surroundings without the burden of duties. There would be time enough in the upcoming weeks to determine how best to use her days as she adjusted to her new role.

Below a long shelf burdened with copper pots, she noticed a board fastened to the wall, with small round metal tags hanging upon it. She bent closer and saw that each tag was numbered. There were many slots, but only six were currently occupied with tags. What were they for?

"Your lunch, signora," said the maid. As she thanked her, Jane saw she wore one of the tags on her apron. But the maid curtsied and scurried off before she could ask about it.

Jane left the house by the kitchen door and was amazed to find herself stepping into a verdant paradise. The gardens and fountains here had obviously been painstakingly designed by some long-ago arborist.

A splendid mosaic floor encircled the base of a burbling fountain, extending nearly twenty feet out from its sides to form a large courtyard. In the center of the fountain, a mischievous Pan stood playing his pipes in peaceful solitude.

She walked the perimeter of the tile floor and saw that it told a mythical history of the House of Satyr. Ships, warriors, fantastic beasts—all were depicted in a continuous frieze of jewel-colored chips set in plastered stone.

Several paths spoked from the mosaic, ribboning outward into expanses of greenery dotted with statues. She chose one lined with lemon trees in terra-cotta pots and shaded by statuesque oaks.

Anxious to explore, she left the path at some point and threaded her way through a sloping carpet of wildflowers. Pheasants strolled about the lawn in haughty jerks, and gazelles leaped past. An iridescent blue-green peacock strutted by, drawing her attention.

At length, she turned to view the castello below. How different its rear facade was from that of the entrance! From the road, it had appeared a forbidding fortress. Yet here, all was delightful. It was as though the castello had two faces—one that repelled, one that welcomed.

Though she hadn't intended to go so far today, she felt the urge to venture on. Leaving manicured hedges behind, she stepped under the leafy canopy of a tangled forest. Overhead, parrots, jays, and rooks flapped their wings and cawed at her intrusion.

She surveyed the forest floor, searching. Here and there, she came across patches of mistletoe, blackberry, juniper, betony, chicory, fennel, rosemary, and saffron. All were plants with magical powers. None were allium moly.

Eventually she sat on a large, flat rock to eat her lunch. At her feet she noticed a grouping of plants unlike any she'd ever seen. She crouched to inspect one of them more closely. It was somewhat bedraggled from the ravages of winter. With a brush of her fingertips she melded, breathing new life into it. The invigoration traveled several yards in each direction, brightening and enlivening. She rocked back on her heels, astonished. One simple touch had never traveled so far before.

An odd sensation of being weighed and evaluated in some way settled over her. Glancing around, she saw no one.

She heard a rustling sound and looked ahead. The trail that had beckoned her forward only moments ago had somehow disappeared! It was as though the trees had closed in to seal off the path and prevent her from invading farther. Only the path behind her lay open.

"I mean no harm," she murmured.

Her way remained closed. She had no choice but to turn back.

When she returned to the castello, Jane was surprised to find she'd pulled three fronds as long as her arm from a patch of ferns.

In the doorway, she swept them across the kitchen step and murmured:

Banish evil with this spell.
Protecting all who herein dwell.

Embarrassed, she tossed the fronds outside and slammed the door on them.

"Foolishness," she muttered. "As if all it took was a broom of ferns."

Since Nick was to return late for dinner, she sought another activity.

"Would you direct me to the library?" she inquired of the first servant she came across.

"But the library door is closed, signora."

"Locked, you mean?"

The maidservant shook her head. "No, signora. 'Tis only closed."

"Then direct me to it, and I shall open it," said Jane, somewhat perplexed.

The maid looked scandalized. "But Signore Faunus says a closed door is never to be opened in this house. No matter what sort of curious noises issue from behind it."

Jane's eyebrows rose. Curious noises? Whatever was she speaking of?

The maid's eyes flicked to the window and back. "Pardon me, signora, but it grows dusk."

Jane looked toward the window, thoroughly confused. Grapevines and olive trees were silhouetted on the hill. Behind them, the sun was setting in strands of vivid orange.

The maid backed toward the door, curtseying with every other step. "I must go. I return in the morning."

Jane straightened in surprise. "Return? You don't live on the estate?"

Now it was the maid's turn for surprise. "No, signora. The master has provided separate quarters for the staff on the outskirts of the estate."

"Separate quarters for all of them?" she asked. She'd never heard of such a thing.

"Yes, signora. We all go. Well, all excepting Signore Faunus. And the master. They stay on overnight."

The maid fingered the numbered metal tag at her collar. It was like those Jane had seen on the board near the kitchen door.

"Why do you wear that?"

The girl looked at the tag and back at Jane. "No one is allowed on the grounds without a tag." She glanced at Jane's chest and colored. "I mean, of course, excepting you and the master. We don our numbers in the morning when we arrive and leave them behind at night when we depart."

"I've heard that miners wear such tags before going into the mine shafts. They must be returned to the board at the end of each day to ensure they have made it safely out."

The maid looked blank. "I don't know about the mines. Here, we hang our tags on the board so Signore Faunus and the master know from the count that all are gone and they are private again."

"And Lord Satyr's brothers? Does their staff operate in the same manner?"

"Yes, signora. Their servants share our quarters. All the staff arrives at dawn and departs by dusk each day."

The maid was now shifting her weight from one foot to the other, appearing dreadfully anxious to depart.

Jane took pity and dismissed her.

The girl rushed toward the kitchen, already unpinning her tag, as if the hounds of hell barked at her heels. What in the world did she imagine would befall her were she to linger past dark?

Jane found the library on her own and held her breath as she let herself in. When nothing unusual happened, she chided herself for letting the maid's nonsense affect her.

Inside, she was pleased to see that her husband's interest in collecting extended to his library. She ran her hands over the gilded leather bindings of books, old and new, shelved in paneled wood bookcases.

A work titled *Curative and Medicinal Herbs and Plants of the Ancient Romans* caught her eye, and she mulled it for some time before replacing it. Other volumes took her interest, but it was difficult to concentrate on one when so many things in the room begged to be studied.

Files with wide, shallow drawers held archival documents detailing centuries of the daily workings of her husband's estate as well as the surrounding hill towns. In other drawers, she found treatises by Byzantine scholars and contracts for the sale of wine from the time of the great Medici family. She vowed to return to them another day when she had more time.

Atop an intricately carved table, an assortment of urns on display drew her attention. Black designs on a golden background decorated the exterior of one tall, handled vase. A border of stylized grape clusters entwined with olive branches ringed its top edge, and below that stood various figures in black silhouette. They were similar to the ones she'd seen on vessels in the more public regions of the castello, but her cheeks flushed when she noticed startling differences.

Pan playing his pipes was easily identified in the group. It was the other figures—naked, bearded men—that she found shocking. They were fantastic creatures with furred flanks and wild hair and eyes. A thin, undulating tail sprang from the tail-bone of each, while an impressive phallus curved upward from the crux of their thighs.

A large, wide-mouthed, terra-cotta bowl was displayed alone, as though it had particular value. She knelt to examine it and saw it was decorated in the reverse—pale figures sculpted in bas-relief were silhouetted upon a dark background. Here, males and females cavorted and drank with abandon. Arms outflung, their expressions varied from ecstatic to demonic. One male held a wineskin to the lips of a female while another copulated with her from behind. In his enthusiasm, the artist had endowed this man beast with a dual set of phalluses, one set just above the other!

Jane swallowed audibly. She turned away and distracted her-self from the disturbing scenes by milling through the book-shelves. When she found the rare volumes 12–19 from Greek botanist Pliny the Elder's *Historia Naturalis*, her attention was caught.

But every so often, she found her gaze straying to the mys-terious vases and their carnal decoration.

13

At dinner Jane's husband was a courteous but distant host. He asked to her comfort and how her day had passed. In return, she inquired about the estate and its history.

"My ancestors located the vineyard on this hillside and walled the grounds for defense reasons," he told her. "The wall encircles two thousand acres of forest, fruit and olive groves, and, of course, the vineyards." He raised a glass of wine to his lips in subtle challenge.

If his mention of the vineyards was verbal bait, she didn't take it. She'd determined that her best course was to simply ignore his profession for the present.

"And your brothers? How distant are their estates?"

"Each is a half hour's journey along the exterior wall on horseback. We'll invite them to visit in the coming weeks. Once we're receiving."

After their honeymoon ended, he meant.

Though she observed him closely, there was nothing in his bearing to suggest he felt any physical discomfort from last night's mutual occupation. Or had he, too, practiced before a mirror until any stiffness left him? The notion had her smiling secretly into her napkin.

His easy, distant manner made it difficult to relate him to the man who had lain with her the night before. Was that why no one spoke openly of what went on in the marriage bed? Maybe the intimacies were blocked out of one's mind in the daytime in order that one might function in ordinary activities.

"Once you've settled in, the household will be given over to your care to whatever extent you wish," he informed her. "You may consult me or Signore Faunus with any questions. He's been my family's trusted servant for many years and will serve as liaison between you and the other staff."

"I do have one question," said Jane. "The staff—why are they are sent away at night?"

As though to delay his reply, Nick blotted his lips with a starched, monogrammed napkin, obviously laundered and pressed by servants. With so little time on the estate, she couldn't help wondering when they found the hours to maintain such perfection.

"A personal preference. You will grow used to it in time."

"It seems strange."

He swirled his glass, and his twin blue mirrors glinted at her over the sanguine wine.

"Strange isn't always a bad thing though, is it?"

At his words, Jane's thoughts spun in a direction she imagined he didn't expect. "I suppose not."

He nodded and returned to his food.

She surveyed him from below her lashes. Did he mean what he said? Was he accepting of that which was truly strange? A glimmer of hope flickered to life within her, refusing to be squashed. Perhaps, just perhaps, she and Emma would find true acceptance here on this land. In this family.

But she must go carefully. She would never consider revealing anything of herself until she knew far, far more of him.

* * *

Getting into her bed that night, knowing the enigmatic stranger who was her husband would likely come to her again, was one of the more disturbing things Jane had ever done. Did she want him to come to her, or didn't she? She attempted to analyze her feelings on the matter and failed.

She'd only just begun to slip under the coverlet when the door adjoining her husband's bedchamber opened. She scrambled to cover herself as he approached.

He appeared unfazed by her haste. His gaze shifted to her nightstand, and he abruptly detoured to her dressing table. She heard the clinking scrape of porcelain. Then he returned to her bedside.

Wordlessly he set the pot of cream he'd retrieved onto the nightstand. His intentions toward her couldn't have been stated more clearly.

As he had the night before, he removed his dressing gown and tossed it over the end of her bed. How easily he revealed his nakedness. How did one become so cavalier as to shed every trace of modesty without a bit of concern? She couldn't imagine.

Though she had cataloged his bodily features the previous night, she now had her wits better gathered to take in the whole picture. He truly was a splendid male creature, she realized, with more than his share of animal grace. Every part of him was well formed, with hard muscle and bone underlying sculpted valleys, hills, and plains.

Without preamble, he joined her on the mattress, folded back the coverlet, and began sliding her gown upward.

She shifted more fully onto her back, preparing to fulfill her role.

It wouldn't be so shattering this time, she told herself. His body was more familiar, and now she knew what to expect from the act. Her aunt had promised it was always worst the first time.

If only he would attempt some sort of reassurance. A few kind words would make everything somehow easier.

As before, he bared her to the waist and perfunctorily parted her knees. His hand lingered, absently caressing a vulnerable spot just behind the bend of her leg. A shiver of awareness prickled over her.

He spoke, his dark voice ripping the silken silence. "I had planned to allow you a solitary night to ameliorate the effects of our joining last evening. But I find myself in need of you. Are you recovered enough to have me again?"

It was obviously a rhetorical question, since he was already moving across her body, settling his brawny thighs between her softer ones.

"Yes, of course," she murmured.

With brisk efficiency, he scooped cream from the waiting pot, spread it over his cock, then smeared the excess through her tender folds. He rubbed the entrance to her passage with a creamy thumb, testing her readiness to receive him.

"Sore?" he inquired, studying her expression.

She flushed, wishing he hadn't spoken of it. "A little. Are you?"

"I?" he questioned in surprise.

"Yes. Are you sore as well?" she asked. "I would suppose so, based on the mechanics of the matter."

He chuckled. "No, I'm not sore, but then, I'm more accustomed—that is—" He shot her a queer look. "Back to my original concern, are you too uncomfortable to mate with me?"

Mate? she echoed silently. An unusual, earthy word. Why was he asking? Would he let her deny him if she claimed to be too sore from last night's masculine assault? No doubt his concern was a farce, she thought in annoyance.

"You may proceed," she assured him in carefully modulated tones. "I won't resist."

His brow quirked. "Grazie." His tone was vaguely sardonic, and she wondered if he'd read her thoughts. Unfair, when she couldn't seem to read his.

Palming his shaft, he guided it to her opening. Softness gave way to hardness as it pressed into her, attempting to encase itself in the passage it had enjoyed the previous night.

Grudgingly, her chafed slit opened. But his engorged tip didn't slip inside with ease.

She flinched.

He stared down at her. "Sometimes the soreness can enhance the pleasure. But you must let me know if it becomes too much."

Pleasure? she wondered. Did he mean he would experience more pleasure if she were sore? Or—

She gasped as, having finally pierced her, he filled her with a long, sure stroke. Her newly sensitized tissues tingled in shocked awareness as she accepted him. Before her body could adjust to the nature of his invasion, the now familiar rhythmic advance and withdrawal began.

She lay under him, hands flat at her sides as he moved on her with intense concentration. Her nether lips dutifully bowed inward with each thrust and pursed outward with each withdrawal.

As had happened the previous night, his steady movements gradually grew more robust in their purpose. The sharp discomfort dwindled, but she assiduously guarded against any unwarranted stirrings of her senses. If she lost her grip on her emotions, no telling what odd behavior might spring forth.

Grasping her thighs, he angled her more to his liking and then tunneled deeper. It took all her concentration to prevent herself from adjusting her position in a way she sensed would bring him into more satisfying contact.

He drove toward his release, seeming to forget her as his lust took control. The contrast between his straining masculine domination and her tense pliancy was stark. Yet he appeared to accept her placid submission as what was expected of her, either unaware of or unconcerned about her feelings in the matter.

Hard fingers seized her hips, and he heaved into her once, twice, a third time, as if he were intent on nailing her to the feather mattress. He uttered a guttural sound against her neck as a series of fierce seminal eruptions jetted hot, milky fluid inside her to mingle with the cream from her jar.

Soon afterward he pulled away and calmly bade her good night before returning to his solitary chamber.

She drew the covers to her chin and stared balefully at his door.

God! The ache. The agony of wanting. Deep in the pit he'd plundered within her, she hummed with it, throbbed with it.

His taking had caused this—this stirring in her. She longed to go after him, to rail at him, to beg. For something. Anything that would relieve her.

A hand crept low, between her legs. His seed was slick. Or was that the cream from her jar?

A finger touched tender flesh, pressed. Her clit pulsed softly. *Mmm.*

Her eyes darted to his door. What if he heard?

The finger rubbed a gentle, slippery circle on the hard nub it had found.

She contracted the muscles of her slit, once, twice. *Mmm.*

The finger circled faster. She watched his door, wary. What if he caught her? What if—

Mmm.

The finger found her slit and dipped inside.

Ahh!

Her channel spasmed on it suddenly, gripping, releasing,

gripping, releasing—like a nursing mouth. When the convulsions seized her clit as well, she rolled to her stomach, burying a moan in her pillow.

The strange sensation pumped at her for long moments and then ebbed and died away.

Eventually she slept, at peace.

14

Over the following days, Jane learned more of the inner workings of the estate and marveled at the complexities involved in its operation. The rules were few but strictly observed.

When her husband secreted himself behind closed doors in his study, the library, or any room, the staff was forbidden to disturb him. Only when the door stood slightly ajar was it permissible to knock and request admittance. The upstairs areas were off limits to the staff after the evening meal, and all were to be off the property by nightfall.

Any questions she put forth regarding such matters were deflected, and the system which had at first seemed unusual soon came to seem normal.

She took her place in the household hierarchy, making few changes and glad to leave its reins in the capable hands of Signore Faunus. The servants welcomed her once they realized she wouldn't prove overly demanding.

This appeared to please Nick. It was as though she'd managed to correctly fit into some sort of niche he expected a wife to fill. And she imagined he was more pleased by that thought rather than any great desire to see his already well-functioning household running more smoothly.

He ventured forth into the vineyard daily, where she presumed he consulted with his brothers on occasion. But the business of the vineyard was kept from her for the time being, as were his siblings.

Aside from household duties, she spent her hours in his library and garden, searching for clues regarding what might be the best brew of herbs for a curative.

Each night after dinner, an ethereal quiet fell over her new home. All the servants departed, leaving Nick and her utterly alone except for the unobtrusive Signore Faunus, who rarely showed himself.

Yet chores got done overnight as though by magic. It was very odd, but any inquiries to the servants on the matter were met with either blank stares or agitation.

Meanwhile, her new husband visited her in much the same way each night, sojourning briefly in her bed and body and then subsequently returning to his own bedchamber for sleep. His swift coupling proved a blessing since it kept him from discovering any hint of her abnormalities.

Or of the relief she found on her own, once he'd gone. She worried this ability was part of her strangeness and daily vowed to cease such behavior.

Her failure to keep such promises was his fault, she'd determined. Before he came to her bed each night, she was resolute that she wouldn't touch herself *there* again. But each time, his taking weakened her will. Her hand often found its way between her legs the very moment the door between their chambers closed behind him.

Nick seemed able to place the routine of his days and nights into separate compartments. His behavior toward her was politely remote during the sunlight hours, making it difficult to equate him with the man who visited her in such a carnal way each night.

However, she was grateful for his example, which she soon copied. In their daily interactions, this arrangement eased any embarrassment she might have felt. It became easy to simply pretend the nights had never happened.

When her monthly courses came a week and a half after their marriage, she informed him with reluctance. Though their time together had been brief, she was concerned he might react badly. He'd underscored the importance of a timely production of heirs. And he'd been working diligently in her bed, unaware that the brew of herbs she swallowed each morning thwarted his purpose.

Surprisingly, he showed no disappointment at her announcement. Still, the delivery of her news resulted in an abrupt change in their routine.

For the first time since their wedding, he didn't visit her bed.

Nick trod the path from office to home, sure of his way even in the pitch of night. His eyes went to his wife's window and saw it was dark. He wouldn't visit her. A woman's blood brought out the animal in him, and he wouldn't reveal himself in that way to her. Not yet. Perhaps not ever.

He'd felt no despair when Jane had informed him of her monthly flux. He was fully aware he hadn't impregnated her. But he planned to, twelve nights from now—in the next Calling. He would have to bespell her in order to ensure her participation. No matter.

He'd never taken a flesh-and-blood woman in the Calling and was intensely curious to experience the spilling of fertile seed in his wife. Because Jane's body was Faerie, her womb should easily accept his childseed, whereas that of a full-blood Human female would have more difficulty.

Upstairs now, he padded down the hall. His nostrils flared as he caught the humid scent of his wife's blood mixed with her inner fluids and her natural, beguiling scent. His testicles bunched and drew up. Within his trousers, his strangled prick thickened and rose, anticipating. He forced himself to pass her door and continue on to his own, if only to prove to himself that he could.

Once in his bedchamber, he bespelled the hallway door as well as the one adjoining his wife's room, bolting them. Crossing the room, he touched a mirrored panel. It tilted, revealing itself to be a hinged door. Slipping beyond it, he found himself in a familiar chamber. The mirror repositioned itself behind him, sealing him inside. He lit no candles. He wouldn't need them.

He tore at the fastenings of his trousers and focused his mind on a point beside the bedpost, summoning. A swirling mist materialized under his stare, where before there had been only emptiness. The myriad of colors coalesced into a female Shimmerskin—one who closely resembled his wife.

Sensing what he wanted, she pressed her breasts to the wall and grabbed two metal rings she found bolted high above her. He lowered his trousers, pressed his cock to her slit, and slammed into her from behind. She was soft, warm, necessary. Disposable. She would feel nothing, demand nothing, and cease to exist when he was done. Fucking her would be as uncomplicated as masturbation. And over as quickly.

His body achieved satisfaction a half a dozen times in the space of an hour. Their couplings were lusty and varied, in contrast to those of late with his bride.

When his mind told her she was no longer needed, the Shimmerskin dematerialized, fading back into the rarified air from which she'd come. Afterward, he returned to his chamber and slept soundly, satiated.

* * *

The following morning he bade Jane farewell and traveled to Florence, where he spent an afternoon at Umberto House with his longtime favorites, Anna and Bella. They were the crown jewels of the pleasure house that employed dozens of talented whores.

He'd selected them carefully a year or so ago after making discreet inquiries. Tales of their greediness in a man's bed had led him to believe he would never have to hold back for fear of causing them distress. He'd been right in his choice and now regularly enjoyed their unquestioning compliance with his sexual whims.

Upon his arrival at their establishment, they'd evinced no surprise that he'd chosen to visit them even after he'd wed. Certainly he felt no qualms about it. Such was accepted behavior for men of his stature in society.

They lost no time ushering him into their quarters and professed to have missed his attentions greatly. Within the first hour of his arrival, he repeatedly relieved himself in every orifice available to him in both of their pliant bodies. As usual, their interplay involved the use of dildos and other curiosities they employed to enhance a customer's enjoyment.

An assortment of such devices now lay haphazardly on various surfaces of the room, tossed there in the throes of earlier activity.

Nick stood from the chaise longue upon which he had most recently fucked Bella while sucking at her companion's slit. As both had screamed with their release, he'd found his yet again.

Pulling a neatly folded square from the stack of linens they supplied for clientele use, he wiped all evidence of them from his face and cock. Then he poured himself another drink.

"Your wife cannot please you as we can," Anna taunted from the chaise longue.

Idly he observed that her slack cunt still pulsed with the most recent orgasm his tongue had provided, while Bella's well-used slit leaked cream his penis had just deposited. The women sprawled seminaked, their breathing still labored from orgasms his body had coaxed from them while his mind and heart had remained disengaged.

He pulled on a robe, feeling mild disgust for both himself and them. He was unaccustomed to experiencing such an emotion after sex, and it momentarily shook him. Surely he wasn't feeling guilty!

"'Tis true," agreed Bella. Her lisping voice had once attracted him, but he suddenly found it repellent.

He disliked hearing these women speak of his wife. Jane wouldn't and couldn't be expected to perform as they did.

The jewels of his family ring glinted as Nick lowered the glass of wine from his lips. "She will please me when she bears my children. That's all the pleasure I require of her."

In the natural order of things, Jane's belly would swell with his child after the next Calling. During the time of her confinement, he would seek carnal gratification with other females such as these.

Once an appropriate interval had passed following the first child's birthing, he would resume conjugal visits to his wife. His father had explained that Human wives desired an ultimate release from such duties. But he would never give Jane one, since regular mating would lend her the protection of Satyr Will.

Bella roused herself and came to kneel at his feet. Her eyes flirted as she parted his satin dressing gown. Her eyeteeth were slightly prominent, lending her a reptilian look.

Licking her lips, she attempted to stroke his satiated penis back to life. Her pointed tongue flicked the long ridge at the underside, lingering at the sensitive spot where it joined the crown. When his arousal instantaneously burgeoned, she smiled at up him through her lashes.

"You're always so flatteringly ready, Lord Satyr."

He could have told her not to be flattered. A hundred others like her could induce the same reaction in him. He felt no special affection for her, he realized, and it was that lack that had tainted today's interlude. Strange that this had never bothered him before.

It was likely time to move on to new pastures.

When her mouth engulfed his length, Nick wove his fingers in her hair to lightly hold her. Dispassionately he watched her thin lips repeatedly engulf and disgorge his cock.

She arced her neck, making his voyage from lips to throat a straighter path. Her neck muscles relaxed, and she exhaled, breathing through her nose and enabling him to drill deeper. The head of his penis dipped well into her throat, quivering at the exquisite stimulation.

Most Human women would choke at such treatment, but Bella was known for her ability to take all a man could offer. He held nothing back, knowing from prior experience that she could handle even his substantial dimensions. She swallowed rhythmically, massaging his tip, cajoling until he sluiced. She held him deep then until the last of his cum made its way down her throat.

Nick pulled free of her, his eyes void of emotion. Her flicking tongue gave his tip a last lick in farewell. He caressed her cheek in brief thanks, picked up his drink, and sat.

Moving behind his chair, she draped her arms over its back, massaging his shoulders and reaching to drag her fingernails in swirls over the stiff nubs of his nipples.

"Not too rough, Bella," Anna reminded in a teasing voice. "The signore might find your scratches difficult to explain to his new wife."

Their amused giggles faded quickly when Nick didn't join in.

He wanted to leave but forced himself to remain, as was his custom. Over the next few hours, he soberly drained his glass as the two women slowly and exquisitely drained his prick again and again. The clock struck midnight when Anna again knelt and smiled up at him with her cat eyes. Pushing his cock high against his belly, she took his balls in her mouth, rolling and massaging them with her rough tongue. He could almost hear her purr.

Dependable as ever, his shaft began to harden.

His head fell back against the chair, and he wondered how his new wife occupied her time that evening.

With Nick away in town, ostensibly on business, Jane spent much of the day in his library poring over yet another book in search of herbal curatives. Many of the supposed cures struck her as worse than the maladies they were said to ease!

One case study had snagged her interest, for it described a woman afflicted with many of her symptoms. The passage claimed a concoction including moly had cured supernatural occurrences in the body of this woman, withering winglike appendages that had grown at her shoulder blades.

The cure was convoluted, involving the use of numerous herbs including varieties of thyme, sage, oregano, mint, dill, and moly—all of which were said to ward off evil.

When she tired of such studies, she finished off the evening writing to her aunt in the salon. Nick had suggested that they might begin receiving visitors, and she was anxious to have Emma with her.

Darkness had fallen by the time she sealed her letter. She set it in the tray Signore Faunus had informed her was designated for outgoing mail.

The house was eerily silent as she took the stairs. It was disquieting to know only she and Nick's estate manager now occupied the grounds. But her husband had assured her other servants could easily be summoned from their quarters should the need arise.

On the way to her bedchamber, she all but ran into a maid she didn't recognize.

"Who are you?" she gasped, straightening away.

"One of the night staff here at the castello, signora," the girl replied. Her dronelike voice held little inflection, and there was an unearthly calm about her.

Jane clutched the book she'd borrowed from Nick's library closer to her chest as a chill shimmied her spine. "I understood all the staff departed at dusk."

"We come when the others go," the girl replied in a monotone.

We? "You're some sort of night servant then?"

The maid nodded distantly.

"Do you live on the premises? Or in the servants' quarters?"

"Signora?" asked another more familiar voice.

Jane turned to find that Signore Faunus had crept up on them.

"Do you require assistance?" he asked, looking anxious.

"No. That is, I was on my way from the library to my chamber when—" She glanced at the strangely placid servant she'd come upon and then back at Signore Faunus. "I had thought the staff departed each evening."

Signore Faunus blanched to the tips of his pointed ears. "Of whom are you speaking?"

"Of this maid, of course!"

"You can see her? Ah!" He rocked to his toes and then back on his heels, nodding as though to himself. "Your heritage. It makes sense." He dismissed the maid, who went on her way, moving in an odd sort of floating glide.

They both stared after her.

"The night staff take direction only from me," the signore informed her. "I will relay any requirements you may have to them."

"I see," said Jane, not seeing at all. "But—"

Signore Faunus clicked his heels and executed a perfunctory bow. "You must ring me if you have needs to be met. We're all here to serve." With that, he twitched his coattails, wheeled around, and dashed off.

Jane watched him go before making her way back to her room. She got into bed and then got back out, crept to the door, and locked it.

Belowground in the cellar of the castello, Signore Faunus played softly on his panpipe, luring the night servants to him. There were over two dozen of them, each one an orphaned dryad who'd been granted shelter after her life tree had died. Once a Satyr lord bestowed caretaker status upon them, such dryads tended his castello and its inhabitants as faithfully as they'd once tended their life trees in the forest of his estate.

"You must take more care to remain hidden," Faunus warned the choir of ethereal faces who gathered around him. "The signora sees but does not yet understand. . . ."

15

Five nights after Jane had announced her temporary indisposition, Nick sensed her blood time had ceased. At twilight, he opened the door that adjoined his bedchamber to hers.

Once inside, he stopped short. He caught her scent, yet she wasn't there. Annoyance assailed him that she was out of her proper place when he was ready for her. It was earlier than he normally visited her bed. But it had been nearly a week. Wasn't she expecting him?

He was about to go in search of her when he observed a puddle on the floor just inside the door to her veranda. A spring storm had come upon them, the kind that would be brief but wild. Surely she wasn't—

When he peered through the door, he could see that she was. Out on the balcony, Jane stood pressed against the stone railing wearing only her nightgown. Wind lashed her, whipping at her hair and gown. One of her hands was braced on the railing, the other hidden from view. As he watched, she tilted her face upward as if she were a flower seeking a drink of life-giving rain.

A part of his mind admired the softly undulating curves of

her bottom, molded by wet fabric. The other wondered at his well-bred, circumspect wife's uncharacteristically uncircumspect behavior.

He opened the door and felt the wind's unseasonable chill. Hadn't she noticed?

"Come, Jane. You'll make yourself ill," he called softly.

She started at his words, whirling around in guilty surprise.

His eyes narrowed with sudden suspicion, and he scanned the grounds beyond her. She couldn't have been engaged in an assignation. One couldn't see more than three yards in the driving rain.

"My l-l-lord," she mumbled, shivering.

He was blocking the doorway. When he moved back and beckoned, she followed him jerkily inside. Her drenched gown clung and slapped against her calves as she went to stand before the fire.

"Do you enjoy storms?" he asked, closing the veranda door and leaning against it to study her.

"They refresh me. I'm sorry," she mumbled, darting a quick glance at him.

She chose to face him rather than the hearth, he noticed. It was out of character for her to display her breasts so brazenly when she must know they were made translucent by the drenched fabric.

She was always scrupulously careful not to show her bared back to him, he realized abruptly. He had an inkling why.

The silence between them lengthened. The feeling of being shut out increased within him, becoming intolerable. He began to circle her.

Nervously she edged away from the hearth, turning as he moved. Always facing him.

He brushed a long wet strand of her hair back over her shoulder, revealing a nipple drawn taut by the cold. He touched a finger to the sloping curve of a breast and then grazed its central nub. She gasped, stepping back and covering the place where his hand had been.

"You may stand in the rain any time you like," he said. "I don't wish to control your every move."

"Oh."

Had she thought that was what he wanted? No. What he really wanted from her was a true and complete knowledge of her talents, freely given. Some Faerie had streaks of evil in them that weren't always sensed on early acquaintance. These were traits he didn't want passed to his children. But asking for her secrets would only invite lies.

She fidgeted guiltily under his stare, and his suspicion intensified.

The Calling would come in seven moons—one week from tonight. His labors with her then would bear fruit. A child. It was premature when he wasn't certain what form her magic took. Yet she exerted a pull over him now, and he wasn't sure he would be able to keep himself from imparting childseed in her once the Calling took his mind.

"I assume your monthly flux has abated?"

She drew her head back as realization obviously dawned that he'd come for his conjugal visit.

Her fingers plucked at the wet fabric that clung to her thigh. "Yes, signore. Give me but a moment, and I will prepare myself to, um, greet you properly."

"You're sufficiently prepared," he growled, crowding her toward the bed.

She pushed at him in protest. "My gown will wet the bedsheets!"

"Then remove it," he suggested. "Or I will."

"I thought you didn't wish to control me."

"Only here, in the bedchamber," he amended. "Elsewhere and in other things, you may exercise greater freedom."

"You're too kind," she snapped.

"Your gown," he reminded her.

With difficulty and purposeful delay, he suspected, she peeled the clammy fabric away. After it dropped to the floor, she sat on the bed and slid backward.

She awaited him there on her back with brittle excitement. Out on the balcony, she'd been stimulating herself—down *there*. Had he seen?

It was the first time she'd touched herself in that way without first having him between her legs. But tonight the storm had called to her, seduced her into it.

Nevertheless, fulfillment had eluded her. She was unsure if it were even possible to achieve that exquisite sensation without the catalyst of prior fornication.

The turbulent emotions the storm and her own hand had aroused still heated her blood. Her void tingled with wanting. When he came into her, would he guess?

Nick dropped his dressing gown and mounted her.

"Cream," she whispered. She was already wet, but maybe the additional moisture would disguise it.

"My apologies." Grabbing the jar on her nightstand, he applied some of the ointment to his penis and then slicked a single finger along her labia to moisten and unfurl it.

Without further preparation, he slid inside her.

Their coupling was the same this time but somehow different. This time, she, too, was naked and felt the soft prickle of the hair on his chest against her breasts. This time, she welcomed the slide of his warm body along her chilled one. This time, his eyes gazed into hers.

This time, she was barely hanging on to her control.

Outside, a flash of lightning illuminated the sky. Wind dashed sheets of water against the windowpane. Nature called to her to join the tumult, to give in to passion.

His cock filled her again and again, pressing at her mons and the needy hooded bud. If she were to tilt her hips, just a little . . .

She struggled to resist. If only he'd given her a few moments to collect herself. Silently, she conjugated Latin. Recited mathematical tables. Called on all the self-discipline she possessed in order to withstand the desire to embrace him. To move with him. To meld.

Her mind played tricks, made promises. . . .

Take what you want of him. . . . It won't arouse your strangeness. . . . Tilt your hips, just so. . . .

And then, suddenly, another voice filled her head, this one deep and masculine.

Yes, tilt your hips just so. Wrap your legs around me. Move with me. . . .

Her eyes widened on her husband's lips. They hadn't spoken. Yet she'd heard the words clearly. IN HER MIND. *Oh, God!*

She was melding with him! Her skin had grown flushed and hot where it contacted his. Her every sense was enriched, attuned to him. She was tumbling . . . *no!*

She flattened her palms on his chest, resisting. Stupid! The melding only intensified.

Her words of rejection were stifled by his lips. His breath became hers, and their tongues danced, mating. As the oils of their skins mixed, so did their emotions, revealing what they would keep hidden from one another.

He was burdened. Yet accustomed to it and strong enough— willing enough—to bear his burdens alone.

She could soothe him. Care for him. So easily. . . .

Let me take the weight from you, husband. You needn't bear it alone. Share with me.

The power of his taking increased. His twilight eyes bore into hers. His promises pierced her mind. . . .

Share your secrets, wife. I will keep them safe, keep you safe.

Passion drugged her. Yes, she wanted to tell. Wanted to

share her burden with him, too. Wanted what he offered.
Wanted him. . . .

Yes, only say you might come to love me one day, husband.

His mind grew wary, distant. Silent.

Hers railed at him.

Then take your enjoyment and leave me whole!

With a strangled shout, he drove deep. She'd taken him off
guard, luring him into spilling before he'd meant to. His slick
desire flooded her, drowning her in his solitary pleasure.

When he left her that night, she had no wayward thoughts
of pleasing herself. Instead, worries darted about her head like
rabbits. She'd thought her ability with Humans was fading, yet
she'd never melded so quickly nor so thoroughly with another
person. Afterward, neither of them had spoken of it. But now it
would be between them.

She sat up. Hunching a shoulder, she explored the area at the
base of its blade. Her fingers combed the feathery down she
found there. Was it her imagination, or was it growing more
rapidly?

What would he do when he discovered her secrets—what
she was? Would he reject her? Cast her out?

Her aunt would have it from him why he'd done so. Con-
demning eyes might then move from her to Emma. Her pulse
tripped and quickened.

She must not meld with him again. She must pretend tonight
had never happened and continue to hide what she was becoming. It was the only way to keep Emma safe.

Her sewing box. She found it on the dressing table and
pulled a pair of shears from within it.

Twisting awkwardly, with her back to the mirror, she stared
at the short hollow quills folded delicately at her shoulder
blades.

Gingerly, she began to snip.

16

Jane ventured outside again the following morning, this time taking a new direction. Now, when she stepped into the garden, nearby plants perked without any effort on her part. Grass underfoot greened and grew lush. Her abilities with flora increased daily.

To lose this aptitude would be akin to cutting off an appendage. But she had to destroy it before her husband noticed. Before outsiders did.

If the herbs she required for a curative were on Satyr land, they would be found in a shady area, not sunlight. She turned toward the forest. Would it part for her this time?

The grass was damp, sodden in places from the violent shower last night, and she occasionally had to circumnavigate a muddy patch. Partway up the hillside, she found a clearing and turned to see how far she'd come.

Outside the castle walls, wind swept dazzling sun across a grassy meadow, bleaching it with shimmering waves of heat. Inexplicably, within the perimeter of the Satyr compound, the temperature remained constant and comfortable.

"Your wife was in the forest this afternoon, near one of the temples outlying the gathering place," said Lyon.

Nick's heart quickened. "What happened?"

"I was fucking. I think she saw me."

"She mentioned nothing of it," said Nick.

"Well, something caused her to faint out there, and—"

"Seven hells! She fainted?"

"I carried her back to your garden," said Lyon.

"Why were you fucking there in the middle of the afternoon anyway?" Nick gritted.

Lyon plunged his hands in his pockets, hunching in vague embarrassment. "As if you'd never done such a thing yourself? Anyway, I had been at work in the vines since dawn. I needed a respite."

"If you were so fatigued, how did you manage to rally the necessary energy required for fucking?"

Lyon shot him a look. "There's tired, and there's tired."

"Damn it all, Lyon!"

"When and where I choose to fuck is none of your affair, brother. I only tell you of this in case Jane raises the matter with you. If she saw the Shimmerskins I conjured, she will have questions sooner or later."

"You're right, of course." Nick rubbed at the tension along the back of his neck. "I don't understand. How was she able to approach you without being turned back by the forest?"

"The forces that protect it may have sensed her Faerie blood and become confused. I don't know. I only know it happened." Lyon hesitated. "There's one other thing. She had a basket with her. It contained sprigs of the ancient moly, taken from our forest."

"The curative? Whatever for?" Nick's eyes went to the door, his thoughts to his wife and their time together the previous night. They'd melded, only briefly, but it had been dangerous. He couldn't trust any woman with his secrets and would be on his guard in the future. Perhaps she was thinking the same way. This morning, she'd seemed wary of him.

"Do you think she might sense the threat and be attempting to ward it off?" asked Lyon.

"What threat?"

"The threat against Jane and her Faerie sisters," Lyon explained in exasperation. "The one to which King Fey's letter referred. Honestly, has marriage addled your brain?"

Nick reddened, reining in his thoughts. "As to the threat, I haven't discovered the facts of it, but I suspect it will issue from within Jane's Earth family."

"At the risk of getting my head bitten off, may I ask whether you ever plan to inform her what she is? What we are?" asked Lyon.

"I'll deal with her in my own way, in my own time."

"Why the snail's pace? She's your wife and must take you as you are. I say get her with child next Calling and be done with it."

"Need I remind you what happened when Raine let his nature get the best of him?"

They were all still feeling the repercussions from that lapse. After Raine's failed attempt to mate his Human wife during a Calling, she had fled into the night. She'd turned up in the servants' quarters, hysterical.

Nick had paid her a visit and managed to mitigate the damage with a simple mindspell. By the time he'd deposited her at her family's home, she remembered nothing save a vague fear of his brother. Nevertheless, she'd subsequently divorced Raine, and rumors had circulated in the wake of the stories she'd told that night.

"Timing wasn't the issue in his case," said Lyon. "His wife was fully Human, and his only error was in not bespelling her."

"Rest assured, I plan to do so when the time comes."

"If it ever does," goaded Lyon.

"We'll see how easily you manage such matters when you have your own wife to deal with," said Nick.

Lyon harrumphed and put on his hat. "Fine. Forego or delay all revelation of your true self as you choose. In the meantime, I suggest you keep her well away from the gathering place unless you intend to her to be shocked senseless by those of us bowing to our natures."

The door slammed behind him.

Nick sat and brooded for a few minutes and then got to his feet and sought out his wife.

He found her in the solarium preparing to work.

Jane started at his approach, hoping he wouldn't quiz her regarding what had passed between them the previous night.

"It's time I take you on a tour of the estate," he told her.

"I'd like that," she said.

Not now, she thought, her toes wiggling inside her slippers. She held the basket of moly she'd gathered earlier that day behind her, out of sight.

Nick looked at the smattering of hand tools at her feet. She was obviously intent on some project in his garden. "Would now be convenient?"

"Of course," she said, sighing inwardly. The plant's roots were wrapped and watered. They could wait until later to find a permanent home in the garden soil.

And if he was suddenly anxious to show her around the estate, she was certainly anxious to be shown. It was an opportunity to learn what other plants might exist. She would be more comfortable exploring with a companion, in view of her recent bizarre experience in the forest.

After procuring horses from his stables, they rode along a rocky trail, ever upward toward the center of Satyr lands. Eventually they dismounted at a pergola of gnarled twisted wisteria vines that covered a stone walkway leading into the vineyard.

They entered its gates and traveled on foot from there. Nick pointed to the various workers they encountered and explained the tasks in which each was engaged.

Jane enjoyed being among the vines, and her interest in the work was unfeigned. Grapes weren't responsible for the brew they became nor how it was used, she reasoned. Men were.

They paused at the crest of a slope, and Jane shielded her eyes to take in the endless stretch of patchworked rows of vines below.

"It's like an enormous living quilt," she said. "And larger than I expected."

"We have eight hundred acres, though less than four hundred are currently under cultivation. Of those, only three hundred are planted in grapes. The rest are in olives and fruit."

Stepping close to a vine, Jane lifted the tiny cluster of small green balls the size of peppercorns. "Are these the grapes?"

"The blossoms," said Nick. "After they flower in June, fruit begins to grow. A hundred clusters can grow on a vine, but the flavor is ruined if so many must be nourished. They'll be thinned until only about two dozen clusters remain."

"You haven't seen signs of the pox?" Jane asked. "I heard others speaking of it at Villa d'Este."

"Not so far."

"How worrisome is it?"

He shrugged. "There have always been diseases and difficulties. If we have too much rain, mildew can set in. If the soil is too rich or the drainage poor, the grapes are puny. Though that's not a worry for us here." He bent and scooped a handful of dry volcanic soil and then let it trail through his fingers to the ground. He stood, dusting his hands. "Water, sunshine, and soil are the ingredients that make the grapes what they are at harvest."

"When is the harvest?"

"It begins in September. Each variety matures and ripens at a slightly different time, so they're harvested one after another. The crush follows. Then in late autumn, fermentation begins."

He pointed to an ungroomed area where vines grew wild. There, ancient millstones sat amid wildflowers and weeds, a testament to the labors of the peasants who'd worked here in years past.

"Those vines are given over to Lyon's menagerie. His pets descend like locusts when the grapes begin to ripen. It's useless to try to keep them out altogether, so we've learned to share."

A well-fed cat wandered by, winding around her ankles. It curled under a vine that was broken and wilting.

Nick was speaking again and had lifted a cluster for her inspection. "See how this cluster tapers upward? The weight of the grapes will turn it downward over time."

While she listened with half an ear, her eyes kept returning to the dying vine.

Noting her distraction and the direction of her gaze, Nick excused himself to speak to one of the laborers. When he turned back, it was as he expected. The struggling vine now grew healthy and strong.

Because of her touch.

Intriguing. She professed to hate the wine the grapes produced, yet she couldn't bear to see a single one of the vines felled.

What was the depth and breadth of her gift with plants? Did she even know herself? He sensed she was ashamed of her talent. Understandable, having lived her whole life in EarthWorld, where it would have been unappreciated.

He smiled and took her arm, and she gave him an uncertain smile in return.

As they passed the knot garden, Nick recalled his time dallying there with the maid in his youth. His cock twitched.

Laborers dotted the slopes around them like ants. Now was neither the time nor place to mate his wife. He forced his thoughts elsewhere.

"You're more curious about the grapes than you admit," he told her, lifting a bow of wisteria so they could pass under a pergola. "It bodes well for our future. My family roots go deep into this soil, this industry. Our wines have graced the tables of the wealthy and royal of this world for centuries."

She remained silent.

He gave her a lopsided grin. "Am I trying too earnestly to convince you of the merit of my heritage?"

"It isn't for me to determine its merit. Intelligence and the propensity for hard work are evident in your family and are admirable qualities."

"So you are no longer concerned you've married a drunkard?"

She smiled shyly. "No. I'm pleased in my marriage."

It occurred to him that she herself was like a grape blossom, grudgingly opening over time, loathe to reveal her special inner self.

"Why did you agree to it?" he asked, suddenly curious.

She shot him a wary glance. "I wanted a family in which Emma and I might make a place for ourselves and be accepted for who we are."

He lay a hand over hers. "You have that here."

She inclined her head, hoping but not daring to believe. "Grazie."

17

Signore Faunus set a silver platter on Nick's desk. "A letter has arrived for the signora."

Nick picked up the folded sealed vellum and read the spidery letters of its address. He tossed it back to the tray. "From her aunt. See that she receives it."

"Certainly, sir," Signore Faunus said, bowing.

Nick gave him a sardonic glance. "Such formality, Faunus?"

"Your signora expects it, and I enjoy it," his servant replied. "At times." He departed with a flourish of coattails, shutting the door behind him with exquisite propriety.

Moments later, Jane was knocking upon the study door. She entered at Nick's summons and burst into speech almost immediately.

"I have had a letter from my aunt!" she said, almost twirling in excitement. "She and Father are taking a villa near Florence for the season to escape Tivoli's heat. And they're bringing Emma! But this is wonderful! I shall have to ready Emma's bedchamber immediately. Which shall we select for her?"

Nick leaned back and smiled indulgently. "Your choice."

Jane tapped a corner of the vellum to her chin, thinking. "She'd been accustomed to sleeping in a room adjoining mine. Do you think—?"

"Such an arrangement could make for awkward moments now that you're married," Nick reminded her.

"Oh, right. Of course. Perhaps the turret then. She'd adore that. She'll require her own nanny and tutors and that sort of thing. Only until she leaves for academy. But I have her with me until then." Jane hugged herself with glee.

"When do they arrive?"

"Within the week. They'll stay several nights with us before journeying on to the villa they have rented."

Seven hells! His estate would be crawling with family during the upcoming Calling night. The forcewall could keep them from the inner recesses of the compound, but it was risky having them here.

And Jane would be unavailable. Any plans to impregnate her would have to be postponed until next month's Moonful.

"What's wrong?" she asked, noting his silence.

He summoned a smile. "Just wondering if we should invite Lyon to sup with us?"

"Yes, and Raine as well?"

"He's away." *Searching for your sister.*

"Lyon, then. We'll make it a family gathering," said Jane. "Oh! There's much to do."

She quit the room without shutting the door, a cardinal sin in his house for which any servant would be roundly scolded. But Nick merely nudged it shut with his mind before returning to his work.

Later, he summoned Signore Faunus to discuss preparations for the impending trio of visitors.

The guests arrived a week later. Baggage was stowed and everyone seen to their rooms to freshen up before dinner.

Jane installed her father in the north wing and her aunt in the south and then escorted her sister upstairs to the third floor. Long habit prevented Emma from hugging her, even after such a long separation. Of necessity, Jane had drawn away from her touch too often in the past.

"It's a princess tower!" exclaimed Emma, running her hand over the curving walls of the turret that was to be her bed-chamber.

"Then you must now be a princess," said Jane. "Because it's yours."

Emma peered from the window to the landscape below. "I shall have to grow my hair."

Jane regarded her quizzically.

"Like Rapunzel," said Emma.

Jane smiled. "Come along, Rapunzel. We shall visit more later tonight. For now, we dine with the family."

"I can't believe we sleep tonight in a true castle!" Emma said on the way downstairs.

At their entrance to the formal salon, Lyon and Nick rose from their chairs.

Catching the tail end of their conversation, Lyon asked, "I hope your sleep will not be disturbed. Has Nick regaled you with the tales of our castles' ghosts?"

Emma was immediately intrigued. "Are there ghosts?"

Lyon nodded, while Nick shook his head.

"Of course there are," said Lyon, "at least in my castle. If you find none in Nick's you'll simply have to come meet mine."

"Are there truly ghosts here?" Emma asked Jane.

Nick answered for her. "Only if you believe the legends handed down by peasants in the surrounding countryside, as Lyon apparently does."

Lyon gave Emma a conspiratorial glance. "Peasants have a sense about these things."

"There are countless stories," said Nick. "Yet in thirty years, I have seen no ghosts myself."

"Of what do you speak?" asked Izabel, coming downstairs with Emma's father to join them.

"Ghosts," said Emma.

"No such thing," said Signore Cova, heading for the liquor cart.

"I beg to differ," said Lyon. "These humble acres of ours have borne witness to much mayhem over the centuries, alas leading to numerous fatalities. Our ancestors battled the Sienese and Florentines and others who sought to gain a foothold here. And on a more personal note, our great-great-great-grandmother, who was beheaded, is said to wander the staircases with her tiara as she searches for her head to place it upon."

"How gruesome," said Izabel.

Jane shuddered.

Emma bit her lip, glancing toward the stairs.

"Perhaps a change in conversation is warranted," said Nick.

Izabel studied him. "I'll begin a direction by saying how well you're looking. Marriage appears to agree with you."

"Tolerably so," said Nick. Over a glass filled with dry wine, he shot his brother a look filled with equally dry humor. "In fact, Lyon hopes to wed soon, don't you, brother?"

Lyon returned Nick's look with an inscrutable one of his own.

Jane sensed an undercurrent of information pass between the brothers, to which the rest of them weren't privy.

"Another wedding so soon?" Izabel asked, looking displeased for some reason.

Lyon stabbed an hors d'oeuvre with a fork. "Let us talk of other things. Dinner, for instance!"

* * *

The following night, Nick and Lyon begged off dinner under the press of business and left Jane and her family to dine without them.

Raine had arrived home from Paris late that afternoon and met the brothers in the gathering place near dusk. Together they took wine made from their own grapes, in preparation for the ritual to come.

"I bring news from the north. The cause of the pox has been determined," Raine told them without preamble.

Nick and Lyon perked to attention.

"The ailment afflicting the vines is called phylloxera. Its cause is an aphid that was recently brought to Europe on an American vine," Raine went on.

"Such a pest could easily spread into our vineyards on a workman's boots or hands," said Nick.

"It's a dangerous time. We can't afford having the forcewall weakened while Raine leaves Satyr land for weeks on end," said Lyon. "I put forth a suggestion that he and I should postpone our bride quests until such time as a cure is found."

Nick twisted the stem of his glass between two fingers. "Don't think to escape your destiny so easily, brother."

Raine looked bleak. "Nick's right, Lyon. This pox could rage for years, while Fey's daughters continue to be at risk."

"Speaking of which, are you any closer at all to locating the second FaerieBlend?" asked Nick.

Raine shook his head. "It's proven difficult."

"Nick found his easily enough," chided Lyon.

"It occurs to me that the reason for my difficulty may be that I wasn't meant for the daughter in Paris," said Raine. He looked at Lyon. "What do you say if I try Venice and you take Paris instead?"

Lyon shrugged. "The other two daughters are strangers to me. Take them both if you wish."

"I think not," said Nick.

"Then it's decided," said Raine, looking relieved. "Tomorrow, I journey to Venice."

They lifted their glasses as one in a toast to the stone god who lorded over them. Together they performed the ancient rituals that would bolster the forcewall around their lands and keep their secrets safe.

Moments later, moonlight bathed them in its fullness. Tunics and trousers fell away. Gilded goblets fell from their fingers to the soft moss, spilling drops of blood-red wine from their cups.

In unison, they raised their faces toward the light, drinking in its power. Their muscled backs arched and their strong arms spread wide in supplication.

Worldly concerns slipped from Nick's mind as the Change came over him, bringing with it both unbearable pleasure and pain. He bent low as his second shaft made its way from his belly.

They were at their most vulnerable now. And Humans were near. He must trust the forest to protect them from the outsiders in the long hours that stretched until dawn. It was his last coherent thought before the Calling overtook him.

In the distance, undetected, someone crept closer to watch. The forest accepted her at first, knew her as maenad worshipper. Avidly she gazed on the debauchery unfolding in the sacred arena.

Her eyes glittered as she observed the lords rut their conjured women. In their condition, they would take any female on offer. They could father a babe—one with Satyr blood in its veins—in her this very night! She stepped forward, already beginning to unfasten her gown.

But the forest suddenly detected her evil. It railed at her intrusion, intent on rejecting her. Insects bit, and thorned vines twisted over her tender ankles. Branches leaned down to lash at her.

Go back! they warned.

She fought their threat for long minutes, desperate to stay. Eventually the will of the forest was too much, and she was forced away.

But the watching had stimulated her. She would need her stepbrother between her legs tonight.

Nick wasn't fond of skulking but found himself doing just that upon his return to the castello at dawn. He would have been in Jane's bed last night, spilling inside her instead of Shimmerskins, had it not been for her family's presence.

Next month, he promised himself. Next Moonful, nothing would prevent him from giving her a child.

Once inside his home, he took the stairs and headed for his bedchamber. At the sound of furtive footsteps, he slid into the shadows.

From an alcove he watched a disheveled Signore Cova pad barefoot down the hall. His hair was askew, and he wore a rumpled dressing gown. Nick looked in the direction from which he'd come. Izabel's sleeping quarters.

There could be only one reason behind this nocturnal assignation between a stepbrother and stepsister. Interesting. Such peccadilloes of nature left him unfazed, but he wondered if Jane knew such a relationship existed between those two. Unlikely.

He moved a few steps along the hall and came face-to-face with the younger sister. She sidled behind him, staring down the hall in the direction from which she'd come. He followed her gaze but saw nothing odd.

"Yet another wanderer," he murmured.

"I was searching for J—Jane," Emma whispered. "I have something I m—must tell her!" She burst into tears and wrapped her arms around his waist.

Some latent parenting instinct had Nick offering comfort.

He led Emma farther along the hall toward a chair. Her hands were small and trusting in his as she told him of her fears.

For the first time, he considered what having children in his household would really mean to his life. The subject of heirs had been an abstract idea before. Now it struck him that children meant he would assume another role—that of father. He would guide any offspring in simple ways as he now guided Emma away from her terrors. And in more complex areas of their lives as well. It was a responsibility he would welcome.

Once Emma was seated, he knelt in front of her.

"Now, tell me again exactly what happened."

"I saw a ghost—the one with a tiara!"

Nick sat back on his heels, skeptical. The child had obviously been spooked by Lyon's stories.

"I d—did!" Emma wailed. "She wore a necklace of tree bark and a tiara of leaves in her hair—"

Nick stiffened. She was describing one of the hamadryad night servants. But that was impossible! She couldn't see them. *Unless* she at least a drop of ElseWorld blood in her veins. He studied her speculatively but detected no hint of Faerie. Had there been another sort of interworld coupling in her lineage at some point?

Jane chose that moment to appear in her doorway. Her cheeks were still flushed from sleep, but she'd thrown a robe over her nightgown. When she saw Nick and Emma, she hurried toward them.

Her eyes swept him, noting he still wore his evening clothes. He read her curiosity but knew she wouldn't think it her place to question his whereabouts during the night. And he'd offer no explanation.

Emma leaped up and ran to clasp her sister's arm. Out of habit, Jane pulled away.

"I saw a ghost, Jane. At first I thought it was Lyon's headless grandmother!" Emma looked around as though to make sure the coast was clear, and then she whispered, "But if it was, I must tell him she has located her head."

"Oh, Emma, do you think it might have been a dream?"

"No, it was real," said Emma. She scratched her knee. "Or it seemed so."

Jane smoothed her sister's hair, tucking flyaway chestnut strands behind her ear. "Could it be Lyon's talk of ghosts that put this idea into your mind?"

Emma shrugged doubtfully and then shivered.

"Come, you're chilled. You must sleep with me, and I'll keep any ghosts away," said Jane. She remembered Nick and quickly clarified herself. "For the remainder of the morning, I mean."

Nick saw them off and then made his way to his chamber to bathe. He didn't need sleep. The Satyr were rejuvenated after a Calling.

While the others slumbered on, he made the rounds of his property. He returned midmorning to find his wife's visitors preparing to depart.

"But I assumed you would visit longer and that Emma would remain with us when you left," Jane was saying to Izabel.

"You promised!" Emma wheedled.

"And I'll keep my promise when the time is right," said Izabel, drawing on her gloves. "But I dare not leave you here until you're older. Why, Lyon's talk of ghosts scared you witless after only one night under this roof."

"I wasn't scared!" Emma protested.

"Hush, girl!" scolded Izabel. "Gather your things and stow yourself in the carriage."

"What's the true reason you won't you let her stay?" Jane asked when Emma had gone.

Izabel's eyes turned sly and elusive. "One of her tender years among so many bachelors here? Her reputation can't be besmirched if she is to make a good match."

Jane tugged Nick's sleeve as though willing him to speak.

He lay a hand over hers and glanced at Emma's father. Signore Cova fidgeted, uncomfortable. Without wine to bolster him, he was weak. The aunt was the obvious one with whom to negotiate.

"Leave Emma here and my wealth will ensure a good match."

Izabel shook her head. "In time perhaps. For now, it's not suitable."

An involuntary sound of protest burst from Jane, and arguments formed on her lips.

"Come now. My wife wants Emma with her, here at Blackstone," Nick coaxed. "How may I bring that about? Perhaps an extended visit is warranted to see how the arrangement progresses?"

"Emma may visit of course, but her father prefers to keep her with him for the present. He so dotes on her. Don't you, brother?"

"Yes, Izzy," mumbled Signore Cova.

Izabel stepped outside. "Goodness! The temperature is so moderate when one is within the grounds of the estate. Yet so hot when one is outside its walls. Curious."

"I suppose," said Jane, hardly noticing. "I haven't been outside the grounds since I arrived."

"Of course," said her aunt. "So recently married. Quite understandable. But you must come to a small party I'm planning in a few days."

18

A week later Jane linked her gloved fingers, tuning out the sea of guests that clotted her aunt's grand salon di festa. Something odd was happening, but she didn't understand its precise nature.

She and Nick had come here to the Villa di Nati, which her family currently rented in Florence, to attend this elaborate party of Izabel's. Jane's visit with her sister had been brief before their aunt had decreed it time for Emma to retire.

Now the festivities were well underway in the villa's salon, and Jane stood among her aunt's friends. Their covert whispers and sidelong glances had grown pointed enough to snag her attention. Jane followed the direction of their gazes and found her husband across the room.

Eveningwear suited him. Though his brand of it was slightly unusual, as always. The cut of his jacket was severe, but the fabric had an iridescent sheen under certain light and was patterned with supernatural beings. It was soft, she knew. They'd had two dances together already, and she'd rested her hand at his shoulder during both.

Watching Nick blend in with society tonight, it was hard to credit that this was the same man who pressed his naked body against her each night while engaging in that unspoken-of activity sanctioned between a husband and wife. It pleased her, this notion of being needed and wanted for a personal service only she could provide for him.

All in all, they'd been rubbing along well together in recent days. She grimaced at her private, unintended pun.

Two attractive young ladies held Nick's attention now. Their feminine cheeks were flushed as they smiled up at him. Many other women here watched him, too, found him handsome.

She couldn't help wondering why he hadn't married one of them. Why had he chosen her when it was obvious other unmarried ladies of his station would have welcomed him?

Beside her, Signora Nesta fluttered her fan in haughty disgust. "Look at those harlots, flaunting themselves. They seek to remind your husband of their existence lest he forget them and remain too long in his marriage bed."

Jane blinked at her, not understanding. "Of whom are you speaking?"

"Those—how do the English say?" She looked at her companions.

"Doxy," supplied Signora Natoli.

"No—mistress," said Izabel.

"Grazie. Mistress," echoed Signora Nesta.

Jane studied the exotic women who stood on either side of her husband. One of them pressed her full bosom against his arm with unsubtle familiarity. He didn't push her away. The other tugged his head down to whisper something, her lips caressing his ear.

Annoyance swept her.

She sensed the two women were aware of her interest and

were flaunting their claim on Nick's attention. She followed the direction of her husband's gaze and found it on her aunt. Some indefinable emotion passed between them, and her aunt's eyes turned cruel.

Izabel placed a consoling hand on Jane's arm. "Poor dear. How can you bear knowing he goes to them?"

Realization struck with the suddenness of a lightning bolt striking her heart. Those women and her husband—

Jane blushed and then paled.

Signora Bich was like a hawk pouncing on the juicy morsel of her ignorance. "Oh! Forgive us!" she said, feigning distress. "You didn't know?"

Jane studied the circle of women around her. They had spoken maliciously, hoping to provoke a reaction from her.

"It's disgraceful," Signora Bich added, her eyes avid.

"It's only natural," Signora Natoli countered. "Lord knows we can't satisfy men as those hussies do. And who would want to?"

Their voices swirled around her, but Jane only stared into the melee on the dance floor beyond. When the colorful kaleidoscope of humanity began to blur, she knew she had to make her escape.

Somehow, she produced a facile smile. "You must excuse me."

She swept away, holding her head high until she had quit the salon. Then she hitched her skirts and scurried along the hallway. A doorknob twisted under her hand, and she slipped inside a deserted sitting room. Only then did she allow her shoulders to bow under the burden of this new knowledge.

While she'd believed the marriage act to be sacrosanct between her and Nick, he'd had in his employ not one, but two mistresses!

She dashed tears away. Hadn't his marriage contract insisted on fidelity? Now that she considered the matter, it had required fidelity only on her part. No such strictures had been placed on his behavior.

Her place in his life, which had recently begun to feel more certain, now seemed shaky, temporary.

All because her husband was doing *that* with other women. He was touching them as he touched her, lying naked with them. Fornicating with them. Finding his pleasure within their bodies.

A wounded sound welled up from her throat, and she stifled it with a fist. She sank down the wall in a heap of satin and petticoats to stare vacantly across the room.

While she had hoped their relationship might deepen over time, Nick had probably never imagined such a possibility. Did he care for her any more than he did those other women?

If there was no hope he could grow to love her, she would never be safe with him. Her position in his home would never be secure. She would feel forever on probation. Never truly a part of his family.

Her head dropped into her hands, and she sobbed, quietly devastated.

"You are upset?" Nick inquired in the carriage on the journey home.

That he'd noticed was unsurprising. Her cheeks were splotchy from tears, and her emotions were simmering.

She lifted a slat of the blinds at the carriage window with a shaking finger. "I have learned some unsettling news," she admitted.

His tone sharpened. "What news?"

She gazed unseeing out of the window, keeping her voice impassive. "News my husband is a philanderer who employs mistresses."

At his silence, she turned accusing eyes on him.

Nick flexed his shoulders tiredly. "I see the cats were out tonight filling your ears with gossip."

"Is it true?"

"Does it matter?"

Hurt filled her, bringing with it anger. "Of course it matters. It was painful to learn of your mistresses, and in such a public way."

He waved a diffident hand, dismissing her. "I assumed you knew."

She looked at him in disbelief. "You assumed I would think you had mistresses? Do you also assume I have male consorts hidden in my armoire?"

He smiled condescendingly, not bothering to answer.

He didn't care that she knew! In fact, he expected her to accept the arrangement. How appalling!

Suddenly she could see how things would be in the years stretching ahead. Nick would keep his mistresses. And keep his wife. Both would remain on their separate shelves, items in his collection neatly labeled WHORE and WIFE. He'd dust them off and use them how and when he wished.

She wasn't sure if she could bear to do *that* special thing with him any longer, knowing he also did it with others.

"Why did you choose me?" she whispered bitterly. "Of all the women you might have chosen."

He stretched his legs out across the carriage floor, irritated. "It was time I took a wife and begat heirs. I believed bedding you would please me."

She tamped down the pain his careless words caused. "And does it?"

"Angling for compliments, Jane?" he reproved.

"I'm attempting to determine how you envision our future together."

"Much as it is now."

She tried another tack. "When I was a child, in happier

times, my parents didn't act toward each other as we do. They showed affection—"

"You wish me to fondle you in public?" he asked.

Jane reddened, embarrassed as he meant her to be, but she forged on. "They were caring toward one another, not lascivious. I know it's hard to imagine, seeing my father as he is now. But at one time, my parents treated each other with fondness."

His brows rose. "And this fondness is something you want to achieve between us?"

She shrugged, embarrassed at her feelings in view of his obvious surprise. "I had hoped it might develop. It occurred to me tonight that the distance I sense between us might be caused by your keeping of other, uh, women."

"It has been my understanding that the fact that a husband keeps a mistress or two is a matter of relief to most wives. Don't criticize me for keeping them unless you're prepared to take their place."

Her cheeks warmed again, but she made herself continue. "I'm simply trying to understand why men in society employ such women. My father doesn't."

"Are you certain?" Nick asked snidely. "You wouldn't necessarily know."

Jane looked at him, aghast. Oh, God, had her father ever—? Did he now?

"Do all gentlemen have mistresses then?" she asked.

He gestured dismissively. "Most of my acquaintances. It's hardly unusual in any case. Surely you were aware of the fact."

"No, I wasn't," she said faintly. "Why?"

"Considerate husbands don't ask their wives to do the things a mistress does," he hedged.

What things? Afraid to voice the question, she instead asked, "Are their wives unwilling?"

He hesitated, flicking her an unreadable glance. "Even the most dutiful wife might find certain acts distasteful."

"Why not at least give me a chance to find out if I could better satisfy you?" she asked.

He sighed, brushing her words aside. "You do satisfy me, Jane. As a wife should."

"If I truly satisfied your physical needs, you wouldn't be bedding other women. And you're wrong in what you said before. I don't find the marriage act to be unpleasant."

His eyes riveted on her in consternation. "You can't mean to imply you're willing to act as my mistress? Willing to take the place of two highly experienced courtesans in seeing to my needs?"

Having taken his father at his word, it had never occurred to Nick that a gently bred wife might find sexual congress a desirable experience if he took more time with her. Or that she might even be enthusiastic. His eyes roamed his wife's shapely contours, allowing himself the leisure to imagine the possibilities.

No, it was unwise. As things stood, he could visit a different bed each night of the week if he chose and display a different side of his need. But if he revealed the entirety of his carnal desires to the same woman, night after night, she would learn too much of him.

Jane wasn't a mistress he could cast aside once she got too close. And he couldn't bespell her into forgetting their every night together.

"I see no profit in continuing this conversation," he said, adopting a bored, supercilious tone. "I recommend you give up these strange notions and accept the natural way of things."

She raised her chin defiantly. "With me as your servant, and you as my master?"

He frowned. "With me as your husband, and you as my dutiful wife. With me employing as many mistresses as pleases me, and with you accepting that my decision is for your own well-being."

A frosty silence settled over them for the duration of the trip. The air outside and within their carriage grew steadily cooler as they rumbled along the cypress-lined avenue leading home.

Home. Was it truly that any longer? Jane wondered. Had it ever been?

As he assisted her from the conveyance, Nick's dark murmur reached her ears. "I'm sorry you were upset by the gossips tonight. I will take measures to ensure that the more sordid activities of my existence won't touch our lives again."

The heraldry on the carriage door blurred before Jane's eyes as she nodded.

Ever the gentleman, Nick accompanied her through the front entrance. Once inside, he gave her a stiff bow. Then he stalked toward his study. She heard its door shut with a firm snap of finality, forming a solid barrier between them. Conversation over.

Nevertheless, Jane didn't think the matter truly settled.

Nick didn't think the matter truly settled. He felt it humming between them during his subsequent nightly visits to Jane's bed. He felt it in her unsure attempts to relax with him, to indicate a hesitant willingness to have him prolong his body's concupiscent visit within hers. These attempts alternated with an agitation that told him she still dwelt overlong on the subject of his mistresses.

Over the following days, the idea of having her take over his mistresses' duties took firmer root in his mind. He found himself watching her on occasion, admiring the way her gown molded her hips when she bent over her garden. Found himself studying the curve of her breast or delicate cheek.

Soon he could think of little else other than the possibility of initiating a fulfilling sexual liaison with the woman who was his wife. He somehow managed to convince himself he could do so while still keeping a rein on the extremes of his baser nature.

After all, he reasoned, Shimmerskins could be summoned to serve those at a moment's notice.

He sought her out in the garden one afternoon and approached her.

"I would speak with you regarding the matter you broached earlier this week," he began.

Jane sank back on her heels and looked at him, her head tilted to the side in question. "What matter, signore?"

"The matter of my mistresses," he returned bluntly.

"Oh, you mean the matter I must accept for my own well-being," she said, returning to her work.

"Yes, well . . ." Her offhand manner disconcerted him. Was he about to make a fool of himself? "I was speaking more specifically of a certain offer you made."

"Offer?"

He grew more discomfited when she kept working and didn't seem to immediately grasp the trend of his talk. "The offer to assume my mistresses' duties."

"Oh, that offer." She studied the hand spade, fiddling nervously with it.

"Upon further contemplation, I find myself willing to more fully discuss the idea," he informed her.

She brightened, looking up. "You are?"

Her reaction strengthened his purpose. Nodding, he proffered a hand. After removing her gloves, she took it, and he led her to walk with him along the brick path.

"However, I think we must first have a conversation regarding certain particulars of the matter. I imagine you have no idea what a man requires—that is, what a mistress's duties entail. And I fear the actuality of those duties might send you into a faint."

She smiled uncertainly as they walked side by side along the sun-dappled path. "Are you willing to dispel my ignorance if I promise not to swoon?"

"Are you certain you want me to? To do so, I must speak frankly," he cautioned. "More frankly than a husband should speak to his wife."

"Please. I'm anxious to know why a husband keeps both a wife and a mistress," she said.

He seated her and then flung himself into a wicker chair opposite hers. It was a feminine chair, and he overpowered it with his masculinity.

"Generally speaking, a mistress is far more adept at exploring a gentleman's passion than a wife," he began in the manner of a professor instructing a student. "With a mistress, a man needn't offer explanations or apologies for his appetites, no matter how carnal. He simply makes demands—physical demands," he stressed meaningfully, "and his mistress undertakes to satisfy them. With every appearance of enjoyment and willingness he might hope for." He fixed a stern eye on her.

"I see." Her brow furrowed. "How does a mistress become so skillful at satisfying a gentleman?"

Heat pooled in his loins at her interest. "Through practice and instruction."

"And are you willing to supply those?" she whispered. "To your wife?"

A silent moment passed in which the sound of birdcalls outside the garden gate seemed unnaturally loud.

Nick shifted uncomfortably, adjusting the lap of his trousers. "I appear to be warming to the idea," he said ruefully.

Her eyes fell to the tremendous bulge that now strained the fabric at his crotch. She glanced away.

Observing her shyness, his contemplation of her grew more overt. He wove his fingers together across his chest and arrogantly splayed his thighs so his arousal became impossible to overlook.

"You've made me stiff with your insistent questions. Now what, Jane? How will you offer me relief?"

She flushed but forced herself to look him in the eye. "What do you mean exactly?"

His dark chuckle heightened her interest. "It's wifely to blush and stammer at such plain speaking. However, if you were my mistress, you would recognize my words as your cue."

"I don't know what to do," she admitted. "Please—it's embarrassing."

He straightened, easing the tension between them. "Then I suppose lessons are in order."

A spark of interest lit her eyes, and she slanted him a glance from beneath her lashes. "Will you truly teach me such things?"

His eyes narrowed on her with a masculine appraisal that seemed to understand more of her body than she did. That he was privy to a wealth of sexual knowledge he would soon share with her was exciting and a little frightening.

"Let's both consider the matter further. If you find you still wish to proceed, we'll begin your instruction tonight."

As he withdrew from the solarium, it briefly occurred to Nick that his garden had never looked finer.

19

That night Jane sat across from her husband in one of his carriages, toying with the strings of her reticule. They were due at a dinner dance being held by a business acquaintance of his in Florence in half an hour, but their carriage was currently proceeding at a snail's pace behind a donkey cart.

Nick scrutinized her dispassionately for the first few minutes of the drive. It startled her when he finally spoke.

"What have you decided, wife? Do you still wish to act in my mistresses' stead?"

Their carriage suddenly found its way around the cart and picked up speed in time with her heart.

She shot a nervous glance at him and nodded. "Yes."

"Are you certain, Jane?" he asked gently. "We can forget this afternoon's conversation entirely and continue as we were. It's what most married couples of our station do for the whole of their lives."

Strangely, his willingness to release her from their bargain strengthened her resolve to see it through. "But it's not what I want."

"Then I may proceed in instructing you in the many ways you might best attend to my sexual proclivities? Consider carefully. I won't be pleased to find you swooning and screaming over any forthcoming intimacies you deem repellent."

She didn't bother to mention she could hardly scream if she were engaged in the act of swooning. More to the point, she asked, "Are you trying to frighten me away from the attempt?"

"No, only to warn you of the daunting nature of the task you seek to undertake. Many of my requests will surely shock you," he said. His gaze dropped lower. "And your body."

"Perhaps you could make a list of your requirements and I could consider them one by one," she proposed logically. "Then we could negotiate them beforehand."

He looked amused. "I think not."

A thought occurred to her. "Am I—? Is a mistress allowed to refuse a particular suggestion posed by her—?"

"Her lover?" he supplied. "I can only state that no mistress has ever refused to attend me in whatever manner I required of her. However, if she were to find an act painful without pleasure attached, I would certainly want to know."

"And if she informed you she was having such difficulties?" Jane posited.

"I would attempt to make the act in question more enjoyable for her," he said.

"And if you couldn't and she refused your suggestion altogether? Would you move on to a more accommodating mistress?" she asked.

"As I say, such a scenario hasn't occurred to date," he hedged.

"Still, it strikes me as eminently logical to discuss these whims of yours beforehand," she continued. "That way I might point out any ideas not to my liking, thus saving us both future embarrassment."

He chuckled. "I promise I won't be embarrassed at anything we do together of a carnal nature. And I suggest you not reject any of my 'whims' out of hand. Some won't be to your liking initially but may prove enjoyable upon experience and repetition."

"I see." She opened her mouth to continue her line of questioning.

He made a slicing gesture with his hand. The discussion was straining both his patience and the lap of his trousers beyond what was bearable.

"Enough talk. Tell me. What have you decided? Are we to proceed?"

Doubt assailed her. Her mind followed various avenues, but she could perceive no other possible way to reach his heart other than to play mistress. And she was curious.

She answered, breathless. "Yes."

He raked her with a calculating gaze, and then his eyes hooded. Though he hadn't moved, his figure suddenly seemed more compelling, the curve of his lips more sensual.

"Let's see how well you mean it," he murmured.

She was so mesmerized at the remarkable change in him she didn't immediately take in his next words.

"You wear the English drawers, do you not? I wish you to remove them," he instructed softly.

"What?" she asked, unsure she'd heard correctly. How did he know she wore drawers? Most women didn't, but her mother had been modest and had raised her and Emma to do so.

"Take them off, Jane, and give them to me."

"Now?" she asked in dawning horror.

"Quailing so soon in the game?" he taunted.

"No—but I hadn't expected—"

His expression turned remote, and he angled his dark head away from her. Tilting a slat of the blinds with a finger, he glanced idly out of the carriage window as though her decision was of no consequence.

She realized he expected her to falter and shrink from the course she'd set. What's more, he would allow her to do so without comment. He would continue to visit both her and his mistresses in distressingly different manners. Nothing would change between them.

His request wasn't so terrifying, really, she reasoned in desperation. Her gaze darted around the carriage, irrationally searching for some screen behind which to disrobe. How far was it to the Cascardis' now? What if there wasn't time to fully remove her drawers? What if the carriage stopped and she was discovered with her underwear caught around her ankles?

She took a fortifying breath. Then, without giving herself time to debate further, she reached under her skirt.

She sensed when Nick turned his head to observe her, and she blushed, keeping her gaze averted.

Carefully arranging the drape of her dress to reveal as little of her elaborate undergarments as possible, she searched beneath the batiste petticoats. Her fingers fumbled and then found the ribbons at the waist of her drawers. She untied them blindly, the task made easy from years of practice. Lifting herself briefly off the bench seat of the carriage, she slid them off her hips. Hurriedly, she shoved the drawers down her legs.

They caught and clung around her ankles with obstinate willfulness. She watched the passing scenery outside the window with growing frustration, trying to determine how close they were to their destination.

With a final yank, she pulled the drawers over her slippers and off completely. Crumpling them into a haphazard bundle, she tucked them on the seat beside her so they were well hidden beneath the folds of her skirts.

Pleased with herself for having met his challenge, she shot him a triumphant look.

He smiled at her in lazy approval, possibly the most genuine smile he'd sent her way thus far in their relationship. He lifted an aristocratic hand and beckoned. "Now fold them neatly and give them to me."

She shrank away, suspicious, clutching the wadded drawers tight to her thigh. "Why?"

"Because I wish it." His hand opened, waiting.

After a long moment, she reluctantly withdrew the fragile garment from its hiding place. Quickly she folded it and passed it to him.

His opaque eyes watched her as he toyed with the intimate garment, feathering it lightly back and forth across his cheek and immobile lips, enjoying the texture.

She told herself he was absurd. Told herself to look away from him. But she couldn't quite manage it.

"Draw your skirts higher."

She looked toward the carriage window uncertainly. Countryside was yielding to cityscape. "I had thought my lessons would be conducted in the confines of our bedchamber."

"They'll take place where I decide," he informed her. "When I decide."

Unable to resist finding out what he might suggest next, she tugged her skirt to reveal her ankles.

He flicked his fingers, indicating she should pull it higher.

Uncertain of what he expected, she tugged again. A few more inches of her calves were revealed.

"Above your knees," he ordered.

Annoyed, she yanked the skirts until they bunched on her thighs. "Is this high enough? Or shall I throw them over my head?"

His smile flashed. "An intriguing suggestion, but that won't be necessary for now." Sitting forward, he wedged a knee between hers and rocked it side to side, nudging her legs apart.

She put both hands on his knee, and he allowed her to stay him. "What are you doing?" she whispered.

"Opening you. I wish to view the place where I come inside you."

Here? In the carriage? Jane couldn't have been more shocked. Suddenly the task of dealing with her husband's sexual proclivities loomed daunting before her.

"Can't this wait until we return home?" she pleaded faintly.

"You may argue as you will about other matters but not regarding your instruction as my mistress."

Slowly Jane released her hold on his knee. Sitting back, she slid her feet and then her knees apart.

"More," he instructed.

She took a fortifying breath, then parted her legs wide. Cool air wafted beneath her skirts to find her most private flesh.

She'd never been so embarrassed in her life.

"Touch yourself."

"What?" She inched farther back. Had he guessed what she did when he left her room each night?

"Here. Like this." He leaned forward and brushed a finger through her pubic hair.

Instinctively she closed her legs, capturing his wrist. Their eyes caught and held.

In truth, she could benefit by his instruction in this. She'd never yet succeeded in coercing herself into convulsing without first having him copulate with her. Was such a thing possible?

"I take it you want to curtail your position as my mistress?" he asked.

She gave a negative shake of her head.

He quirked a brow.

Hesitantly she released his hand and allowed her legs to sprawl.

He braced them wide with his knees and then shook one of her hands from its death grip on her skirt. Her teeth tugged at her lower lip as he stroked her fingers through the crisp thatch of hair, playing. He circled her finger over her clit. Once.

Twice. Softly. A shiver of forbidden excitement trilled through her.

She closed her eyes to distance herself from what was happening. But this only increased her susceptibility to the titillation. Shifting her hips, she found herself riding her hand, cupped in his.

Two fingers pushed inside her, one his, one hers. They rocked her, simulating the motion of coitus. Moisture seeped from her inner cave, easing the inexorable ingress and egress, ingress and egress.

The rumble of his voice reached her, urging her on.

"Is it good, Jane?"

Ummm.

He angled their hands in a new way that exposed her clit to the rub each time their joined fingers intruded. "Tell me."

"Oh, no," she moaned. Her tissues tingled. It was going to happen—! That thing. That glorious thing.

The carriage lurched. Nick glanced outside and then drew their hands away from their task. When her eyes opened, he was wiping his fingers and hers with his pristine handkerchief. He stroked it over her slit, cleansing away that shameful moisture.

"Alas, we must call a halt," he told her. "You don't want to arrive at the Cascardis' smelling of sex."

"Hush," she hissed, pushing him away. She slammed her legs together, and shoved her skirts to her ankles. Her flesh tingled with frustrated wanting. Appalled, she ignored it.

She craned her neck to stare out the window, her thoughts swirling madly. "How close are we?"

"I believe you were *quite* close."

He dared make sport of her? "My drawers. Return them to me," she demanded.

He held them out of her reach and brushed them over his cheek, shameless. "They smell like you. Warm and sweet."

Her gaze flicked to the scenery passing outside and back to him. A wife would scold him. But, tonight, she was a mistress. She tried to take his behavior in stride, keeping her voice level as she sought to reason with him.

"Please, Nick," she implored. "I see lights ahead. We're almost there."

He glanced out the window. "So we are," he agreed. Before she could react, he unhurriedly tucked her garment under the seat cushion beside him.

She gaped in disbelief. "Why ever did you do that?"

"Because I prefer you without them. It's more expedient for my purposes as your lover if your . . . womanly charms . . . are readily accessible." A knock sounded on the carriage door, and Jane jumped.

"Ah! We've arrived," Nick announced. He alighted from the carriage, obviously in good humor at having gotten his way.

Half dazed, Jane stared at the cushion under which her drawers were concealed. She could grab them, hide them in her purse until such time as she could slip away and . . . Her hand reached.

"Come along, my dear," said Nick, turning to help her out.

Reluctantly she took the masculine hand that had so recently been between her thighs and stepped outside.

"You aren't to wear drawers again unless I specifically request it," he informed her when she drew close.

She pulled away to see his expression. "Are you jesting?" she returned in horrified fascination.

"I assure you I'm not." He settled her on the pavement and gave her buttocks a surreptitious squeeze.

"Stop that!" she scolded, nodding to indicate that there were onlookers.

He merely smiled and slid a hand to her waist, ushering her up the steps to the villa.

The lace and embroidery stitching on her petticoat delicately abraded the skin of her bare bottom and legs where they were exposed above her gartered stockings. The tender void high between her thighs pulsed with each step, begging for relief. She longed to bury her hand there. Or his. Both. His phallus. Something!

"Later," he whispered.

Then heavy doors swung open, and they were swallowed into the awaiting gaiety.

20

Upon their return to the castello, Nick followed her upstairs. Once inside her bedchamber, he leaned back against the door to the hall, shutting out the world and its expectations.

Trying to conceal her growing excitement, Jane went to her dressing table and began removing the pins from her hair. He came to tower behind her, looking immense and powerful.

"Will you assist me?" he asked, extending both wrists toward her where she stood at her mirror. She turned and unclasped the gleaming studs at his cuffs and then clinked them on the table's glass-topped surface.

"Why do you dismiss the servants every evening?" she asked, watching his reflection unfasten its clothing. "They should be here now, seeing to your comfort."

He shrugged out of his shirt. "My ancestors set the rules centuries ago. It's our way."

"What of the night servants?"

His eyes sharpened on her, and secrets shifted in their depths. "Ah, yes. Faunus told me you'd become aware of them."

"And?"

"They are a wary sort. It's best they're left under his supervision. Relay any direction you have for them through him, at least for now."

"A rather inefficient way to conduct a household."

"It's our way," he repeated bluntly. His hands came to rest on the points of her shoulders, and he fingered the straps of her gown.

He would see nothing of *her* secrets, she reminded herself. Her gown had been designed to rise higher in the back than was fashionable.

Dark sapphire met emerald in the mirror.

She'd been tense the entire night at the Cascardis', waiting for him to do something scandalous. He hadn't. But now, she sensed the moment had come.

"May I undress you?" he asked, already releasing the copper hooks cleverly hidden along her back.

She raised her brows. "My duties as mistress are certainly proving light. So far, you're doing much of the work."

"You may be sure I'll find duties for you in the hours to come. But for the moment I find myself in the mood to rediscover you. To make love to you not as a wife but as a mistress." His voice was full of wicked promise.

"How do the two methods differ?" she asked in fascination.

"For one thing," he murmured, "a man doesn't always make love to his mistress in bed as he would his respectable wife."

He finished his task and brushed the fabric at her back wide to reveal her corset and chemise. Her bodice fell forward. She caught at the neckline and then let it gape and fall to the floor.

The back of his fingers stroked down the corset's threading. "Shall I unlace it?"

She nodded. "But I'll keep my chemise," she added quickly.

He frowned, annoyed. She still hid her back from him.

His hands shaped her nipped waist, but her flesh was so constricted she barely felt his touch.

"Then you must also keep your corset as punishment," he told her.

"What?"

A finger hooked itself under the crisscrossed lacings at her back and tugged. "They're loose," he noted.

"They loosen as the night wears on," she said.

He found the leading strings. "We must tighten them."

"But why, when the night is over?"

"In such matters, a mistress does as instructed," he told her. "Now brace yourself against the dressing table and breath in deeply."

Curious to see where it would all lead, Jane leaned forward, flattened her hands on the table, and dutifully sucked in. At his firm tug, the laces cinched aggressively. She silently cursed the metal eyelets that had come into use a few years ago. Before that, her corset could never have been tightened so decisively without ripping the surrounding fabric.

In the mirror, she saw that her breasts had been shoved violently upward. When she stood, they plumped above the top of the corset like a voluptuous shelf.

She raised her palms to cover them.

Nick tested the taut smoothness of her waist.

"How does it feel?"

"Too tight, of course. Will you untie it?"

He stroked her upper arms, looking contrite. "I'm sorry, but I don't think I can allow your flesh such freedom. Unless it proves deserving of a concession."

"Deserving?"

"If it performs well for me, it will earn leniency. However, if it fails me, you may sleep in your satin prison tonight."

To her astonishment, his words excited her. It was a tremendous relief when she could remove her corset each night. The idea of being forced to sleep in it should have incensed her.

He reached his hands around to slide beneath hers. Taking the weight of her breasts, he gently kneaded. Lace scratched and teased at the nubbed tips. Her breath hitched.

Something queer was happening. Her nipples had begun to burn, licking fire straight to her core. She ducked her head and watched in horror as an unearthly glow began to suffuse them, turning their tips the palest of blue, almost silver. Oh, God, yet another part of her body now betrayed her!

Her eyes met his in the glass. He'd seen.

Would he cast her out now? Call her witch?

He did neither.

"Well, Jane?" he said, his voice gruff and low. "Do you think your flesh desires freedom enough to perform as I require?"

A dizzying relief swept her. He wasn't even going to mention it!

"I'll do my best," she managed. "But it may prove a bit difficult to breathe during, uh, strenuous activity."

"Ah, yes. Strenuous. Exactly."

Suddenly she had an inkling of what he was planning. Would he take her here, where they stood? The vision she'd seen weeks ago in the tent returned, dashing her with images of his body hunched, straining, sweating, working in passion.

His fingers toyed with her sensitive nipples, now dipped in blue silver. The light was obviously some sort of gauge of arousal. Did it happen to all women when they were sexually stimulated? No one had ever mentioned it, but then, except for that one brief conversation with her aunt, no one had ever spoken of sexual things to her.

Lips traced the juncture of her neck and shoulder, distracting her. His hand slid lower across her abdomen and beneath her chemise to stir the curls between her thighs. Lower still, her private flesh contracted, a wanting void.

"I enjoyed watching your fingers here earlier tonight," he said. "How did it feel?"

"Strange," she admitted.

"What else?" he asked.

She averted her eyes.

"Stirring?" he prompted.

She nodded.

"You must learn to say it. To please me."

"Stirring, then."

The two long fingers of his left hand pressed against her pubic bone, pulling upward at the same time. Her slit lengthened, tautened. The fragile hood retracted from her clit, baring it.

His other hand palmed her pussy. A finger flattened horizontally along her opening, as though measuring its length. It pressed inward. It retreated and then pressed again, initiating a rhythm of moist suction. With each inward press, the fleshy mount of Jupiter at the base of this forefinger rubbed her naked clit.

Her head lolled back against his shoulder. From beneath her lashes, she watched the hands that were tucked between her legs flex with the movements of his finger.

This was stirring her, if he really wanted to know. The words were still difficult, so she tried to tell him with her body, adjusting her legs wider and curving her hand to his thigh behind her.

His finger advanced and retreated, flexing, drawing moisture from her depths. It pressed at the far end of her slit and then dragged the wetness forward to paint slick circles over her clit.

"Oh!" she breathed, beginning to understand the thrilling depths of what his touch promised.

"Rest your palms on the table," he murmured at her ear.

"Will you take me here?" she asked, brittle with excitement.

His heated gaze met hers in the mirror. "If you will allow it."

The sound of her hands slapping the table was audible.

A much larger hand pressed the table alongside one of hers. His body hunched, forming a cage around her back. Reaching between them, he unfastened his trousers. His shaft sprang free, and its greedy thickness nudged between her legs from behind.

She tensed, expecting him to push inside her.

Instead, he palmed his cock in his free hand and rubbed it along her wanting folds like a plow trenching a furrow but not yet digging deep enough to plant a seed. In the mirror, she watched its ruddy head peer rhythmically from the thatch between her legs, like a prairie animal peeking from its burrow and then ducking away. It was big as a plum and shiny with her desire.

"Good. You're slick," his voice rumbled at her ear. "It'll be easier to fuck you."

She gasped. The word wasn't unfamiliar. Guttersnipes and servants—even her own father—had uttered it within her hearing. But it had never been spoken directly to her before. Somehow it excited her under these circumstances to hear his dark, urgent voice use it to describe his plans for her.

His lips caressed the spot behind her ear, his breath hot on her skin. "You'll let me fuck you, won't you, Jane?"

"Yes. But—wait. The cream," she begged, uncertain of what was to come.

"We won't need it. Trust me."

She wanted to.

He stroked her, whispering explicit, forbidden words in her ear, describing how touching her this way excited him, how soft her body felt against his harder one, and how much he looked forward to coming inside her, to spilling his seed in her.

Their bodies swayed as one, in time with the rhythm of the

cock's thrust between her legs. Long strands of her hair tickled her cheek, and her skin grew dewy and flushed.

Within the confines of her stays, her breath was shallow and quick. "My corset. I can't breathe."

"It's exciting that way, isn't it?" he growled softly. "The restriction, the limits, the lack of air so necessary for survival."

She wavered, light-headed, stirred beyond reason.

"Don't faint," he murmured. "You'll miss everything."

His words shocked her as he'd meant them to. If she fainted, would he truly continue on this path without her conscious involvement? How deliciously appalling.

A rising tide of sensation shuddered along her dripping slit.

"Come for me, Jane," he whispered. "Let it happen. Let go."

At his words, her slit clenched fiercely, as though inhaling a deep breath before—before what? When he slicked the ridge of his crown over her defenseless clit, she knew.

That thing was going to happen. Now. With him.

She arched as her tiny bud seized tighter and tighter, leaving her teetering on a dagger's edge of want. Then it seemed to implode. A series of violent spasms took her breath, stilled her heart and then set it speeding. She fought for consciousness. Still, the wrenching went on and on and on.

The dizziness passed, and she came to realize that his body now rocked hers gently. Between her legs, his touch had grown soft—designed to enhance each convulsion, make it last.

Eventually her breathing slowed, and she lifted her head. "Now *that* was stirring." It had been far more glorious this time with him inside her than it had been as a solitary occupation.

His smile came and went in a flash. All business now, he shoved his trousers lower, to his knees. Gripping her hip bones, he found her opening with his cock and pushed into her feminine channel, fathoms deep.

Her trembling tissues balked, unsure how to handle so much fullness but given no chance to reject it.

The dusting of hair on his powerful haunches rasped her inner thighs as he retreated, only to return for another taste of her. And another, and another.

Then he separated from her slightly, penetrating less deep for a time. The cloth of her chemise fluttered delicately as big, sure hands smoothed it upward. As though hypnotized, he watched the play of moonlight across her lower back. Watched her flesh gulp and disgorge his penis.

The vision she'd had at Villa d'Este had become reality. His eyes were predatory and hooded, his features rigid—exactly as she'd seen him then. The sculpted muscles of his shoulders and chest flexed and tensed as he worked in her. But now the sight was accompanied by sensory details—the ram of his invading cock, the lewd slap of their flesh, the heat of him at her back.

His passion tightened, and he moved impossibly close between her legs. His body was a furnace, his hands iron. His thrusts were powerful strokes that had her bracing a hand on the wall.

Their eyes met in the mirror and clung. Their bodies strained together, reaching. . . . She watched him climax, saw his features contort with it, and she gasped as orgasm rolled through her again, echoing his release.

Later that night, Nick opened the door adjoining his room, preparing to leave her at last. The family crest of the ring on his finger winked in the firelight as he rested his hand on the doorknob. His expression was enigmatic as he turned back toward her.

"Will you wish to continue in this vein after tonight?" he inquired with remote politeness.

Jane sat up in her bed and grasped the covers to her throat.

Held it to skin that bore marks made by his mouth. Did he mean his tone to imply he didn't want to?

Between her legs he'd left copious evidence he'd been eager. He'd enjoyed her before the mirror and thrice more since in her bed. And he'd removed her corset after their first coupling, which implied her flesh had indeed satisfied him as required.

But had he gotten enough of her? She couldn't bear it if their relationship reverted to its previous state.

"Yes, if you want me to," she hedged carefully.

He nodded. "You must let me know if at any point in the future you decide you'd prefer to relinquish the role of my mistress."

"All right," she agreed, her eyes lowering to the bed.

"But don't delay too long," he advised softly. "We'll soon reach a point of no return."

21

Nick did his best to ignore Lyon's smirk when they met the following day in the grotto overlooking the vineyard. It was obvious his brother had an inkling of what had transpired the previous night. Sometimes the sharing of emotions engendered by the linking of their Satyr blood had its drawbacks.

Lyon lounged on a stone bench, stretching his hands high before folding them behind his head.

"How's Jane settling in?" he inquired with a knowing grin.

"Fine," said Nick, flinging himself upon a bench directly opposite his brother.

"Good to hear it," said Lyon. "I, uh, somehow sensed you two were getting along. It bodes well for the next Calling."

Nick sent him a warning look. "Go ahead and mock. The boot will soon be on the other foot."

But Nick was more worried than he let on. Worried at his impatience to have Jane last night. His impatience to have her again. Her. Not just any woman. Her.

It was unwise. Dangerous to become so needful of one female. So distracted by one.

A part of him had always held lust in check, mastering it so he could calculate how much of his need a woman could take. He prided himself on keeping a cool head in the heat of passion.

But last night, it had been all he could do to leave her instead of rutting the night away until she was bloody and raw from his taking. He'd wanted to act the animal. He'd barely restrained himself and couldn't help fearing what tonight would bring.

When Jane's monthly courses came again that afternoon, Nick seized the chance to keep from her in order to regain his equilibrium. How pitiful he was. How his brothers would laugh if they learned what he'd become.

"I'm sorry," Jane said miserably when she informed him. "I truly am."

He lay a hand on her shoulder. "A child will come, Jane. Don't worry."

At his kindness, a sob escaped her.

Startled, he drew her against him.

"Excuse me," she said. "I'm often weepy at this time." In truth it was guilt at the lie she must perpetuate that had her crying. If only she dared tell him why they must wait for a child and that she took herbs temporarily to prevent one.

"Jane, when I said I expected heirs of you, I didn't mean you had to supply them with miraculous haste. You'll be a mother soon enough, I promise you."

She moaned against his chest, dabbing his proffered handkerchief at her watery eyes. "Even you cannot control such things, signore. Some women never can conceive, you know. What if I'm one of them?"

He tilted her chin and found her gaze with his. "You have my solemn word I shall get you with child within the month."

She rolled her watery eyes at him, thinking he teased.

22

Some weeks later, Nick found her in the library at midday, her brow knit as she gazed unseeing at the yellowed pages of a tome of some kind. Something was preying on her mind. Secrets she hadn't shared.

Would she ever confess her strangeness? It grated that she had not.

She registered his presence and quickly shut the book, shunting it aside. When her eyes met his, she emptied them of whatever disturbed her. So. She would share her body with him but keep her thoughts private. It had been thus with many other women before her. But he'd never cared before.

"You're home early," she said in surprise.

"And it's your fault," he informed her.

"Mine?"

"Don't look so innocent," he said, circling closer. "It's surely your fault I find myself thinking of you during the day when my thoughts should be on other business. Thinking of wicked ways I'd like to pleasure you and have you pleasure me."

Jane smiled uncertainly at his use of the word wicked. It reminded her of a matter that had caused her concern of late. When she was with him, what they did together seemed right. But when she contemplated it later, she worried it was not. Having always been out of step with others, she wasn't certain what was normal, only that normal was something she wished to be. Was it abnormal to reach such heights of desire and passion? Did it happen to everyone?

"I'm delighted to hear you think of me when I'm not with you," she ventured.

"Do you think of me, Jane?"

She sighed. "Yes. More than I should. In ways I probably shouldn't."

"Ways that would shock your relatives, I hope?" he teased.

"No doubt," she agreed, taking the hand he offered and allowing him to pull her lightly against him.

His fingers pressed over the ribs of her back to draw her nearer. Her eyes lost his as his mouth slid lightly down the side of her throat to nibble along her shoulder.

"Tell me more," he prodded.

Knowing how fond her husband was of hearing her speak frankly about such matters, Jane attempted to explain without subterfuge. "Sometimes my body experiences an insistent craving to join with yours when you're nowhere in the vicinity." She darted an embarrassed glance at him.

His lips paused on her shoulder, and there was a gleam in his eyes when he drew back to look at her. "Intriguing. Be assured my body experiences a similar craving for yours."

"It happens at the most unlikely moments, does it not?" Jane inquired conspiratorially. "When one can do nothing to requite the longing."

"Describe what happened the last time such an event occurred," he instructed as though embarking on a scientific investigation.

"Well, at my aunt's tea yesterday morning, for instance," she confided. "I let my attention drift from the conversation for just a moment, and from the window I chanced to see a gentleman, whose broad shoulders resembled yours. I found myself thinking of you. Remembering the previous night when we . . . And it was almost as though—that is, my imagination began to conjure memories of you moving inside me, which in turn created a pleasant . . . yearning sensation."

She bit her lip at the erotic image she'd conjured.

"Fantasizing about other gentlemen you chance to see from the windows of respectable lady's parlors? For shame, Jane. I believe you must be reprimanded. What shall be your punishment, I wonder?"

"Whatever are you talking about?" she protested. "I merely spoke of noticing a gentleman who bore only the vaguest hint of your build. And I wasn't fanta—oh you're teasing."

His eyes widened in feigned surprise. "I'm seldom accused of such a thing. No, this conversation has been most enlightening. And it has given me a yen to have that wanton aspect of your nature better revealed." He toyed with a button at her throat until it freed from its fastening.

She flattened her hands over her chest in dismay and looked toward the sunlit windows. "In the afternoon?"

He pulled a silk handkerchief from his pocket with a flourish.

"Close your eyes," he told her. "And I will make it night. A night of pleasure and exploration of the senses."

His gaze was distant as though he envisioned embarking upon a path ahead she couldn't yet imagine. She felt herself begin to pitch down a sensual tunnel of his design. Even knowing she might regret her behavior later, she was helpless to pull back.

"This sounds promising," she murmured. Her eyelids fluttered shut.

He spun her around, and she felt the silk cloth being wrapped around her eyes and secured behind her head.

Her fingertips touched the silk. A blindfold. It reminded her of blindman's bluff, an innocent game she'd played in childhood. She smiled slightly at the fond association.

"Come, Jane." He took her arm and led her to the door.

"What of the servants?" she managed, holding back.

"There are none about," he assured her.

He led her upstairs, the warmth of his hand at her waist her only guide. As though hypnotized, she followed, doing as he asked. They entered a room, and its door snicked shut behind them.

"Where are we?" she asked, staying his hands when he began loosening her buttons.

"My bedchamber," he responded. His hands pushed hers aside and busied themselves with her buttons, obviously intent on disrobing her.

She'd never entered his chamber before, and now to have her eyes covered! How disappointing.

"Don't peek," he warned, as though reading her thoughts.

Together, they made quick work of her clothing. She sighed with relief when he released her flesh from the confines of her corset but hugged her chemise when he made as though to remove it as well.

"We must keep the chemise? You still insist?"

"Yes," she murmured.

"Very well." Leaving her dressed only in the thin covering, he lifted her in his arms. The fabric of his formal shirtfront rasped against her seminudity, somehow emphasizing his power and her vulnerability to it as he carried her across the room and placed her on his bed.

"Lie back," he instructed.

"Yes, sir," she mocked lightly.

"Your obedience is gratifying," he said easily. "And just what I had in mind, as it happens."

While she pondered the meaning of that, he wrapped something that felt like a scarf around her left wrist and tied it. By means of pulling its other end, he raised her left arm above her head and then secured the bond somewhere above her.

Not understanding what was happening, she turned to look, recalled why she couldn't see, and reached to push the blindfold aside.

He caught at her, making a tsking sound. "Ah! What did I say about peeking?"

Raising her free wrist above her head, he knotted another restraint around it and tethered it fast above her head as well.

She tugged on her arms, heard the responding creak of the bed rail, and knew herself to be tied to it. Tugging harder, she quickly discovered that she couldn't break free.

The bed shifted, telling her he'd moved away.

"I'm not sure I like this," she said uncertainly into the potent quiet that had settled over them. "Why have you restrained me?"

The silence stretched. A frisson of awareness sizzled through her as she heard the bolt on the door slide home. He never bothered to lock doors.

Footsteps approached, and the mattress dipped as Nick sat next to her again.

"What are you planning?" she asked.

His continued silence heightened the growing tension between them. It permeated the room, nearly suffocating her with anticipation.

Something touched the tip of a breast through her chemise, and she flinched. A tongue? A fingertip?

"I'm planning to enjoy you," he said at last. "It happens my afternoon is free." He massaged the nipple between a thumb and finger but too lightly to suit her.

Her breath caught and quickened. "That sounds agreeable enough." The tiniest flicker of guilt that what they embarked upon was wickedness tried to flare within her, but her eagerness to follow where he led stamped it out before it could grow.

"I'm glad you find it so." His tone was laced with amusement, and she felt him studying her body.

It was exciting, not knowing what he would do, where he would touch her next. Denied sight, she found that all her other senses became heightened, expectant.

His hands dipped under the hem of her chemise, rucking it high on her chest. The cuffs of his shirt brushed her skin, reminding her he was fully dressed while she was virtually naked.

He squeezed her exposed breasts lightly, testing their weight and texture as though they were new to him. Her nipples tightened and heated in a way that told her they had begun to give off the soft bluish glow. Though she knew he enjoyed this evidence of her excitement, her hands strained to cover her chest in a reflexive action that jerked at the restraints.

"You have lovely breasts," he told her, rubbing the pads of his thumbs across her jutting nipples. "Plump, yet firm in texture. Fair in color and tipped with delicate nubs. The kind of breasts many men might enjoy. In fact, I believe they were the objects of more than one lustful glance at your aunt's villa the night of her party. Did you mark Signore Mosca ogling them spilling forth from your gown?"

Jane stiffened in affront. Signore Mosca was a stuffy man who thought himself superior to others. She couldn't imagine him deigning to ogle any woman's breasts.

"He wasn't!" she denied in embarrassment. "Besides, the amount of cleavage my gown displayed was perfectly within the bounds of acceptability, as you're well aware."

Nick grunted and continued lightly fondling her curves, sensitizing them and making her yearn for a firmer caress. "Nevertheless, I'm certain the signore spent a good part of his evening imagining you exactly like this. Wishing he could see your lush flesh uncovered, bared for his pleasure. Wanting to touch your nipples as I am now. To lick them. Would you let him, Jane?"

"What?!" she asked, shocked. "No, never. Of course I wouldn't!"

"Even if I asked you to?" Nick coaxed, his velvet voice lowered in dark enticement. "Instructed you to do so as a feature of your employment as my mistress?"

Jane's thought processes halted, shifted, and moved tentatively down the new, uncertain path upon which he sought to lead her. "Would a gentleman really require his mistress to do such a thing? To let another man touch her?"

"If it appeased his sexual appetites to do so in a given moment."

"Have you done such a thing before?" she asked.

"A true gentleman never tells," he answered obliquely.

"Did your mistress enjoy it?" Jane demanded, assuming the worst.

"Speaking hypothetically, I believe a mistress might enjoy such a thing. But any mistress of mine would no doubt allow it regardless of whether or not it stimulated her own pleasure response. She would allow it if she knew it might please me to watch her perform with another man. Or to imagine her performing with one."

The fabric of the chemise poofed softly as it was lowered to veil her again. His big hands wandered over her, tracing along her ribs, abdomen, and hip.

Jane fought against falling under his thrall. "I prefer not to accede to that particular whim."

"I understand completely," Nick hastened to assure her. "However, it isn't so much my whims we must consider. It's a matter of scrupulous politeness."

"Your suggestion is quite beyond the bounds of mere politeness!" Jane exclaimed.

"Only imagine if Mosca were here at Blackstone as our guest. As mistress of the household you would see to his needs, wouldn't you?"

"I—"

"Say yes, Jane," he advised smoothly. "Even if you do not mean it."

She hesitated, wondering where this might be leading. "Yes, then."

"And if he asked to fondle your breasts and tug at your nipples, what would be your answer?"

"No!"

"Jane, Jane," Nick chided. "You're displaying an appalling lack of hospitality. If Mosca were our dinner guest, and he asked you for a serving of fruit, would you refuse his request?"

"Of course not, but breasts are hardly fruit," she retorted.

He chuckled. "But yours are rounded and delectable, like *melone*. I can see why Signore Mosca might desire them."

"He doesn't!" Jane exclaimed.

Nick's hands left her. "I believe we must endeavor to improve your manners without delay. With practice, you may become more properly prepared to make yourself agreeable to my guests."

"And thereby more agreeable to you?" she retorted.

"Precisely. Now repeat after me, and be certain you get the words correctly," he instructed her in the tone of a tutor. "Signore Mosca, you may lick my breasts."

A silent tug of wills ensued. Eventually curiosity led Jane to break it.

"S—Signore Mosca," she repeated haltingly. "You may lick my breasts."

Nick planted a quick kiss on her lips and then drew back. "Excellent, Jane. But it isn't quite right. Let us try it this way. 'Signore Mosca, you may lick my *tette*.' You know this word?"

Jane shook her head.

"This is the naughty Italian word for breasts. It will excite the signore to hear it on your lips."

Jane repeated the words, her voice a near whisper.

Moments passed in which nothing happened. Her senses heightened with the waiting.

Cool air wafted over her as the hem of her chemise was lifted again. The thin material dragged and abraded her sensitized skin, catching on the tips of her breasts before sliding free to lie just above them on her chest.

Nick's tone altered slightly to that of a man speaking to a male companion. "Please do proceed, signore."

Seconds later, a pair of prim lips introduced themselves, suckling lightly at first one nipple and then the other until both were puckered and begging. A dry sandpapery tongue fondled them attentively, swirling in broad, flat strokes.

"I think that will do, Mosca," Nick announced briskly.

The chemise lowered to settle over her again.

"Thank Signore Mosca for licking your *tette* so nicely," he instructed.

"Grazie, Signore Mosca for licking my *tette*," she repeated, warming to the game.

"Well said, Jane! Now, of late, Signore Mosca has oft been in the company of one Monsieur Lemieux due to a matter of business."

Jane's brow rumpled as she rifled through her mental catalog, trying to match the name with a countenance. She called to mind a large, hulking Frenchman, with lank, unruly hair in need of a trim. He had sparse conversation, and little interaction had occurred between them on the occasion they'd met.

"I can't precisely recall his features," she admitted.

"And no doubt you're too much the lady to mention those features you might recall. But I recollect him as thick and muscular—his overall shape fashioned in a most ungentlemanly way. And you're too well bred to remark on his manners—

brutish, as I recall," added Nick. "Nevertheless, we can expect that Signore Mosca might bring the monsieur as his guest when he visits. And in that event, you would be also obliged to extend your hospitality in a new direction, wouldn't you?"

"I suppose."

"After observing your generosity toward Mosca, Lemieux would almost certainly want to fondle your breasts as well. However," Nick cautioned, "it's likely he wouldn't request permission."

As his words died away—

Rough hands cupped the underswells of her breasts through the fabric of her chemise, squeezing and remolding their contours with scant consideration. They pressed until her areolas met, positioning her nipples for the descent and easy ravishment of a voracious mouth.

The crests of her flesh were drawn deep into its warm, wet prison and then released and drawn again. Under the strong nursing her chemise grew sodden, a stimulation in itself.

The lips pulled away, and Nick confided:

"I fear I was correct regarding the monsieur's behavior. In fact, I believe he might abuse your breasts in other ways before he leaves you. But no matter how unmannerly his touch, don't complain, Jane. Bear in mind he's our guest."

Jane yelped and strained at her tethers as her sensitized nipples were peremptorily tweaked and pinched. Teeth bit and nipped along the curves of her breasts. The lecherous attention stirred her blood, and a corresponding echo of sensation twinged between her thighs. How was it that such ill usage could invoke this secret shameful enjoyment?

Abruptly the sensual attention ended. Hands and lips departed, leaving damp circles on her chemise and a tingling remembrance.

"Now, Jane, thank Monsieur Lemieux for teasing your nipples."

Vastly irritated at having such stimulation withdrawn before it could be properly analyzed, Jane remained silent.

"Jane?" Nick scolded softly.

"Merci, Monsieur," she said grudgingly.

"Said like a good, obliging mistress," Nick approved.

"Yes, well . . ."

"Lemieux has another request to put forth for his additional entertainment," Nick interrupted. "Do you think you might accommodate him further?"

"In what manner?" she hedged.

"The next request he might put to you would surely be an uncouth one. Don't be shocked if he asks something truly wicked."

"Puis-je avoir la permission—may I view her cunt?" an accented male voice inquired.

"Nick—no!" Jane pressed her thighs together. The thought of showing herself to strangers was so abhorrent she momentarily lost sight of the game.

Nick made a tsking sound of disapproval. His palm cupped her cheek in a comforting way. "Impulsive and forward of him, I agree. But I'm proud of you, cara, and therefore find myself strangely willing to show you off. You don't want to displease me, do you?"

"No," she whispered.

"Then display yourself. *Faccia come dico.* Don't keep our guests waiting."

After a moment of indecision, Jane rallied her courage. She let her legs fall open. Unseen hands pulled her knees upward and apart with brisk efficiency, splaying her as wide as her body would allow.

Cool air found her private slickness, and she sensed eyes inspecting her. Hard knuckles stroked through her labia, nudging at her slit.

"Am I not fortunate, gentlemen?" Nick asked, fatuous pride evident in his voice. "This is mine to enjoy whenever I wish. Do you not envy me?"

Jane's inner muscles tightened at the casual touch along the folds gating her vaginal opening. She murmured appreciatively.

"With such visual provocation, Mosca has been emboldened to make a new request," Nick informed her.

"Con permesso. May I taste it?"

"And what do you reply to that, Jane?"

Jane groaned, squirming closer to the tantalizing rub between her legs.

The clever fingers were withdrawn.

"Answer the signore, Jane."

She should have been shocked. But his tone soothed and lulled, and she craved more contact.

"If my lord wishes, you may, signore," she replied.

"Such compliance!" Nick told her.

"Proceed, Mosca," he suggested, his tone brimming with jovial male camaraderie.

Long seconds passed. Jane lay tense with expectation. . . .

The merest butterfly touch of a tongue came, tickling her clitoris. So light she wasn't sure if she'd only imagined it. Her legs drew inward reflexively.

Gentle thumbs spread the delicate hood protecting her clit. The touch came again, still light, but firm enough to be more certain of it. When she didn't twist away, the hesitant tongue seemed encouraged. With tender precision it began to lap at her, laving first with only its tip and then with the full stroke of its raspy warmth.

"That's good," she breathed, shivering.

With a final lingering lick, the tongue dragged away.

Only then did Jane realize her legs now lay sprawled, wide and welcoming.

"After observing such a wanton display, Monsieur Lemieux will be anticipating another turn," Nick told her softly. His fingers combed through her silvery hair where it lay on the pillow.

"Puis-je—may I suck it?" a gruff voice inquired.

"Please, yes, monsieur, I would be delighted for you to do so," Jane answered.

"I believe your manners are improving greatly through this exercise," Nick told her. "But remember, Jane. Monsieur Lemieux has already shown himself to be exceptionally brutish."

Before she could formulate a reply, hot, moist breath fell on her as a wet, greedy mouth descended to feast at her slit—sucking, slicking, tonguing. Hands clasped the underside of her thighs, lifting her closer, and she jerked in helpless response.

All too soon, the mouth pulled away.

Jane made a yearning sound. Her hands strained, retesting her restraints.

Nick brushed the dampened curls over her mound. "What is it, cara? Is your pussy hurting?"

"No!"

"Lonely, then?"

"Yes! Please cease this game. Come into me? I beg you."

"I regret that I cannot," he commiserated. "Though I desire nothing more fervently than to accommodate your request, you must acknowledge how rude it would appear if I attempt to relieve myself with you while our guests go wanting."

Jane gritted her teeth in frustration.

Nick caressed her hip consolingly.

"But happily, I see Lemieux has a solution to offer. Put your request forward, Lemieux."

"Avec permission, Monsieur Satyr. May I poke my cock inside it?" the French voice asked.

"Ciò è ingiusta! Why should Lemieux do so when I was here first?" Mosca rightly demanded.

"Gentlemen, please. I think I can speak for Jane in this matter," Nick said in a conciliatory tone. "I happen to know she's well acquainted with such matters and much enjoys the feel of a stiff cock inside her. As to the question of who shall be first? I shall decide quickly if you will but pull your shafts from your trousers and allow me to assess them."

The rustling sound of clothing being adjusted followed, loud in the otherwise quiet room.

"Ah, and Signore Strand has joined us. Do reveal your shaft, sir, and join the game," Nick invited.

"Jane, can you handle three unfamiliar cocks tonight?"

"Yes, signore," she replied.

"Generous girl," he said, patting her thigh. "Then it's only left to decide whom Jane will service first."

After quick consideration, he reached a conclusion. "Signore Mosca, you're the smallest. Therefore you may apply yourself first, thus preparing her for others of more robust proportions. I'll allow you to put yours all the way inside her. But only once."

There was a pause.

"Don't grumble, Mosca," Nick admonished. "I am being an exceedingly agreeable host, after all."

Jane held her breath, tantalized with the knowledge that a "stiff cock," as her husband described it, would finally be forthcoming.

Beside her, the bed shifted, and her flesh felt the warmth of someone nearing. A man's body hovered and then settled between her legs.

Fabric burnished the inside of her thighs. Though he still wore his trousers, the flap of cloth at his crotch sagged open. The velvet tip of his shaft dragged down her abdomen, leaving a snailing trail of pre-cum. His male thatch brushed her skin as he fumbled and poked, as though trying to locate her entrance. The inexperienced prodding was somewhat uncomfortable, but at last his crown found her.

Her slit parted. Then came a rigid, welcome invasion that filled her by slow inches.

He lay within her for long seconds, his breath harsh and steady in her ear. The buttons of his shirt remained fastened and pressed uncomfortably in a line along her abdomen and chest. They dug deeper still when he bucked once against her, as though to retest her depth.

Then came a reluctant, lingering slide, and his length found its way back out of her body. Her vaginal walls clenched, trying to imprison his shaft for a longer stay, but to no avail. The thick head of his cock popped from her, leaving her gaping.

It wasn't enough.

"Enough," announced her husband.

The body left her and the bed.

"Ooh, please, cease this teasing," she begged.

"Silence!" Nick scolded sharply. "Don't be unseemly, Jane."

"Monsieur Lemieux," Nick continued, his tone now colored with boisterous fellowship. "You may proceed next. Your cock is the largest, so I'm sure you'll understand when I say you may only insert it to a shallow depth on the first thrust."

"Then may I pump her?" Lemieux inquired.

"You may, but ten times only," Nick stipulated.

Without warning, her chemise was shoved well over her head to join the bonds on her wrists. The mattress dipped, and a man's body dragged voluptuously along hers until their genitals were aligned. His trousers were carelessly bunched around his calves and ankles, leaving his hips and thighs bare.

His knees drove hers wider, but he didn't come into her. Instead, his fingers opened her labia so its squishy wetness might better massage his straining erection.

Willingly, she aided him in mimicking the sex act. He grunted in savage pleasure, tickling her ear with gutter French. Hands lowered to cup and squeeze the contours of her bottom, forcing her hips to move in time with his. Utterances of the most forward nature issued from his lips, assuring her of the delight his flesh found in the grinding.

He folded his arms and tucked them to her ribs, hooking fingers over her shoulders to hold her. An eager cock nudged her entrance.

Jane quivered, anticipating.

He entered her in a single onslaught, but it was shallow as her husband had dictated. Mere inches lay inside her for a moment, until she thought she might be driven near mad with the need for a deeper thrust.

She turned her head, and her lips brushed his jaw. "Please," she begged.

The thick head of his cock drew from her, suctioning. Quickly it rammed into her again, this time plowing so hard and deep that her body was forced a few inches toward the head rail.

It was good. Full, heavy. Her eyes closed, and she wrapped her legs over him.

His mouth nipped the side of her neck. Teeth grazed. Sucking, he marked her skin.

He pulled from her completely, dislodging her legs. Then he pumped her again with Herculean vigor. And yet again. Her inarticulate murmurs urged him on.

With each intrusion, he expressed his hot enjoyment of her flesh with coarse, carnal epithets. His words would have shocked her at any other time, but strangely, at this moment they only intensified her desire.

Aloud, he counted each rut: . . . huit . . . neuf . . . dix!

When he eventually departed, she pleaded for more. He'd taken her roughly. Odd that she'd found pleasure in it.

Nick drew an unsteady breath, loud in the silence of the afternoon.

"Lord Strand," he finally managed, finding a businesslike tone. "I believe it's now your turn. And to express my gratitude that you have recently ordered a vast supply of our vintage, I will grant you a special favor. You may put your cock inside my mistress and pump her until you're thoroughly satisfied."

"Jane, will you invite our favored guest into your body?"

"Certainly," she agreed with alacrity. "Signore Strand, I would be honored if you would put your shaft inside me."

Nick patted her ankle. "Your compliance pleases me, Jane."

A fully naked body settled over her, and she welcomed its male strength between her thighs. Warm lips nuzzled her neck, giving gentle apology to the skin which had so recently been marked.

Fingers sluiced through her ruffled furrow, testing her readiness. Long seconds passed as he fondled her, keeping her balanced upon a knife's edge of wanting.

Finally, just when she thought she might expire from need, a solid, sure cock began to enter her. It filled her slowly and with painstaking precision, until the joining was as complete as possible.

A back-and-forth thrusting commenced. The strokes were capable but measured and slow. Again, her passion built, pushing her toward the precipice of orgasm.

Nick's disembodied voice whispered in her ear. "I can see by Signore Strand's expression that you're pleasing him. Does his cock fill you differently than mine? Are you enjoying it, Jane?"

"Yes! It's good," she moaned. Her fingers clenched at the taut fabric of the scarves that held her. "So good." Her legs wrapped themselves around the hips rhythmically flexing into hers. Seconds later, a violent climax shook her.

At her cry, the cock plunged deep, anchoring her to receive a series of searing, furtive spurts. "Chiavata!"

Lips dragged across her cheek to meet her mouth. Hips subtly rubbed, helping them both to draw out their mutual climax, to savor it.

She was still relishing the last echoes of her orgasm when the body disengaged and left her.

"Thank Signore Strand for giving you his semen," Nick instructed from beside the bed. His voice sounded unnaturally low and gravelly.

"I thank you for your semen, Signore Strand," she managed.

Nick smoothed her hair and jaw. The caress was perfunctory and didn't linger. "I'm pleased you're becoming such a talented and dutiful wife."

She smiled, listening to the comfortable rustling sound of clothing. He was dressing.

"Mistress," she corrected lazily.

He chuckled. "I find that the delineation between the two is becoming more delightfully blurred with each passing day."

Her smile widened. Patiently she awaited the removal of the wrist bindings she assumed to be imminent, frowning when her husband's boots instead moved away.

"I shall see our guests out and return momentarily," he told her.

It seemed the game wasn't over.

"Wait! Nick! Release me before you go. Someone could find me like this."

His footsteps paused briefly, and she felt him studying her. She imagined what a picture she must present, lying bound on the bed amid the rumpled covers, her legs splayed, milky wetness on her inner thighs.

She shifted, closing her legs. "Release me," she whispered.

His footsteps continued to the door, and she heard it open.

"Nick! At least cover me," she begged.

In disbelief, she listened to the door creak wider and then shut. She heard his footsteps in the corridor outside, moving away.

"Come back," Jane whispered, knowing he wouldn't hear. She lay on the bed for long seconds, feeling bereft and far too exposed. A chill drifted over her as her body cooled in the aftermath of heated lovemaking.

Using her feet and legs, she haphazardly gathered and shifted the covers to hide herself.

He deserved to be slain for this.

The muted thunk of two boots hitting the carpet woke her. How much time had passed? Moments or hours? The mattress depressed beside her. Cool air drifted over her as the covers were pulled back.

"Nick?" she murmured. She'd twisted her bindings so she was now lying on her side with her knees curled to her chest. He joined her on the bed, tucking a pillow between her knees and tucking himself at her back.

She tried to turn within his arms, but he forestalled her. Fingers slid from behind to touch her moist triangle of curls. How dare he, after he'd abandoned her!

"For pity's sake, Nick," she gritted. "Untie me. Anyone could have found me in this state while you were gone."

No answer.

"Nick? That is you, isn't it?" she asked, trying to annoy him into speech.

His finger dragged through her folds, bringing on one last spasming remnant of her earlier orgasm. She tried to tighten her legs and trap his hand, but the pillow prevented her.

Shockingly, she heard him smack his lips, tasting her on his finger.

"Signore Strand asked me to thank you for making him come so adequately," he told her at last. "I can taste his salty semen on you. Did you find his cock to your liking?"

"Untie me and perhaps I'll tell you," she said.

Ignoring her suggestion, Nick dipped two fingers partway inside her, drawing jism. He stroked it over her, toying, until she began to move with his hand.

"Umm," he murmured appreciatively. "You're nice and slick

with other men's leavings. I think I'd like to come inside you, too, where those other men have had you. May I?"

"Yes, of course."

"There's no 'of course' between us, Jane. Do you want me?"

She weighed his question. Before, he'd always taken what he considered his right. It seemed a favorable development that he now considered and even needed confirmation of her feelings in the matter.

His arousal pressed against her, already heavy and thick. Why deny what she wanted?

"Yes, always."

His lips nuzzled her neck, kissing, and then he reached to remove her blindfold. "I would have you certain whose cock you pleasure this time."

Drawing his hips back, he tucked the tip of his cock inside her and pressed inward. His hand draped over her waist and slid lower to rub and fondle between her thighs. His lovemaking was a gentle rocking this time, his thatch massaging her bottom with each thrust.

"Tomorrow morning, when you're bound up chastely in your tight laces and layers of dresses and petticoats . . . and when your legs are primly pressed together hiding your secrets as a well-bred wife should . . . I'll be thinking of this," he whispered. "Of the fucking we're doing now. Of you like this. . . ."

23

The next morning, Jane could barely look Nick in the face when he entered the breakfast salon. Since her gaze refused to rise above his collar, she quickly noted he was attired for his day in a striped jacket of superfine. Its restrained design was uncommonly plain considering his usual taste, as though he had been thinking of other things when he selected it.

Her cheeks pinkened, and she poured her tea with unusual concentration.

He chose his repast at the sideboard and sat across from her, opening a journal. After a moment he lowered it. "You pleased me last night, Jane," he admitted stiffly.

She blinked at him. "And you me," she whispered.

He nodded, beginning his breakfast.

Jane sipped her tea without tasting it. Her stern husband was back. How could he alter his demeanor so greatly between day and night? It was confusing.

Across from her, Nick was even more confused than she. The sight of her dining on tea and toast with jam had him hardening in his trousers after he'd just spent an entire night in her bedchamber. He'd always known himself to be depraved, but now his body was insatiable. It yearned to spend both day and night fondling, tasting, fucking. And not fucking just anyone. It was she—his wife and only his wife he craved.

Desire was something to be controlled and compartmentalized. He couldn't allow any woman to weave a spell around him. He would rule his feelings and rule her, taking her as he needed.

Jane pressed a linen napkin to her lips and spoke to the maid, who brought in a new teapot.

He tamped down the threatening erection and forced himself to form a coherent reply when Faunus appeared with a question on a business matter. Her voice and scent tortured his senses. His arousal strengthened. His cock would soon be peeking from his waistband.

Intolerable!

He slammed his chair back and stalked from the room, leaving Jane, Faunus, and the maid staring after him in surprise.

What he needed was a distraction, he decided.

The journey to the villa the Covas had leased in Florence took less than an hour on horseback. When Nick was shown into the salon, only Izabel awaited him.

Refusing her offer of a seat, he got to the heart of his business with her. "I've come to petition you again to allow Emma to make her home with Jane."

From her seat on the dais, Izabel studied him where he stood at the hearth. "Why come to me? Why not ask the girls' father?"

"Signore Cova obviously defers to you in such matters."

She inclined her head regally. "I'm loathe to let Emma go. I fear we will see little of either of my nieces if we allow both to live apart from us. Her father would miss her, and so would I."

"Perhaps I can offer solace for your loss." He picked up a small jade figurine from her mantel and turned it round and round in his hands. "What would induce you? More jade? Gold? Jewelry? Lands?"

Her eyes swept him. "Shall I be blunt?"

"Please."

She rose and moved to stand before him. "I'm a lonely widow," she told him. "With needs."

"Needs."

The word hung over the room, like the stink of smoke left from a dung heap fire.

Izabel interrupted the silence. "I invite you to discuss the matter of Emma with me in a more intimate setting."

"Your bedchamber?" Nick guessed.

She smiled up at him. She was still an attractive woman.

"And will your opinion of my suitability as a guardian for Emma alter in any way through my visit to your bed-chamber?"

Her smile turned flirtatious. "That depends upon how obliging and persuasive you show yourself to be."

Nick kept his distaste from his expression. "So, to put things plainly, you want me come upstairs with you now. To fuck you. And if I fuck you well enough, you will then turn your youngest niece over to Jane's care? I may take the girl with me when I leave here this afternoon?"

She eyed him, toying with the fringe of her wrap. "No."

"No?"

"In exchange for so great a boon as Emma, you must enjoy my hospitality throughout an entire night. A special night. When the moon is full."

Unease prickled Nick's spine. She knew. But how? And what to do about it?

He straightened. "I believe I have had all the hospitality I can tolerate for one day."

She cocked her head. "Come now, are you refusing?"

He moved close to tower over her. "Emma's affections already lie with Jane. I'm willing to pay her bridal price when she comes of age and to settle any amount on you. You could have the finest of villas, a castle. All in exchange for releasing Emma into my care."

She placed a palm on his chest over the fabric of his waistcoat. "You've heard what I require of you. You have slain hundreds of women with your cock if the legends are to be believed. What is one more?"

"And if I say I'm now true to my wife's bed?"

She gave a snort of laughter, which quickly faded as she read the sincerity in his face.

Nick wasn't sure who was more shocked by the truth of his claim—he or dear Aunt Izabel.

Sudden rage filled Izabel, spilling through her veins, inciting her to destruction. But she merely gave his shirtfront a pat, and turned away. "I see. I didn't realize my niece had so thoroughly bent you to her will."

"And now that you're aware of it, may we speak more reasonably regarding the disposition of her sister? Jane pines for her, and it pains me to see it. I have the wealth to buy you other men—anything you desire."

"I ask for one night together with you under a full moon. There's no other price. If you don't meet it, Emma stays here."

"I can apply to the courts for her. They will be interested to know of Signore Cova's nocturnal wanderings when you last visited Blackstone."

Izabel sucked in a breath.

"And failing that, in a few years Emma will be of an age to choose for herself," he went on.

"Before you could convince the courts to intervene, I would see Emma wed to the most despicable of men."

He stared at her, not understanding her determination. "Why?"

She turned to the window, giving him her back. "You've heard my terms. Until you're prepared to meet them, we have nothing more to say. Good day, signore."

24

Jane scooted a stool over so she could reach for a book on the library's highest shelf.

Here it was at last! The book of herbal curatives she'd sought. It had been in her husband's splendid library all along.

Nick was at his desk behind her, attending to business while she browsed. She'd taken his books before but wasn't sure if he was aware of it or if he approved.

She held the herbal out for his inspection. "May I borrow this?"

"My library is your library," he told her.

She hesitated, and his expression turned curious.

"My father says women should be kept ignorant," she explained. "He believes too much information would taint our minds and render us barren."

Nick leaned back in his chair, an indulgent expression on his handsome face. "I'm sufficiently confident in my ability to sire children. You may make free with my library."

Jane shrugged away the niggling guilt that always accompanied the mention of children she knew were not forthcoming.

"Thank you. Another husband might not be so generous with his literature."

"You must remember to thank me properly later," he told her. "Toward that end, you may want to take special note of my collection of erotica."

"You're too kind," Jane said, refusing to blush. "But I believe I will stick to your botanical tomes for the moment."

"Perhaps you'd enjoy my botanical erotica?" he commented, drawing her startled glance.

"Is there such a thing?"

He came close and reached over her head for a slender volume. Gilded letters on its spine read *Sermo de structura florum* by Sébastien Vaillant.

"Vaillant's early comparisons between the sexual reproduction of plants and human reproduction are believed to have influenced Carl Linnaeus to later make more robust comparisons," he told her.

"I'm familiar with Linnaeus's theories."

"Then you're aware he studied flowers intimately," Nick went on, "procuring thousands to learn their methods of procreation. He examined their genital organs—both stigmas and stamens—and made conclusions regarding their sexual reproduction, which both shocked and repulsed his contemporaries. He even claimed that simple marigolds kept both concubines and wives."

"Linnaeus's work has always been of interest to me. But I admit to surprise at learning you know it so well. Tell me, do you skim the text for titillating carnal references or study it more thoroughly for the benefit of your vines?"

He grinned, setting the book aside. "Both, truth be known. However, I can't take full credit for my library's contents. As with most of my collections, it was begun by my ancestors. I merely continue their work, adding items of interest when I can."

"Out of a sense of familial duty?"

"That may have sparked my initial interest, but collecting has become a passion."

"Your passion for collecting encompasses a great many objects. Glassware, pottery, artwork, swords, books."

He slid his hands along her ribs, caressing. "I enjoy possessing beautiful and curious objects. And I'm fortunate to have the wealth to indulge my whims."

Jane crossed her arms over the herbal and pressed it to her chest, a barrier between them. "Is that why you married me? To add to your collection?"

His hands stilled. "I beg your pardon?"

"It occurs to me you had an available space in your castello museum marked WIFE, and so you sought to fill it."

"In a sense that's true. Yet, not any woman would have filled the position so adequately. Of all the items in my collections, you are the one that gives me the most pleasure."

Warm fingers traced up her spine to toy with her hair.

She tilted her head and studied him curiously. "Pleasure. You use the word to divorce yourself from any stirrings of love."

He released her. "You grow sentimental."

"And you remain intentionally distant."

"I recall a distinct closeness between us in your bedchamber on regular occasions. We may retire there now if your memory needs refreshing."

"You seek to compartmentalize our lovemaking as sport or a meaningless bodily function incapable of touching your heart."

He shot her a look meant to belittle her notions. "Pleasure can be had between two people who don't love."

"Can't it also be experienced between two people who do?"

"Don't love me, Jane. I cannot reciprocate."

She sucked in a breath and shoved the pain of his words into a small compartment to be pulled out and examined later. "Cannot or will not?"

"It wouldn't be safe for either of us. I must concentrate on keeping my heritage and this land intact for generations that follow."

"And if I want more? If I say what you offer isn't enough?"

"I apologize if you object to the manner in which my body must use yours. You did agree to the requirements of wife and further request the duties of mistress. Are you reneging?"

"No," she mumbled. Never.

His eyes slid over her clothing, and suspicion dawned. "You've been out. Speaking to other ladies who have colored your view of our arrangement. Did they tell you it isn't proper to enjoy the touch of a man who doesn't proffer protestations of love?"

She stiffened. "I haven't been out. But since you bring it up, I imagine most ladies would take my side in this."

He snorted.

"It's just that I'm not certain how to be what you require in a mistress and also remain a lady."

"You can't help but be a lady, Jane, even when you're performing the tasks of a mistress. It's in your nature to be kind, intelligent, and giving in both spirit and body. These are the traits of a true lady, not fabricated societal manners."

Jane searched his expression, weighing his sincerity.

"I do need you, Jane. You, no other." He pulled her against him, and she felt the bulge between his thighs.

"Your apparatus needs me certainly."

Nick smirked. "My apparatus? Come, cara, you must learn the proper terminology. A mistress must apply more titillating words for the appendage between a man's legs. Try cock. Prick. Belino. Grillo. Uccello."

"I know what it's called in lower circles."

"I assure you it is called by those names by many in the upper classes as well."

She shrugged, unwilling to admit her naiveté.

"You think yourself worldly?"

"I have certainly become more so since falling into your clutches."

His chin nuzzled her hair, and a teasing note entered his voice. "Thus far, I have played nice with you. I believe it's time now to further open your eyes."

"What do you mean?"

"Come." With a hand at her waist, he led her upstairs. Her heart began to pound when she saw their destination. His bedchamber.

Once he shut the door, he strode to the large mirror on the far wall. To her surprise, it opened, revealing itself to be a portal that connected his room to a hidden chamber.

He lifted a candelabra and beckoned. "Enter. I will show you more of what I truly am."

The intimate compartment was smaller than his bedchamber but more lush. As her eyes adjusted, she saw that small statues and other antiquities adorned it. But, here, they were more blatantly lewd than those in the rest of the house.

"They're relics from an ancient temple fallen to ruin in the Satyr forest," he said, noting her interest. "Do they shock you?"

"Is it your intention to shock me?"

"Their intention isn't to shock but rather to instill thoughts of a lustful nature. You must let me know if they succeed in their purpose."

Her eyes darted around the interior of the room, finding something strange and illicit in every corner. Metal rings were attached at intervals high along one wall and in the ceiling. There were leather straps, knotted scarves, feathers, strands of pearls, a pommel, a bed of furs. There were devices whose purpose was unclear but whose delicate menace gave her an uncomfortable shiver.

"What is this place? Another museum?"

"Of a sort. A very private one created by my ancestors in which to explore mutual pleasures."

He pressed a panel in a red-lacquered cabinet, and a drawer jutted forth. "Now," he said, "tell me what you think of these."

Jane moved to his side and peered into the drawer, where a series of cylinders ranging in size and shape lay neatly lined in a row. She gasped when she realized what they were.

"Phalluses?"

"Some. Others are dildos, designed to closely resemble phalluses."

"Are they intended to be ogled or utilized?"

"Both, I suppose. Viewing them is a stimulation in itself." He selected a small column with a tanned, mottled surface and held it out to her. "It's the phallus of an ancient beast that no longer lives. Touch it."

Hesitantly, Jane brushed its surface. It vibrated under her fingers. She snatched her hand away in surprise.

"Even after centuries, it still hums with the warmth of the beast. The vibration provides a strong stimulation when inserted into one of the lower orifices."

One of the lower orifices? Whatever did he mean?

"It seems cruel to kill an animal simply in order to use its parts in such a narcissistic way."

He shook his head as he replaced it in the drawer. "The humming would cease forever if the beast had been murdered. Only when they die of natural causes is the phallus removed to create such a rare instrument."

"I see."

"It is said to have the power to bring an immediate orgasm upon its insertion inside a woman. If it isn't removed promptly, the user can suffer a fatality from successive orgasms. Never use it alone," he cautioned. "I wouldn't want you to injure yourself, even in the throes of orgiastic delight."

Jane rolled her eyes. "I promise to bear that in mind."

Her gaze fell on an elaborately carved stool with a suspicious hole in the center of its wooden seat.

Noting her glance, Nick took another of the dildos and inserted it from below the stool so it protruded upward through its middle.

"A woman wears such ridiculously wide skirts that a man could easily work such a device beneath them while she was seated on the stool next to him. Imagine, in polite company, having to pretend calm while such a cylinder was thrust through the seat and into your body. Imagine it briskly working, stimulating you. You would have to remain so quiet and motionless. No one must know the truth, save you and your sequestered tormenter."

Moisture pooled between her legs. She swallowed and looked away.

Peering into the drawer, she lifted the largest of the phalluses from it. Its silver-veined, marble surface begged to be touched, and Jane slid a finger along its cold smoothness.

"That one is purported to have been chiseled from the stone of a sacred altar and polished by a goddess."

It was so outsized she shuddered, imagining. "Aren't you the tiniest bit jealous?" she teased.

"It would fit inside you," Nick assured her. "With enough prior stimulation and lubrication."

She replaced it in the drawer and took a step back. "Impossible!"

"The body is more elastic than you think."

She stared at him in fascinated horror. "But why would you wish me to consider such a thing?"

"It gives me enjoyment to explore the limits of a woman's pleasure."

"Will you require me to find pleasure here in this room?" She made a sweeping gesture with one hand.

"On occasion, I hope to introduce you to some of these utensils and their intimate uses. The question is, would you allow it?"

She surveyed the room. Something about it repelled her. Something about it thrilled her as well.

Slowly she nodded. "But not all at once," she quickly amended. "And not all of them."

He smiled. "Most certainly not all at once. And not all of them. Only those to your liking."

"How will I know which are?"

"Over time, your curiosity will grow, and we will experiment. You will find me a willing partner, open to any suggestion. You have only to indicate an interest in any direction and I will try to satisfy it. There is no rush. We have a lifetime to explore such things."

"What if a whim takes me to explore your body with some of these devices?"

"I will accommodate you, within reason. It's difficult for me to give up control."

"Perhaps we can work on that. Here in this room."

"Perhaps."

He broke eye contact, but her heart had lightened at his admission. It felt like the beginning of trust. And maybe something more.

25

Jane sat amid the trees of Satyr forest, feeling excited and afraid.

She was coming to love this land and its owner. Emma would join her here one day. And if she allowed him to, Nick would give her a child to love as well. The makings of a true family seemed within her grasp.

But if she couldn't shake her curse—and soon—it would all fall apart.

She broke the brittle stems she carried in her basket, letting the dried herbs flutter into the bowl she'd placed on a flat rock. Over the weeks, she'd managed to gather all the ingredients the curative had specified. Several had proven difficult to obtain, and then she'd had to wait for them to dry.

One by one, the herbs found their way into her mortar. With her pestle, she crushed them together, watching their rainbow colors mix.

Carefully she lifted the prime ingredient from her basket—allium moly. She had plucked it from her garden and wrapped its roots in damp cloth just prior to coming here. Her reading indicated it must be served fresh.

She tore off the flowers and dropped them into the bowl, grinding them with her pestle into a smear of yellow.

Last of all, she added dewdrops collected that morning from the leaves of a plant known as flowering lady's mantle. She mashed the entire concoction into a paste.

When the potion was ready, she took it all, finding it bitter on her tongue.

Afterward, no thunder sounded. No crack of illumination filled the forest. There was nothing to mark the occasion.

All had been done according to the ancient book, she reassured herself. The philter would banish her evil taint. She had to believe it.

The book had said the effect of the curative would take several hours. She could only wait. Jumping to her feet, she decided to walk the perimeter of the grotto.

Stepping close to one of the caryatids, she studied its graceful contours. She wasn't certain why she had come here to take the potion. It was the place where she'd once seen that trio of lights take female shape. This place had frightened her then but no longer.

She yawned, growing sleepy—a side effect of the potion she'd taken. She sat beneath a tree in the well of a natural chair formed by its root structure.

It was afternoon when she woke. She straightened, remembering. Hoping. Hastily and with little care for her gown, she lowered its sleeve. Her hand trembled as she reached, seeking along a shoulder blade.

When soft fluff tickled her fingertips and quills pricked, her heart stilled and then wrenched with the agony of failure. The curative hadn't worked.

She yanked at the quills, whimpering at the pain, trying to

rip them away. But she had tried that before and only succeeded in bloodying herself. They would only sprout again.

With a cry, she flung the basket and its remaining ingredients across the path. She tore through the trees, stumbled down hillsides, falling here and there and scrabbling across fields, then the lawn, then pave stones and mosaic. Finally she let herself into the castello.

She rushed to her chamber and fell on the bedcovers, her mind racing. She wouldn't give up. There was too much at stake. She would have to begin again. Find a new curative. She had to, if only for Emma's sake.

She could remain with Nick, she told herself, even tainted as she was. She'd hidden what she was from him this long.

But one day soon they might produce a child despite her efforts to prevent it. And any child she bore might also be freakish, forced to grow up holding herself or himself apart from the world in fear of discovery.

No! She couldn't take the chance.

She would have to leave here. Leave Nick. Search for a cure elsewhere.

She curled into a ball and wept at the pain of impending loss.

26

Nick entered her bedchamber that night as she sat in a tufted chair, reading. With resigned calm, she folded her book shut and set it on the side table. Her last-minute study of an herbal from his library hadn't offered a glimmer of hope.

She knew what she must do.

Nick strolled aimlessly about the room. He'd been agitated about something all afternoon. She'd only just noticed because her mind had been preoccupied with searching for a way to inform him of her intentions.

"You're restless. What disturbs you?" she asked.

His glance was hooded. "I'm attempting to make a difficult decision. And I'm not inclined to make the choice that considers your best interest. It troubles me."

"If the matter concerns me, may I assist in the process of the decision making?"

Nick studied her, so beautiful and ethereal, so prim. Determination rose within him. Tonight was the Calling. A special one—that of the second May moon. A blue moon, the villagers called it when a single month had two moonfuls.

The time had come to beget an heir. How best to approach it?

He'd originally planned to take her to the glen tonight without her knowing. To subdue her with an ancient spell so she would cooperate but afterward remember nothing. It was what his father had done in order to sire his three sons. It was what his brothers expected him to do.

So where did this notion come from that she should be given a choice in the matter? Where did this need come from to have her with him tonight, in body and spirit, reveling in the full experience of the Calling?

Would knowing the truth of what he was repulse her? Send her screaming into the night?

Within minutes, he would know.

Jane drank in the sight of him, dreaded seeing his desire for her turn to disgust. Months ago at her aunt's home, he'd informed her in no uncertain terms that he expected a child of her. And she'd agreed. He would be angry when he learned she'd changed her mind.

He would tell her to go, she knew. To leave him and his home. For Emma's sake, she would lower herself to plead with him for funds enough to help her and her sister to make a home for themselves elsewhere. Surely her service to him thus far was worth that concession.

How she longed to go on as they had been. But she must not. The herbs she took each morning would fail her eventually. Coupling with him tonight or in the nights to come could result in a child. One tainted with whatever unearthly plague she carried. Leaving him was the only decision she could make in good conscience. He would have to accept it.

Her lips parted, to tell him.

* * *

"I wish to leave you with child tonight," Nick said before she could speak.

"I know you want an heir above all things," she said, contrite. "And I'm hopeful that you will have the child you desire someday soon. However—" She took a breath and stood, willing herself to say things that would forever sever their ties.

He brushed her words aside. "You misunderstand. I'm asking your permission to leave you with child."

"You speak as though my permission is all that stands in the way of conception."

"If you wish it, I can make conception happen. Tonight."

Something in his eyes frightened her. "You can't know that."

"Yes, it's something I know with absolute certainty," he said. His voice was calm, sure. "If I lie with you tonight, you will conceive. You can turn me away, Jane. I won't force this on you if you aren't ready."

"I've wanted your child—" she began.

"Even if I can't guarantee it will be Human?" he challenged.

"What?" She took an involuntary step away from him, a sudden chill skittering down her spine. "What else would it be?"

"Part Human. Part—something else."

Their eyes locked. He knew. Somehow he knew.

Blood and oxygen ebbed within her and then gushed through her tissues in a wild, erratic dance. The sudden exposure of her closely guarded secret left her raw. Needing to escape.

When she backed away, he followed.

She licked her lips. "How did you—?"

"Did you think I wouldn't guess your secrets?" he chided. "I had hoped you would confide in me."

"Don't. Please." Fear and humiliation washed over her in waves. She held her hands toward him, palms outward as though to halt the onward march of his body and his words.

But both continued to stalk her.

"I know of your uncanny insights, your unusual abilities, and your physical abnormalities. I've seen your breasts glow with a passion not of this world, and I suspect I know the reason you keep your back turned from me."

"Stop!" she whispered. His every syllable was a dagger in her heart. She took a step toward the door, but a heavy hand flattened on it, cutting off escape.

She wrapped her fingers around the doorknob and yanked, knowing it was futile. "Let me go. I'll get Emma from my aunt's and go."

He grasped her shoulders from behind and gave her a little shake. "You're going nowhere."

Though she tried to wriggle free, a hand tugged the material at her back lower, ripping the fabric of her soul until her shoulder blades were exposed.

She curled into herself, dying a thousand silent deaths, biting her lip to keep from crying out with shame. She held herself brittle and distant as he surveyed her back, waiting for him to shatter her with condemnation.

But he only stroked the hideous, delicate down. Petted its fragile snowy softness.

"I know the origins of your secrets. Of this," he said in a voice as gentle as rain. "Shall I tell you?"

"No!" she breathed, twisting in his hold to face him. "How can you know?" She pulled her sleeve higher, covering herself.

"You can't run from what you are, Jane. I'll tell you whether you think you're ready to hear it or not."

"What then!" she shouted, hitting his chest with a fist. "Go on. Kill me with your words. Tell me the origin of my wicked strangeness. If you know. If you must."

Nick pulled her close, stilling her fury. "You're neither wicked nor strange. And don't ever speak such again."

"Whatever the case, I only beg of you this one thing. Don't

tell anyone else what you know, for my taint doesn't affect only me. Think of Emma."

"What you are doesn't touch Emma."

Her eyes came up to meet his, a question in them.

His grip on her tightened as though he expected his next words to set her struggling again.

"You're Faerie, Jane. Born of a Fey father."

"What?" She laughed at him. "That's ridiculous. My father—and Emma's—is a drunk. A Human man. And this isn't Ireland. There are no faeries here. Nor anywhere else."

"Faeries no longer inhabit Ireland, though I assure you they once did and were freer with their magic there than in other places. More to the point: Signore Cova is indeed Emma's sire. However, your father was of the same world as mine. A place called ElseWorld."

"You make fun of me. What I am is repulsive to me and must be to you as well."

"Know this, Jane. Believe it. My knowledge of your heritage doesn't repulse or frighten me. It's because of it I searched you out."

"What do you mean?"

"It was no accident we married. Shortly before we met, I received a letter from your father informing me of your existence and that of your two half sisters."

"Sisters?"

He nodded. "Raine searches for one of them even now. Lyon will eventually seek out the third. They will be brought here as you were and placed under Satyr protection."

"I don't want this." Jane tried to shrug him off, but he caught her wrists and held her.

"It is truth. Inescapable."

"Are you saying you and your brothers are like me?" She gestured toward her quills. "I've seen no evidence of it."

He shook his head. "Our abilities are different. You have Faerie blood as well as the Human blood of your mother in your veins. Both Satyr and Human blood flow in mine. A mix of the three strains will fill the veins of our children. You once said you desired those children. Does this change your mind?"

Jane rubbed her forehead, willing her brain to work more efficiently. "I don't know. I had thought to leave you when we spoke tonight."

His head jerked back. "Seven hells!"

"Not because I wished to, but because I thought my strangeness abhorrent."

"And now?"

She stepped away from him, shaking her head. "Now I think that this is too much to consider at once. I need time."

Nick's gaze shifted to the window. When his attention returned to her, he seemed to loom larger and more dangerous, as though he'd been concealing the reality of himself until now.

"Do you know of the Calling?" he asked.

She shook her head.

"It afflicts the Satyr once a month. At Moonful."

Her eyes darted to the window and its glowing night eye. "You mean at the full moon? Tonight then?"

He nodded. "When the moon is heavy and round with light, the Calling occurs. It engenders within me and those of my kind a desperate desire to mate. Our bodies alter. Our carnal needs grow more robust."

Jane's mind clicked back over the past two months. "But while I have been married to you, at least one full moon has passed. How did you hide this from me?"

"I left you and went to a place in the forest. There's a gathering ground there ringed with statues built by my ancestors."

"I've seen it, or at least its outskirts," she admitted. "Lyon was there."

"Yes, he told me," Nick went on. "In the same way as you

saw him that day, I have gone there and mated with Shimmerskins."

Jane crossed her arms as jealousy rose. "Mated?"

He waved a negligent hand. "Don't concern yourself. Shimmerskins are merely pleasure women conjured from the mist to perform as Satyr desires dictate. If we were to take Human women in the Calling, we would reveal the strangeness of our natures. It would put us and our land at risk."

"What sort of strangeness is it that must be kept so secret? I don't understand," she said.

"You're capable of understanding, of accepting my ways—my needs—if you are willing. Now that we're wed, I am driven to mate with you during the Calling. Each Moonful, it grows more difficult to keep myself from you."

"I didn't ask you to do so," she told him.

He took her hands and flattened them on his chest under his.

"I had planned to take you tonight as my father mated my Human mother, by first bespelling her. But I've discovered a desire to have you accept me with full knowledge of what transpires between us. So I offer you the choice. Shall I go to Shimmerskins tonight, or shall we make a child together?"

"I've been taking herbs." The confession blurted from her, surprising them both. "To prevent conception."

His eyes darkened, withdrawing.

She grabbed his shirtfront, willing him to understand. "Not because I didn't want your child. But out of worry over what sort of children I might give you. I didn't want our offspring to live as I have, never daring to touch the skin of another human being."

His reply was forestalled when a shaft of moonlight struck him. His voice turned urgent. "My childseed will overcome any preventive potions. The hour of Calling grows near. Tell me—am I to leave you for the forest, or do you offer yourself?"

Tense silence fell between them.

Would his strangeness unleash more of her own? Would he then find her objectionable? Would she find him so tonight?

Nick moved as if to leave her.

"I offer myself," Jane said quickly, not knowing from where the words came but knowing they felt right. "Don't search out others to give you pleasure."

His hands cupped her jaw, and he gazed down at her, the mirrors of his eyes becoming pools of desire. Softly he asked her, "Shall I tell you what is to come, or shall we take it a step at a time?"

"The latter," she whispered. "I want you, need you. Stay."

He pulled her close, his cheek pressed to hers.

"No matter what passes between us this night, remember that I'll take care of you. You'll suffer no permanent harm," his velvet voice promised.

"You begin to frighten me," Jane said, pulling back with a nervous laugh.

"'Tis not my wish to." Nick flicked another glance at the waning daylight. The thick vein along the side of his neck pulsed. "My time draws near. Come."

He led her to his bedchamber. Closed the door.

Inside, a young maid wearing a crown of leaves awaited them, her face ethereally beautiful.

When the creature approached her, Jane instinctively shied away. "A—are you one of the night servants?"

"Si," the maid replied. Her voice was melodious, soothing. "Do not fear me. I am dryad, here to serve."

"Let her help you with your toilette," Nick coaxed. "Time grows short."

Jane backed against a wall. The dryad's fingertips were cool and insistent as it began to undress her.

"Are you from ElseWorld?" Jane asked her.

The leaves in her hair rustled as the girl slowly shook her head. "From the forest. I was once hawthorn but no more."

Beyond them, Nick went to a cabinet and thrust an ornate key into the lock. He removed a bottle and poured a measure of liquid into two goblets.

When her dress had been removed and a robe donned, the dryad stepped away. Jane's thanks was met with a placid expression.

As the creature slipped from the room, Nick handed one of the glasses he'd poured to Jane.

"Drink."

He threw his back and was quickly done, setting his goblet aside.

Jane took a hesitant sip and wrinkled her nose. "Wine?"

"Of a sort." He nudged her glass. "Take more of it."

She held it away, shaking her head. "You know I don't drink spirits."

"It's necessary. 'Tis a special elixir with magic properties that won't addle your mind but will aid you in performing as I require."

Jane's eyes widened, her pupils dilating. "Now you are frightening me, Nick. Maybe you should explain what's going to happen between us after all."

Again he glanced toward the blackened window, and his voice turned rough and urgent.

"It's too late to renege. I need you. Drink. It will make you desire what I offer."

She stared into his eyes.

His mind pushed at hers. *Trust me.*

As though with a will of their own, her hands lifted the goblet to her lips. Wordlessly she took another sip.

Nick moved closer and loosened the tie at her waist. The gap at the front of her robe widened, and he brushed it from her shoulders to catch at her elbows. Her nipples tightened in the cool air, begging. He took one in his mouth.

An arm circled behind her under her robe. She swallowed a gulp of wine just as he ran a finger along the crease between her buttocks. Sputtering, she clenched her muscles and tried to pull away.

"Later, then," he murmured, withdrawing his touch. "I'm too eager."

He tugged the length of her hair forward, over her shoulder exposing her back. Gently, he stroked the soft down of feathers struggling to grow.

She snapped away, pulling the robe back into position.

"No barriers tonight," he warned. "I want you as you are. Not as you wish to be."

He let her go then, beginning to undress himself. She watched, her eyes reflecting her growing tension.

He nodded toward her drink. "Finish. Night comes."

She stared at the ruby liquid swirling like blood in the goblet. So often she'd warned herself of the evils of liquor and had made herself frightened of it. But her eyes fell on Nick, and she saw the need in his eyes.

"Your father isn't the Human sot you once believed," he reminded her. "The elixir will not make you an addict."

Did she dare? Could she trust him? He'd seen her differences and accepted them. Accepted her. Perhaps it *was* time to trust. To love.

A feeling of something momentous falling into place came over her, as though she'd found the missing pieces in the puzzle of her life. Self-loathing fell away. The beginnings of self-acceptance blossomed, taking its place.

The robe slipped lower and then pooled at her feet. Holding his eyes, she lifted the goblet to her lips. The potion slid down her throat easily now, warming her.

The next time he approached her, he was naked.

This time, when he slid a finger along the cleft of her buttocks, she scarcely registered it. He dipped a thumb in a shallow dish of oil the dryad had prepared and slid it inside her there.

She clenched her muscles, halfheartedly defying him. The thumb slid deep, plugging her untried portal, and then out to gather more oil before intruding again. Her head lolled against his shoulder.

"What are you doing?" she murmured.

"More," he coaxed, tipping the glass to her lips when she began to forget.

She drank until the goblet was empty, while his oiled thumb tried her anus a dozen times or more. She stroked the pad of a finger over her nipple and sighed. Inhibitions were sliding away.

The goblet dropped to the floor as two slickened fingers replaced his thumb and tried to screw their way inside her. At this, she wanted to squirm away, but other fingers were pleasuring her clit and she was loath to dislodge them.

Sudden, intense need ripped at her, and she turned her lips to his throat.

"Join with me," she pleaded in a husky whisper.

"Soon," he growled.

Distantly she noted a new change in his body. The pelt at his groin had spread. A matted, downy fur now covered his haunches and calves. He was as furred as an animal.

"You're different," she said, skimming a hand along his thigh.

"A trait from my ancestors that occurs each Calling," he murmured. "Does it offend you?"

Her calf hooked over his, rubbing sensuously.

"No, I find it oddly pleasing," she said.

Idly she noted yet another difference against her belly. When she drew back, her eyes widened. His already generous cock had assumed new and slightly monstrous proportions. It had grown at least an inch in length, but its more impressive increase was in its girth.

She cradled it in her palm and found it heavy, smooth. She looked at him in question.

"Another feature of the Calling. I like to think of them as bonus inches," he teased.

All humor abruptly left him. His eyes dilated, and his jaw hardened to granite. Staggering, he clutched his belly, folding forward as a cramp seized him.

"What is it?" she asked, leaning close.

He bit off a snarl, unable to form words.

Moments later, he straightened again, and stood.

Another even more dismaying change had occurred in his body, she saw. Scant inches above his cock, a second shaft now protruded from the region of his pelvis. It was a duplicate of his other penis, though slightly smaller.

Striated with purpled veins and crowned with plump reddened heads, both cocks strained eagerly toward her. A tickle of fear penetrated her slumberous desire. But her need to have him come into her overrode it.

"Do it," she begged. "Whatever you must do to me, do it. I can't wait a moment longer to have you."

He groaned and drew her to him. "Thank you, Jane. I swear you will find some enjoyment in it."

She eyed his cocks warily. "I'll keep you to that promise."

He carried her to the bed, positioned her on all fours upon it, and then knelt on the mattress behind her. A hand hooked around her hips to hold them high and another pressed between her shoulder blades. When he had her in the position he desired, her face was in the pillow, her legs widespread, and her bottom was offered up to him.

Cupped fingers came between her legs, sluicing oil as they swept her from clit to rear cleft. A knuckle nudged her anus.

"I'll take you here only once this night," he told her. "Upon achieving a single satiation, my pelvic cock will be gone again."

Grasping her hips, he nestled close. His new fur tickled, causing her labia to contract in greedy anticipation. The heads of his cocks found both her gates. And punctured. Prodded. Stretched.

The bedcovers bunched under her hands.

In her need, her body might have taken his enlarged man cock with no trouble. That is, if it weren't for the other, second intrusion he was attempting at her rear.

"No! Stop!" she demanded, attempting to lunge away. "Truly, I'm sorry, but I fear I can't."

His big hands held her still, in position. "'Tis the heads that are the hardest to take. Once they're sheathed, the rest will go more easily."

"No! Truly. It's too awful," she cried, succeeding this time in pulling away. She twisted on the bed to stare up at him.

A light sheen of sweat glistened on his forehead and chest, and he appeared almost to be in agony.

"You must take me, Jane." His voice was graveled. "I've imprinted on you. It's too late to go to another for relief."

"I don't want you to seek another. But, oh—"

His hands grasped his cocks at their roots and swept outward, massaging pre-cum over their tips. Her slit pulsed at the erotic sight.

His eyes beguiled her with wicked promise. "Try again. I swear on Bacchus's name I won't injure you."

"May I have more elixir first?" she suggested.

With admirable stoicism, he left her and made his way to the cabinet where he sloshed another goblet half full. She looked away from his astonishing proportions as he rejoined her on the bed.

He held the cup to her lips. "Make haste."

She gulped the brew in a panic, willing it to help her withstand the ordeal ahead. The wine swirled through her system, sending with it a blast of euphoria. She drank again. The sense of wanting strengthened, enveloping her once more.

The goblet slid from her fingers, leaving ruby droplets on the pristine bedsheets. He brushed it to the floor and gazed at her hungrily. She smiled coquettishly at him.

She sat on her haunches facing him, combing her fingers along his furred thighs. Leaning over his lap, she touched her lips to his smaller pelvic shaft, sucking lightly.

His head fell back, and he groaned.

She sat up and raised a hand to smooth his jaw. "Come inside me. I need you," she beckoned.

His eyes blazed into hers. With hands that shook, he pulled her close and kissed her mouth. Then he returned her to her former pose and quickly reseated the heads of both cocks at her openings.

Again came the pressure. But this time she only murmured as it increased, thrashing her head upon the pillow and tilting her rear to give him better access. The elixir was bubbling in her veins, and her body craved him.

"Hurry," she begged.

His fingers gripped her hip bones convulsively. Both cock heads opened her, nudging until her body gulped and took them. The sharp bite of dual penetration gave her momentary pause. The sting continued as he advanced, stretching her almost beyond endurance.

Though his body urged him on, Nick went slowly, giving her time to accustom herself to him. His journey seemed endless. He roamed his hands over the convex curves of her buttocks, pressing ever onward. Finally his thatch mingled with hers.

"Ahhh, fuck." His eyelids drooped, and his lips took on a

sensual curve as pleasure seared his soul. He'd heard that the Calling fuck was more intense with a true wifemate. It was true. He had never known such exquisite sensation.

"You were correct. The first was the worst." Jane giggled. "Ha! I rhymed."

He grimaced in a parody of a smile as his cocks began to work her slick passages in unison. Each of them could feel the other moving within her. The massage was like nothing he'd ever experienced. The mind-body completeness of this taking was heaven.

Her inner juices released, easing his way. "Full, so full," she murmured.

Soon he was delving even deeper, pounding his flesh into her like the rutting animal he'd become. His eyes darkened at the sight of the twin globes of her bottom quivering and yielding to his hot hardness.

He leaned close and pressed a palm to her belly, holding her for his rough, pagan mating. Anchoring her as his body hunted its pleasure within hers. He fucked her fiercely, grunting his enjoyment, speaking to her in an urgent, arcane language that ratcheted her passion ever higher.

Yearning toward fulfillment, she rose to all fours, arching into his rhythm.

His furred thighs and hips slammed against her, and the velvet sacks of his testicles slapped her with each fuck.

Sensation licked at her nerve endings, coiling, amplifying. She churned with it. Burned with it. Reached for that wondrous feeling that was just . . . out . . . of . . . reach. . . .

She shrieked at the suddenness of its attainment, at the coming of her first full-body climax. It quivered her thighs and buckled her arms. Shuddered at her nipples until they glowed the feverish silver-blue of the night's moon. Both her channels tightened and released in a powerful rhythm that milked him, beguiled him—promising him ecstasy.

Her flesh mastered his, drawing him inexorably into the velvet maelstrom. With a great final thrust, Nick seated himself so deep that the slit of his tip kissed the lips of her womb. He knew a suspended moment of perfect joy.

Then his features contorted. And he exploded, blasting the seeds of life into the waiting mouth deep within her. Like a fountain in sunlight, his childseed sparkled into her, pulsing over and over again until, finally, he was drained of it.

And he rejoiced.

He was a father.

He sheltered her back with his body, his breath sawing in and out of his lungs as though he'd run many miles.

Sometime later, Jane squirmed, her anus involuntarily clenching as his pelvic cock receded from her squishy-wet rectum. Now that it had gotten its way, the shrunken cock disappeared meekly back into his skin.

His lips brushed her shoulder. "My second cock is quenched," he told her. "It will trouble you no more this night."

He made no mention of the fact that his other oversize cock remained inside her vagina, poised and throbbing.

She wriggled against it. "I thought I felt, that is . . . Didn't you spill inside me?"

A hand stroked her rib. "This is the way of the Calling. My shaft won't grow flaccid until sunrise."

She smiled at him over her shoulder. "Excellent."

"I'm glad you think so." He grinned and withdrew only to turn her to face him and slide into her again. Wrapping a hand under her bottom he lifted her slightly, tilting her hips forward.

He fucked shallowly for a time, letting her opening massage the swollen plum at his tip, watching her accommodate it over and over. The petals of her labia folded inward with his taking and then blossomed outward with each retreat. His hand slid higher along her hips, and he pressed closer, watching her face.

"The elixir did its work then? My second cock didn't cause you too much distress?"

"No, you were right. It—ahh!?" Startled, she cried out, trying to sit up and scoot away. "Something is—ahh!"

An unidentified serpentine instrument had unfurled from below his scrotum to tickle its way inside her anus! She wiggled her buttocks in confused delight as more of the tonguelike protrusion made its way into her rear entrance.

"Oh! What is that?" she asked, sighing despite the strangeness of it.

"The Seeker. Another feature of the Calling," he informed her with a rakish smile. "One females are said to greatly enjoy."

The long appendage slithered within the crimpled crevice of her buttocks, licking up his deposits and healing her abraded tissue.

"Stop, oh, god, that's so—"

A second climax surprised her in mere seconds, and her tissues coaxed Nick into tumbling over the edge with her.

Catching the scent of their arousal, the tonguelike protrusion slid from her rear portal. It encircled the root of Nick's cock like a curling vine, licking at her vaginal opening as though begging entrance.

Nick pushed it away, his expression intent as he concentrated on the pleasure engendered by their mutual orgasm. "Not yet."

The protrusion seemed to take the hint. It uncurled and moved on to swirl around her clit, tickling, licking, tantalizing.

Jane gasped. "What is it doing?"

Nick answered carelessly. "It's meant to soothe any distress my body causes yours during this night. To keep your arousal at a pitch that ensures your willingness to mate with me for the length of time I require."

"How does it do that?" asked Jane.

"It deposits a secretion that heals any small injuries my continued mating causes within you. You will grow to appreciate it as the night wears on."

He was right.

After their tenth mating, Jane lost count of how many times he fucked her and in how many ways. Damp tendrils of hair framed her flushed face, and her breath came in pants. But she was neither chafed nor sore.

His two appendages attended to her throughout the night, and she to them. She willingly took him as he needed and by morning felt thoroughly explored.

With the coming of dawn, all stimulation desisted. The Seeker tucked its length under his ballocks and retracted inside him until it disappeared.

Sighing, she fell asleep in his arms.

When she awoke it was nearly noon and Nick was gone.

She moved cautiously from the bed. Her muscles protested, but she wasn't as uncomfortable as she should have been after a night like the one that had just passed.

She gazed into the mirror. Surprisingly, her neck and breasts were unmarked by his lips. Nowhere was her skin grazed or bruised. Only a mild, pleasurable sensation within both her nether channels remained as vivid reminders of the night.

The Seeker had done its work well. So had her husband.

She was happy, she suddenly realized. There was a new lightness of heart within her, resulting from a great burden having been lifted. It seemed Emma was in no danger of becoming like her. For no tainted blood flowed in her sister's veins.

And now she had a name to put to her own strangeness.

"Faerie," she whispered into the freedom of the cool morning air.

27

When Jane joined Nick at breakfast, he kissed her in full view of the day servants. Though it was a shocking departure from the norm about which she should have delighted, she found she could only return his embrace listlessly.

The euphoria she'd experienced upon awakening had quickly passed. With startling speed, another feeling had taken its place.

Nausea.

It roiled in her belly now, threatening her enjoyment of breakfast. The aromatic concoction of eggs and tomatoes on the platter repulsed her. Even the lightly spiced tea sickened her. She pushed it all away and made a face.

"You aren't hungry?" Nick asked in surprise. No doubt after last night's exercise, he expected her to be ravenous. In fact, she was. Yet food repelled her.

"I am. I can't think what—"

Suddenly, her color faded to a pale green, and her eyes widened in horror. She pushed from the table and dashed through the kitchen to the garden, where she was promptly sick in a bed of peonies.

"Is the signora unwell?" she heard one of the servants ask from behind her.

"Bring water and linen," Nick directed.

With his assistance, she rose and was situated on a stone bench. She slumped with her forearms resting on her thighs, so wan and dispirited she scarcely noticed when he stroked her hair.

Footsteps clattered over the mosaic tiles toward them. It was the servant bearing his requests.

"Set it there and leave us," he ordered. "All of you."

She heard the door shut, and they were alone.

A fresh, dampened cloth ran over her mouth and face, bringing cool, welcome moisture. Nick handed her a glass of water that she drank thirstily.

She leaned against him, and he wrapped an arm around her. "I feel dreadful," she told his buttons. "Perhaps the elixir last night didn't agree."

Nick glanced down at her. "It's not the elixir that makes you ill," he informed her baldly. "It's the child I gave you last night."

She looked up at him with a startled laugh. "Even you can't manage to know such a thing so quickly."

Dipping a hand inside her bodice, he lightly grazed her nipple.

"Oh!" She jerked and placed a hand on the fabric over his to stay his touch. "I'm tender."

"Because you are with child."

"More likely because of your recent attentions."

His broad hand left her breast to spread over her abdomen, testing its contours through her skirt. "It's more than that. Your belly and your breasts are swelling already. You have conceived. Your body knows it even if your mind hasn't yet accepted it."

She shook her head against his shirtfront. "It's too soon for such outward changes. If I'm showing signs, conception must have happened between us some weeks ago. The herbs must have failed."

In his certainty, Nick easily ignored such speculation. He'd known the exact moment his childseed had pulsed into her womb last night. But to share this physical confirmation of it with her was surprisingly enjoyable. He rested his chin atop her head, content.

"Jane, this is wonderful. Truly joyful news."

When she made no reply, he pulled away to look down at her. "Aren't you pleased?"

Her eyes were troubled when she spoke. "If it's true, I'm pleased, of course. It would be a promise kept."

He brushed the back of his fingers along her cheekbone and then encircled and caressed the back of her neck under the fall of her hair. "But other than that, are you pleased? Do you want our children, knowing they will have other than Human blood?"

"I will love any child of ours. But sickness consumes me, and motherhood seems distant at this moment."

"Not so distant," he murmured. "Satyr children are eager to be born. It will only be a matter of . . ."

She missed the remainder of his words as a new concern reared its head. "Does my condition mean you will discontinue visiting my bedchamber?"

His hand stilled on her neck.

"What I mean to ask is, will you visit me nightly as you have been? I apologize if my questions are inappropriate, but I don't wish to be kept in suspense on this matter."

He planted a brief kiss on her lips and then tucked her head to his chest. "I won't come to you during your confinement."

She flinched.

"Not because my desire for you will lessen," he assured her. "Rather because it is the ancient way."

"But how will you manage without my, uh, attentions—in the bedchamber?"

"It won't be easy." His hand curved her belly again, rubbing in gentle circles. "My desire to mate will only heighten during your time of gestation. However, I'll manage. I have no choice."

The way in which he would "manage" was precisely what concerned her. "Couldn't we contrive some method of carnal relief short of an actual joining? Surely you're creative enough to offer suggestions in that area."

Yes, he had many suggestions he would like to offer her in that area. Even after last night, his cock throbbed with want of her.

Half a dozen Shimmerskins at once had never given him the pleasure his wife had given him last night. It struck an odd sort of fear in him. Perhaps it was best that circumstances forced him to distance himself during the child's incubation. He couldn't afford to become so besotted that he forgot other obligations.

"Denying myself is a necessary part of the process. It will lend strength to our offspring if I keep myself from you until its birth."

It was what she'd feared he might say. She'd once overheard a maid complain to another that her husband didn't find it enjoyable to couple with his breeding wife. So, in this matter, Human and Satyr were apparently alike.

"Very well," she whispered, nodding. "Thank you for your consideration."

He squeezed her against him, and briefly she felt cherished. "It is I who thank you. Only think, Jane, we're to be parents."

Jane hugged him back. She was delighted, but she was also afraid. How would her virile husband possibly do without sex for nine months? What if he sought out other women?

* * *

Six nights later, Jane lay abed with her back curved along her husband's chest. Nick slumbered peacefully, wearing trousers as he had every night since he'd become aware of her pregnancy.

And she truly was with child. It was certain now. She saw new evidence of it daily.

Ironically, now that he'd proclaimed her untouchable, Nick had begun sleeping in her bed throughout the night rather than in his own. Though she welcomed his presence, it frustrated her almost beyond endurance. Want of sexual congress with her husband hounded her, keeping her from sleep.

Night and day, she thought of little else. His breath at her neck, a casual brush of a hand on her skin, or the shift of his warm thighs against hers—all were sensual torture.

Even now, the warm bulge at his crotch prodded her longingly through the fabric that confined it. It had been thus every night. Unable to bear it a moment longer, she reached a hand between their bodies to find and stroke him in the darkness. He was thick, ready.

She needed to touch skin.

Stealthily she unbuttoned his trousers. It took some minutes, but he didn't awaken. She widened the gap she'd created in the fabric and fondled the column of hard heat she found within. When he groaned and rolled to his back, she took quick advantage.

Twisting, she ducked under the covers and moved lower over him. When her tongue found his tip, she swirled it over him. A fierce dart of lust flickered between her thighs. Never had she needed him more.

Abruptly, he came awake. He wrested himself away, his knee bumping her chin in his haste to withdraw. Strong hands reached below the coverlet and grabbed her armpits, hoisting her into the cool air.

Through the dimness, accusing sapphire met emerald need.

"What are you doing?" Nick demanded.

"Didn't you like it?"

"Of course I—that's not the point."

He'd inadvertently aligned her crotch to his, and she help-lessly rocked against him. His fingers flinched on her, but he didn't push her away.

Sensing a chink in the armor of his resistance, she slid her arms around his neck and stroked her lips along his jaw.

"It's been almost a week," she cajoled. "I know you're hurt-ing. Won't you allow me to lessen your strain?" His shaft twitched under the wet stroke of her labia.

He groaned, his will obviously weakening.

Lifting, she sought his crown with her frilled opening. Her private flesh was an aching void, pulsing with want of him.

She found him. Their eyes caught.

She read his grim desire and sensed impending victory. "Why not take the relief I offer?" she whispered, caressing his face. She spread her knees, letting her weight take her lower on him.

When her nether lips gapped over his crown, he came back to himself. He grabbed her hip bones and caught her to still-ness.

"No, Jane," he said firmly. "Though it pains me to say it."

Miffed, she yanked herself away and grouchily watched him refasten his trousers. "In denying yourself, you deny me as well. Yet I have no say in the matter?"

He ran a hand over his face. "Don't you think I find it equally difficult to keep from you? For the good of our unborn child, we must deny ourselves gratification. In any form. That means you must not stimulate yourself by your own hand ei-ther. Do you understand?"

"How can this unnatural abstinence be of any benefit to our unborn child?" she argued.

He gestured futilely. "It's not something I can explain. I can only say it's the—"

"—Satyr way," she interrupted. "I know, I know."

Feeling rejected, she rolled away from him. Tears of frustration clung to her lashes, but she pressed her face into the pillow before they could fall.

Nick pulled her into the hollow of his chest, lending comfort in spite of her stiff resistance. Tucking her to him, he wrapped an arm over her, securing her wayward hands under his at her breast.

His voice was soft at her ear as he dropped a kiss. "It won't be for long. We will bear it."

Within seconds, he fell asleep, leaving her to endure the frustration of his nearness.

Thirty minutes later, his lips caressed her shoulder as he murmured in his sleep.

An hour later, his thighs slid along hers, momentarily forcing the hardness of his shaft into firmer contact with her wanting valley.

She sighed.

It was near dawn before she slept.

28

Three weeks later, Jane stepped out of a carriage at Izabel's villa in Florence. She gripped the railing as she ascended the front stairs, her step ungainly and slow.

The butler's eyes widened as he admitted her. "The signora is entertaining this afternoon," he informed her doubtfully.

"And Emma?" asked Jane.

"Away," he answered vaguely.

A letter had arrived that morning from Emma, begging Jane to visit. Though there was no particular news, the tone of it had been strangely worrisome. So worrisome that Jane had ventured out without consulting Nick, hoping to speak with her sister.

After traveling for hours, she refused to be deterred. "I'll see myself into the parlor then, to speak with my . . . aunt," she told him.

She stumbled over labeling Izabel as her "aunt" now that she knew it for a lie. However, she and Nick had agreed that the lie must be perpetuated. If the truth were known, Izabel would likely never allow Emma to come live at Blackstone.

Jane found her way into the parlor where her erstwhile aunt held court with several of her dearest friends. Izabel was the first to notice her. Her eyes fell to Jane's waist, and she stood, her napkin tumbling from her lap. Her face was a picture of shock.

"You're with child!" she blurted. "But my God. So huge!"

Her companions turned to stare with rounded eyes.

"Twins, from the look of you," said Signora Bich.

"Or triplets," said Signora Natoli.

Izabel and her friends exchanged loaded glances.

Jane hugged her bulky waistline self-consciously. She'd wondered if it hadn't had swelled more quickly than should be expected. The women's obvious dismay exacerbated her concerns.

Izabel's expression quickly turned to one of delight. "But this is wonderful!" she said, moving toward her with outstretched arms.

The other ladies surrounded Jane, oohing and ahing. They patted her belly through her dress with overfamiliar hands, testing its shape and size as though it were an object apart from her. She felt disturbingly vulnerable without her stiff, protective corset, which she had of necessity abandoned weeks ago.

She sat down to escape their touch. "I have come to visit Emma, but your butler tells me she isn't at home today?"

"Signore Nesta brought his children to visit. He and his mother have taken Emma out for the afternoon," Izabel explained.

"Oh."

Jane felt like crying at finding Emma gone. But then, the least thing made her a watering pot these days. Another effect of her condition was apparent in the greater opulence of her breasts. They'd become so sensitive that they tingled at the slightest rub of fabric. However, worst of all was the constant state of arousal Nick insisted she abide in.

The threat of the pox was a great weight on his mind, and vigilance against it kept him in the vineyard later and later. Each night, he returned home weary and fell to sleep with ease. Unlike her.

Was such abstinence truly necessary?

As the other ladies settled back into their circle of button-tufted chairs, Jane realized this was her chance to ask. It was an indelicate issue, but one that such experienced ladies could shed light upon. All had been wed at one time, and most had children.

"Am I unusually large then?" she ventured.

"You have the belly of a woman in her final month," Signora Ricco informed her, popping a sweetmeat between her lips.

Jane swallowed. As the mother of six, the signora was in a position to know.

Signora Natoli nodded. "At this rate, you'll be big as a house by the time you're ready to give birth."

Jane blanched.

"Stop frightening the girl," Izabel chided. She inched forward in her seat and took her niece's hand.

Disturbing, erotic images flashed in Jane's mind at the brief contact. She drew her hand away, pretending to straighten her skirts. She was rarely able to meld with flesh other than Nick's any longer, and only when another's emotions were unusually strong.

"A woman was meant to be a vessel for her husband's passion and to birth his children," Izabel told her. "Motherhood is a blessing, isn't it, ladies?"

The others in the semicircle dutifully bobbed their heads.

"We didn't mean to cause undue alarm," said Signora Ricco.

"No need to worry," added Signora Bich.

"I'm trying not to," said Jane. "It's just that I've grown large so quickly. Nick has advised against it, but I wonder if I shouldn't consult a physician?"

Izabel shot her a look. "Your husband knows what is best. You should obey his wishes."

"I know he means well."

"Is he a considerate husband then?" asked Signora Natoli, her eyes sharpening with interest.

Jane shifted uncomfortably. It was an opportunity to voice her concerns about Nick's inattention in their bed, but she was reluctant. "Yes, most considerate."

Signora Ricco leaned forward. "In all things?"

Jane looked around the circle of women. Their gazes were avid.

"Come now, speak frankly," said Izabel. "We have all lain with men. And you're no longer a maiden."

Signora Bich glanced slyly at Jane's belly. "Well, that's obvious!"

The others tittered, and Jane felt tears gather again. "I shouldn't speak of private matters."

"Come, come, you're now a seasoned wife. There is no harm," said Signora Ricco.

"No harm indeed. Surely you must have questions about the impending birth of your child," said Signora Bich. Her eyes surveyed Jane's girth. "Or children."

"Don't leave them until it is too late and you're in childbed," Izabel advised. "It's best to be prepared."

The others clucked their agreement.

"I do have one question," said Jane. "I hope it won't shock you."

"Yes?" asked Izabel. Though no one moved, Jane felt suddenly crowded. She plunged ahead.

"I—is it necessary for a husband to abstain from physical relations with his wife during her confinement?"

A hush fell. The women stilled, awaiting Izabel's decision in the matter. Odd, since Izabel was the only one of them who hadn't borne children.

"That depends upon the size of her husband's male organ," Izabel lied smoothly. "Is Lord Satyr especially well endowed?" She took a sip of tea.

"I have nothing to compare him to," Jane murmured, growing ever more discomfited.

"More than seven or eight inches in length is considered quite well endowed," said Signora Natoli.

Jane's eyes widened.

Izabel returned her cup to its saucer with deliberate care before lifting her gaze. "Is your husband's length greater than seven or eight inches?"

The women held their breath in unison.

"I haven't, um, measured," Jane hedged.

"Estimate," suggested Signora Bich.

Jane shifted to the edge of her chair as though making to rise. "The hour grows late."

"Wait! Don't you have questions about the birthing itself?" asked Signora Ricco.

"Shall I attend you then?" asked Izabel. "Perhaps I should accompany you home and await the birth."

"Capital idea, Izabel," said Signora Bich.

Jane shook her head. "I haven't yet thought of such things. I'm barely a month into my pregnancy."

Signora Natoli choked on her tea. "A month! But—"

"Dear God!"

Jane swiveled on her chair to find Signore Cova standing in the doorway. His mouth hung open, and his astonished eyes were riveted to her enlarged waistline.

Izabel leaped to her feet and hurried toward him, skirts flapping. Wordlessly she steered him from the room. His voice echoed through the marble foyer beyond, returning clearly to be heard by everyone.

"That slut!" he accused.

Izabel's reply, when it reached their ears, was an unintelligible murmur.

"You're wrong! No one could get that brat-swollen so quickly," Cova replied, his words like cruel darts. "And why else would Satyr have wanted her if not that she carried his bastard in her belly?"

Jane blanched. She set her tea aside and awkwardly attempted to push herself from the chair.

The other ladies offered assistance.

Again, Izabel's soothing tone, but not her words, floated to their ears.

"Then another man plowed her if Satyr did not!" Cova bellowed in reply. "She was obviously already breeding when he offered for her. Even if he'd impregnated the very night of her wedding—"

Izabel's voice rose on a sharp note. "Silence, Pier! This is no time to be upsetting the girl. I'm sure she's developing at her own pace."

Their voices faded farther away.

Jane made her way to the door and peered out. They were gone from sight.

Signora Natoli patted her hand where it rested on the doorjamb. "My dear, don't let this upset you. Men sometimes lack understanding."

Jane slid her hand from the blue-veined clasp. "I must go."

The ladies followed as she slipped from the room and across the foyer to the front entrance. The butler opened the door, his smirk telling her he'd heard everything.

She stiffened her backbone.

The ladies trailed her onto the front porch. "You must come to any of us with any further questions," one of them called after her.

"Thank you for your kindness," Jane replied as the coachman assisted her into the carriage.

She wouldn't return. But she would ask Nick to write to Izabel and request a visit from Emma, pleading his wife's confinement as reason.

As her carriage pulled away, she hugged her belly as though to console her unborn child.

"Don't worry what they think. I promise I'll care for you and protect you. And I'll love you," she whispered. "No matter what you are."

The women chattered busily in the wake of Jane's departure.

"She'll die birthing this one, mark my word."

"As long as the child doesn't die, her demise would serve our purpose."

"How large do you suppose Lord Satyr's cock is anyway?"

"Far larger than eight inches from the look on the girl's face."

"It bodes well for his offspring's proportions."

They snickered.

Izabel reappeared in the doorway, smiling broadly. "Ladies, things are progressing at an unexpectedly swift pace. It would appear we must step up our schedule."

29

The evening sky was painted with slashes of deep purple and orange by the time Jane returned to Satyr land. The day servants were gone by that hour, and there was only the coachman to help her. With his assistance, she struggled from the carriage and moved partway up the front steps.

Signore Faunus hurried out to her aid, waving the coachman away. She accepted his arm gratefully, and they made their way toward the ornate front doors.

"The master has been waiting," he scolded anxiously.

"He has returned from the vines?"

"Si."

"But he has tarried there well into darkness lately. I assumed he'd linger."

Nick's voice reached them. "Jane!"

As they stepped inside the front doors, Jane glanced up to see her husband beckoning to her from the balusters at top of the stairs. His face was wracked with pain, and he was paler than she'd ever seen him. Though it was barely past dusk, he already wore his dressing gown.

"Are you ill?" she asked. Behind her, Signore Faunus locked the heavy doors and withdrew from them.

"Where have you been?" Nick growled down at her.

"To my aunt's," she admitted, hurrying as best she could to join him. "To Izabel's, I mean. To see Emma, though she wasn't there after all."

"Seven hells, woman! You shouldn't have ventured so far in your condition. But we will discuss your foolishness another time. Come." He pushed her along the hall toward his bedchamber and then ushered her inside it.

Slamming the door behind them, Nick reached for the buttons of her gown, a salacious glint in his eye.

Jane grasped his wrists. "What are you doing?"

His lips caressed her throat, and he whispered, "Removing your clothing, wife. It's the Calling. We must mate."

She batted at his hands and whirled away, warding him off with an outstretched palm. "You said we were to abstain."

"No longer."

"But Izabel agreed it was wise."

He hunted her, his gait stalking. "Fuck Izabel."

"Nick!"

She backed around his bed and found herself cornered. His eyes glittered, scalding her where they touched.

Hard hands reached for her and then checked as sudden moonlight bathed the window glass.

A vicious cramp rippled over his belly, and he staggered, his white-knuckled fingers clutching at a bedpost. Grimacing, he hunched forward.

Jane leaned over him, wrapping an arm around his back. "Shall I summon help?"

He managed a negative shake of his head. After long moments, he regained control, uncoiled, and stood. From the divide of his robe, two penises now strained upward, their bulbous crowns rich with blood. Each extended well beyond Izabel's stated requirement.

"Jane! Do as I bid you," he snarled. "I'm dangerously in need."

"But you said we shouldn't. I assumed you would take Shimmerskins—if you became desperate while I'm breeding."

He shot her a disbelieving look. "I can't go to Shimmerskins this night. A mating must occur between us."

She shook her head. "But—"

"You doubt me?"

"I believe you would say anything to get your way when you're in this, uh, condition."

He sliced the air with his hand. "Enough. I will have you with or without your cooperation," he gritted. "I would prefer the former. Which is it to be?"

He towered over her, and she felt a shiver of distress. She'd never seen him like this. His every muscle was tense, every sinew coiled. His nostrils were flared and his eyes wild, as though the animal in him had overtaken the man.

She glanced toward the door. He stepped closer, watchful.

Her hands went to her buttons. Reluctantly she began removing her clothing. When she was finally naked, his eyes and hands worshipped her belly as though it was a celestial globe and he was seeking the location of a particularly beloved star.

"Don't look at me!" she said, trying to shield herself. The last time he'd seen her unclothed body, her waist had been slender.

He shot her a quizzical glance that said women were beyond his understanding. Then he shed his robe, helped her onto the bed, and knelt on the mattress, waiting.

Jutting from his thatch, his twin cocks were hard, unforgiving instruments, ruddy and thick. She reached for a jar of cream on his night table. For the first time since she'd agreed to become his mistress, it would be required to facilitate their joining. With shaking hands, she sluiced it over his crowns. The slurping, smacking sounds were stark and arousing. Her fingers smoothed over twin ridges and followed twin lengths toward his thatch.

Without conscious thought, she began to meld.

Cruel emotions rushed at her. Anguished need. Tortured desire. Her fingers sprang away, unable to bear it.

Desperate hands threaded her hair, and his mind touched hers.

Trust me. Take me.

Mesmerized by his desire, she turned and slid under him, assuming the pose she knew he required for the first mating of the Calling. Kneeling, she lowered her face to the pillow. Her buttocks were raised, both of her nether openings easy plunder.

Nudging her thighs wide, he took her from behind, groaning in satisfaction as his twin penises were sheathed. The cream eased his way, but his rut stretched her, going deep.

Her fingers fisted the sheets. "Not so deep, Nick. Take care."

It was as though he hadn't heard. He settled into a robust, almost punishing rhythm, punctuated by a slew of grateful curses and ancient words that were foreign to her.

Her worry increased in proportion to the strength of each ensuing stroke. She held her swollen belly protectively in one hand and braced the other on the head rail.

"Nick, not so vigorously! What of our child?"

The pillow muffled her breathless voice. She turned her head and repeated herself more loudly. "Nick!"

Immersed in a primal, desperate need to mate his fecund wife, he seemed incapable of understanding. His body continued to slam into hers.

He would hate himself if their child were injured. And surely this exercise could not be good for it.

Eventually he achieved his first spill. She was furious with him and frightened. But her channels had minds of their own. They convulsed with him in harsh spasms that wrenched at his cocks. Like hands gloved in wet velvet, they milked strong spurts of his cum.

Her moan of pleasure mingled with his of pleasure-pain as the smaller penis retracted within the haven of his pelvis. Though her tissues were still pulsing, he was already busy at turning her onto her back for another taking.

He sat on his haunches and pulled her thighs over his so she straddled him.

Tilting his penis lower with a thumb, he curved a palm under her buttocks. The head met her slit, and he pulled her forward, driving into her again and again. Transfixed, he watched her mounded belly shudder with each thrust.

"Nick," she whispered, grabbing his wrist. "Please have a care. Our child."

"Our child," he echoed in bemused wonderment. His hand touched her belly reverently as he kissed her . . . and immediately climaxed.

Again, she fell over the edge with him.

Throughout the night, he would often kiss and caress her abdomen in this way and took obvious care not to directly impact their child. Nevertheless, she worried. How could she not?

In spite of her concern, her body achieved orgasm with reluctant consistency. It was as though each new gush of his cum sent her passage into unwitting convulsions.

When the first fingers of dawn touched his back, Nick rolled away from her at last, breathing a contented sigh. Having drained himself in her innumerable times and with regularity throughout the night, he was finally sated. He levered himself on one elbow to stare down at her.

She lay amid the tumbled bedcovers, thoroughly replete. Somehow she dredged up the energy to turn her head toward him. Her eyelids fluttered up.

His gaze on her was blazing, intense. Whereas she was utterly exhausted, he was energized, expectant.

She blinked.

Something wasn't quite right. But she was too tired to figure it all out. Perhaps when she awoke. . . .

Sleep called to her, and she slid into a light doze.

Sometime later, her eyes flew open to find him in the same position, watching. What had awakened her?

Pain.

A terrible cramp belted her midriff. She placed a hand over her belly and felt the muscles bunch unnaturally.

The convulsion was quickly followed by another. Then another.

Instinctively she turned on her side and curled into the hollow of her husband's chest. "Nick!"

"I'm here." His hand found her lower back, massaging.

"Something's wrong."

"Shhh. It's your time," he said.

The twinges continued to strike, developing an unrelenting, excruciating rhythm. Soon they were coming close together, on top of one another. She scarcely had time to pant between waves of pain.

"A doctor," she gasped. "Please, Nick. Fetch a doctor. I—"

A strong cramp hit her, worse than all those that had come before. Under her hands, a fierce undulation of muscle rippled through her abdomen.

"Oh, Nick, the baby," she sobbed. "I think we're losing the baby."

"No," he soothed. "Everything's going as it should."

"What? This can't be right. It's happening too soon—ah!"

Another seizure hit, galvanizing her into action. Instinct drove her to rise on all fours like an animal. Nick assisted her. He murmured encouragement and stroked her hair back.

She rocked forward and backward on her hands and knees,

moaning at the overwhelming need to expel—something. She reared up, arching her neck at a sudden stab of pain more torturous than the rest.

A warm gush of silvery blue liquid poured from between her legs, drenching her thighs and the bedcovers.

She crumpled against the pillow, sobbing.

"Oh, Nick! We're losing our child."

"What?" He sounded preoccupied. "No, Jane, I assure you everything is taking its natural course. Calm yourself."

He cleansed the strange moisture from her and moved the soiled covers aside. The sheets were dry below them. He turned her to lie on her back and slid a pillow under her hips. Widening her knees, he knelt between them. He obviously expected her to miscarry and was planning to help.

"Have you ever done this before?" she asked.

He looked startled. "Of course not. I've never given my childseed to anyone but you."

She searched his face. Why wasn't he upset? He'd wanted an heir above all things, and now they might be losing all hope of one. It made no sense.

Sudden, acute agony knifed her, and Nick flinched at her scream. A heavy, fistlike fullness migrated from her womb into her channel, nearly suffocating her with pain. The urge to expel gripped her, and she bore down mightily. As the fullness left her, she screamed again and then collapsed, panting and exhausted.

Nick withdrew from the bed.

Jane lay a forearm over her eyes, unable to look, to accept what had happened. Silent tears leaked from the corners of her eyes into her hair. Her baby was dead, and it was her fault. She should have refused Nick tonight. Knowing it was a Calling, she should have hidden from him.

When another cry mingled with hers, she looked up in disbelief.

Nick's face swam into her vision. He looked—pleased. And he was holding—a baby! A live, squirming baby!

She raised on one elbow and clutched her belly. The swell of her pregnancy had gone.

"Is that our baby?"

He laughed, sounding joyful. "Who else's?"

She struggled to sit upright.

He flicked her a frowning glance. "Lie still."

She subsided on the pillow but held out her arms. "Is he—she all right? Let me see."

"We have a son, Jane," Nick said with evident pride. "And he's perfect."

He brought the child to her, placing him in her arms. Then he lay beside her, wrapping them in his warmth.

Jane inspected the tiny child with sable hair and olive skin. When his blue eyes opened, her heart contracted. "I don't understand. How could I have borne a healthy child in so little time?"

"It's the way of the Satyr. A child is conceived in one Calling and then birthed at sunrise in the next. Only one month of gestation is preferable to the Humans' nine, don't you agree?"

"You should have told me," Jane murmured, too sleepy to conjure up true annoyance.

"I did!" he protested. "That morning in the garden, after you conceived. I'm sure of it."

She remembered she'd missed some of what he'd said that morning. "You expected me to listen? I was sick." Her eyelids fluttered, and she yawned. "Oh, I can't stay awake."

"Rest then."

She shook her head, fighting to keep her eyes open. "There's too much to do. The baby . . ."

"Sleep, Jane. It's tradition. The wife of a Satyr does the work of gestation and birthing. Then her husband takes over the Bonding."

"Hmmm?" She yawned again, and her eyes closed. She heard him rise and begin moving busily around the room. "The maker of the urns in your library didn't get it wrong after all, did he?" she mumbled abstractly. "The Satyr do have two phalluses and a tail."

Nick chuckled. "Only on special occasions. Now rest and let me work."

But she didn't hear the last. She'd fallen asleep.

Nick smiled fondly at her as he bathed their child in a basin. Satyr men were never tired after a birthing, but their women often slept for a day or more afterward.

As Jane slumbered, Nick assumed his husbandly responsibilities. He bathed her with a sponge and removed her to her bedchamber where he placed her amid clean sheets. Then he brought the baby to her.

It was his task to get the child fed while his wife slept. Though how she could slumber amid this racket was beyond him. By now the baby's cries had reached an astounding volume. His son was lusty for sustenance only a mother could provide, and Jane's breasts were firm with milk.

He lay next to Jane and tucked their child between them. "I hope you have some idea of what to do," he told his son. "For my instructions to you will be limited."

He placed the baby's lips at her nipple and waited. The child latched on and began sucking but quickly let his displeasure be known.

"Trouble?" Nick asked, pulled the red-faced boy away. He massaged and squeezed Jane's breast, but the milk still refused to come. The baby's cries turned pitiful. In desperation, he resorted to laving her nipple himself. He pulled the tip of her breast deep into the cavern of his mouth and worked it with a suctioning motion.

Finally he was rewarded when a warm liquid spurted onto his tongue. Milk.

He set their son at her breast again. The tiny lips rooted for the nipple and began to feed with gusto. Jane murmured and shifted at the unfamiliar sensation, but she didn't awaken.

When their child was somewhat satisfied, Nick joined in the feast, pulling Jane's other nipple into his mouth. He quickly brought down the milk this time and then settled the boy at the second breast to finish feeding.

He positioned a pillow at the headboard and lay against it. As he watched his wife give sustenance to their child, he stroked her hair. Something shifted inside him, and the darkness lifted just a little. Sunlight fell across the bed, and he felt it enter his heart.

The hours passed, and he saw to it that their child fed several times. The nursing served a dual purpose. As a result, Jane's body would be largely mended by morning.

He kissed her hair as she slept.

"We've made a beautiful son, Jane."

30

"Let me in at once, fool!" hissed Izabel.

Jane hurried down the stairs to intervene in the scene unfolding at the front entrance of the castello. Signore Faunus held Izabel at bay while she attempted to cow him into admitting her.

Over his shoulder, Izabel spied Jane. Her face paled when she took in the new slimness of her niece's waist.

"You've lost the child?" she asked tremulously.

Jane avoided the question. "Signore Faunus, please allow my aunt to enter. She is unwell."

Noting the older woman's pallor, Nick's servant reluctantly moved aside, and Izabel rushed past him into the grand entry.

"Do sit," Jane told her, indicating a chair.

Izabel sank into it like a deflating balloon, her anxious eyes fixed on Jane's flat belly. "I came to inquire as to your health, but it appears I have left it too late. The child is gone?"

Signore Faunus hovered in the doorway.

"Some tea perhaps, signore?" Jane told him.

He puffed up, readying a protest, but her glare banished him to the kitchen.

Jane turned back to Izabel, who had begun to weep.

"These things happen," she told Jane. "You must get with child again as soon as possible." She grasped Jane's sleeve, her grip surprisingly strong. "Promise me you will try."

Jane was reminded of another promise—one she'd made to Nick that morning before he'd slipped into the forest. A threshold secreted in the sacred gathering place would give him passage to ElseWorld, he'd told her, and he would return to her tomorrow morning.

She'd given him her word she wouldn't tell her family of the birth just yet. Though he'd bespelled the servants into thinking her pregnancy had lasted the expected nine-month term, he would have to be with her in order to work his magic on the minds of other Humans they encountered in the outside world. Once bespelled, they too would accept the notion that she'd conceived on their wedding night and carried her babe a full Human term.

A sudden, faint cry echoed down the stairs, forestalling any attempt Jane might have made in keeping her promise.

Izabel's chin lifted, her expression suspended like that of a surprised deer. The cry came again, and her head swiveled in its direction. Jumping up, she gathered her skirts and raced upstairs.

Jane followed, wringing her hands and watching as Izabel tried one door after another. She finally yielded to the inevitable and opened the door to her bedchamber.

Izabel swept inside and over to the crib that stood in one corner. She clasped its railing and gazed at the child with an expression akin to reverence.

"Yours?" Izabel breathed. She read the truth Jane wasn't skilled enough to conceal.

Jane waved the day servant away so that she might say what she must. "Tell no one, Aunt. The birth must remain a secret."

"I understand. An early child."

Jane disliked having to confirm such suspicions, but to protect her new family and honor her husband's wishes, she kept her lips firmly sealed.

"A son?" Izabel asked hopefully.

Jane nodded. "Vincent."

Izabel flicked away the small blanket, uncovering him. Tears filled her eyes. "He's beautiful."

For some reason, the sight of the older woman's hands on her son unsettled her. Jane gathered the bedclothes around him and lifted him from the crib.

"Thank you," she murmured, tucking him close.

Izabel seemed to come back to herself. "You must bring him to the villa for a celebration of his birth."

"Soon. When I'm certain the world won't look upon him and label him a bastard."

"You'd wait so long? Your father will be anxious to see him."

A denial that Signore Cova was her father crowded her throat, but Jane held it back. "I doubt he'll want to see me or my child. He made his opinions quite clear when I last visited."

"You must make peace immediately," Izabel urged. "If you aren't careful, you'll have him forbidding you to see Emma."

"No, Aunt. Nick has my promise on this."

"Can't you reason with him?"

"Perhaps. But he's away at the moment."

A cunning look flashed in Izabel's eyes, gone before Jane could analyze it. "Where to?"

"I can't say," Jane hedged.

"I suppose there are women whose favors may be bought in many locations."

Jane gasped, hurt by the insinuation. "You don't know what you're talking about."

"His kind are never satisfied with the attentions of one woman. In fact, he came to me recently, and we discussed the possibility of a visit to my bedchamber at a more opportune moment."

Jane stepped back, her arms clasping her child so tightly he squirmed. "Leave this house."

Izabel's expression turned menacing.

"Signore Faunus!" Jane shouted.

They heard his prancing footsteps on the stairs, taking them two at a time.

"I'll see myself out," Izabel said. With a last look at the child in Jane's arms, she swept past Signore Faunus and his tea tray, downstairs, and out of the castle.

From her window, Jane watched Izabel's hired carriage depart. A flash of bright blue darted from it into the garden, startling her. A face peered up at her from the shrubbery and then ducked away. Emma?

She left Vincent in a servant's care and hurried downstairs to investigate.

Something stirred in the night, awakening her. Half asleep, Jane rose from her bed, instinctively making for her child's crib. Her hands fumbled amid the blankets for him, growing panicked when he wasn't there. Instantly alert, she swept her palms over sheets still warm from Vincent's small body.

"She's awake," said a voice.

Jane whirled around, her eyes quickly locating the figures of two women through the gloom. She'd known Izabel would return but not so soon. And not by dead of night, with others.

"What have you done with Vincent?" Jane demanded.

"Signora Bich has him," said the other figure—Signora

Nesta. "He's a darling. Barely fussed at all when she stole him. Not colicky like some babes."

"Signore Faunus!" Jane shouted toward the hall.

"Now, Faunus was a different matter," tsked Signora Nesta. "Pitched a veritable fit until we knocked him over the head and tied him."

Jane reeled with the knowledge that her child had been stolen and her guard incapacitated. Until Nick returned tomorrow night, or Raine returned from his travels, only Lyon remained as a distant protector. Nick had bade her to summon him on the slightest pretext of concern, but it was impossible to do that without Signore Faunus or servants available.

A candle was lit, and tension tightened its screw within her. She must find a pretext to draw them into the hall before they saw—

She moved toward the door. "Take me to Vincent. Once I see he is unharmed, we can discuss whatever it is you have come for."

Izabel snapped her fingers, and Signora Nesta scurried to block the exit.

Thwarted, Jane whipped toward Izabel. "What do you hope to gain by stealing my son?"

"You took something that belongs to me," said Izabel. "It's only right that I take something of yours."

"A fair exchange," agreed Signora Nesta. "Vincent for Emma."

"Where is she, by the way?" demanded Izabel. "Emma!"

"Aunt?" Emma sat up in the bed she'd been sharing with Jane. Swallowed in one of Nick's shirts, she looked younger than her years, defenseless.

"There you are, dear," said Izabel.

Emma hugged her knees guiltily. "Don't be angry at Jane. I sneaked a ride here from the villa on the back of your carriage this morning. She didn't know I was coming."

"Get up now, there's a good girl," Signora Nesta told her, rousting her from the bed.

"I'm not a baby," said Emma. "Please don't speak to me as though I am."

Signora Nesta's eyes permeated the dimness to study the girlish curves of Emma's ripening figure. "No, my son will be glad to know you're growing up quite nicely."

Emma's eyes rounded. She dashed to Jane's side, and Jane tucked an arm around her protectively.

"What does she mean?" Emma whispered.

"You are to marry my son in but three years," Signora Nesta explained.

"No!" breathed Jane.

"I can choose my own husband if I want one," cried Emma.

Izabel ignored their outbursts. "Jane was promised to Signore Nesta but married another," she told Emma. "The family honor rests on you taking your sister's place."

"But he's twice her age! She's only thirteen," Jane protested.

Signora Nesta shrugged. "He will keep himself busy with the whores while he waits for her to ripen."

The door adjoining Nick's room opened, and all eyes turned to see Signora Ricco step through.

"I don't find it," she told Izabel.

Izabel bit off an expletive and then took both her nieces' arms to drag them toward Nick's door.

"Show me the hidden chamber," she said, all but throwing them into his room.

"What?" asked Jane.

Izabel calmly slapped her, leaving a bright red mark on her cheek. "Don't waste my time with evasions."

Emma shrieked, rushing at her aunt, but Izabel easily subdued and held her.

"I won't help you until I have Vincent," said Jane.

"Your sister will pay for your reluctance."

Jane had never seen Izabel's eyes so pitiless. Thinking to buy time, she gestured toward the mirror. "The chamber I assume you seek is behind this mirror, but I don't know how to open it."

Signoras Ricco and Nesta hurried to the mirror and began working manicured fingers around its edges, eventually finding the latch. When the mirror opened, Izabel waved them all inside.

Jane balked. "Emma's too young for such things."

Izabel smiled cruelly. "Let your sister see what you get up to with that husband of yours. Then we'll see how eager she is to remain with you."

Jane tried not to panic as she and Emma found themselves ushered into the secret chamber. She was Emma and Vincent's only ally here and had to keep her wits.

Izabel and Signora Ricco explored the chamber with euphoric wonder. Jane's eyes flicked to the entrance. Signora Nesta stood sentry, bodily blocking it.

Emma's intelligent gaze roved the room curiously. Jane sensed the questions forming on her lips.

"Look away, Emma," she murmured, pulling her sister close. "This isn't for young eyes."

"Let her look," said Signora Nesta. "I'm sure my son will appreciate any education she receives in this area."

Izabel and Signora Ricco sniggered as they haphazardly gathered an array of devices into slipcovers they had torn from Nick's pillows.

"How did you know of this room?" Jane demanded.

Izabel smiled wickedly. "I had your husband's father in my bed many years ago."

"I see."

"The Satyr are so annoyingly closemouthed. But between the sheets, he was quite free with family secrets, thinking no doubt to wash my mind clear of them with a potion he offered me afterward. I took the potion. He insisted. But I tricked him and didn't drink it. My mind remained clear, and I remember everything I learned that night."

"And what was that?"

"Don't pretend ignorance," said Izabel. "I know how Satyr change when their lust peaks."

Jane pressed her hands over Emma's ears, and Emma struggled in annoyance.

"I know the Satyr aren't Human," Izabel went on. Her eyes narrowed on Jane. "Just as I know you are not."

"Later, Izabel," cautioned one of the other ladies. "Remember our true purpose here tonight."

Emma shook off Jane's hands, frowning at her. "I hate when people do that. I'm not a baby to be shielded."

"I'm sorry. I thought it for the best," Jane told her.

Izabel moved to the side of the room and lit the candelabra. When she lifted it from its sconce, a door Jane hadn't known existed swung open, revealing a spiral stair leading downward.

Izabel smirked. "I see by your expression I know more of the workings of the castello than its mistress. Come."

Holding the light, Izabel took the lead, and the others trailed her. The stair swept them downward, far below the castello. Eventually it ended in a cool, dark crypt. Its walls were lined with double rows of barrels stacked on their sides three high as far as the eye could see.

"It's cold," said Emma, her breath making small puffs of fog. "And spooky."

"Hush, girl," Signora Nesta chided. "Spooks are spirits of the devil. Never speak of them."

"There *are* spooks in this castle," said Emma. "I've seen one."

"Hush, I say, or you'll get a smack," said Signora Nesta. "I look forward to the day you're given over to my son's care. I'll see that you're guided by a firmer hand than you're used to."

276 / Elizabeth Amber

Intent on her objective, Izabel ignored her friend's subtle insult. She led them unerringly along the corridor until it eventually opened outside and they entered copse surrounded by a ring of statues.

Emma shivered. "What are all those statues? Where are we?"

Izabel exhaled reverently. "The sacred place."

Under her feet, Jane saw the grass brighten. Tiny, gray mushroom caps reared their heads. The others would see!

She had little time to register the scene or to worry. A sudden mist descended, obscuring the statues and the landscape they graced. As the fog shifted and swirled, various portions of the stone bodies came and went from view.

"What a ghastly night it's suddenly become!" groused Signora Nesta.

"Almost as bad as London," Signora Natoli agreed, appearing from the mist. "My skirts grow damp."

Izabel laughed, her gaiety echoing eerily along the stones of the glen. "They won't trouble you for long, cara."

The others chortled.

In the distance, Jane heard Vincent cry out. A woman's voice soothed him.

"Vincent!" She darted into the mist, turning in circles and quickly losing her way. "Where are you?"

Another woman stepped from the fog. Signora Bich. Ignoring Jane, she spoke to Izabel. "I've given the child a dose so he'll quieten."

"Good. There's nothing worse than the cry of an infant to spoil a mood," said Signora Nesta.

"Where is he? Take me to him," Jane demanded, her eyes threatening. She lay a hand on Izabel's arm, hoping a melding would help her learn his location.

Izabel thrust her away. "Don't try your sorceress tricks with me. Take us to the place where our world meets that of the other. Then you may have your son."

Jane had no idea where the door between the two worlds occurred on Satyr land. But if Izabel realized her ignorance, she might decide her usefulness was at an end.

Jane took her sister's arm and began to walk, with no idea where she was going. The group followed them.

"If you find a chance, run and hide," she whispered to Emma. "Remain quiet and Nick or I will find you later."

"What about you?"

"I'll rest easier once I know you're safe," Jane told her.

"Stop your whispering!" Izabel commanded, pulling them apart.

"She's leading us in circles," complained Signora Nesta. "Leave it for now. There's time enough to find the opening ourselves when the fog lifts. After our ritual."

"Agreed. I grow randy," said Signora Natoli.

"It's this place," said Signora Ricco. "It's meant for fucking. What say you, Izabel?"

"Very well," said Izabel.

All eyes turned to Jane.

"Remove your gown, niece."

Aghast, Jane flattened her hands on her chest and glanced toward her struggling sister. Signora Ricco held her now with a hand covering her mouth.

"If you want my cooperation, let her go," said Jane. "I mean it."

"Take the girl into the forest and tie her fast to one of the oaks," Izabel told Signoras Ricco and Bich. "Not too distant. I want her to enjoy her sister's moans."

Though Emma scratched and bit, she was no match for two grown women. Once she was ushered into the fog, Izabel turned back to Jane. "Now then."

Jane stood, unmoving.

"Shall we bring Emma back and dally with her first?" Izabel threatened.

With leaden fingers, Jane began to unfasten her gown.

When it fell away, the other three women moved behind her, whispering in wonderment. Fingers roved her back, making her skin crawl as they examined her quills as though she were a bizarre species of bird captured in a foreign land.

Izabel curled around to face her, leaving the others to their petting. Her eyes were dilated, her lips eager to spill her evil.

"Don't be shy," she said softly, cupping Jane's cheek. "I have seen you like this before, many times. In the bath. At your toilette."

"How?" Jane cursed the tremble in her voice.

"Remember the holes Emma found in your bedchamber in London?"

"The spy holes? You said they'd been made by a servant. You closed them."

"Yes. But there were more. Not made by servants but by my own hand when I visited. Through them, I watched you struggle with your powers. Saw the feathers awaken. Longed to touch."

"Did my mother know?"

"She watched with me and was afraid," Izabel told her, each word a stab at Jane's soul.

"No," Jane whimpered.

Izabel settled a kiss on her lips. "Poor Jane. When the changes first began, you didn't know to hide them. In your innocence, you asked questions that terrified her. She sought my help, and I counseled her on how to handle you. We became close for a time. But I knew all along she would eventually have to go."

Jane's head snapped back. "Are you saying you had a hand in her death?"

"I had to punish her," Izabel explained with a self-righteous air. "She married your father and took him from me, foolish creature."

Rage flared in Jane, bringing with it a strange fluttering sensation along her back. Behind her, Signora Nesta gasped. "The feathers—they're moving!"

"Step away," Izabel warned. "We must begin. Show Jane what we have planned for her, Signora Natoli."

Signora Natoli obediently came forward and lowered the front of her bodice, displaying twin silver rings hooked in the center nubs of her massive breasts.

Izabel looped a finger through a ring and tugged, stretching the large brown-colored disk in the center of the signora's breast.

Signora Natoli sucked a quick breath.

Izabel smiled into her eyes and then released her.

Her gaze slid to Jane's. "After we mark you in this way tonight, you will be one of us."

"No!" Jane struggled against the other two women who now held her. The unusual sensations at her shoulder blades increased.

"Calm yourself," Signora Natoli crooned at her ear. "The power of the ancient rings will convince you soon enough."

Izabel's lips closed over one of Jane's nipples and then the other, sucking until they sprang obediently to attention. Then she took both tips between a thumb and forefinger and pinched hard. At Jane's cry, she made a moue of commiseration. "You should thank me. The numbing helps dull the pain of piercing."

Jane had never been more thankful she could no longer meld with anyone other than Nick, for she wanted to know nothing more of these women.

"Where are they?" Signora Nesta wondered impatiently, looking in the direction Signora Bich and Ricco had taken Emma.

"Find them," said Izabel. "I'm anxious to begin, and they carry the rings."

"Ladies!" called Signora Nesta.

There was no answer.

"Perhaps they are dallying with the younger girl," suggested Signora Natoli, glancing toward the forest.

"No! Emma?!" Jane shouted.

Still no answer.

"Join us," Izabel told her, "and your sons will be the beginning of a new race, one beyond mortal. We will guide them, worship them with our bodies. One day, they'll be feared, powerful beyond measure."

At the full revelation of Izabel's plan, Jane was flooded with guilty horror. If she'd never wed Nick, his land wouldn't have been invaded, his secrets laid bare, his child threatened. She pushed away fear and sought a plan.

"You're right in what you said before. The Satyr are vigorous and inventive lovers. My husband has led me along a sensual path that I have at times feared bordered on wickedness. It has given me a taste for it. If you can sincerely promise more of such things, I'll join your society."

Izabel's hands stilled on her. "Do you think me daft that I would believe such a turnaround in your behavior?"

Jane tried not to let her distress show. "Come, let me prove it to you by explaining how to use some of the accoutrements you found in his pleasure room."

"I think we can figure them out for ourselves," scoffed Signora Natoli.

"But Nick has shown me their secrets. You might never guess them without instruction."

"Release her," said Izabel. She waved Jane toward the devices, her eyes challenging.

Jane was careful not to go directly to the devices she most wanted to show them. Instead she picked up one of the small whips and handed it to Izabel. "Each of these imparts a special taste on impact."

"Test it on me," Signora Nesta said, eagerly offering her back.

Izabel took the whip and snapped it, her eyes sparkling. It cracked against her friend's bared back.

"Peach!" shrieked Signora Nesta, smacking her lips. "I taste peach! Your niece doesn't lie."

Three sets of eyes fell on her.

"What else? Show us, girl," said Izabel.

Casually Jane led them to the cylindrical devices. "My husband particularly desired me to examine these."

"Dildos," murmured Signora Natoli.

Jane pointed at one. "This was the phallus of a beast from that other world you seek. It still vibrates with the creature's lifeforce."

She held her breath, keeping her expression innocent. Would Izabel take the bait?

Izabel raised her skirts to employ the device but then drew back, her eyes slitted. "You are too eager for me to try it. And I shall. But first you will lubricate it for me. Lie back."

Bark scratched Jane's skin as she half reclined against a tree trunk.

Izabel shoved the cylinder between her niece's legs and inside her, watching her expression closely.

Though Jane's passage was dry, the beast's phallus brought forth moisture and engendered instantaneous delight. She arched, groaning. Embarrassed, she looked away from the salacious gazes of the other women.

As she built toward unwilling climax, she divorced herself from it, staring high into the branches of the tree upon which she leaned. An elder. Amid its bark and branches, a kind face stared down at her, offering comfort. Was she hallucinating?

"If you rest under the Elder tree, it will bring drugged and dangerous dreams of faerieland," Jane murmured, recalling an old childhood verse.

Hands were touching her, petting, stroking the device between her legs. These hands were no strangers to poisonings. Murder. Blood. People had died under their delicate caress. The cries of tortured victims rang in her ears. Long ago, their cries had gone unheard amid the crash of cymbals and drums in the seven hills of Rome.

What was happening to her? Her orgasm crested and broke, shattering the frightening images into hundreds of colored shards. But her wanting didn't ease.

"Again," she moaned, craving more.

"I think not." Izabel wrested the device from her.

Bewildered at its loss, Jane sprawled in a boneless heap at the foot of the tree.

"Are there any more like that one?" Signora Ricco asked. It seemed Signoras Ricco and Bich had rejoined them while Jane had been distracted. Jane managed to turn her head toward the forest. No sign of Emma.

The five women sorted eagerly through the dildos. They each chose one of the beast phalluses and tucked it beneath their skirts, lying under the elders.

"Help me," Jane whispered, gazing into the mysterious faces in the trees above.

Overhead, branches rustled an answering chorus of murmuring voices. Dryads crooned to her, their song comforting. Though there was no wind, their leaves drifted softly over her, forming a light blanket.

Drawn by the dryads' call, vines crept and curled over the elder's gnarled roots and then around ankles and under petticoats. Surreptitiously, they wrapped around shins, thighs, wrists, and waists, pinning the five signoras fast before they became aware of their presence.

"What's happening?" Signora Nesta squealed. Silver rings

were tugged from four sets nipples, and the phalluses were pulled from the cunts of all but one victim.

A vicious snaking vine curled itself around Izabel's windpipe once, twice, a half dozen times or more, growing ever tighter. Her hands ripped at it, clawing for breath. The phallus throbbed inside her, giving her orgasm after orgasm after orgasm. It remained in her long after she was overwhelmed by its stimulation. Long after her heart ceased beating and her skin grew cold, her eyes fixed and dilated.

With the morning, Nick came, finding Jane sleeping in the cocoon of leaves and enfolding her in his arms. Lyon gathered Emma and Vincent from the forest, where dryads had watched over them, and saw them safely in their beds.

The figures of four sleeping women and one dead were gathered and deposited in the grotto of Izabel's childhood home. When they awoke, days later, the four signoras were bewildered and changed, the rings at their nipples gone. Their minds were washed of the events of the night as well as any evil.

The fifth's evil had died with her. Only her stepbrother cried piteously over her when she was discovered dead in the garden of the home where they'd grown up, and in their own twisted way, loved.

31

In the following days, two more missives from ElseWorld arrived. Nick grew more tense with each. When a third came in as many weeks, Raine returned from Venice, and the three brothers met at Blackstone to discuss a course of action.

"The unrest in ElseWorld is intensifying in the aftermath of King Feydon's death," said Nick. "His sons and daughters vie for control."

"All this could have been avoided if Feydon had left directives regarding a line of succession," Lyon said in an aggrieved tone.

Raine picked up one of the missives, studying it. "Do they still respect our right to vote in the election of a new king?"

"Yes, though some view us with growing suspicion, believing we hold Human welfare above that of creatures in Else-World," said Nick.

"The makings of war are brewing," said Lyon. "ElseWorld factions will soon challenge Human control of EarthWorld to enhance their worthiness as potential rulers. Our role as a buffer between the worlds will be tested."

Nick shrugged his massive shoulders tiredly. "I'll depart for the conclave in ElseWorld two days hence, hoping to calm the waters. I fear for Jane's safety while I'm away."

"You don't believe the danger to which Feydon's letter referred passed with her erstwhile aunt's demise?" asked Raine.

"It has lessened—" Nick began.

"But something remains to disturb the calm," Lyon finished. "I've sensed it, too, and wondered if the danger to your wife is truly over."

"Have you considered taking Jane with you through the worldgate?" Lyon suggested.

Nick shook his head. "My focus must be on the negotiations. I won't be able to adequately guard her from those who would try to harm me through her."

"I'll postpone my bride search to remain here while you're gone," said Raine. "Lyon and I will watch over her."

"But will it be enough?" asked Lyon.

A potent silence fell, taut with unspoken words. Their thoughts took them all along the same path.

Finally Raine broke the tension. "There are ways of better protecting her."

Nick nodded reluctantly. "The ancient ritual. I have considered it."

"And?" prompted Lyon.

"She won't easily participate. But I must contemplate what is best for the family. And for her."

"Tomorrow is the Calling. We'll await your decision," said Lyon.

"I'll sleep on the matter," said Nick.

A sparkling of dew had begun to settle the following evening when Nick led Jane from the castello by way of the back garden. It was July now, and the rest of Italy was parched by the heat. But temperatures on the estate remained constant and mild.

Her skirt fluttered in the sultry breeze as they followed the brick of the garden path until it blended with lawn. Nick continued on through the grass and wildflowers that caught at her ankles. Just ahead, oak, olive, and elder loomed, thick and tangled.

Nick tugged on her hand when she held back at the forest edge.

"Where are we going?" she asked.

"You will see. Come."

The forest opened and quickly swallowed them. Jane sensed none of the uncertainty the giant trees had once shown toward her. There was only acceptance.

All was inky darkness within the landscape of silvered trunks, but Nick moved quickly, propelling her forward with a hand at her waist, sure of his path. Now and then he pressed at her shoulder to duck under a hanging branch, some instinct enabling him to dodge obstacles she couldn't see.

"A torch might have been useful," Jane said when he saved her from tripping on an oak root.

"I've been this way countless times," he murmured. "I could tread it blind."

They continued on for some minutes in silence, when Jane again asked their destination.

"Tonight is the Calling," he replied obliquely.

Her pulse quickened. "Yes, I know."

It would be the first such time since their child had been born. Her body was eager, anticipating what would happen between them. She'd seen that Emma and Vincent were in bed early and well looked after by their new dryad nannies. The night was hers and Nick's to enjoy.

A stray shaft of starlight fell across Nick's brow, and he shot her a look filled with meaning she couldn't interpret. "It's my brothers' Calling time as well."

An image of Nick's reticent brother Raine leaped to her mind. It was difficult to imagine him involved in a carnal mating ritual. Lyon was a different matter, but her mind veered away from envisioning either brother in the throes of passion.

"I never thought about them . . . doing that."

"They require the same release at Moonful as I do. During the recent Callings, when I remained with you within the castello, they met at the gathering place in the forest without me."

"But they aren't wed. Who do they—?"

"They join with Shimmerskins."

Jane digested that for a moment.

"When it happens, I experience their passion," Nick added.

"How do you mean?"

"Satyrs are bonded by blood. We know when the others achieve physical fulfillment."

"If you know when your brothers are having relations, does that mean they know when we're—?"

"Having relations?" he asked, lifting her over a narrow brook. "They don't know specifics, only that you're giving me pleasure."

"Oh," she said faintly.

"Don't be embarrassed. When one of us is stirred to arousal, the others are only too glad to benefit."

"I wonder if I'll have such telepathic kinship with my half sisters."

Nick's interest perked. "An intriguing thought. You will have to tell me after they join our family and are mated to my brothers. We've lived with this sense so long between us that it is second nature. But it is particularly strong in the Calling. And, of course, the Bacchanalia."

"As in a celebration of the wine god, Bacchus?" asked Jane.

Nick held aside a silvery branch grown thick with olives so she could pass before replying. "That's right. It's a three-day rite held at the vernal equinox."

"Is it anything like the Calling?"

"Wilder. Even more passionate."

"I wonder if I'll survive it," she teased.

He paused and drew her close, his palms shaping her ribs. She felt his fierce erection at her belly as he murmured into her hair. "Physical joy will swell within us in harmony with the reawakening of the vines in anticipation of the grapes that will eventually swell to bursting—ripe, juicy, and sweet. The passion is stronger. Indescribable. You will see."

He pulled away, leaving her breathless. Taking her hand, he led her deeper into the woods than the forest had ever allowed her to penetrate. Overhead, the trees rustled in greeting. Ferns and thicket parted for him.

Finally the forest thinned and they entered an expansive clearing. Pale statues loomed from the night, forming an eerily silent ring around it. Tendrils of mist curled and snaked among the dozens of granite figures. Simple stone altars dotted the landscape of the central glen, like ancient picnic tables in a public park.

Her eyes grew accustomed to the starlight, and she was able to see more clearly. This was the place Izabel had brought her that awful night.

As they moved farther into the clearing, she saw that the statues depicted creatures both fantastic and real, all shaped in lewd poses.

Rock-hard Satyrs entwined themselves with multiple female partners, feasting on their breasts and enthusiastically filling their every orifice in one lascivious way or another. Carved nymphs cavorted in orgiastic fervor. And, everywhere, wine—petrified in stone—flowed from flagons and decorative urns.

She felt guilty for studying the figures and for the moisture that formed between her legs at the sight.

"Why have you brought me back to this horrible place?" she demanded.

"It's the sacred gathering place," he told her. " 'Tis here that the Bacchanalia I spoke of will occur."

"Tonight?"

"At September's end."

"For what purpose have you brought me here tonight then?" Was the Calling to take place here in this strange, wild arena?

The moon chose that moment to show itself, filtering through the foliage overhead to bathe them in its glow. Nick groaned and lifted his chin upward to receive its sacred energy. Light bleached his skin, silvering his features, until he appeared almost a demon.

He lowered his mirrored eyes, and his hands traced the curve of her waist to mold her back. "I have brought you here tonight," he said, "for a Sharing."

Jane frowned, not understanding. Before she could ask him to explain, she heard the crunch of footsteps. Turning, she saw Raine and Lyon enter the far side of the sacred ring.

They stopped just inside the perimeter, as motionless as the statues. Their figures were poised and expectant, their gazes riveted on Nick.

Realization began to dawn, and with it came instantaneous repudiation. "You don't expect me to disrobe in front of your brothers, surely. And we won't make love here in the open while they—watch?" Her voice rose on the last word, suddenly fearing that was exactly what Nick planned.

She saw the answer in his eyes, felt him willing her to agree.

"Absolutely not!" She shook her head wildly, pulling away from him. "Why would you ask me to do such a thing!"

"It's our way."

"I grow weary of that explanation."

Nick sighed and cupped her shoulders in his hands. "It's necessary. They'll think nothing less of you for it. Quite the opposite, in fact."

"No, Nick. You should have told me your plans so that we might have discussed it before we came here."

"I didn't wish to alarm you."

"Well, now I am alarmed. The idea of disrobing in your brothers' company is scandalous."

"It's commonplace for females to disrobe before family members in ElseWorld," he went on. "Women of this world wear far too many clothes."

"You've never complained about my clothing before. Why now?"

He spread his hands as though at a loss to understand why she didn't grasp the necessity of his intentions and go along. "It's a Sharing."

Jane peeked around him. Raine and Lyon hadn't moved.

She searched his eyes. "What does that mean exactly?"

"My brothers will share our pleasure with us."

"I said *exactly*. What *exactly* do you imagine will occur here tonight?"

"They will touch you as I do."

"Touch? You mean, touch my body?" she squeaked.

He nodded.

"Couple with me?" she hazarded.

He nodded again.

"You wish to share me in that special way? With your brothers?" she whispered in disbelief.

His jaw hardened, but he only nodded a third time.

She stepped back from him and looked in the direction from which they'd come, at the unbroken line of trees. Where was the path? "Take me back."

"Jane—"

She stalked from him, but an arm scooped around her waist,

halting her. She twisted in his grasp to scowl at him. "If you truly cared for me, you wouldn't suggest such a thing."

"I do care for you. It is part of that caring that allows me to set my jealousy aside. I don't want to share you with other men. Not even my brothers. But it is for this night only and for your good that I make such a sacrifice."

"For my *good*?" she mocked. "Oh, please."

His brows snapped together. "You doubt me? 'Tis true. I must leave soon for ElseWorld, where I'll be unable to sense you. I worry for your safety."

"The threat from Izabel has passed. What do you imagine could happen?"

"Any number of things! ElseWorld is on the brink of war, and the gate between our two worlds lies on Satyr land. There are those who would dare an attack upon us to wrest control of it. A Sharing will forge bonds that link you with my brothers, as I'm linked with them. They will sense if you're in trouble while I'm away."

"No."

"Jane, see reason."

She tried a different tack. "What if your brothers get me with child?"

He took her hands in his. "It goes without saying that they will withhold their childseed from you tonight, as will I. I wouldn't have you burdened with overly quick birthings."

Jane closed her eyes, wishing this nightmare away. When she reopened them, nothing had changed. Her husband still gazed upon her with expectation, and his brothers still lurked in the shadows beyond.

"I don't want this, Nick. I'd rather remain at risk."

"And thereby leave our son at risk while he's under your sole care?"

Jane hesitated.

She felt the strength of his will cajoling at her mind, pushing her toward compliance. "Stop that. I never should have melded with you."

Nick chuckled. "You will understand in time. But I dare not wait. We must undertake to safeguard you before I depart on the morrow."

She felt a tug at her dress and realized he was prompting her decision in the direction he desired. She was being disrobed.

Beyond him, she saw that Raine and Lyon had taken his actions as a signal and had begun to remove their clothing as well. Chests emerged from tunics, appearing wider and stronger when revealed in the moonlight. She wanted to continue thinking of them only as brothers, not carnal men with desires of the flesh. She looked away.

All too soon, she and Nick stood naked within the hush of the glen.

Raine and Lyon left their clothing draped over one of the altars and joined them. The moon chose that moment to bathe them all in its fullness, and she silently cursed it. She tried to scuttle her way behind Nick. But he put a hand at the small of her back, refusing to allow it.

He kissed her with an air of finality and a whisper of gratitude. Then his hand slid from hers.

Her fingers made an abortive attempt to maintain contact and then fluttered to her side. She crossed her arms over her chest, feeling abandoned and horribly embarrassed as he moved to stand with his brothers.

The three giant males stood shoulder to shoulder, staring down at her. Their muscled torsos gleamed in the gauzy murkiness like those of the stone statues. They presented a united front, and she felt small and alone.

Lyon smiled at her encouragingly.

"She's shy," explained Nick.

"But willing?" asked Raine.

All three males looked at her.

Her teeth worried at her lip, but she jerked her head in assent, careful to avoid glancing anywhere below their naked chests.

Nick gazed at her with approval. Underlying it, a haze of passion filled his eyes. She knew that glazed look. There would soon be no reasoning with him. He would listen to nothing but primordial desire.

She searched his brothers' faces and saw they were similarly afflicted. The hypnotic spell of the Calling was overtaking them all.

The day had begun so well. How had it come to this—that she found herself alone in a sacred glade with three muscle-bound, lust-crazed, naked men? She shivered.

"She will take the elixir?" asked Raine. His voice was somber, urgent.

Nick caught her expression and saw the uncertainty. He nodded.

The brothers quickly poured and partook of the elixir from their own glasses and then set them aside. A fourth mixture was poured into a goblet and handed to her.

Her breasts shifted and bobbed as she reached for it. Three sets of male eyes fell to them, like iron shards drawn to magnets. She shrank from their stares, but they missed nothing of her movements as she drank.

Liquid fire slid down her throat, and she welcomed it. Moonlight winked in the ruby sheen. As the last drops burned their way inside her, her eyes narrowed.

At her wedding and all the times they had met afterward, these men had known that someday this night might come to pass. All three of them had known but hadn't seen fit to tell her. No doubt their silence was "the Satyr way."

She slammed the empty goblet onto a nearby stone. The

brothers took no heed of her disgruntlement, intent only on their own objectives. Lyon took the goblet and replaced it in some hidden nook.

Silence fell as they all waited for the elixir to stir her blood. Long moments passed. The fog threaded her legs, brushing her body with its swirl.

Her movements grew languorous, and she swayed. She raised a hand to her neck, rubbing sensuously under the fall of her hair. Her breasts were thick and heavy, her nipples puckered and tightened. Her slit moistened, and her labia plumped. Deep inside, her core began to tingle, and she squeezed her thighs together in an effort to capture the sensation.

Her every murmur and undulation were duly noted.

"Take care with her," Nick muttered.

Jane turned slumberous eyes on him, wondering what he meant.

Raine nodded wordlessly. He stepped forward, his body claiming her attention as it blocked his brothers from her view. Footsteps padded across the ground behind him. Nick and Lyon were moving away, leaving them alone.

Raine looked somewhat apologetic, yet when he took her arm and guided her across the length of the clearing, it was with determination and purpose. Easily led, she breathed deep of the orchid air. Beneath her bare feet, the moss was spongy soft.

He paused before the largest statue at the end of the arena. She followed his gaze and looked up. And up. Above them, haughty Bacchus reigned over the glen, a grin slicing his face.

Grape clusters, vines, and leaves entwined the locks of his hair, curling in wild abandon. His pose was confident and lavish in its nakedness, proudly displaying his most prominent feature—an enormous phallus that curved high, like a corpulent scabbard.

Maenads and nymphs caressed the god with delicately wrought hands and lips. He took their attentions as his due, scarcely acknowledging them. Instead, the concave pits of his eyes seemed focused on her.

Warmth surrounded her as Raine came to stand at her back. She braced her palms on top of the stone pedestal as his hands at her waist lifted her high to lean against its side.

"Find the footholds," he instructed.

Her toes scrambled until they found purchase in two notches about fifteen inches from the ground. The footholds were an arm's length apart and held her legs splayed. There were similar notches at varying heights and intervals ringing the base of the statue. Always in pairs.

She felt Raine hoist himself into position behind her. Muscles bunched along the front of the masculine thighs that aligned with the backs of hers.

A heavy palm pressed between her shoulder blades, stirring her quills. It pushed her forward until she was bent at the waist over the statue's base. Her position was one of worship, of supplicance. Had she tried, she could have reached out and traced the web of ivy at Bacchus's feet.

The stone that met her breasts had been smoothed in subtle twin indentations. How many other women had been taken here by Satyr males over the centuries? she wondered. How many other breasts had rubbed here and slicked the stone to this sheen?

She started in surprise as a finger and thumb opened the cheeks of her buttocks. Something nudged at the puckered aperture revealed in her rear divide.

A penis.

It prodded, seeking trespass.

Another, simultaneous stab came at the shadowy slit between her thighs.

So it was to be a dual mating. She hadn't ventured to look but had wondered if Nick's brothers' bodies changed in the same way as his during the Calling. Now she had evidence they did.

The velvet crowns pierced her, stretching her openings beyond what seemed possible and then proved possible as Raine pressed on. He cleaved himself to her by slow inches, taking care as Nick had requested.

Some of the sensual haze faded to be replaced by fear and uncertainty. His body felt unfamiliar. Wrong.

Jane's breath caught on a sudden sob.

The prodding abruptly ceased. Raine curved his palm over her hip bone, lending comfort. She only sobbed harder.

"The elixir," he said in a kind voice. "We thought—but I'll wait and let it take full effect. Tell me when you're prepared."

He stood motionless for several moments, with only the first few inches of his cocks lodged in her intimate compartments. Occasionally his sex twitched, and she knew his desire to complete the act must be great. His restraint was admirable, but she couldn't fully appreciate it in her current distress.

The elixir pumped more strongly through her veins, bringing with it calm and willingness. Her passages moistened. She'd agreed to participate in this. She tried to relax for him.

Raine's knuckles whitened where they gripped the stone on either side of her, and she sensed his growing desperation. "May I proceed?" he asked at length, his cultured voice strained.

She took a shaky breath and then nodded. At the first agreeable inclination of her head, he thrust deep. This time she didn't quail as his appendages sought haven in her body.

He sank home. She shuddered. Like his elder brother, he filled her beyond what was comfortable.

Almost immediately, his hips pulled back, only to push flush against her again. He handled her with the rigid bearing that typified him. His withdrawal and penetration were controlled, rhythmic.

Thoughts whirled in her head as he worked. Was she really

here in this forest being fucked by her husband's fastidious brother? And her husband condoned it? Watched it, in fact? Over and over, what had once been unimaginable often became truth here on Satyr land.

Eventually Raine commenced bucking with less consideration for her comfort. Reluctant groans were torn from him.

The swells of her breasts polished the stone surface as he pounded her. Again she wondered how many other women had been impaled here on this altar. With their husbands' consent, had they sought their pleasure here with men who weren't their husbands? She felt a burgeoning kinship with them.

Raine murmured low words in what she knew to be the Satyr language. They touched a chord deep within her. Her mind and body were relaxed now, accepting.

His large hand wrapped the length of her hair around his wrist to hold her for his increasingly powerful taking. Her neck arched, and her head lifted to meet Bacchus's gaze. He smiled benevolently down at her, approving of her sacrifice.

When release threatened, she fought it. It had been a game before when Nick had mated with her under the guise of being other men. But this was all too real. She wouldn't enjoy another male's caress, even under her husband's instruction. She would not.

"Let go," Raine prompted, his tone grim. "Your ultimate enjoyment is necessary to complete the Sharing."

"No," she moaned, clenching her fists.

Masculine hands slipped beneath her arms to find her breasts. They plucked at nipples already taut and distended, carefully pressing them to the stone surface so it abraded them in time with his luxuriant thrusts. Lust shot straight from her breasts to her core.

When orgasm could no longer be held at bay, she gave in to it. Raine felt the milking begin, and his hands tightened on her hips. He drove deep in one final, smooth stroke.

With a muted bellow, he creamed, spurting warm, brotherly semen inside her. From above, she felt Bacchus's pleasure wash over them.

Hands stroked her, she knew not whose. Nick and Lyon had returned even while her tissues still pulsed around their brother's cocks. Raine stayed firmly nestled within her as three voices joined together in some sort of chanted ritual unfamiliar to her. At its completion, a strange feeling came over her like a light, comforting veil of magic.

Then Raine perfunctorily withdrew. She clutched at the stone surface to retain her balance and blinked after him as he and Nick departed.

Leaving her alone with Lyon.

Though Nick had appeared to be suffering the tortures of the damned, he'd offered no words of comfort or love. She felt abandoned.

Lyon tugged her from her perch. She fell against him but quickly pulled away from his brawny heat.

"Come," he told her, taking her hand in his large pawlike one. "We shall tease Nick a little, eh?"

"I'm not sure that's wise," she mumbled.

As they walked side by side, the joggle of her naked breasts embarrassed her, as did the new slickness between her thighs and rear cleft. All she could think of was that he'd just seen his brother fornicate with her. That he was planning to do the same.

She watched the ground pass under her feet. Fragrant Corsican mint and blue-spiked lavender grew thick in low mounds edging the mossy path. From the corner of her eye she saw Nick and Raine a distance away, observing them. Could Nick see the residue that clung to Raine's shaft as a result of their joining? Did the scent of her arousal on his brother's body torment him?

Lyon led her to a different place upon the altar of Bacchus

where stone formed an arched bridge over a series of small pools. Here a fountain of fresh water trickled from gourds held by three nymphs with beguiling features and lichened hair. It cascaded over the edge of the bridge in a wide sheet that spilled to the pools below.

He held out his arm as though assisting her into a carriage. The gentlemanly gesture struck her as ridiculous in such circumstances, but she took his hand nevertheless.

With his support, she stepped upward onto the stair wall that edged the pool. Where her ribs met the bridge, the waterfall halted and found a new avenue, easing around her to dribble down her sides.

This new perch held her facing outward, toward the open glen. The bridge obscured only a narrow strip at her waist. When she looked straight ahead, her gaze tangled with Nick's. From where they stood, he and Raine had a direct frontal view of her breasts, hips, and legs!

She glanced at Lyon over her shoulder and tried to step down. "Not here. They'll see too much."

"The place is mine to choose," he told her.

Before she could argue further, Lyon's feet found a larger step that jutted from the pool's rock-wall base just below hers. The warmth and scent of him engulfed her as he swung up behind her and pressed himself along her back.

He flexed his knees and dipped lower behind her. He paused, purposely giving his brothers ample time to view his engorged cocks through the window created by the inverted vee of her legs.

Slowly he straightened. His twin penises greeted her unguarded gates. At Lyon's carnal puncture, she saw Nick start forward and then check himself. Lyon was either very brave or very foolish to incite his jealousy by this blatant display.

Slowly, slowly he speared her. Her tissues were tender from Raine's attentions, and she felt every inch of his ingress. He was gargantuan, but her body, her mind, didn't resist. Eventually his thatch met her bottom, and he sank to the hilt.

The heat and musk of him surrounded her. The sudden sensation of fullness and captivity was too much. She whimpered.

Lyon's palm slid over her belly, fingers wide, laying claim. Nick wouldn't miss the possessive gesture.

Jane heard him snarl and saw Raine restrain him.

Lyon moved his lips next to her ear. "Don't hate me, sister. In a Sharing it is best to arouse a husband to jealousy. It's strange to you, I imagine. But it's our way."

Jane rolled her eyes at this all-too-familiar disclaimer, but positioned as he was, Lyon didn't see.

Getting down to business, he began to rut on her with vigorous strokes. Again, she felt the difference—the shape and size of a man to which she was unaccustomed and who wasn't her husband. His furred thighs pressed hers wide and chafed silkily as he shoved and retreated. Hands at her pelvic bones arched her hips back, opening her for his surging cocks.

Bacchus watched this coupling from a different angle than the last. She felt his avid eyes on her bottom jiggling in sync with Lyon's rhythmic heave.

Her breasts dangled over the stone, slapping and sliding in the slick sheet that cascaded over it. The frenzied shine bubbled, bathed, and soothed. She cupped her breasts, lifting them away from the titillation, refusing it. But when Lyon's thrusting intensified, she lost her grip and simply endured the stream's chilly caress.

This was a man who delighted in fornication and wasn't afraid to show it. He reveled in his task and shouted his enjoyment of her body for all the world to know. Compliments and encouragement punctuated their coupling, urging her toward pleasure. His brothers might not catch his every word, but his relish would be apparent.

Lyon's vocabulary devolved as his need overtook him.

"Umm, fuck. Good," he murmured. Then, "Come for me, sister."

Jane was chagrined to again feel arousal burgeon. Even though she knew the elixir was responsible in part, she rejected the ecstasy his fucking of her was causing. She shook her head, fighting the rising tide of release.

His fingers parted her wet curls, searching. Her neck arched, and she hung suspended on a precipice of need. Then he lifted her clit and rubbed oh-so-softly. She cried out.

Through misty lashes, Jane saw Nick reach the end of his tether. Raine barely held him back as orgasm tore through her. It milked Lyon into a fierce ejaculation. His spurting warmth flooded her to mingle with that Raine had already deposited. He was still shuddering out the last of his cream when Nick and Raine rejoined them.

She remained draped, limp, and docile over the stone bridge with Lyon at her back. More of those guttural Satyr words were chanted over her. Again, that strange sense of melding drifted over her.

Then Lyon was gone.

Familiar arms closed around her. When she fell into them, Nick caught and lifted her down, crushing her to him. His hands stroked her damp hair and slicked over her wet skin. She relaxed against him in relief.

The sticky wetness was more profuse now. It clung to her thatch, dribbled from her apertures, and smeared her inner thighs as Nick led her away. Dazed, she went with him, scarcely knowing where.

At the entrance to a cave, three ancient trees bowed low, forming a live arch that nearly obscured the rock opening. Gnarled roots of oak, ash, and hawthorn intertwined to form stairsteps so beautiful in their design that they appeared planned by a skilled artisan.

"Where oak, ash, and thorn come together, faeries be found," murmured Jane, quoting from England's legend of the faerie triad.

Nick gave her arm a reassuring squeeze.

Their quartet passed through the opening the trees provided and then entered a dim cloistered room. It smelled of an ancient ferment of mosses, herbs, grapevines, and beloved souls, and she sensed its sacredness.

As her eyes became accustomed to the absence of moonlight, she saw she now stood before a low altar in the middle of a path. The path continued some distance ahead, ending in a void from which a strong aura of magic emanated.

A warm body knelt behind her. Nick. He grasped her hips and pulled her to her knees before him.

"Where are we?" she asked, her tone hushed.

"At the place where EarthWorld and ElseWorld meet," he told her. "I have chosen this—the most sacred of all joining places—to close the circle of the Sharing."

Raine and Lyon stood on either side of them, watching as she was bent upon this final altar. Something tickled her breasts. She patted her hands lower, finding the cushion of faerie thyme and fragile moss that covered the altar.

Twin penises found her vaginal and anal openings. Her flesh was tender, but she knew this body well and welcomed it. Her husband.

Nick groaned his relief as he drove inside her. His brothers' leavings paved his way, making this third joining an exceptionally easy one. It was a fact he couldn't miss. He fucked her hard and with little mercy. The strength of his coupling was, she suspected, motivated by his desire to stamp her as his own.

She looked down at her breasts and saw they were now tipped with that strange silver-blue glow. Embarrassment that his brothers witnessed it might have come at another, former time. But not now.

Nick saw and was driven wild. His thoughts pierced hers.

It didn't happen with the others. Only for me.

Only for you, her mind echoed.

Orgasm swelled quickly between them, each sensation building on that the other experienced. It crested and then crashed as his seed blasted into her channel to dash against her womb.

She could feel each drop of his jism meet and bond with those of his brothers. Three separate masculine potions mixed together within her to form a powerful blend that prolonged her inner convulsions until she found herself sucked into velvet blackness.

When she resurfaced, the pungent tang of fresh earth and moss filled her nostrils. Above her, low words were being spoken by three male voices. Their chant wove itself around her, sealing her within the protection tonight's Sharing had constructed.

Without voice, she accepted what they offered and felt their gratitude in return for her understanding. Raine and Lyon withdrew from the chamber, moving out into the moonlight.

Nick grunted as his second penis retracted into his pelvis. His other penis remained thick and ready, still lodged in her quivering slit.

"A respite, husband," she whispered.

He withdrew from her and folded her against him. "I'm sorry. You're small, and we've been too eager with you."

Over his shoulder, through the frame of trees that formed the door to the chamber, Jane watched Raine and Lyon move into the glen. Watched the mist around them glisten and then solidify into female form. Watched Shimmerskins materialize out of thin air.

One of them sank to her knees before Lyon. Her hands stroked over his furred thighs as she took his ready cock in her lips. His palms cupped each side of her head. Holding her steady, he began to fuck her mouth.

Another Shimmerskin stroked Raine's chest, brushing his nipples. He cupped her bottom to lift her. She wrapped her legs around his waist and parted her labia with one hand while her other directed his cock inside her. His eyes fell closed as he seated himself deep and began to rock her.

Jane gasped.

"Are you all right?" asked Nick. She pressed her blue-tipped breasts against his chest and let his body hair massage her.

"I can feel their arousal, or something of it," she said in surprise. Her brow knit. "It's a peculiar feeling. I'm not sure if I like it."

Nick sat and lifted her to his lap, and she felt his hardness against her hip. "It's the result of the Sharing. You're now linked with all of us. It will grow to feel normal over time."

"I don't want to physically join with them again."

"There's no need. You're now sufficiently protected by the irrevocable familial links formed tonight. I'm content that you will remain safe in their care whilst I'm in ElseWorld."

"I feel the truth of that. This has all been so strange. I never thought to mate with a male other than my husband."

"I imagine you've done many things you never thought to since coming to me," he said. "Any regrets?"

She smiled at him and slowly shook her head.

Jane heard Raine groan in the distance and started at the responding sensation she felt in her clit. Her hand moved downward, but she caught herself before she could rub at it, too shy. His hand pressed over hers, moving their entwined fingers sensuously through her slickness.

"It's like an echo of their pleasure," she murmured.

His breath was a hot whisper against her neck, his hand urgent over hers. "I feel it, too. An enhanced stirring that spurs me toward release."

"A useful physiological occurrence meant to perpetuate your race, I presume." She moaned at the sensation their fingers were causing.

"Speaking of which . . ." He lay her on the soft mossy bed, obviously planning to continue their coupling in the privacy of the cave.

"Will there be more surprises?" she asked, encircling his neck with her arms.

He kissed the side of her throat. "Undoubtedly."

She tapped his chin with a fingertip. "In the future, perhaps more warning?"

He grinned at her. "Consider this a warning then. Something is about to surprise you."

Ahh! She gasped as the Seeker made its way inside her vagina, lapping up cream and tending to abrasions.

She relaxed into its attentions. "A welcome surprise, husband, for I'm sorely used."

He kissed her forehead, contrite. "I'm sorry."

"It was difficult," she said, writhing. "*Ahh!* —but I begin to heal."

Moments later, the Seeker's work was done. Nick batted it aside and slid over her.

"And now, wife, be warned that my tongue, fingers, and cock plan to surprise you repeatedly over the coming hours until dawn is finally met."

She widened her thighs and smiled at him, inviting. He spread the ruffled folds of her labia, displaying her most vulnerable heart for the kiss of his lips, the stroke of his tongue.

Sighing, she relaxed into it and let her fingers sift through his hair. When they fisted there, he rained soft kisses up her body. As his shaft found and pierced her nether heart, joy pierced her soul.

Tonight she'd truly been accepted into his clan in both mind and flesh. He had trusted her enough, cherished her enough to choose this place that meant so much to him and his kind to mate her.

"How lucky I am to have found you," Nick murmured.

Lucky. He hadn't said he loved her. But he needed her, at least for this. Because she'd become his preference for carnal engagements and the mother of his child, he'd offered her a home and his protection. She and Emma would be cared for just as if they'd been born into this family.

It was what she'd longed for her entire life. She would not be greedy. She would let it be enough. For now.

"I, too, am lucky," she whispered.

That night he departed for ElseWorld through the joining wall in the cave, leaving both her and EarthWorld behind.

32

Jane hummed to herself as she and Emma left the castello garden and entered the forest the next morning. They were going in search of flowers for Emma's version of Linnaeus's clock. They lacked only two now, having found the other ten, whose petals opened and closed in time with the hours.

Her mind brimmed with thoughts of the previous night when she'd fully embraced her special brand of sexuality and that of her husband. Carnality was theirs to explore in the years ahead. In time, she hoped he would come to love her. But in this moment, she was content.

Had she not been preoccupied with such ruminations, she might have noticed they were being followed. After they entered the forest, their pursuer finally made himself known to them.

"Papa!" Emma breathed in surprise.

Jane whirled to find her father—no, Signore Cova, who was not her father—appear behind them, a barrier between them and the castello.

"Where did you come from?" she demanded, not understanding why the forcewall had allowed a stranger to invade the forest.

"Followed you," he mumbled.

He'd been trailing them. Because the forest now accepted her and Emma's right to enter, it must have accepted someone it perceived to be their companion without question.

Cova stared around the glen, weaving on his feet. Drunk. She'd never seen him so rumpled and unkempt.

"Filthy place," he muttered, ". . . taken my Izzy . . . gotta pay . . . godforsaken place and its heathen owners."

Jane and Emma drew closer to one another, watching him warily.

"Nick had nothing to do with Izabel's death," Jane ventured.

Cova pulled a small wooden box from his pocket. "A pox on all the Satyr houses!" he misquoted woozily. He opened the box, turned it upside down, and let the crumbled leaves within flutter forth on the wind.

Jane watched, not trying to prevent him, not understanding the full import of his actions until it was too late.

The empty box fell from his fingers to the ground. He giggled drunkenly. "Pox in a box."

Sudden horror dawned, and Jane whirled around, gazing at the bits of leaves skittering and floating to the ground on the breeze. There were hundreds—too many to collect, now that they'd blended with the ground cover.

"What have you done?!" she shrieked.

Emma dropped her basket, clasping her hands. "What? What did he do?"

"He brought the pox here on those leaves. Purposely, to infect the vines," said Jane.

"You always were a quick study, harlot daughter," said Signore Cova. "So hear this: As the vines shrivel and die, so will your husband. And his brothers. Izzy said the Satyr need those vines to live. My poor, dear Izzy. *Ohhh*." At the memory of Izabel, he took his head in both hands and dissolved into sobs.

"Is it true, what he says?" Emma asked Jane.

"Run to the house and fetch Signore Faunus," Jane urged. "Tell him—"

Cova knocked Jane aside and grabbed Emma's arm, his tears quickly drying. "I'll not have you stay here in this wicked place, girl. You'll come home with me and serve your father as a good daughter ought."

Emma looked at Jane, unsure. "Must I go?"

Everything within Jane rebelled. Emma must stay with her, safe on Satyr land. As a terrible anger rose, the quills at her back stirred.

"No. Not now," Jane breathed, feeling the change and fearing what might happen next. Unbidden, the feathers ripped from the back of her dress and sprang forth. They unfurled gloriously into translucent fluttering wings! At their movement, her feet lifted a few inches off the ground.

Emma stared at her, shocked into speechlessness.

"Let her go," Jane hissed at the man who held her sister.

Signore Cova shrank back in fear and then fled, stumbling his way from the forest. "Witch! Witch! I'll tell! See if I don't!"

Jane called after him. "Only remember everyone will say that if you're my father, you must be tainted as well. And a witch, too." She only hoped the threat would censure him.

In the wake of his departure, the feathers at her back folded together as neatly as a lady's fan and slipped back into her skin. Her feet touched down to earth. She darted a glance at Emma, dreading the rejection she was prepared to see in her eyes.

But Emma was grinning! "I knew you could make the plants well. But I didn't know you could do that!"

Jane laughed in relief. "To be honest, I didn't either. Come, let's go for horses. Nick and Raine are away, but we must check on Lyon and inform him of what has happened."

Together, they raced back downhill toward the castello.

"When did you guess about the plants?" Jane asked breathlessly as she ran.

"Long ago. I could tell you were embarrassed about it, so I didn't let on. But I didn't know about the wings. Will I grow them, too?"

"No. Nick tells me I have them because my father was in fact someone other than yours."

"Oh," said Emma, sounding disappointed as she digested that.

Jane couldn't help but smile. "For years I've worried that you would exhibit signs of this taint. And now you say you wish for it?"

"Why wouldn't I want wings? They're beautiful," said Emma. Then her brow creased with worry. "But if Papa isn't your father, are we still sisters?"

Jane nodded. "Always. We're half sisters by blood and full sisters by love. You will live at the castello with me from now on."

Emma's small hand slipped into hers as they reached their home. "I'm glad."

The next morning, Jane paced before the entrance to Else-World in the sacred cave deep within Satyr forest. She'd been there since dawn awaiting Nick's return. Yesterday she and Emma had visited Lyon and found him already ill from the early effects of the pox. She'd left Signore Faunus and Emma to care for him before coming here.

Raine was away, and she had no way of knowing if he also weakened. But it seemed likely. Was Nick ill, too? She couldn't sense him, far away in that other world. Should she go to him there? Lyon had made her promise not to, for he said it wasn't safe.

Now and then, as she paced, she heard shouts of revelry

from vineyard workers in their quarters outside Satyr land. A local festa was underway, so they wouldn't come to the estate today. Their gaiety seemed surreal in view of her terror.

It was late afternoon when Nick finally stepped through the gates into EarthWorld. His face was haggard, his body exhausted.

He slumped against the cave wall and held a hand to his head. "I'm ill, Jane. Poisoned. I feel my brothers' illness as well. What's happening?"

Jane wrapped her arms around him, wishing she could take away his pain. "It's the pox. It's come on the estate and is sickening the vines. Sickening you and your brothers."

"Fuck."

She reached for her basket. "I've brought a mixture of herbs. A curative I've given Lyon. You must take it. I'm hoping—"

"No. It won't suffice." He turned his head away from the offering and pushed off the cave wall, heaving against her, one arm slung around her shoulders. "Take me to the vines high above the gathering place."

"But—"

"Please." His voice was a fragile, husky whisper.

Jane put an arm about his waist, and with a strength born of terror guided him from the cave. She led him past the statues with their solemn stares and far beyond the glen. His footsteps were leaden and unsure. As they climbed, he stumbled over a root and staggered, taking them both down.

"Rest," he begged. His shoulders were bowed, hopeless.

"No! Come on!" she shouted, shaking him. She dragged him to his feet, and they trudged on.

At the entrance to the vineyard, the gates swung open, knowing and welcoming him. By the time they reached the vines, her entire body ached from supporting him.

Nick collapsed at the edge of the vineyard, falling to lie on his back upon a patch of bare soil between the rows.

Jane knelt beside him, praying he hadn't come here to die. "What now?"

He didn't answer. His body was lifeless, his breathing labored.

She cupped his stubbled jaw and tried to meld with him. Under her hands, she felt his mind slipping away.

"You can't leave me, Nick," she sobbed. "We have yet to raise Vincent. And what of our other children?"

"We have more?" he asked. His voice was slurred, disoriented.

"I speak of the children not yet conceived. Now, tell me! Why did we come here? What can I do?"

She forced herself to calm. His pain would debilitate her if she let it in. To save him, she had to keep her wits.

"Heal," he muttered.

"Heal? HEAL?" What did he mean? She rocked back, and her hand inadvertently brushed a five-pointed leaf. It perked, filling with new green life. But the color only extended a few inches beyond the leaf onto its stem.

She stood and looked over the endless rows. "I can't touch them all. Not in time."

". . . nourished through soil . . ." he muttered. ". . . roots go deep . . ."

The phylloxera had infected the vines through the soil! The soil is what her body must cleanse.

Quickly she began ripping at her clothing. Her dress and petticoats were tossed away. Her corset was impossible. It remained.

She stretched out, her skin pale upon the warm, crumbled soil. As her body melded with the earth, she willed new life to suffuse the vines' roots.

Their pain scorched her, weakened her, but then the pox's poison passed through her and was gone, leaving her as she'd been.

She stood again, shading her eyes to survey the hillside around them. The vines sprang green and refreshed, rejuvenated. But then she looked farther, to the next hill. The vines there remained black and withered. As did those on all the surrounding hills.

Nick murmured something.

She dropped to her knees beside him. "I've failed. I'm so sorry."

His hand moved hers from his chest and lay it over his crotch.

She snatched away. Even near death, he wanted sex? "Nick! Don't be ridiculous."

"Heal them . . . through me." He cupped himself through his trousers. "Seed—life. New. Fuck."

Suddenly she understood. His lifeblood was intertwined with these vines. Would their mating, here on this land, breathe new life into the vines and thereby into him?

She yanked at the fastenings of his trousers, tearing them in her haste.

He chuckled and touched a fingertip to her nipple. "Wanton."

"Hush."

When his trousers opened, she nearly cried. His shaft was limp!

She took it between her hands, rubbing, gently tugging. Not a twitch.

She tried her mouth, working him with her lips and tongue, simulating the sex act.

He began to swell. Was it enough?

"Nick! Come on top of me," she told him. "I need to lie on my back for full contact with the soil."

"Can't," he mumbled.

She lay on her back and attempted to roll him over her. Impossible. Desperate, she straddled him instead and then moaned in despair. He'd wilted.

His lack of interest terrified her. Always before, he could be counted on to be ready for every aspect of carnal behavior.

Determinedly she slicked herself over him, teasing him with her cunt. She leaned close to whisper low, raw sex words—the kind he liked. She taunted, begged, coaxed.

Under her, his shaft thickened and distended. She lifted over him to find his tip. With her hand, she forced the semisoft shaft several inches inside her channel.

His hands lifted to her thighs and squeezed. His eyes opened.

"You look tired, wife," he murmured.

He was silly, unmindful of their situation. But he was coming to life.

Her knees were bruised from scraping on the volcanic soil at his sides. "Roll over me. Can you? I need you to be on top."

"So submissive," he teased. His eyelids fluttered closed.

She smacked his shoulder. "Move, Nick!"

"Ow!" He looked at her, his expression hurt.

"We have to switch positions. I need greater contact with the earth."

Awareness flickered in his eyes. With a mighty breath, he heaved himself from the ground and reversed their positions. It took much out of him, and he fell on her, forcing his cock deeper. Then he lay on her, unmoving.

She ran her palms over his muscled back and buttocks and let her fingers trace the furrow at his rear. A fingertip prodded his puckered opening.

He jerked, and his cock strengthened. He managed to move his hips in the barest of push-pull rhythms.

Straining, she reached to gain better access. He gasped as her finger moved knuckle deep, sodomizing him.

"Cream," he protested against her throat.

"I have none."

"Then, enough." He forced her hand away. But the thrusts of his hips had grown stronger and more controlled.

Now that she had his cooperation, she shifted her concentration. Her mind drifted, willing the soil to accept their offering. Willing it to meld with her. Willing it to sharing their fecundity, share her love for him.

Her back grew hot, and she felt the melding begin. Felt the soil's pain, knew the roots and the vines and their sickness. Offered to lessen it.

Her chin filled the notch where his shoulder met his neck. She smelled rain in the air, saw raindrops sweep the forest and reach the vineyard gates.

Nicks movement within her remained slow but steady.

"Is that the best you can do?" she taunted. "Fuck me, husband. Fuck me as I desire. Or shall I leave you and find my satisfaction with another?"

He growled, and she felt strength and determination rise up in him. His fingers dug into her hips, and he began shafting her with increased fierceness.

"You must let me in as you did the day we met," she whispered at his ear. "Don't shield yourself from me. I don't have enough to give the vines alone. They need us both."

Had he heard her?

Yes! She felt his mind come into hers. Bringing warmth. Caring. Love!

The rains came, slicking their bodies as they mated with each other and with their land. Together they writhed in the life-giving soil and became slathered with it. Mud sucked at Jane's body, pulling her deeper, taking what she offered and giving her husband life through her in return.

Above her, Nick bucked hard, newly invigorated. When he finally drove deep and shouted his release, the last of his pain drained from him, washed over her, and faded into nothingness.

All around them, woody canes firmed and straightened. New blossoms burst from healthy vines now flowing with sap.

Nick clasped her to him. Above them, the rain slackened to a diamond mist that drifted its veil over them from the sky.

I love you, his mind whispered. His kissed her deeply with rain-slicked lips. Then he spoke aloud. "I love you."

"And I you," she echoed.

The earth that smeared them both was dry by the time they left the slopes. Far below them, Jane watched the forest part and saw stone and shingle come into view.

And knew it to be home.

EPILOGUE

Greenery sprang to life everywhere across Satyr land.

Bees hummed at the vines. The grapes were beginning to ripen. Soon it would be autumn and harvest would begin.

In the castello garden, Jane heard laughter and turned to watch Emma instructing Lyon on the proper way to wield a baby carriage across the lawn. Even the servants smiled at their antics, caught up in the sheer joy of their happiness.

The outward normalcy her new extended family presented to the world was something Jane reveled in. Any Human chancing upon the idyllic scene would think nothing unusual. Hers could be any of hundreds of well-heeled families in Italy on a summer afternoon.

But here on Satyr land, all was wonderfully unusual.

Life here suited her as that outside Satyr walls never had. EarthWorld had once seemed such a hostile place. And Nick's home had sometimes seemed darkest of all. Now she knew it was a haven. A place of acceptance. Her home.

Soon, the Satyr clan would expand. Raine was even now

gone in search of his FaerieBlend wife for yet a third time. His brothers had teased him mercilessly about his inability to locate her as quickly as Nick had found Jane. Though Raine moved more carefully and methodically than the others, Jane had no doubt he would eventually succeed at his task. Once he had, Lyon would go in search of his bride.

Would her sisters be like her? Nick had explained that magic found its outlet differently in each of the Faerie. Her gift was a facility with plants. It remained to be seen what her half sisters' abilities might be. She looked forward to welcoming them into the fold.

Jane's eyes strayed to the clock Emma had completed only yesterday. The passionflower was in bloom. It was nearly time for Nick's return. After an absence of a week, her husband would be randy.

She rubbed a hand over her flat belly. Nick had promised her a second child a year after the birth of their first. It would be many months before then. For now, Emma and baby Vincent kept them busy.

Joy bubbled through her veins at the knowledge that their children would grow up here, safe, accepted, and loved. And free of the restrictions the world outside Satyr lands imposed. Here, in this inner sanctum, there would be none to condemn them for their strangeness. They had only themselves to please and would hurt no one else in the process. There was no false piety here, no useless societal rules to govern them. There was only the private, secret wonder of their lives.

She heard the soft pad of footsteps across the lawn and felt Nick come to stand behind her. Unsurprised, she leaned back against the heat and strength that was her husband. Muscular arms came around her, and Nick nuzzled his chin in the nook of her shoulder.

"I am returned," he murmured.

"I'm glad," she said.

"You knew I would come," he teased.

"I knew," she murmured on a soft smile.

Tonight there was to be a full moon. A Calling night. She looked forward to it.

AUTHOR'S NOTE

Grape phylloxera is a tiny aphidlike insect that feeds on the roots of grapevines, stunting their growth or killing them. The pest was accidentally imported to England and France on American vines around 1862. It reproduced with devastating speed, and by the end of the 19th century, phylloxera had destroyed two-thirds of Europe's vineyards.

For the purposes of this story, the date of the infestation is set at approximately thirty-nine years prior to the actual date of the infestation.

Turn the page for
a sizzling preview of
BLOOD ROSE!
On sale now!

1

THE HUNTERS

London, October 18th, 1818

Sex. She wanted sex. But she wanted this anticipation, too. Serena Lark stirred sensually on the bed, enjoying the feel of silky sheets beneath her bare skin.

A candle lit the room—it could only be one, for the light was weak and the candle must be close to guttering. Golden light wavered on the wall and danced with the reflections of silvery-blue moonlight.

Serena's hands skimmed her tummy and touched—boldly stroked—her cunny, which ached in delightful agony.

Shadows swept over her. She saw the sudden darkness cross her belly, and she looked up. Her heart hammered but she smiled a greeting at the two masked men who strolled arrogantly into her bedchamber. Lord Sommersby and Drake Swift—the Royal Society's two most famous and daring vampire hunters. Both men were dressed for the hunt, though masked, and they swept off their greatcoats as they crossed her threshold.

A gold mask framed Swift's glittering green eyes, and a deep royal purple mask clung to Lord Sommersby's face. Swift threw his hat aside, revealing his unfashionably long white-blond hair. He dropped a crossbow on the floor, followed by a sharpened wooden stake. He lifted a heavy silver cross from around his neck, let the chain pool on the floor and the cross fall with a clunk.

As dark as Swift was fair, his lordship gave a courtly bow and doffed his hat. Thick, glossy, and dark brown, his hair tumbled over his brow. Her breath caught at the heat in his eyes—the deep, delicious color of chocolate.

Serena crooked her finger and both men came to her, tugging their cravats loose as they prowled to her bed. They tore at their waistcoats, their shirts, and stripped to the waist. She could barely breathe as she drank in the sight of two wide chests. Swift's skin was bronzed to a scandalous shade, which brought the gold curls on his sculpted muscles into stark relief. The earl was massive, possessing a barrel chest and biceps as big as her thighs. He looked like a giant, one with a body honed by battle with the strongest creatures on earth.

She was dreaming. Even lost in it, she knew somehow. And in this dream, Serena had no idea what to say—what did one say when two men came to one's bed for the first time? Words seemed inane. She was most terribly shy. And as a governess, she'd been well trained to be a silent servant. But she gave a welcoming moan—the prettiest, most feminine one she could muster.

Tension ratcheted in her. Desire flared as the men approached. They would touch her. Her heart tightened with each long, slow step they took. *Yes. Yes!*

Laudanum. Even here, in her dream, she remembered the laudanum. A few swallows in her cup of tea because she couldn't sleep.

Mr. Swift paused to yank off his trousers, and he flung them aside as he stalked toward her, his ridged abdomen rippling. He wore no small clothes. His magnificent legs were formed of powerful muscle, lean and hard.

And his cock. Serena couldn't look away. It curved toward his navel, thick and erect and surrounded by white-blond curls. She knew it would fill her completely, stretch her impossibly, and she knew it would be perfect inside.

Mr. Swift reached the bed first. He smiled, his teeth a white gleam in the darkened room. His hand reached—she followed the arc of his fingers with breath held—and he touched her bare leg. *Oh!*

"Miss Lark." He dropped to one knee. "Let us dispense with the pleasantries and begin with the delights." And with that he parted her thighs and dove to her wet cunny.

Candlelight played over his broad, tanned shoulders and the large muscles of his arms. His tongue snaked out, slicked over her, and Serena arched her head back to scream to the ceiling.

So good!

Boot soles sharply rapped on the floor. Leather-clad knuckles gently brushed her cheek. Lord Sommersby. She flicked her eyelids open as Mr. Swift splayed his hands over her bottom, lifted her to his face, and slid his tongue as he tasted her intimate honey.

Lord Sommersby looked so serious, but he never smiled. He required encouragement so she held out her hand to him, but her smile vanished in a cry of shock and delight as Mr. Swift nudged her thighs wider, until her muscles tugged, and feasted on her. His lips touched her clit, the lightest brush, and pleasure arced through her. She tore the sheets with her fisted hands, heard silken seams rip.

Then squealed in frustration as Lord Sommersby lay his strong hand on his partner's shoulder and wrenched Drake Swift from his work.

"She is a woman beyond your ken, Swift. A woman to be both pleasured and treasured."

Pleasured and treasured. Serena could not believe she'd heard those words from the cool, autocratic Earl of Sommersby's lips. He thoroughly disapproved of everything about her, didn't he?

And then the earl was gloriously nude. The hair on his chest was lush and dark, and the curls arrowed down his stomach into a thick, black nest between his thighs. His cock was straight and hard and remarkably fat, and it pointed downward, as though too heavy to stand upright.

A sweep of his lordship's arm and his rich purple mask flew aside, revealing dark brown eyes, narrowed with lust, and a predatory determination in his expression that made his fine features harsh. "Out of my way, Swift."

"I think the lady wants *me* to finish, Sommersby." With an insolent grin, Swift rolled back onto his lean stomach and lowered to her sex once more. She lost all her breath in a whoosh.

To have two such beautiful, naked men argue over which would lick her to ecstasy . . .

It was almost too much to bear.

Lord Sommersby bent and licked her nipples. Of course this was a dream, for she lifted her breasts saucily to the earl and spread her legs wider for Mr. Swift. His lordship sucked her nipple at the exact instant devilish Mr. Swift slid fingers in her cunny and—dear heaven—her rump.

Her heart pounded; her nerves were as taut as a harp's strings. "I will let you bed me," she gasped, "if you let me hunt with you."

Drake Swift laughed, and thrust *two* fingers in her quim and ass. "You were made for this, lass. For naughty fucking. Not for hunting vampires."

How illicit and wonderful it was to be filled, to feel invaded with each thrust of his fingers. Serena looked to Lord Sommersby.

"I would never risk your life," he said.

"But you know it is what I want most of all," she whispered.

"Is it?" Drake gave a roguish wink that set her heart spiraling in her chest.

In the blink of her dreaming imagination, both men were kneeling on the bed at her sides, looking down on her, their smiles hot and wild.

Mr. Swift's cock approached her mouth from the right, his lordship's from the left. The two huge, engorged heads met in the middle, touching right over her mouth.

Serena had never seen anything so erotic—so wildly arousing that she forgot about decorum, about bargaining, about hunting vampires.

What would it feel like to run her tongue around and between the two heads?

Their fluid was leaking together, making them deliciously wet and shiny—

What on earth was she doing? This was scandalous!

Her mouth opened to protest.

They moved to push their cocks in, parrying for position. Serena lost herself to the moment, shut her eyes, and stuck out her tongue—

Something sharp pricked her tongue. She pulled back, shocked by the pain, as thick liquid spilled into her mouth. Hot, with a strange yet impossibly familiar metallic taste.

Blood.

Icy horror snaked through her veins, and she forced her eyes open.

The men were gone. They'd vanished and a young girl sat on the bed in front of her. A child dressed in a fragile white nightdress with loose, tangled, golden hair.

Anne Bridgewater. Little Anne, who had died young—she remembered holding Anne's cold hand, laying her face to the girl's quiet chest . . .

As though floating over the scene, she saw herself twine the blond hair around her wrist to expose Anne's slim neck. Anne cocked her head, and her sweet scent of youthful skin flooded Serena's senses. Pain lanced her jaw and fangs shot out.

She was a vampire! Serena tried to resist, tried to fight, but she saw herself press her pointed canines to the girl's fresh, clean skin. The pulse thrummed beneath, fervent and strong, and the rushing blood sang in her ears.

Against her will, she bent to the young girl's neck . . . but everything tilted and a sudden light poured into her room. Havershire Manor. She was in her old bedchamber, and Mrs. Thornton was tossing her half-packed case out the window while Mr. Thornton paced in front of the fire. Neither seemed to care that she wasn't wearing a stitch of clothing, and she desperately tried to cover her body with her long black hair.

"You are in love with her!" Mrs. Thornton screamed at her husband.

Serena fought to protest, but she could not force the words out. She had done nothing wrong . . . nothing but read poetry with Mr. Thornton, and walk with him, and fall in love with him . . . and let him kiss her once—but nothing more.

Mr. Thornton raked his hands through his hair. "The wretched girl bewitched me."

His wife wheeled around and pointed at Serena. Her triumphant laugh rang out around her. "You'll starve in a week, you little fool."

She woke on a scream. Serena found herself bolt upright, sheets tangled around her legs, sweat pouring between her breasts. She pressed the flannel to her skin to soak up the rivulets as she gulped down air.

Not again! So much for dosing herself with laudanum—it hadn't helped at all. Foolishly, she ran her tongue over her teeth. No sharp points, of course. No fangs. And she had never, ever hurt Anne Bridgewater.

Serena kicked back the covers and jumped down from her bed. She rubbed at her eyes, scratchy with sleep. She hadn't slept properly for four weeks. Not since coming to London, meeting Althea—Lady Brookshire—and joining the Royal Society.

She flung open the velvet drapes. Her bedroom in Brookshire House overlooked Hyde Park. Beyond the line of trees, pink touched the sky, promising dawn. How could she look upon the rising sun if she were a vampire? How could she stand in the sunlight?

But the erotic dreams of the magnificent Lord Sommersby and that enticing rogue Drake Swift—didn't they prove she was not a normal, proper Englishwoman?

She leaned against the window, staring out at the shadowy green park. She had promised she would not give in to her baser nature this time. Twice she had fallen in love and she'd ended up in disaster. She thought she'd loved William Bridgewater, Anne's older brother. He'd come to her bedroom, kissed her senseless, and she wanted him. Wanted him with the same urgent fiery need she felt in these dreams. And that need had got her banished from the house. Then there had been Mr. Thornton, and his poetry, his brooding pain as they walked together, his stories of his wife's madness and rejection. She, the simple governess, had fallen deeply, impossibly in love—

She was never going to do that again. She could never do that again.

With the daylight spilling over her, Serena folded her arms beneath her breasts and paced to her bedside table. She slid open the drawer and drew out the small stack of folded pages. The edges were torn and curled and smudged by tearstains.

> *My dearest A,*
> *I am writing to express my fears in regard to the behavior of S.L. She shows an unhealthy interest in men; she*

is brazen and wanton and disobedient. Often she slips out of her room at night, and returns only at dawn. One afternoon, a fortnight prior to my writing here, S.L. pricked her finger on a rose's thorn. She put the wound to her mouth and suckled—not of great concern perhaps—but I saw her return to the same place in the garden the next afternoon, deliberately wound her finger, and delight in suckling the blood from her flesh—

I greatly fear that your concerns are quite accurate estimations of the truth. You do see, do you not, why I beseech you to bring her to London, to keep her under your watchful eye? Dear Anne is devoted to her and the child is fragile and impressionable. I am not at all certain how to proceed—I have raised S.L. as a daughter, but she is not normal. Subhuman, in my opinion, and I fear, a danger to us all—

I must fervently await your reply,
  Yours in devotion and admiration unsurpassed,
  Mrs. Ariadne Bridgewater.

Every instinct inside her yearned to rip the words to shreds. But she couldn't do that—she needed these copies she'd made. There'd been so many of these letters, written to *dearest A.* She'd found them last week, neatly filed away in chronological order, in one of the bookcases in the Society's vast library. Letters written by Mrs. Bridgewater, the woman who gave her food, shelter, the woman who had raised her—the only "mother" she had ever known. A "mother" who thought her subhuman.

Who thought her a vampire.

Serena tipped her face to the weak strands of daylight, closed her eyes. Still hazy from the opiate, she struggled with the questions that plagued her day after day. "Dearest A" was the elderly

Earl of Ashcroft—the most powerful man of the Royal Society for the Investigation of Mysterious Phenomena.

To think she'd believed every word of Lord Ashcroft's story when he'd brought her to London two months ago. To think she'd believed he would teach her to slay vampires. *A tragic secret has been hidden from you, Miss Lark ... the truth is that vampires killed your parents ... but I will help you learn the truth, if you serve the Society.*

Lies. All lies. She'd been so thrilled to come to London, to stay with Lord and Lady Brookshire, to join the Royal Society. Ashcroft must have known she had been tossed out of the Thorntons' home without a reference and had no place to go.

Worse, her parents hadn't been killed by vampires. The letters had made it clear. Serena's throat closed. She shuffled through the copies she had made but didn't look down at the words. She didn't need to; she'd cried over them so often the words were burned in her head. *I suppose this is exactly the kind of behavior we should expect,* Mrs. Bridgewater had written, *from the daughter born of a vampire and a mortal.*

Serena shoved the letters back into the drawer and shut it tight.

What did Lord Ashcroft want with her? Why had he kept her alive?

Was he waiting—waiting to see if she changed?

Would she? For all the books in the library she'd pored over, she didn't know. She didn't know if she could start out as a mortal and become a vampire without being bitten.

Serena stalked back to the window and pulled the curtains shut, filled with a sense of purpose. She was not going to wait; she would not be meek and docile and simmer in fear. If she wanted the truth she would have to bargain for it. And the journal of Vlad Dracul would be a temptation Lord Ashcroft wouldn't be able to resist. Once she had it, she would trade it for the truth about her parents, the truth about herself. And her life, God willing.

All she had to do was break into the brothel to find the journal. It was a deadly risk, but worth it. She had to find out the truth.

Was she the child of a vampire or not?